The room spun madly, whirling and raging.

Sparks from the dim light floated down onto Valin, spreading across his flesh, taking away his voice in the very moment he knew he must scream or die. They wrenched from him his humanity, and he screamed voicelessly to feel it go, leaving behind only the pain of the ripping as all his bones broke apart and reformed. He heard his spine crack, like glass crushed.

He opened his mouth again to scream, but no sound came out.

The room whirled faster and faster. Gray chasing gray, chasing gray. Gray haze and red agony. Tendrils of fire spread into his limbs.

Valin tried desperately to breathe. He tried to cry out, and now he had his voice, full and roaring . . . Crysania!

The room spun faster until finally—an hour, a day, an age later—his screaming became silence.

NOVELS

CHAOS WAR SERIES

The Doom Brigade
Margaret Weis and Don Perrin

The Last Thane
Douglas Niles

Tears of the Night Sky
Linda P. Baker and Nancy Varian Berberick
Available October 1998

NOVELS

Tears of the Night Sky

by Linda P. Baker
and Nancy Varian Berberick

For Larry,
whose belief and faith rivals Crysania's
—L.P.B.

To all the bright spirits who will turn these pages
and walk this road with me.
Thank you for your companionship on the journey.
—N.V.B.

Chapter One

A tall figure came out of the darkness. Man or woman, the dream did not show.

In the dream, rain fell from the sky. Droplets as silken as tears and tasting of honey. In the waking world, Crysania lived in velvet blackness, blinded by the gods, blinded so that she might better see how dearly compassion was needed in the world around her. It had been a hard lesson, but that lesson did not exist in this dream. Here, in this sleeping world, she had sight, and she delighted to see rain sparkling like diamonds.

The tall figure came out of the darkness, hands cupped, as if bearing a gift. The dream being's mouth moved to shape words Crysania could not hear above the sweeping sigh of rainfall. Straining to catch the silent words, she turned her face up to the sky and tasted the cool, wet rain. It soaked her skin and mixed with the real tears running down her face. She, who knew her every emotion from source to end, didn't know why she was crying. Not knowing filled her with dread.

"Who are you?" she cried to the creature in her dream.

Rain hissed like snakes and rushed like fire.

"Paladine?"

She spoke the god's name softly, investing it with her every hope. Her words fell soundless from her lips, creating a silence that rippled outward like a stone tossed into a pool so that the whisper and sigh of falling rain stilled.

The being looked at her long, then vanished like mist rising up to an unseen sun.

"Wait!" Crysania called, and with the word still on her lips, she woke to the swelling heat of another day.

Tossing in restless sleep, she'd flung her bedclothes aside. Her nightshirt clung to her, wet with sweat; her eyes stung, hot and dry. The sun had yet to rise, but all the heat of the day before and the long night hung in the chamber. Out in the streets beyond the Temple of Paladine, the sound of the city rousing swelled up, washing in through the window of the bedchamber like the sound of a distant sea. The business of the day was starting—carters shouting to their horses, peddlers beginning their rounds, children running and shrieking at play in the coolest part of the day. An hour after sunrise, the air would burn like the hottest noon of the longest summer day. In the marketplace, the sellers of fabric and baubles and tools flung the shutters wide to open their stalls, glancing uneasily at the booths that remained dark and closed.

Anyone who remembered springtime remembered it from another year. This year had forgone that tender season, bringing burning sun but no rain, no rain. Crops had burned in the fields; pigs and cows and chickens died

2

of hunger and thirst. What food farmers managed to grow, what beasts they kept alive, they held for themselves. Very little remained to bring to the market in Palanthas, and this caused people to look around themselves and wonder how bad winter would be. Encircled as it was by the Vingaard Mountains and the Bay of Branchala, Palanthas provided her people with little land for farming, save for backyard plots. The city depended on trade for its food.

The ruined spring and this terrible summer were the hottest Crysania had ever known. The dwarves in the city were calling this the Anvil Summer, and it seemed as good a name as any she'd heard. It had rained in her dream, but in the waking world, no one had felt the kiss of rainfall in a long time, and all of Palanthas seemed to burn like iron stock being beaten on an anvil's hard breast.

Into what are you shaping us, O gods?

Crysania left her bed and crossed the marble floor, gritty with dust. Someone would sweep the floor today, and again this afternoon, and once more before night, but still the dust returned. It had rained in her dream, but no rain would wash away the dust in the waking world.

And Paladine . . . Paladine might well have spoken to her in her dream, the god standing in the sweet, soft rain, offering her something, a gift, a mere word, but in the waking world, she had not felt the gentle warmth of his loving presence in a long time.

No one knew that, of course. No one must. And perhaps he had spoken to her in this rain-filled dream. But if he had, she hadn't heard his words.

No matter, she told herself. If I could not hear his words, then I must divine his meaning from the images.

Once a small girl had asked her, "Lady, are dreams messages from the gods?"

Crysania had smiled and patted the girl's hand,

charmed by the question and the little lisping voice. "Sometimes," she said, "they are indeed messages, child. Other times they are the effect of too many sweets before bedtime."

The chubby little hand had closed around her fingers, trusting. "But how do we know which ones are messages and which ones are too many sweets?"

"We watch and look around ourselves and see what we can see. The wise eye will find a clue in time."

I will do that, she told herself, slipping out of her uncomfortable nightshirt, slipping into a light robe. I will look around me and see what I can see. A blind woman who could see nothing, she smiled at the thought. Still, there are ways of seeing that did not need a keen eye. She would listen; she would learn all she could. She would see. Even as she determined to do so, a prickling ran up the back of Crysania's neck.

Last night's dream, with its confusing images, left a dry, dusty taste of warning in her mouth. Of what did it warn?

Tying her robe loosely, Crysania crossed the room to the wide windows from which the sound of the waking city entered the chamber. She had long ago arranged her furnishings in such a way that she could easily make her way around the chamber. The unbroken order assured that she could walk without bumping shins and stubbing toes. Hers was a simple chamber, simply furnished, large enough for a bed and a small dressing area. It had the same white marble walls as all the other bedchambers in the temple, the same elegantly carved friezes at the corners where ceiling met walls, the same smooth, polished gray marble floor. Furnishings were plain heavy wood, her bedclothes sweet, cool linen. The only unusual feature was the stretch of floor-to-ceiling windows along the length of one wall. It was the one indulgence she'd allowed herself when the Temple of Paladine was rebuilt after the Blue Lady's War. Though she couldn't enjoy the view, Crysania loved the smells carried on the breeze through open windows, the scents of gardens and people and the salty tang of the Bay of Branchala at the edge of the city.

Now, as she stood before the windows, she felt the sun rise. She used to be able to track its rise by the heat moving up her body. No more. Heat, these days, was unwavering heat, never changing, ever present. Still, she felt the sun rise by some sweet sense within her, some knowing born in all creatures who live by the sun's grace.

Came the sound of hammers on wood, the murmur of voices like the voice of the bay's restless waves.

Out there, she thought, beyond the market, past the empty cattle yards, and in the great square, they are making ready for the Festival of the Eye.

She heard the hammering and the voices of many people walking along the street in front of the temple as they headed for the palace gardens. A child's voice piped high above the murmur, chanting a song of summer's blessings. These were the sounds of anticipation.

They are so full of hope, the children and their elders, as though Paladine himself lives in each of their hearts. What would happen to that hope if they knew that the god had not spoken to his Revered Daughter for so long?

By midmorning, the crowds would be uncountable, all of the people waiting for her to greet them and bless the Festival of the Eye. She would lead them in offering thanks to the gods for the passing season of growth and in prayer for the coming season of trade.

Crysania lifted her face to a stray breeze, one smelling of the city, of crowds of people, of gardens barely alive. A great surge of pity rose up in her, pity for those who would trust and for those who had, perhaps, already fallen from hope. How hollow would their prayers ring? How well would the people accept her message when she reminded them that the gods always had a purpose for what they did. She would say, "There is always a lesson to be learned." And she believed that—even in the silence of her god she believed that—but she could not understand what lesson was being taught in this Anvil Summer.

In the east rose the sun. Crysania turned her back to the window and faced west. There rose another trouble, one as frightening as drought and the specter of winter famine.

Palanthas, set as it was in the Vingaard Mountains and at the head of the Bay of Branchala, had always enjoyed year-round traffic from the rest of the continent. Visitors to the city were not so numerous during the War of the Lance, but afterward, as peace returned, the major overland route into the city became busy once again with traders and travelers and couriers. The majority of those travelers, regardless of their religious preference, visited the magnificent Temple of Paladine. Thus news, official or otherwise, had never been difficult to come by.

Until this year.

As the unprecedented heat baked the roads of Ansalon, travelers became fewer. Two weeks ago Crysania had asked among her clerics for volunteers to travel to the High Clerist's Tower to seek audience with Sir Thomas in hopes of finding out what was happening, or at least to learn that knight's thinking on whether rumors of troop buildups in the Khalkist Mountains were to be credited and what to make of the strange, destructive weather. The human woman, Nisse, and the hill dwarf, Lagan Innis, had willingly taken on the work. They were good and canny people, those two. They would make the journey to the Vingaard Mountains together in good company. And, Crysania had hoped, in good time. But though Crysania had expected them back before Festival Day, neither had returned, and not one message had come from them in all the time of their absence.

Now, as every day in the hour of her morning prayers, Crysania's thoughts were with them. Her fingers went to the medallion she wore always around her neck—a dragon simply wrought in beaten gold on a circle of solid silver, suspended from a fine gold chain.

"Paladine's blessing be on you, my friends," she whispered as she sank to her knees, facing the warm sunlight and the still air of the garden.

For some in the temple dedicated to the worship of the god of goodness and light, the ritual and ceremony of prayer was an important part of their faith, and she loved the beauty of ceremony no less than others. Yet she often craved the peace of being able to kneel on the floor with but a humble windowsill as a rest for her forehead. Today, this hot and burning morning, peace was what she most needed. In peace alone she hoped she would find her god—his peace, his wisdom, his all-embracing love.

Crysania covered the medallion with both hands. The sounds of the city faded, and she waited for the warm glow to pour forth from the golden dragon as it had so many times in years past. There were many things her mind had forgotten through the years of blindness. Colors blended and warped. Faces faded or were reshaped by her memory. The sight of the medallion, glowing warm, bright with Paladine's presence, was something she would never forget. She saw it as clearly in her mind today, in darkness, as she had in her youth.

Crysania took a deep, cleansing breath. She waited for the medallion to grow warm, for the tingling sensation of the god's nearness to fill and fulfill her. She found only the chattering of her mind telling its worries. A hot breeze blew in from the window as she willed herself to relax, and the willing itself was a distraction.

Good enough, she said to herself. I will walk away from what troubles me.

She rose and circled the room, feeling the gritty dust beneath her feet, letting the rhythmic sound of her robe whispering around her ankles lull her. Her mind was distracted. She was too caught up in the worries of the day, too concerned about the weather, anticipating too greatly the festival and the crowds. She was not emptying herself, not making herself a proper vessel for her beloved god to fill.

Again she knelt at the window, and now the sounds and scents of the city faded. The medallion lay heavy in her hand as quiet, like a balm, settled upon her. She did not form the god's name; she kept still and silent.

Was that the dream's message? Be still! I will enter in . . .

Soft at the edges of her mind came a tingling, the barest presence, as if Paladine were aware of her, but from a great distance. She willed herself to be still. The warmth of the medallion grew, but only slightly. She stayed where she was for a long time, but she felt the god's presence only barely. Her voice gave no cry, her lips formed no words. Her heart, though, ached with loneliness.

What had she done—what had they all done?—to merit the aloofness of their god?

There was a reason, always a reason, for the actions of the gods. It was her responsibility to learn and explain, to help her people appreciate whatever lesson was being laid out for them. Crysania lifted the golden dragon to her lips and whispered words of hail and farewell as she always did when her prayers were complete.

Wherever he was, she must trust that Paladine would continue to guide her.

From outside her bedchamber came the sounds of the waking temple, of voices calling softly one to another: "Is she awake?" asked one. "I don't know," replied another. Steps to the door, listening silence, steps away.

Crysania arose from her prayers, smiling, to whisper, "I am coming."

From a small wardrobe, she selected a cool linen robe, plain except for the silk ribbons woven into the neckline and hem. She ran her fingers over the row of belts, one covered in fine embroidery that felt silky under her fingertips, one thick with needlepoint, one of softest leather. She selected the one decorated with delicate metallic threads.

She washed and dressed with swift, economical movements. She combed her hair and chose a comb of polished platinum, Paladine's metal, to hold back the heavy mass of her hair. She reached out and touched the slick surface of the mirror over her dressing table, left there for the convenience of those who sometimes helped her fix her hair or her clothing. There had been a time, more than thirty years ago, when she had taken great pride in her appearance. She had gazed at herself in mirrors and been pleased by the reflection that stared back: milky pale skin, shining black hair, and startling eyes as gray and soft as a dove's feathers. Her attendants told her she was beautiful still, that her black hair had only a few strands of silver woven through it, that her skin was as smooth as that of a woman half her age. She appreciated their kindness and always smiled her thanks, not for the compliment but for the gift of their affection.

And that is a gift indeed, she reminded herself. Paladine's gift. With such friends, how can I doubt that he heard my every prayer?

So she breathed deeply and drew her faith about her like a cloak. She would meet the day with a smile; she would enjoy the festival. And she would, find the right words with which to frame her blessing for the people.

She would guide them and remind them that Paladine still loved them.

Soft came a tap on her door. She smiled again, already knowing who knocked. She would have known from the rhythm of his fingers on the wood, even if not for the fact he was always the first to greet her in the morning.

"Good morning, Valin," she said as she opened the door.

It was easy to smile in his presence. He was her grand experiment, a mage set among clerics, and it pleased her to know her experiment was working well. A bold experiment indeed, one mounted with the help of the Conclave of Wizards. The time has come, she'd told them months ago at winter's end when all hopes seemed possible, to bridge the gap of mistrust between clerics and mages. Arched brows, murmurings, and outright proclamations of distrust greeted this announcement on all sides. Dalamar himself, in a move unusual for him, had come down from his tower and managed a small oration on the subject of his doubts, but Crysania had prevailed, offering to take a white-robed mage into the temple. "For a time, to see what mages and clerics can learn from each other." Valin, desert-born mage, had been reluctantly chosen by the conclave.

Valin felt no reluctance at all. In the five months since her meeting with the Conclave, he had become as much a part of the temple as she, as trusted an advisor as her own clerics.

"Lady," he said, his voice low and, grave, "I've brought you a message."

Crysania's heart lifted. "From Nisse and Lagan?"

"No, lady. I'm sorry. Not from them. From Lord Amothus." He put a roll of parchment into her hands, not to read but so she might feel the seal and know from whom the message came. Later someone would file it or archive it or tidy it away.

"Thank you, Valin. Join me in my study."

He moved to let her pass, then followed, a tall man at her heels. His scent, something musky that reminded her of wood oils, drifted around her.

Like her bedchamber, her study in the outer room was specifically arranged, the furniture never out of place. Crysania went to the small grouping of chairs before her desk with as little effort as though she were sighted. There she found a silver pitcher on the table and two cups. The water was warm, but she offered it to the mage as though it were freshly chilled with mountain ice.

Valin thanked her and poured two cups.

"We'll be glad when the weather breaks, lady."

She frowned, remembering the dream of rain and the unusual sense of dread to which she'd wakened. Then she smoothed it away, assuming the calm expression she knew she must wear throughout her day. He put a cup of water into her hand. Their fingers touched, but before his could linger, Crysania withdrew, cup in hand.

She was, she knew, careful of being touched. So many times during the day hands guided her, dressed her, helped her to find her food, her drink, her hair combs, her sandals, her way. She appreciated those touches for the help they gave, but she'd found herself, over the long years of blindness, welcoming the peace of an untouched moment, reluctant to share it. Others, though, others liked to linger, to touch the Revered Daughter as though they might well be touching Paladine himself.

"Why, Valin," she said lightly, "I'd think you'd welcome the heat. It must remind you of home."

He laughed, a husky, warm sound. "It does, and here I thought I was leaving the desert sands to find shade. Instead, it seems I brought the sun with me."

"Now tell me, friend mage, what has Lord Amothus written?"

She heard the scroll unrolled, heard the small sounds of him reading, slowed breath, a tapping of one finger on the parchment. In a moment he said, "The lord wishes to speak with you before the blessing, lady. He doesn't say why, but he asks that you grant him this request."

"I will, of course. He says no more?"

"Only that."

A small tightening of concern pricked her. Whatever he had to say, Amothus would not confide it to parchment, for that would be the same as confiding it to whoever would read his letter to her. What was it the Lord of Palanthas had to say for her ears only?

Crysania took a sip of water then set aside her cup. "Are we all ready for the ceremonies, Valin?"

"We are, lady. We wait only you."

"Then you will wait no longer."

On Valin's arm, she went out into the wide hall of the temple. Seralas, a longtime friend and one of her oldest clerics, greeted her. With him were three other clerics of her household. Their murmured greetings were almost lost in the bustling activity in the hall, the comings and goings, the brushings and straightenings, the excitement of a festival day only a little tinged with uneasiness.

Paladine, Crysania whispered, her voice the silent one of prayers, O Father of Light and Goodness, be with me this day as I am with you, in trust and faith.

But did he know she was with him, the god who had lately taken to not answering her prayers?

Crysania shivered, an odd feeling on so hot a morning.

* * * * *

She walked through marble halls of the Temple. Crysania trod lightly on thick, soft carpets woven in far

12

places. She went in darkness through corridors sweetened by incense and the dried rose petals of a season ago, and this felt like floating to her. She was going to her people bearing the blessings of Paladine. With Valin on one side and Seralas on the other, she went through her temple and felt it surrounding her, embracing her. Soon the burden of her questions, the burden of her fears, fell away. Her heart eased and opened, ready to receive joy, ready to offer it.

No other place could ease her heart as her beloved temple did. She cherished it as much for its peacefulness as for the sweat and tears she had invested in its creation, the lifting of it from ruin to glory. The great temple that stood here now was the second raised up to Paladine. The first had been broken and burned in the Blue Lady's War when dear Elistan, the head of the church and her mentor, had been killed. Crysania's sight had been newly sacrificed to the gods as penance for her ambition, some said, and so she had then believed. As a gift, she now knew, a way to see more deeply into the hearts of others, a way to find within herself the ever-filling well of compassion Elistan himself had always known was there.

Her first chore as Elistan's successor, the leader of the worshipers of Paladine, had been to rebuild the great temple. It had been a labor of love, one into which she'd thrown herself with an enthusiasm bordering on obsession. She knew every stone that had been laid for the foundation, the feel of every type of marble used for the floors and the thick walls. She knew the scent and texture of every tree that had become a chapel pew or a hall bench. She knew the width and length of each corridor, the floors and walls, every painting or decoration. Elistan had been buried in a deep vault in the echoing basement. As his teachings had become part of Crysania's heart, so now was his body part of the great Temple of Paladine.

No better place could he have rested.

"I have heard he was a great man," Valin said. The statement startled her, and he laughed. "Forgive me, lady. I can see Elistan in your expression each time you speak or think of him."

Behind them, the clerics who attended her kept a decent distance, letting her conversation progress unhindered.

"Am I so transparent, Valin?"

"No. Not usually." His voice still held laughter, but now it was a rueful kind, as though he shook his head over some foolishness of his own.

"Yes," she said. "Yes. He was a great man. Great in his mildness, beautiful in his humility." She sighed small sigh. "I miss him very much."

"Ah, you make me envy you, lady, for you have known so many great people."

She had, and she had known—she knew!—a god's touch upon her heart.

Valin stepped ahead of her now to open the wide doors leading onto the lawn. A dry lawn, a brown lawn— the temple suffered in appearance for that—but Crysania had months ago insisted that water, soon to become scarce if rain didn't fall, was better used for drinking. She stepped out into a blast of heat that would have been unusual at the height of summer. A sheen of sweat slicked her skin before she'd taken even a step.

"Ah, lady," Valin said, he who enjoyed describing all that he saw. "The streets are busy, filled with people passing by. Do you hear?"

She heard voices and shufflings and the sound of leather sandals slapping on cobblestones. Wagons creaked, horses whinnied, and knights—she heard their armor clanking—walked past.

"Bless the knights for their devotion," she whispered to Valin. "That they would go abroad on such a hot day,

14

clanking and banging. And, no doubt, polished and shining."

Valin chuckled and stood near her as she let the sounds wash over her, the excited laughter of children, adults calling greetings to each other. Festival Day was a happy day, meant for celebration and joy. Like the knights in their armor, no one seemed willing to let the heat spoil the occasion.

On Valin's arm, Crysania led her little cluster of clerics down the wide walkway and out into the street. As she passed, the knots of people stepped aside, making way for her as they always did. They loved their lady, their Revered Daughter of Paladine. She whispered a word to Valin, who spoke to the clerics behind them, and they took a longer route to the palace than might have been necessary. The shorter way led past Shoikan Grove, the dark and haunted wood that warded the Tower of High Sorcery. The cold emanating from there—even in this terrible Anvil Summer!—would chill the heart of anyone but the master of that tower, the dark elf Dalamar. How he stood it no one knew, and this was not a thing Crysania liked to think about, not even to marvel.

She had been in that grove once a long time ago. Sometimes, in nightmares, she went there again.

The crowds swirled around, their voices running high and excited. Valin moved closer, protectively. This mage, born in the wide desert where no one could see the horizons, never relaxed in the crowds of Palanthas. The Dawning, just a month previous, had been his first, and it hadn't been this raucous. Crysania smiled up at him with easy reassurance. She knew the streets of the city of Palanthas almost as well as she knew the temple. This was comfortable territory to her, filled with the people she so loved. She had no fear of walking among them.

"It's all a tangle of byways and roads," Valin had once said to her, "and I don't know how anyone finds his way."

She had laughed and told him he must think of the city of Palanthas as a great wheel, one having eight broad avenues radiating from the palace and its gardens.

"You'll never get lost as long as you remember that, friend mage. One road or another will lead you home."

"Eventually," he'd said.

"Well, yes. Eventually."

It was one of those avenues, tree-lined and neatly paved, that led them to the palace grounds, where the air was a-hum with people, electric with anticipation. Now Seralas stepped out of the crowd of clerics and walked at her right side, Valin's complement. In this way, they went to the Central Plaza, parting the crowds who stopped to wish the Revered Daughter good day, to call cheer to her on Festival Day.

"The grounds are very pretty today," Valin said, bending a little to speak close to her ear so she could hear above the noise. "The trees are all hung with colored ribbons. The fountains don't run, but the palace is decorated with lights of all colors. A gift of the mages, perhaps, for they don't flicker like fire. They are as round as balls and sliding up and down the walls." He leaned closer still, his breath warm on her neck. "Why, it's nearly as colorful as the lord himself."

Crysania tilted her head toward him, not quite sure what he meant. Seralas supplied the answer. "The Lord of Palanthas, my lady. He's wearing green and gold satin. His cloak must weigh ten pounds, for all the embroidery and gold beads. And his tunic flows with gold fringe."

"In this heat!" Crysania said, laughing softly as she imagined Lord Amothus sweltering in full dress.

16

Like magic, she turned her laughter into a smile of greeting as the lord and his retinue approached, pages and ladies and serving people chattering like a charm of finches in the eaves.

She moved, standing free of Valin and Seralas.

"My lord, I give you good day." She extended her hand and he bowed over it.

"Lady Crysania." His voice was incongruously deep and rough, for all his cultured tone. "Thank you for coming to grace our Festival Day." He turned, drawing her hand to the crook of his arm. "Will you walk with me?"

"Of course." Crysania gestured, a small movement of her hand, to indicate that her retinue need not follow closely. Valin stepped away. She could feel him leaving. Seralas edged aside, too. Neither went far. Smiling, she said, "Come, my lord. I will take you for a stroll."

Amothus murmured an absent gallantry and walked her away. "Lady, you received my message?"

"I did indeed. How may I help you, my lord?"

He shuffled and took a deep breath, which he let out slowly. "I have heard disturbing rumors of war. More than just the whispers of a buildup of troops that have been familiar to us since the winter."

Crysania stood still and lifted her head, as though to hear more. In her heart, she fretted, wondering where her own news of the troop buildup had got to. Nisse and Lagan had been gone for many days now. Paladine is with them and so they are well, she assured herself as Amothus guided her through the gates separating the palace gardens from the Central Plaza, helped her to weave in and out among the people spreading picnic blankets and the children running across the ground.

"My lord," she said, her voice low and private, "at the temple, we've heard these rumors, too. I've sent two

17

clerics to the High Clerist's Tower to speak with Sir Thomas. He will know the latest developments. I assure you, as soon as they return, I'll send word."

He took in another deep breath and let it out. "I would be grateful, lady. Especially if you hear anything about mages who wear gray robes, who fight—"

"Gray robes?" Crysania stopped in midstep.

"A rogue *order*, Lady, adhering to no rule but that of their own ambitions."

Crysania nodded. "Yes. I have heard of this before."

Amothus glanced around nervously. She felt his movements. All eyes were upon them, certainly. How could they not be when the Lord of Palanthas and the Revered Daughter of Paladine strolled and conferred?

"Lady, this is not the place to discuss it. There is already enough unrest."

Crysania frowned, trying to stretch out her senses, trying to know what she could not see. She heard only the crowd, the voices, the shufflings.

"The worshipers who come to the temple are concerned, but I would not say there is unrest."

The lord shrugged, chuckling with a weary resignation. "They come to the temple seeking guidance and prayer, lady. From me, they expect a different type of aid. And while they would not demand immediate attention from their gods, they do demand it of the lord of their city.

"Naturally the people are afraid, lady," he continued. "This heat makes tempers short. Travel into the city has fallen off in the last few weeks at an alarming rate. The merchants and traders are feeling the effects in their pocketbooks, and their concern trickles down to their customers. The rumors say the plains have been devastated by this early heat. The people are beginning to ask questions. What will happen if we have no trade this year? The stalls in the market are not filling up with farmers and their produce. If the weather continues, what will happen to our own crops? How will we supplement our supplies? When people start to worry about how they will feed their children—"

"Please, my lord. A moment to let me think."

What if, what if? What if—a small dark voice whispered in her heart—what if the gods will not send rain? O Paladine, where are you?

They passed under a fluttering banner and out of the sun's reach. The relief was immediate and welcome. The lord steered Crysania to a bench of smooth, polished wood placed before a table covered in a soft cloth.

"I've had a tent set up for you, lady. We've ordered refreshments. Let me know if the breeze grows too strong and I'll have the sides unrolled."

Crysania managed a smile, for the watching crowd, but not from her heart. "I can't imagine any breeze could be too strong. I thank you, though, for your concern."

Amothus leaned close and whispered, "I wish we could have canceled this Festival Day."

"Oh, no," she protested. "This is important for the people. Coming together and giving thanks."

"Your faith is to be commended," he said wryly. "But I can't think it will do anyone good to bring people together to compare their miseries. Now, lady, you must excuse me. I have others to greet."

She said something gracious, something absent, and he moved away. Almost at once one of the young clerics brought a plate of pastries to the table, along with a glass of water. Crysania thanked her and heard the sound of food being transferred from one plate to another, and then Valin slid a plate against her mug. She passed her fingers delicately over the contents, soft rolls with a selection of textured surfaces. She chose one and took a bite she never tasted.

No harm could come from gathering to receive the blessings of the gods, surely, but Amothus's own fears had planted the idea in her mind of a disturbed, agitated crowd. She tuned out the soft conversation of her people around her and listened instead to the more prevailing sounds of laughter and the rising hum of voices. To the movement of people. Was it her imagination, or did this festival have a different sound to it than previous ones—a more restless sound? Was the conversation more subdued, the adult laughter more forced?

"Is all well, lady?"

Valin's deep voice, his desert accent, brought Crysania away from her thoughts. She tried to smile, but she couldn't shake the memory of Amothus's fears.

"Valin." She motioned the mage closer.

He came around the table quickly, knelt at her side.

"I want you to do something for me."

"Of course, lady. Anything."

She leaned close enough to him that she could smell him, a peculiar mixture of Valin and sweet rolls and wine. "Go out into the crowd. Walk about. Listen. See if you can divine their mood."

Valin stood. "I will return as quickly as I can."

She couldn't hear him walking, so loud was the noise of the crowd, but she felt him leave. In his absence, Crysania asked Seralas to accompany her as she strolled to the edge of the tent. There she heard a group of children playing nearby, their shrill shrieks and shouts of pleasure drowning out the more contained voices beyond. It would be easy to let Amothus's fears color her perceptions, but she refused to do that.

All is well, she told herself, all is well, and one day soon it will rain and wash away Amothus's doubts.

What, though, would wash away the truth of the storm clouds of war massing over the Khalkist Mountains?

Paladine, be with us, and, dearest lord, you don't have to speak a word to me if only you will stay near!

Soon came a heavy step behind her and the scent of Valin on the barely stirring air. She turned, reaching her hand out to him. "What have you found?"

The white robe came close, lowering his voice. "The mood seems strange, lady. I don't know your people, but if these were mine, I would say they seem almost overly anxious to have a good time. They are laughing, playing, enjoying themselves, but it seems forced."

They are in fear, she thought. My people are in pain. How can I heal this?

She smiled, just a little, feeling a sudden brush of warmth in her heart. She could heal by offering Paladine's blessing.

"Valin, please leave me a moment in peace."

He left, but he didn't go far. His scent told her that. He gave her enough room for quiet thinking, though, and so she sat alone in the shade and prepared herself for the coming ceremony. She kept her breathing light, her thoughts simple. Prayers for prosperity and happiness ran through her mind, the words a comfort, the rhythm a blessing of its own.

The crowd began to move closer. A boy shouted, "It's time! Is it time?" His father hushed him. Crysania heard his mother's fond laughter as she counseled patience.

It was time, though. The boy was right. Time for the blessing, time to embrace the people and gather them into Paladine's loving arms, by her words, by her faith, by assuring them that all would be well.

Crysania stood, a signal to her people that she was ready. Her entourage gathered around her, Valin on her left, Seralas on her right, the others behind her. Lord Amothus awaited her at the foot of the steps, his people gathered around him in the same manner, an escort of honor for the Revered Daughter of Paladine.

"The crowd is very large, lady," Seralas murmured as they started up the steps. Ahead of her, she heard the Lord's entourage whisper as they ascended the stage, moving into their places. Valin and Seralas had dropped back to climb the steps side by side behind her. When she stepped out from under the vast awning into the heat and the open air, the sound of the crowd rose up in front of her as a solid wall.

Cried a voice from right below, "The lady! Oh, look! The lady has come!"

Another raised up, a child's voice piping, "The Lady Crysania!"

In another voice, a hope edged with something as dark as desperation. "Paladine, bless us!"

For this, Crysania had come, to offer hope and the healing that might come with it. Lifted up on their voices, lifted up on her own trust and faith in the god she loved, Paladine so long and strangely silent, she raised her arms and held out her hands, palms up to the heavens. Quiet fell about her like silently falling snow.

"Citizens and visitors of Palanthas," she began, raising her clear voice so that it projected all the way back to the plaza wall and bounced back at her. "I welcome you to the opening of the Festival."

She had not known what she would say until this very moment. Speaking to her people was such a joy, such a blessing, that the words always seemed clumsy if she rehearsed them. Ever she spoke of faith, trusting. Never had her trust been denied.

"I know many of you come here today with questions in your heart, with concerns about the weather and crops. I know that when you are concerned about your families, it is difficult to fathom the workings of the gods. I cannot tell you that the weather will not be harsh or that we do not have hard times ahead of us."

She paused to take a breath. She would say nothing about the rumors of war on her mind, on the mind of the Lord of Palanthas, surely on the minds of many who stood now before her. She would offer hope, and so she paused to let the joy of blessing rush into her and fill her.

"Dear ones, I can only tell you that Paladine loves you as you love him, and that he will continue to watch over us. That is why is it so important we gather here today to ask that the blessings of Paladine be upon us, to thank him for the blessings he has already heaped upon us, and to ask that he continue to shine the light of his boundless love upon us."

And yet, in spite of her joy, her words rang hollow in her ears. In times past, she would have brought the crowd a specific message from Paladine, words of hope and confidence and direction. Yet she did not—could not—say she had communicated recently with their god. Never would she lie, not even to offer balm.

The crowd sighed and shifted as Crysania raised her hands to begin the blessing.

A shout, like a thunderclap, rang out from the mass of people below.

"Lady, tell us what Paladine has said to you!"

The man's voice came from near the middle of the crowd, loud enough to be heard by her and all those around him. Behind her, clerics and the lord's retinue stirred. Someone—Valin, to be sure—took a step forward, then halted.

Crysania ignored the question and the motions of those behind her. She lifted her hands to begin the benediction, but the insistent question came again, silencing the murmuring voices in front of her.

"How does Paladine allay our concerns about this heat? Of rumored war? What does he say about all these rumors we hear, of which none will speak?"

The questions were her own, couched in other words, spoken to no one but herself and her god in quiet dark nights. The voice before her, speaking her own doubts, sounded familiar, yet she couldn't place it. She gave a quick twitch, turning her head a little to the side, and mouthed "Who speaks?"

Once again the questions, insistent, and now in other voices. Men's voices, women's voices, some sounding as rough as a fishmonger's, some sounding as smooth as a courtier's. On her right, the lord stepped closer, tense and annoyed. And the original questioner lifted up his voice again, asking what all wanted to know.

What has Paladine said of the incomparable heat? What does the god say about the rumors of war?

Crysania reached out a hand to still Amothus, but either he didn't see it or he ignored it.

"You are unwise, Sir," the lord said firmly, loudly enough for all to hear. "The lady is giving us a blessing."

An answering murmur washed up from the crowd, in some quarters agreement, in others disgruntlement. Crysania hesitated, grateful that the lord's intervention gave her a moment to think.

That voice! That insistent, questioning voice. She knew it, a name to place with it hovering in the back of her mind, just out of reach.

Like the restless waters out on the bay, the crowd murmured and moved, shifting and rising, falling back, coming close.

On her left, Valin came close enough that she could feel his warmth near her, her good and faithful friend. The remainder of her people and Amothus's fanned out behind her. It had, she hoped, the appearance of being

24

part of the ceremony and not a protective gesture.

Valin's words came to her, almost unintelligible, as if he spoke with his head down. "The man who spoke is dressed roughly. A farmer or a worker of some sort."

Ah, but that wasn't the voice of a farmer, nor the voice of a countryman rough with shouting at cows and herding geese. That much Crysania knew, though no more yet. Turning her attention back to the crowd, Crysania quieted the lord with a gesture. "I will endeavor to answer the man's question."

She turned back to the crowd, her heart beating so hard she was sure it must sound like a drumbeat to all who stood near. No matter, let them hear.

"Dear ones," she said, her voice low so they must be quiet to hear her. When silence fell again, she went on. "I do not pray to Paladine of weather and such everyday things. I speak to him of our souls and our faith. I ask him what we may do for him, not how I may keep myself comfortable." She kept her voice soft and clear, without censure. "Each day of our lives is a test, of our faith, of our will." She moved forward, lifting her arms to the sky, to the god who must surely have good reason for his silence. "This I know: The gods will not always give us gentle rain and cooling winds. Our crops will not always flourish. Our neighbors will not always be kind. We will have heat and storms and battles. Our faith will be tested. Our resolve will be tested. And we will come through all the stronger."

She opened her arms wide as though to embrace the entire crowd in the warmth, the joy of her faith and trust. "Together our faith will be strong, and Paladine will look down upon us with pride."

Crysania paused, feeling the crowd settle and sigh. They were not simply lulled by her voice, but filled and uplifted. The surge of emotion that buffeted her was almost palpable. She swayed on her feet, moved by what she felt, for the first time in a long time wishing for her sight that she could see the light of trust dawn on the faces of those to whom she spoke.

"Dear ones," she said, "my dear ones, Paladine's blessing upon you all."

A profound silence followed her words, unbroken by any sound.

One of her clerics touched her gently in the small of her back, moving with her, guiding her backward. Then Valin was beside her, offering his arm, and the lord was talking to the crowd again, telling them about the festivities—musicians playing in the palace gardens, ale and food available in the market.

"Quickly," she said.

At the bottom of the steps, her clerics surrounded her, a wall of whirling white robes that separated the Revered Daughter Crysania from the crowds. The quick walk back to the temple was one of the most miserable of her life. Never had she left a festival before midafternoon, walking at length among the crowds, speaking freely to the citizens of her city, touching the heads of small children whose parents asked for a blessing. Never before had she felt the need to cut herself off from them.

And yet, as Paladine seemed to have removed himself from her, so must she remove herself from her people. Lonely! How lonely it felt! Did the god himself feel thus? Did he miss her and all those who loved him?

Oh, Paladine! If I could only feel your healing presence!

On the heels of her silent cry came a sudden, unlooked-for understanding. She knew who had called challenge to her from the crowd. She knew that disguised voice!

Hope rose in her suddenly, flushing her cheeks. She knew him, that heckler. He was an unlikely presence at the festival, just as unlikely a source of help and hope, but Crysania did not stop to question.

"Valin," she said.

He came close. "Lady?"

"I have a favor to ask of you."

Chapter Two

Mistress Jenna walked the quiet streets, heat rippling around her like the shimmer of magic. She missed the usual knots of people bustling in the streets, seamen on their way to the docks, knights shining and clanking, clerics like white ghosts in their temple robes going to and from the Temple of Paladine. Not a dwarf was to be seen in the Street of Anvils. No elves walked in the Gardens of Grace, murmuring to each other as though to tell secrets. Most people, citizens of the city and visitors, were still at the festival, eating and drinking and no doubt talking about the disturbance before the Revered Daughter of Paladine offered her blessing. Naught but a gully dwarf or two did Jenna see, skittering in the alleys as they hunted their supper. Now and then their prey, one fat rat or another, ran dashing across Jenna's path. Then she'd

28

step back, wait for the inevitable chattering gully dwarf to follow, and continue on her way.

Though Jenna had forgone her usual cloak and worn her lightest robe, it had made little difference. Her red robe hung damp with sweat, and sweat inelegantly defeated Jenna's soaps and perfumes. She had long ago grown weary of smelling like a dockworker. She lengthened her stride, hurrying to get out of the bitter sun and into the relative coolness of her mageware shop. Another street, another alley cut through, her footfalls echoing on the deserted New City street, and at last she came in sight of her shop, The Three Moons.

Over the door, the sign that wore the symbols of the three moons of magic—red Lunitari, black Nuitari, and silver Solinari—sat sullen and immobile without the usual sea breeze to stir it. Softly whispering, Jenna spoke spidery words of magic, a spell to unweave that which guarded the door. A little bell, crystal tinkling, sounded as she pushed open the door. Except there was no real bell, not one to be seen with the eye, only a minor spell set to make the sound when anyone opened the door. It was a small spell, but it pleased her.

Jenna stepped into the darkness, breathing in the cooler air and the woven scents of her wares, spell components from throughout the world. Like the bell, the well-ordered shop—the quiet interior, the magical supplies all in their places on the shelves—pleased her. Bottles and boxes and books all had their places, lining the walls with their colors and varied textures of the earth, wood and grain and soil and paper. Here, neatly stacked upon shelves, were all the possibilities of magic, ready to unfold to the mage who understood how to use them. She looked around at the peace and the order, and she took a long, deep breath.

It had been a strange festival, with the heat and the uneasy crowds. Strange was the demanding question flung out from the crowd during the Revered Daughter's blessing—who, though, wouldn't wonder what gods had to say about this long, hot season? Something about the questioner had pricked Jenna's curiosity. That was one of the reasons she'd left early, to find a place to think in quiet, to decide whether she wanted to ponder this incident on her own or to lay the strange event before Dalamar to see what he'd have to say. Some things she shared with her lover and some things she didn't. She never liked to share doubt with him unless she could couch it in phrases to make doubt seem like observation.

Time enough, she decided, to go to the tower this evening and speak with its master.

Jenna stepped into her back room, splashed water over her face, caught her long red hair into a knot atop her head—and stopped still as the bell tinkled above the door. She'd not raised the shade to indicate that the shop was open, and so she stood quietly at the curtain separating the shop from her back room, taking a moment to observe who was bold enough to enter The Three Moons when the shop was so obviously closed.

In the dimness, a tall human man stood, dressed in the rough brown trews and tan shirt of a farmer. Those long-fingered well-tended hands weren't a farmer's, though, of this Jenna had no doubt. Nor were his a farmer's eyes, for they did not sit in nests of wrinkles as would the eyes of a man used to squinting at the sky and toiling in the sun. Jenna arched a brow. Here, in her own shop, was the man who'd started the festival crowd questioning the Revered Daughter Crysania. She was not a big believer in coincidence, rather choosing to think that all things converge which must.

Stepping into the shop, she said, "Good day to you, master farmer. How can I help you?"

The man took a step toward her, letting the door close

behind him. He moved with a certain elegance, and all of a sudden Jenna recognized him. Still, she stood where she was, delaying his moment of small triumph for just a moment simply because she could. At last, low and soft, she said, "Good day to you, my dear."

The man lifted his head to smile, though his eyes held little warmth. He had his vanities, this one, and Jenna had pricked one. Words of magic fell from the man's lips, words like dust soon blown away. Jenna listened to the changing spell but did not try to remember. It would have been a waste of time. Words of magic vanish from the memory of speaker and listener in the moment they are given voice. More interesting to her, far more exciting, was to see the power those words engendered.

A dark, raw force hummed in the room, and the air became charged, as though some black bolt of lightning had torn through it unseen. Jenna's skin prickled, and her heart rose as though she had just come into her lover's arms. This was magic to her, practiced and watched, like making love.

The "farmer" stood surrounded in a cone of sparkling colored light, blue and green and red and gold. The light began to swirl, first earthwise and then counter, growing brighter all the while even as the colors came together to become white. Then the light fell away, dropping down the length of him until it lay in a pool at his feet.

Out from the pool of light stepped the Lord of the Tower of High Sorcery, Dalamar the Dark, dressed a soft black robe stitched at hem and sleeves with silver runes.

Jenna laughed and complimented him on his entrance.

The dark elf swept her a low, ironic bow. He brushed at an imaginary speck of lint on the spotless robe. "I missed you at the festival, my love."

"Did you? I didn't miss you. Nor," she said pointedly, "did most of the others present. You don't expect your little charade will hold for very long, do you? The Revered Daughter is no simpleton."

Dalamar adjusted his robe on his shoulders. "Hardly that."

Lips curling slightly, his version of a smile, he came into the shop, brushing his long fingers across Jenna's arm as he passed. She lifted her face and he kissed her lightly.

"Tell me," she said, breathing in the magical smell of him, "what did you discover with this stunt? What did you hope to accomplish?"

He paused in the basement doorway, his shape lost in the shadows, only his voice to be heard. "There was nothing to accomplish. I just wondered how she would answer my question."

Perhaps, Jenna thought, and perhaps not. She hadn't heard many proclamations of Nuitari falling from Dalamar's lips these days. Probably as few as those heard by Paladine's clerics.

"Does that mean you didn't get what you wanted? Or that you're not going to tell me your true goal?"

"There is nothing to tell. I simply wanted to know if the lady Crysania is as concerned about things as we are." Dalamar slipped behind the curtain and walked down into the darkness of the basement and Jenna's lab.

He might have added, Jenna thought, that he had indeed gotten what he wanted. He'd seen the reaction, the concern on Crysania's face when he called out to know what Paladine had to say about the terrible summer and the rumors of war gathering like storm in the west. He had his answer from the look on her face: The Revered Daughter of Paladine knew no better than he, Dalamar the Dark, what the gods had to say about anything.

This cannot be good, Jenna thought. This cannot be good at all.

32

* * * * *

"This cannot be good," Dalamar muttered. He took the steps down to Jenna's basement laboratory two at a time, easily, as a boy might.

Where were the gods? Cold suspicion crowded him like the shadows on the stairs. More to the point, what were the gods up to?

He flung up a sphere of light to see by and looked around at Jenna's laboratory, the place below as neatly organized as the place above. Here she worked her spells and experiments, here she searched as diligently for answers to the mysterious silence of the gods as he did. Had she found anything? He doubted it. Some things Jenna withheld from him, but this—this silence of the gods—disturbed her as deeply as it did him. He knew, he who knew his lover well, that she had learned nothing more than he. Nothing more than the Lady Crysania, who hid her uneasiness behind blind eyes and yet smelled of that unease across the whole festival crowd.

Where were the gods? What were they up to?

Paladine was silent. Dalamar's own dark god, Nuitari, had not communed with him in weeks. When wars were brewing, as rumor said was the case these days, Takhisis could always be counted upon to summon her forces, those who worshiped her and strove to do her will. Yet even the Dark Queen was silent.

This could not be good.

And yet when he remembered the look on Lady Crysania's face, that pale, calm expression behind which she tried to hide the loss of her god's company, his blessing, his guidance, he thought there might yet be a way to learn what was afoot.

The dark elf took a long breath, slow and deep, and put into his mind the picture of the Tower of High

Sorcery. He saw Shoikan Grove, the fearsome wood that the god Nuitari himself had commanded to grow around the tower. Within that grove existed terrible things—the dead, the undead, ghosts and daemons and creatures worse than they, creatures who should never have been given life. These were the wardens of the tower, past which none could go without Dalamar's leave. Another breath, as long, as deep, and the black robe called into his mind the image of the tower itself, grand and high and bristling with battlements. Of this great fortress he was master; in this fastness he ruled as kings ruled in lesser places.

In the cool and quiet darkness beneath The Three Moons, Dalamar held these images easily in mind. He let go a deep breath, and in doing so breathed life into spell words and gave himself to the magic, let it blow him along the roads of enchantment that would take him to the Tower of High Sorcery.

In a measureless moment, Dalamar's feet touched solid marble at the foot of the long winding staircase leading up to his own chambers.

As he climbed, he met a red-robed mage on her way down. The young woman spoke a respectful word of greeting to the master of the tower, then slipped by, past Dalamar's grim silence. Dalamar never looked back nor ever spoke. He kept climbing.

Yes, he thought, yes. This might work. He might soon be feeling the chill touch of Nuitari's regard, the delightful tingling up the spine that told him he and his god were in communion. He missed that communion, that drawing of strength from Nuitari's dark well. More, he missed knowing what was going on in the world. That was the true sting.

Dalamar's chamber sat high in the tower. The walk was long, one he enjoyed, ascending to the seat of his power. In between the landings, darkness as thick as night hid the steps. That mattered little to him; he knew each step and could have walked them with his eyes shut tight. Many levels up, he came to his laboratory. Outside the great door, a torch burned brightly. Two disembodied eyes floated in the shadows beyond the flaring light.

"This way is forbidden," the specter intoned, "even for you, Master."

No one could pass this way, not even he, and that was as it should be. Past that door lay the portal through which the Dark Queen had once entered the world. Through there she'd been driven back again. Beyond that door lay the Abyss. Once Lady Crysania herself had passed into that place and out from it again. Sighted, she'd gone in. Blinded, she'd come out.

"I do not seek entrance," Dalamar said easily. The memory of his own words came back to him, as if he had spoken them only yesterday instead of years ago: *Take this key and keep it for all eternity. Give it to no one, not even myself.* "I came only to assure myself that none has come here, that none has disturbed anything."

"None has come this way, Master."

Satisfied, Dalamar returned to his own chamber. Magic warded that door, too, visible as a shimmering in the air. As he saw the shimmer, so did Dalamar feel a slight tingling on his skin, a spidering up his arms and spine. This was the silent whisper of magic, the wordless voice of a powerful artifact kept safe and hidden in the quarters of the master of the tower. Now the master smiled, as one does who reviews and finds in order the final details of a newly hatched plan.

His outer chamber was lightless. The tingling on his skin became pricking. Softly he spoke a word of magic. A globe of light sprang to hand, pushing away the shadows, and he crossed to the far side, to his broad desk set beneath a wide window. Upon that desk lay a tower of books, and atop the books two stones, rough-edged, never worked, uncouth as rocks just dug from the ground. From these came the prickling, the edgy song of magic playing on his skin.

They had fallen into his hands months ago, as rain falls to the ground. He'd found them sitting upon this very desk one morning months ago. From where had they come? No one knew, not the wisest mage in his tower, not the least, not the most innocent, nor the most suspicious. The stones, for all anyone knew, had simply appeared upon the desk of the Master of the Tower of High Sorcery. Dalamar had chosen to think of them as a gift.

Ah, but a rough gift. The vibration emanating from one stone hummed gently. It had no alignment to either of the three gods of magic; it simply vibrated with undifferentiated power. That coming from the other, though, that was a harsher magic for Dalamar to feel. This close to the stone, the power clawed at him, raking his nerves till they cried out in pain. Here was a magic no Black Robe could bear to feel, for all the warmth and strength of goodness poured out from the second stone. Still, he'd touched them both when first they'd appeared, curious, wanting to see what he could see and not caring about the pain. The first time he put his hand to them, he heard a name whispered softly:

Dragon Stones.

He began at once to hunt down their history. With all the resources he had at his command, he soon learned the sketchy lore of the stones from books, from rumor, from whispers of ancient legend. There were originally five Dragon Stones, one for each of the chromatic dragon colors. Two of those he had now.

In the weeks after the finding, he'd worked with the

two he had, testing them, prying to see what would come loose of magic. Nothing. From these he learned little. They tingled always; the one raked him with pain each time he touched it. Once they had glowed a little. No more than that had he gotten from these mysterious stones, and now they rested atop the tower of books, useless as anything but paperweights, their magic alive in them and resisting his every attempt to free it.

The first starlight fell pale into the room, shining a little upon the two stones. It was said, between the lines of lore, in the margins of rumor, that the mage who mastered all five Dragon Stones would hear the voices of the gods and that mage would have more power than anyone before him and need not worry about the power of anyone to come. Dalamar's heart thumped, sending the blood rushing through his veins.

He needed such magic! And he might well find it, following the paths of marginalia on the pages of rumor. Following, or setting someone else to follow. He was, if nothing, a patient man, not given to leaping after the short term gain. Better, far better, to look to the long term.

Dalamar stroked the spines of the books upon which the stones lay. One was bound in leather as gray as the eyes of the Lady Crysania herself. That one spoke of the Dragon Stones in a way no other book had, and what it said held the promise of the great power he craved.

The dark elf moved the books aside, stones and all, and sat down, his back to the high window. The vibrations from the good-aligned stone raked his nerves, but he did not withdraw. He closed his eyes and saw in memory the Revered Daughter of Paladine, hungry for word from her god. What a charming thread Crysania would make in the tapestry of his plan. Her image faded and now he saw the Dragon Stones glowing not in memory, but through his very eyelids.

* * * * *

Valin ar Tandar strode through streets emptied by the festival. Long purple shadows fell gently upon the cobblestones. They offered shade but little coolness. The sky, burning blue all day, had a softer glow to it now in the twilight hour, but still heat poured down on the city. Not even the darkest part of the night would offer relief from the burning and the sweltering humidity that promised rain and ever failed to keep that promise. Sweat slicked his skin and made his white robe cling to his back, made him long for the clean, dry heat of his desert home. And yet, long as he did, he couldn't see himself leaving the city.

Palanthas the Beautiful. Said to have been constructed by dwarves in the image of a fabled ogre city, both New City and Old City were remarkable for their loveliness. Sunlight reflected brilliantly off the streets and walls and ornate marble buildings. People of every kindred and kind filled the streets—humans, elves, dwarves, even a minotaur or two if one looked in the right quarters. All this was exciting to Valin, making his memories of home sweet but never so alluring that they'd send him from the city.

Not all his memories of home would ever entice him from the Temple of Paladine, from his work there. Never would they send him from his lady.

A young woman sitting in the shade of the wall that separated Old City from New City smiled as Valin approached, raising her eyebrows in a way that communicated frank interest. Her white skin shone with sweat; the flaxen hair so common here and virtually unknown among his desert kin spilled like running gold down her back. He stopped only a moment to smile, then he walked on.

38

There would have been a time, not so long ago, when he'd have done more than smile and pass by. He'd have gone to sit beside her, talked with her and listened to her, or found a cool place to lie with her, whatever her mood willed. He'd have taken joy in her and she in him. Perhaps they might have forged something in the cool shadows to last beyond a quick grab for passion. Perhaps that would have happened one day a long time ago, before he met the lady. His dear Crysania.

He named her so boldly, in his heart. Her grand experiment, she called him, all the short half year he'd been at the Temple of Paladine. Friend mage, she often addressed him.

"My lady," he said back to her aloud. My dearest Crysania, in his most secret heart.

Who knew that love could sparkle in the blood as brightly, as sweetly as magic itself did? Not Valin—certainly not he—until he became the Revered Daughter's grand experiment.

A desert son, he had seen courage, known and loved it as it burned in the hearts of his tribesmen, shining as they breasted the winds, the storms of sand, as they faced each other, tribe against tribe, in battle. Never had he seen such courage as Crysania showed today, the lady straight and tall before a mass of people she could not see, for whom she brimmed with love. Each one of their woes she would erase if she could. Each one of their sorrows, their aching doubts, their griefs, she would heal if she could. For this woman, this beautiful Revered Daughter of Paladine, he would go anywhere, he would do anything.

Past darkening alleys he went, past huddles of clothing that might have been sleepers or beggars collapsed from hunger and heat, all the while watching his way. He'd not been to The Three Moons before, only knew the way by his lady's direction. When at last he found the place, he was surprised to see the tidy storefront, the neatly painted sign showing the moons of magic.

What is dark does not always seem so, his lady said. What is light may often be hidden. As ever, she was right.

A bell tinkled softly overhead as Valin entered the mageware shop. A heady aroma flowed out the door, like arms to usher him inside, the intoxicating scents of herbs and spices and tanned leather and acrid liquids. Valin breathed again deeply, enjoying the tapestry of magic's scent. He stood in the main aisle of the small shop, surrounded by shelves filled with jars and bottles and boxes and pouches. At the back of the shop, glass cases sparkled, meticulously clean, reflecting beams of sunlight in which dust motes swirled and sparkled. A wall of spellbooks, neatly shelved, looked so old they might crumble if touched. Upon another shelf were books so new he yet smelled the fresh parchment. He ran his fingers along the spines of these, imagining the ecstasy of learning the spells, lips moving as he memorized the words, his skin prickling as he cast magic!

A mage among clerics at Paladine's temple, he'd had little chance lately to practice his art. The last spell he'd cast had been the tiniest of things, a few words to fling light before his lady when a torch blew out. Not light for her to see by—ah, no, she needed none of that. Crysania went in darkness as others went in sunlight, easily, confidently. The light had been for him, so that he could see her, the grace of her walking, the beauty of her standing before the door of one of her clerics as she knocked to enter.

He missed the magic and often thought he'd traded it for something else. For his Lady Crysania, who smiled at him as she would a friend, who called him her grand experiment. Who did not know how dearly he loved her.

Soft, a footfall. Gentle, a woman's strong, clear voice. "How may I help you, sir mage?"

Valin started, then inclined his head in a courteous greeting. Here was the mistress of The Three Moons, Jenna, who was the lover of Dalamar the Dark. They were well matched, those two, each full of power, each ambitious. Once Valin had heard a cleric at the temple say that it was a good thing those two had come together. Together they would watch each other, checking the balance of their power always. What would our lives be like if they were at odds, one trying to have it over the other?

That cleric had been Lagan Innis, the hill dwarf, gone these last weeks to the High Clerist's Tower. A quiet one, as most hill dwarfs are, Lagan was a keen observer. His droll remarks often amused Valin, who had quickly become friends with the dwarf. An odd friendship, some thought, the dwarf and the desert mage, but as Lagan himself had said, "We're a pair of oddities, my friend Valin and I, for who would expect to find a hill dwarf serving as a cleric of Paladine? And if that didn't strain credulity, there's the even greater oddity of a mage of any stripe in a nest of clerics. Yes, we're well matched, we two curiosities, fated to friendship."

Now, from new habit, Valin offered a prayer to Paladine for his absent friend's safety even as he smiled at Mistress Jenna.

"Good evening to you, Mistress Jenna. I'm Valin. I—"

She offered her hand, smiling. "From the temple."

He returned her smile, for it was lovely. "Yes, from the temple. You flatter me, mistress, for I'm not such a mage as anyone would have heard of."

"Indeed? A white-robed mage living in the Temple of Paladine is certainly of interest in magical circles. How does the—" she paused, as if choosing her next words "—how does the experiment fare?"

A prickle of warning skittered up Valin's neck. He was certain she'd almost said "the grand experiment."

"Well enough, I suppose. My lady continues it and seems pleased. I confess it isn't so difficult as one would imagine. In the desert tribes, mages and clerics hold each other in high esteem. I started with less prejudice than most."

Again she dimpled. Such a dazzling smile!

"How fortunate for you. And for your lady."

"Yes," he said coolly. He had the feeling that he was as transparent as glass, that she knew exactly why he stayed on at the temple. He took a small breath, refusing to show this wizardess more than a polite smile.

Yet now she had what she wanted, he was certain of that. Like her lover, Jenna was a collector of information and observations. One way or another, everything she saw and surmised would serve her, later if not sooner.

"Now, sir mage, tell me what brings you to my shop? How may I help you?"

Valin kept his expression neutral. "The Revered Daughter Crysania has sent me with a message for Lord Dalamar."

Jenna nodded easily, as though this were no uncommon occurrence. "I see. I'll be happy to take it to him."

Perhaps she was just being prudent, Valin thought. He knew that Dalamar and Crysania sometimes communicated on matters of importance, and perhaps Jenna was accustomed to relaying those messages. Nonetheless, Valin had his instructions.

"You are kind to offer, mistress, but I was asked to speak with Dalamar himself."

For a moment, he thought Jenna would protest, but she only nodded. "Of course. I can take you to him now."

He waited while she crossed to the door and drew the cloth across it to signify that the shop was closed. Then she murmured words too low for him to hear and moved her hands along the door, setting a ward to seal it. When she was done, he saw the trembling aura of the spell, twining motes of magic around the door.

She came back, briskly sending a swirl of dust into the air as her robes brushed the floor. "We'll go through my laboratory."

Valin followed Dalamar's lover down a staircase into the basement. Shadows cloaked the steps. He moved slowly, feeling his way along a cool, damp wall. As he stepped onto the hard-packed ground at the foot of the staircase, Jenna disappeared ahead.

Valin saw but the barest hint of light in the small room. Natural curiosity made him want to move around, to peer into the shadows, but he was a mage, and so he had prudent respect for another mage's laboratory. He waited in the cool blue light that illuminated the area around him, his hands at his sides. After a moment, he heard Jenna's soft voice. As with the weaving of the ward, he could not distinguish her words.

A moment later she returned. "Dalamar awaits."

She held out her hand, and as he stepped toward her, Valin saw the circle of salt in which she stood. The outline of a transport spell. He lifted his robe, careful not to disturb the mineral as he joined her inside the circle. So close did she stand that he felt her breath against his chest. She took his hands in hers, her fingers cool, her grip strong.

"If you close your eyes, you won't be dizzy." Then she spoke words that chased through his mind as quickly as sand swirling before a desert storm.

Valin had no intention of closing his eyes. He loved the transport spell, the glory of the wild ride along the roads of magic.

The cool blue light became bluish purple and then deep purple, which changed into red purple and finally red, like the unraveling of a rainbow. A cool wind, so welcome after the city heat, caressed his eyelashes, ruffled his hair, rustled his robe round his ankles. The wind grew into a roar, then, as suddenly as it had begun, it died away. The colors swirled together into blackness, and Valin found himself once again standing on solid ground.

Not really ground, he realized as he glanced down and saw a finely patterned rug beneath his feet. A floor. Polished granite, strewn with colorful rugs, rising up into pale gray walls covered by exquisitely woven tapestries. He was in a study, or a sitting room, where one wall was filled with rows of books, another was dominated by a high, deep fireplace. In the firebox, ashes lay dead and cold. Opposite the fireplace stood a small couch, two chairs, and a low table. Everywhere lay spellbooks and wands and bottles sealed with wax and decorated with twine. Silver and crystal spheres sat beside marvelously carved wooden boxes.

So bright and lovely a place for Dalamar the Dark! He'd imagined worse, with darkness and shadows and danger in every corner.

Well, there was still that last to consider. What is dark, said his lady, doesn't always seem so.

In the moment he thought so, Valin saw a motion to his right, a sparkling of light, like dust motes, only silver, swirling and spilling and spinning until at last an elf, tall and slender, stood before him. Beautiful, in the timeless way of elves, he wore a black robe of a soft cloth embossed with arcane symbols, some of which Valin recognized, some of which he did not.

"Welcome to the tower, Valin. I am Dalamar." The elf's voice was strong and clear, his tone polite with the welcome one stranger offers another.

A safe enough tone, a decent enough greeting, but when Valin met Dalamar's eyes, he knew all the stories he'd heard about the dark elf had to be true. Dalamar's true power was in his eyes, in his gaze. Valin felt as though those eyes could see through any artifice, could probe beneath the skin and scorch his soul.

Well, search all you like, sir mage, he thought. I have nothing to hide.

As though he'd heard that thought clearly, the Master of the Tower of High Sorcery invited Valin to speak his message.

Valin inclined his head, a small bow to the master mage, all the courtesy due, but no more. He was, after all, the messenger of the Revered Daughter of Paladine.

"The Lady Crysania sent me to ask a favor of you, Lord Dalamar."

Dalamar's smile receded and the ambient light of the room suddenly waned, as if banished by some power of his expression.

A small clutch of fear took Valin in the stomach. He turned to look for Jenna, but she was studiously looking away from him. For a moment, silence sat thick and heavy as a pall upon the room. Then Dalamar said coldly, "Go back to your mistress and tell her I will speak only to her. I will, of course, be happy to consider any favor she asks, but she will have to ask it herself. I do not deal with servants."

Valin drew himself up, squaring his shoulders. This might be how one addressed a servant, and no matter if the dark elf thought him so, but this was no way to answer a message from the Revered Daughter of Paladine.

Before Valin could draw breath to speak, the dark elf waved to Jenna, indicating that she should take him away, back the way they had come. Valin started to protest, but Jenna laid a soothing hand on his arm, applied a slight pressure toward the door.

As Valin turned to go, Dalamar stopped him. "Tell your lady to come herself. Tell her to come alone." As if in afterthought, Dalamar added, "Oh, and tell her I have a gift for her."

Saying no more, he left Valin standing silent and thoroughly dismissed.

Chapter Three

Crysania settled herself in the small chapel.

Several such places existed in the temple—quiet, smaller, more personal rooms than the great hall where she commonly held services. Here, more intimate service was often held, ritual for a few worshipers. Four short benches provided seats for the attendants, while one small dais stood in the center of the room for the cleric. Someone had served ritual here not long ago; the room smelled poignantly of recently snuffed candles.

Crysania breathed deeply, letting the peace of the place settle on her to ease her cares and tensions. In the hours since the festival, she'd done nothing else but talk with the clerics who each had some rumor or another to bring to her. They'd been out in the market in New City at her bidding, gathering information, listening to the gossip and speculation. All they found, they brought back to their lady, and all they found came to this: As the Lord of Palanthas had said, people were becoming uneasy, in some quarters fearful. Though she showed her true heart to no one, here in the chapel, Crysania allowed the admission that she, too, felt uneasy. That unease had only deepened after many hours spent at prayer.

Paladine was somewhere far away, a dimly glowing ember in the distance rather than the roaring fire that he had been in her heart. She had searched her soul, wondering whether something she had done, some thought or deed, made her unworthy in Paladine's eyes, but soon realized that this was the reaction of a child. Paladine's love was boundless, not a thing to fall away because of one misdeed, a small doubt. He must not be judged on human scale, and she must be patient. Her god would come to her.

This afternoon, after the festival, some of her clerics had asked for council—even Aras, who had been with her from the beginning, one of the earliest believers to step forward from the fires of the War of the Lance; and Seralas, who had toiled by her side as they rebuilt the destroyed temple. A handful of others had come to her with doubts as well, younger and newer to their faith. They were all concerned. In their prayers, they received no comfort from Paladine. Aras, like Crysania, confessed that he had raked his soul, wondering what he had done to cause Paladine to frown upon him.

She had advised them to practice patience, to wait for the god's return. "We are not his only concern in the world, my children. Perhaps he feels he can depend on our patience and trust while he deals with other things."

That advice had comforted some, even Crysania herself, for a time. But she could not deny, in the peace and privacy of this chapel, that something was terribly wrong, something more than the unseasonable heat and the rumors of gathering armies.

She started as the door opened, tamped down her irritation as Valin's deep voice dropped into her silence.

"Forgive the disturbance, lady. I know you are praying, but—"

"Yes, Valin?" She sat up straight, her annoyance disappearing as hope flared that he came with a message from Dalamar that might help make sense of all that was happening. "You've come from Dalamar?"

Just as she was not able to keep the hope out of her voice, Valin could not keep the anger from his. "I did not deliver your message, lady. The dark one asks me to inform you that he will not speak to a servant."

Just for a moment, silence fell between them.

"Is there more, Valin?"

"Yes. He says that he will consider any favor you ask of him, but that the request must come from you in person. And he also told me to tell you that he has a gift for you."

Unbidden, an image from haunting dreams came to her, a tall, shadowy figure coming out of the rain, his hands cupped as if to offer something. Startled, she thought, Never tell me I've been dreaming of Dalamar all this while! She almost laughed. Almost. No, there had not been darkness clinging to that mysterious, beckoning figure. No matter what Crysania didn't know about the dream, that much she did know.

"What gift, Valin? Did he say?"

Valin snorted, a soft, disparaging sound. "Not to me, he didn't." He came close, his footfalls soft on the marble floor. "The dark mage draws considerable pleasure from being cryptic."

Crysania nodded. "Yes, he does." She gathered the folds of her robe in her hands and stood.

"Lady, I don't think you should go to him. It was arrogant of him to demand it. And I—I don't like this gambit of his."

Now Crysania laughed, a light, lilting sound in the confines of the little chapel. How could she not? Valin's mood was so uncharacteristically grim, his fear on her behalf so out of proportion to the moment.

"Not arrogant, Valin. He simply wants to speak with me on the high ground, his own territory. Very well, let him have that if he needs it." He stiffened, ready to object again. "Valin, what do you imagine, that he will lure me to his tower and hold me prisoner for some evil purpose of his own? No, we understand each other, Dalamar and I, at least so far as to accept hospitality, one from the other." She put her hand on Valin's arm, directing him. At her touch, he gave way, backing up to allow her to leave the narrow space between the benches. "I will go to him. After all, it is I who seeks a favor of him."

Valin and his disapproval followed her into the hallway, where an acolyte waiting to assist Crysania, fell into step behind them.

Through wide and airy halls they walked, Crysania thinking, Valin and the acolyte respectful in their silence. As she went, she considered Valin's message. No doubt her estimation was true, that Dalamar wanted to deal with her on his own ground. She had not been to the tower in over thirty years, not since her fateful trip through the portal. The Tower of High Sorcery was the last thing she had ever seen with her eyes. The last thing in this world. Of that other world, that horror beyond the portal—of the Abyss—she had long ago trained herself not to think. Dalamar's territory was not a place she would like to be, yet the images of her dream haunted her now, the offering hands, the secret giver. She was curious to know why the master of the tower suddenly offered a gift to her and why that haunting image would not let her refuse.

Smiling secretly, she thought, He is not shouting his messages to me, my beloved god, but it might be he whispers in my dreams.

Crysania stopped in her walk, took a few steps to the left, and her hand found the small fluted column she knew would be there, a divider between one alcove and another where, in kinder seasons, one could stand and look out upon the temple's vast gardens. Right below lay the herb and vegetable gardens, those plots to which all water went these days, leaving the flower beds to fare for themselves in the Anvil Summer. They did not fare well, and it had been a long time since last she smelled the heady scent of roses and peonies and wisteria.

"Valin," she said softly, turning her face from the hot breeze of evening. "I will go to Dalamar in the morning. I'd like it if you came with me."

"I am yours as ever, lady."

Was that a small satisfaction she heard in his voice? Perhaps.

"Good enough. Go find your rest, friend mage, as I go to mine. Our day has been long and wearing. Call for me after the morning service."

He swept her a bow. She heard the soft sound of it, his robes whispering against his skin. She felt the stirring of the air before her. As he had said before, he said again: She need only ask a thing of him and it would be done.

* * * * *

In the hour after morning prayers, Valin went to his lady to conduct her to The Three Moons. Once outside the temple gate, he offered his arm, as he always did, and she took it. Her touch, light and trusting, moved him deeply.

She did not cling, nor did she start at each sound or change of surface beneath her feet. She trusted her guide and went on through streets wide and narrow, past noisome alleyways and dry, burnt gardens. Even in the unfamiliar surroundings of Jenna's mage shop, she needed little more than the increased pressure of his hand on hers to guide her.

She lifted her head, listening, and smiled graciously when Valin said, "Mistress Jenna, my Lady Crysania has come."

Jenna, her green eyes bright with curiosity and some glint of satisfaction, bowed to the lady and murmured welcome. "How may I help you, Revered Daughter?"

Valin glanced at Crysania and caught her small, knowing smile. Of course Jenna understood well why the lady was here.

"Mistress Jenna," Crysania said, "I have come to see Dalamar. Will you take us?"

"I will, lady."

Her voice sounded weary; her eyes were not as bright as they could be. Long nights bred such looks. Valin wondered whether Jenna's had been a long night of magic or a long night of love in the dark elf's bed. Perhaps both, he thought, or perhaps just a night of wondering what her lover was up to. It could not be easy, he thought, always obliged to keep a close eye on the balance of their power.

Jenna motioned to a young red robe to take her place behind the counter. As the mage ushered them toward the basement, Jenna raised her eyebrows questioningly at Valin. Crysania was to come alone, said that warning glance.

Valin stared back at Jenna, daring her to speak, but she only shrugged, as if to say his disregard of Dalamar's order was his to explain and no concern of hers. She held out a hand to lead Crysania, who willingly followed.

"There are stairs, lady," the wizardess murmured as she took Crysania to the top of a stairway. "Count to twelve, and the thirteenth will be the floor."

Crysania made the passage easily, Jenna before her, Valin behind. Once in the laboratory, she followed Jenna's instructions to step within a circle. Both mages offered their arms, but she waved them away.

"I advise most people to close their eyes as I cast the spell, lady, to avoid dizziness, but you will come through fine. Simply stand still and face straight ahead. You will feel a sensation of falling, but you may trust me when I say that you will not, in fact, fall."

Valin stood close beside Crysania, his heart swelling with love and pride to see her. The spell words fell around her, and she never wavered as the wildly colored lights and all the energies they represented swirled around them. She might have been standing in her own garden, her face caressed by a sweet spring breeze, as Jenna's transport spell blew them along enchanted paths. Only once did she react, and that to smile, when she felt once again a solid, cold floor beneath her feet.

She reeled for a moment. Valin caught her arm. "Lady?"

"The tower . . . I've never forgotten the smell of it."

And she hadn't been here in thirty years, not since that day she came sighted and left again blinded. How dark and frightening it must have seemed to her then, filled with terrors and dread in every corner.

"You did not have me with you then, my lady," he whispered, low for only her to hear. "You need fear nothing now."

She lifted her face to speak, then fell silent. All in a breath, Dalamar was at her side, taking her hand and bowing. Valin expected to see a mocking light in the dark elf's eyes, and he did. He saw, too, respect.

"Revered Daughter, I hope you are well."

53

She lifted her head, and her dark eyes glinted with unvoiced laugher. "Ah, my lord. It sounds as though you are well. I had wondered. When I heard your voice in the square yesterday, it sounded . . . hoarse. I hoped you weren't falling ill."

He looked at her long, his eyes glittering, his lips turning only reluctantly to smile. "Was it so easy to know me, lady?"

"No. Not so easy to know Nuitari's servant when he comes asking after news of Paladine."

Between them, the air became electric with unspoken challenge. Valin stood close, her protector at her side.

Silken-voiced, Dalamar asked, "What news, then, lady?"

"The very news you imagine, my lord."

"I see. Well, then I am glad I asked you to come, and I thank you for granting my request."

"You left me little choice," Crysania murmured, allowing only the barest trace of sarcasm in her words. "You would not speak with my messenger."

"Ah." Dalamar tucked her fingers into the crook of his arm, led her across a smooth surface and up a flight of steps. "It was only that I have come across something that you and I need to discuss. Actually it is something that I think you ought to have. And I wanted to present it to you in person," he said lightly. "I see, though, that your chosen messenger elected not to deliver that part of my message in which I bade you come alone."

Valin kept his stride, as though the dark elf had not spoken.

Crysania only laughed, as at news of an amusing misdeed. "No, he didn't. But it doesn't surprise me. My people are as protective of me as yours are of you." She gestured pointedly at the red-robed mage who was trailing quietly behind them.

54

Dalamar shrugged. "Oh, you mistake my Jenna, lady. She's told me she has little time for me this morning and must return at once to her shop. Isn't that so, my love?"

Oh, they are good, Valin thought, watching one toss the ball and the other neatly catch it. Jenna actually twinkled when she said, "No time at all for you, Dalamar."

"And Valin can wait with you, can't he?"

He stood in the darkest tower of all, in the presence of the darkest mage of all. Nonetheless, Valin held his ground. "No, my lord," he said, grimly respectful. "Valin goes nowhere unless his lady says so."

Dalamar cocked an eye at him, a long slow moment of seeing. Then he shrugged and said to Crysania, "Direct him, lady. If you trust him with your secrets, then I certainly have no objection if he accompanies us. If you don't—"

Crysania reached back, and her hand found Valin's arm. "This man is one of my most trusted advisors. I have no secrets from him."

"Well, then, I shall hold none from him either."

No one believed that or even pretended to. In grim, unyielding silence, Valin followed his lady and Dalamar the Dark up the winding staircase, high into the tower, all the way to the dark elf's chamber.

* * * * *

The master of the tower lived well, Valin thought as he looked around him. Chairs were large and deep and cushioned. Carpets, woven in far places, softened the floor. Candle after candle burned, upon tables, upon windowsills, in brackets tucked into high corners of the room. One large, tall pillar burned upon Dalamar's desk, a lone light in that dark space, glinting from the embossed bindings of a high stack of books.

"A chair for you, lady," Dalamar said, amused to play the part of Crysania's affable host. "Would you like some wine?"

Crysania accepted the chair, she welcomed the wine, and she gestured to tell Valin to come stand behind her. This he did, keeping close enough to see the candlelight on her skin, to smell the light scent of her dark, spilling hair.

"Your hospitality is generous, my lord," Crysania said. She sipped her wine. "I won't prevail long upon it. I will be frank with you, and I hope that you will be with me. I came to speak with you about what happened at the festival. You have answered my question, and perhaps I have answered one you may have had. And so we both wonder why the gods have fallen silent."

"Yes," Dalamar said, "we both wonder. And we will wonder about other things, you and I, before the day is done." He leaned forward and placed a small, smooth box in her hands. "I do hope your servant"—he glanced darkly at Valin—"managed to tell you the part of my message about this gift I have for you."

If Crysania felt Valin's restless stirring, she made no sign. She settled back in the chair, willing to wait the game through. "Yes, he did say something about it. You are generous, my lord."

"I like to think so, but I can't take credit this time. I believe this gift was left here for you."

Crysania cocked her head. "Indeed? By whom?"

Candlelight and shadow ran on the dark elf, hiding his expression. "I don't know, lady. Perhaps you will know when you see what lies in the box."

Head up, alert, Valin watched as Crysania examined the small porcelain box, flipping the tiny metal catch. Two small stones lay within, neither remarkable, each looking like something found in a farmer's field. Crysania felt inside, touching one stone and then lifting a hand as if in question. When no answer came, she touched the other. She sighed when her fingers closed around the second stone. Valin, beside her now, saw the same expression in her dark eyes that he was used to seeing when she touched her dragon medallion, a suffusion of joy. She did not speak, but her lips formed a word, a beloved name.

Paladine.

A candle hissed, flame encountering a faulty wick. Light leapt up and fell again, making shadows scurry up the walls. Across from Crysania, Dalamar settled in watchful silence, his face as still as a mask. Beside her, Valin laid a gentle hand on her shoulder as if to say, "I am here, lady."

She never moved to acknowledge his touch, she simply lifted her head and turned to where she'd last heard Dalamar's voice. That blind stare could be daunting, Valin had good cause to know. Dalamar did not react.

"You tell me, Dalamar, that these stones appeared here . . . mysteriously. But why do you imagine they're meant for me?" With her thumb, Crysania traced the irregular smoothness of the more powerful stone.

Dalamar lifted a glass of ruby wine and held it before the light of a candle to admire the effect. A bit of theater. "I'm sure you can detect the power of the one. And I'm sure you can imagine why it would be of no use to me."

He has put too fine a point on it, Valin thought. Even the smallest artifact of goodness would resist the machinations of a dark wizard. This stone, radiating all the energy of goodness, would be worse than useless to Dalamar. Valin imagined that it would be poison to the mage if he touched it ungloved.

"For whom else would such an object of powerful good be intended?" Dalamar asked. He stopped, considered, and went on. "I believe these are Dragon Stones.

57

Not all the Dragon Stones, for there are more than these, but here are two of them." He rose and went to his desk, plucking a book from the stack. He dropped it on the low table between their chairs. "Since I discovered these stones, I have gone to my books and researched them as best I could. Do you know the legend of the Dragon Stones, lady?"

Crysania reached to touch the stones. The tense line of her shoulders eased as though she heard whispered words of comfort. "Entertain me, my lord."

"It's not a very well known legend," Dalamar said, flipping open the book and riffling pages. "Except among the elves. In the Age of Light, in the time of Silvanos, the great elven leader, the elves came together for the first time, unified as a nation. They settled in the south, in an enchanted wood in what we now call the Khalkist Mountains. But the land was home to dragons, who, as you might suspect, objected to the elves' choice of home. So there was war."

"The First Dragon War," Crysania said, remembering the legends carried down through time by bards.

"Yes. The elves allied to fight the dragons and to drive them from their chosen land. It is told that the three gods of magic walked the face of Krynn then, and that they made a gift the elves of five magical stones. Stones of great power, that the elves might defeat the dragons. The stones had the power to capture the dragons' souls, and when the elves used them, the magic turned the dragons' great bodies into rock.

"There the stories diverge. Some say the stones became jewels embedded in the eyes of the stone dragons. Some say that the elves flew far away on the backs of griffons and threw the stones into bottomless pits in the tall mountains. The gods of magic were then banished from walking the face of Krynn for their interference in mortal affairs."

Crysania waited, absorbing the story. Beside her, Valin stood, untiring, listening. Dalamar didn't hasten to his tale. From outside his chamber drifted the sounds of mages coming and going through the tower, muted voices, the crash of something heavy, secret laughter in the halls of power.

"It is told," Dalamar said at last, "that almost one thousand years later, the dwarves found the magical Dragon Stones the elves had cast deep within the mountains and, shunning magic as they do, gave the stones to a red dragon, who in turn ordered that the stones be hurled into the caldron of a dormant volcano called Darklady. Darklady then erupted, forming the Lords of Doom, the ring of volcanoes that surrounds Sanction. It is said the explosion of color from the stones became the eyes of Takhisis's constellation."

Valin moved closer to his lady, a chill creeping along his spine when he heard the name of the Dark Queen.

"My lord," Valin said, pausing until Crysania gestured that he could continue. "If the stones exploded in the volcanoes, how could these stones be the very same?"

"Quite right to ask," Dalamar said, his expression belying his words and saying clearly to Valin that the white robe had overstepped. He tapped the open pages of the book. "The references I've found do cite an explosion of color from the stones, and I can't help but wonder, does that mean the stones themselves exploded and were destroyed? Or perhaps they were shattered, and there were pieces of them left behind.

"We have spoken of things we wonder about, lady, and here is one. I have read in this book an interesting tale of how a powerful mage found a magical artifact in the Khalkist Mountains hundreds of years ago."

He paused for a moment. Crysania handed the box and the stones to Valin and said, "Please go on."

"A mage of great integrity, she recognized how dangerous this artifact could be should it fall into the wrong hands. Using the power of the artifact itself, she cast a spell upon it."

Valin protested, "But here are two stones, not a single artifact."

"Yes, on the face of it, this story doesn't seem to match. Until you hear the spell she cast."

On the table, a candle failed and darkness spilled over the book. With a small gesture, Dalamar called the flame back, making it leap high and burn brightly. With an ironic smile, the dark elf turned the book so that Valin could read.

"The first spell was an obscuring," continued Dalamar, "to change the appearance of the artifact. The original Dragon Stones were the colors of the dragons—red, green, blue, black, and white. So if the appearance was changed, these could very well be the same stones."

"I'm not expert at reading these old languages, lady," said Valin, "but I believe this says that the final spell was a 'binding.' "

Crysania shook her head. "I'm afraid I still don't understand."

"What it actually says," Dalamar corrected, "is a 'binding together.' "

"And the mage wouldn't have cast a 'binding together' on one item," Valin finished.

"Yes, that is the obvious conclusion. But you apparently have some knowledge of ancient eleven languages. Read more closely, sir mage."

Valin ignored the condescending tone and moved the candle closer so he could read the faded script. It was a mediocre translation, but close enough to the real meaning. He put the box back into Crysania's hands, the gesture careful and gentle as he said, "I believe, lady, that this is the true tale of what happened to the Dragon Stones, or the remains of them, after the great explosion of Darklady. How these two have now come to be in Lord Dalamar's possession, however, I confess I do not know."

"Why, they have come here mysteriously," she said, sweetly gentle as she matched, for the moment, Dalamar's irony.

Valin almost laughed to see the dark elf's expression as his eyebrow suddenly raised. As though she sensed his sudden mood, Crysania lifted a hand to still him.

"Lord Dalamar, I know there is goodness and kindness in you, and so I know you will forgive me for questioning your motives."

If not your story, Valin thought, narrow-eyed and watching as Dalamar chuckled at Crysania's words, plainly enjoying the polite sparring.

Crysania lifted a hand to brush a stray wisp of dark hair from her cheek. "I know you say that this stone would be of no use to you, but I cannot imagine your giving it to me without a reason. There must be something you hope to gain."

Dalamar laughed indulgently. "Ah, how could I expect to conceal my motives from you, lady? I confess, I hoped to find the dark stone that is supposed to be part of the set. And I might have hoped to see all five stones rejoined."

"Rejoined?" Crysania sat forward. "Do you know where the other three are?"

"I know as much as rumor and old legend inform me." He paused.

Valin sat forward, listening carefully to what he was sure would not be a satisfactory reply.

"You have heard that the Conclave of Wizards will convene shortly."

Crysania never moved or even changed her expression. And so Valin knew she was listening with all her attention.

"I have heard so. I have also heard that you meet to discuss certain important matters having to do with the buildup of troops in the east. Perhaps you will discuss this Anvil Summer and this silence of the gods."

"No doubt we will discuss many things, lady."

It was the best answer she'd get from him, and not such a bad one at that. Crysania sat back and folded her hands in her lap. "And I have heard of the gray mages. Perhaps you will discuss this."

"Have you heard that? Hmm. So have I."

Dalamar leaned forward to refill her wineglass. "Yet as you see, with the Conclave meeting in a matter of days, I cannot go to retrieve the lost Dragon Stones." He kept silent for a brief moment, then touched her hand, his fingers closing round hers. "These stones appeared mysteriously, as I say. I will swear any oath you require to testify to the truth of that."

"Any?"

"All."

She believed him. Valin saw it. She, in her goodness, never failed to find even the smallest capacity for truth in anyone. "Go on," she said.

Candlelight flickered across the mage's face, shadow and light breathing on him. "I won't trust the matter to any of my mages, but I would trust it to you, lady, and so I beg you to consider accepting these stones and taking on the search."

Valin returned to his perusal of the book, but he did so with ears cocked.

"I particularly thought you would be interested once you heard more about the power of the stones. If I am interpreting the text correctly, the spell placed upon them all those years ago would allow a cleric to communicate directly with one of the gods."

Crysania closed her hands over the box.

Dalamar smiled and continued. "It's said that the person who gathers all five of the stones will be able to use them to contact the gods and speak to one of them more directly, more intimately, than any mortal could ever manage on his own."

Crysania touched the medallion on her breast.

"No," Valin said quickly. He ran his fingers to the bottom of the page he'd been reading, turned it to look at the next page, then flipped the pages back. There was a small piece of paper tucked into the pages and covered with writing. "No, lady, you cannot think to do this." He turned the book so that it faced Dalamar again. "Do I misinterpret this enclosure?"

"What are you talking about?" Crysania turned her head from one to other.

Dalamar shrugged. "My own decoding of an ancient map. From all indications, the remaining stones are in Neraka."

Chapter Four

Dalamar watched as Crysania kept her expression carefully neutral. To see her eyes, so dark and still, one would think he'd not spoken the name Neraka. One would think he'd named Solace, or Elm High, or any other city. Yet calm as her face was, Crysania's hands moved, one to cover the other where it lay on the porcelain box.

No one, not even Lady Crysania, could hear the name Neraka spoken and not react. In Neraka lay the ruined Temple of Takhisis, a place of dark and deep evil. Since before the War of the Lance, the city had belonged to the Dark Queen. It was her domain, and only her servants lived there. Set in the heart of the Khalkist Mountains, surrounded by bubbling volcanoes, Neraka was as unholy as its mistress. No one who did not follow Takhisis would go near it.

The white-robed mage's reaction was as satisfying as Crysania's, if easier to determine. Valin glared at the dark elf with the eyes of hatred.

Well, Dalamar thought, rising to stand with elaborate nonchalance, this one is as easy to read as the book in his hand. Very useful . . . very useful indeed.

"Of course," he said, as though no one had reacted in any way at all. "Now that I've told you where the stones are, and you are properly pleased and grateful for the knowledge, I'm sure you'll agree that it is only fair that you do something for me. In exchange for giving you these two stones, I ask that you accept a guide of my choosing, who will take you to Neraka and help you find the missing pieces of the artifact."

"No," Valin growled.

Crysania quieted the mage with a gesture. "Assuming that I am willing to make such a dangerous journey, why would I want a guide whose first loyalty would be to you?"

Her tone was suspicious, but Dalamar was sure she was already committed. He smiled, not bothering to mask his triumph.

"The guide's first priority will be your own safety, I assure you, lady. Since there are five Dragon Stones, I'm sure you agree that five would be the correct number of people for your party. I choose only this one, the guide. The others will undoubtedly be the most brave, the most qualified, the most loyal of your retinue."

A flicker of emotion passed across Crysania's face. Was it impatience, the realization that at some point she had lost control of the situation? Indeed, for resolve followed that impatience, and she stood, smoothing the folds of her gown, smiling graciously as she said,

"Thank you for your hospitality, my lord. The wine was good and the conversation fascinating. I will certainly consider your proposal."

She closed the porcelain box and handed it to Valin, who came around the table, offering his arm and still glaring at Dalamar.

"Sir mage," Dalamar whispered to the desert mage as they passed by him for the door, "I would like to get to know you better. Come see me tomorrow, Valin, and let us talk as one mage to another."

Valin opened his mouth to say something, then refrained. Crysania must have overheard, but she, too, said nothing as they left. The good host, the careful observer, Dalamar followed. As he knew he would, he found Jenna waiting outside his chamber, still and patient in the light of a torch hung on the wall.

His voice low and smooth for the benefit of others, Dalamar said, "I thought you had returned to your shop, my dear."

Jenna smiled coolly. "And here I am again to guide your guests back."

"Well, your timing is impeccable, as ever. The Revered Daughter is ready to leave now."

Jenna moved to lead the way down the long staircase, but Dalamar held her back with a light touch and let Valin find the way for the moment. She leaned close to Dalamar, her hand on his arm, her green eyes alight. "And what tricks are you up to now, love?" she asked.

He slipped an arm around her and gave her a quick squeeze before pushing her gently toward the pair. "No tricks. Only tossing pebbles into the pond and watching the ripples." He put a finger to his lips. "Watch. I'll toss another." Leaning over the railing, he watched Crysania pass into the clinging shadow below. Then he called, "My lady?"

Crysania looked up, her pale face white in the darkness. Beside her, Valin tensed.

"Our conversation moved so quickly that there is something I had no chance to mention." He let silence hang for one long moment. Then he said, "The mage who set the spell upon the stones. She was of my order. It might well be that whoever finds the other three stones and matches them to these will find herself calling upon the wisdom of Takhisis."

He heard the hiss of indrawn breath. At his elbow, Jenna echoed the sound softly. "Hush," Dalamar whispered. "Simply watch, my love."

Footsteps rang on the stone steps as Valin started angrily toward Dalamar. Swiftly Crysania grabbed him back, pulling sharply on his robe.

"Valin, be still!"

Dalamar chuckled, feeling the mage's anger rising, watching him be forced to stand still, the Revered Daughter's obedient servant.

"Think!" Crysania whispered. "He can kill you with a word."

Jenna came quickly down the stairs, her robes swishing, her footsteps tapping. Behind her, the dark elf stood on the landing, barely visible in the shadows.

"Oh, no, my lady. You misjudge me," he said, smiling still. "I can kill him with much less than a word."

Valin tensed and took another step forward, but Crysania tightened her grip.

"Valin," she warned.

Was he actually grinding his teeth? Dalamar chuckled, but silently. Indeed he was. For all that, though, the white robe never left his lady's side.

"I will return," Valin said, staring up into the darkness as if ordinary eyesight could pierce the gloom.

Dalamar feigned surprise. "Do you threaten me?"

"No, sir mage," Valin said coldly. "I say a thing, and then I do it."

Then Jenna was there, stepping in front of Valin, ushering him away. "Come with me. Now! I'll take you

back." Her quietly authoritative voice drowned out whatever comment Dalamar made in reply to Valin's vow.

* * * * *

Dust lay thick on the street outside The Three Moons.
Humidity hung in the air like a pall. It seemed to Valin
that the smell of the city grew worse every day, every
hour. Refuse rotted in the cans outside the little shops and
houses, animals dead of the heat festered in the gutters.
Palanthas the Beautiful was beginning to seem like a
lovely corpse too long unburied.

Valin went in silence beside his lady, anger still roiling
inside him. How dare the dark elf treat the Revered
Daughter of Paladine as he had? How dare he summon
her only to lay before her such a plan as he did, suggest-
ing that she pick up and go off to unholy Neraka in search
of artifacts that might—if rumor and legend and guesswork were true!—put her in touch with the Dark Queen
herself?

He glanced at Crysania, so clearly lost in her thoughts,
and a chill spidered down his spine.

"My lady, you aren't thinking—you aren't going to
take up this foolish quest, are you?"

She lifted her head to indicate she'd heard him, but
she spoke no word.

Valin's heart thumped hard in his chest. She *was* considering it!

"My lady, please . . ."

Dust swirled around the hem of their robes and rats
skittered in the alleys. In the brazen sky, the sun beat
down, pitiless as a hammer on an anvil.

Crysania patted his arm absently. "I'm thinking,
Valin."

"Thinking of what?"

"Thinking of a dream I've been having . . . one that returns to me time and again."

She said no more for a long moment, and Valin thought she might be getting ready to tell him the dream, but in the end, she only shook her head.

"We've heard some fine stories today, Valin, and some rumors and guesswork. What stays with me, though, is this question: If the Dragon Stones were meant solely for evil purposes, wouldn't Dalamar have kept them for himself? He says he won't trust the mission to one of his mages, but I don't believe that. He trusts them with all manner of things there in his tower. What is clear is that not one of his mages would be able to use the stone we have here." She lifted the box in her hand. Sunlight beat upon the white porcelain, glinted off the golden catch. "And so no mage of his would be able to reconnect it to the others."

Valin snorted. "Nor will you be able to connect these two to the one imbued with dark magic."

"Well," Crysania replied, allowing herself a smile, "you'd be right if I were a mage of your order. But I am no mage at all. It would not be pleasant for me to handle the dark stone, but it would not be as painful, perhaps deadly, as it would if I were a white robe."

It would not be pleasant. Valin shook his head at the vastness of her understatement. She would find it more than unpleasant to handle the dark stone. It would be nightmarish. Yet she was right; it would not be fatal.

"But, lady, why would you do that? Why work for him?"

Crysania turned her face up to him. It was as though she were looking right into his eyes. "I have no mind to work for him, my friend. No more than he is minded to work for me. It's a matter of faith, Valin. For me, all things come to matters of faith."

"But—"

"Valin," she warned, patting his arm as though he were a small child overspilling with questions. "You must let me think now."

Valin bit his lip and fell into step beside her. He said no more as they walked through the streets thick with people, only guiding her as he always had. But his mind was indeed overspilling with questions, and his heart—with each step he took—his heart grew heavy with foreboding.

* * * * *

Crysania sat in silence, her study empty of acolytes and aides and clerics. On the desk before her lay the porcelain box with the two stones Dalamar had given her. Her hands upon the white porcelain box, she opened her heart, her very soul, to the resonating power of the stones within. One stone sat silent, neither malignant nor benign. It simply sat, humming to itself over its muted power. But the other—ah! The other was not silent at all. It sang in muted tones. Almost she heard Paladine's voice, his beloved voice, speaking to her through that stone.

Breath held, with great gentleness, she lifted the box's lid. In the same moment, she lifted her heart in prayer.

O Paladine, O Father of Goodness and Light, is it you I dream of at night? You standing in the rain, holding out your hands with a gift for me?

O Paladine, O Fountain from Which All Goodness Springs, is this journey the dark elf has set before me the gift you offer?

It might well be. Who knew better than she that all gifts don't seem fair at first? Who would have ever called her blindness a gift? And yet it was, for over the years, in her forever darkness, she had learned what she most needed to learn—compassion for those whose griefs, whose pains, whose bestormed hearts blinded them to the goodness and the hope that lay all around them in the world. Far from being a loss, her blindness completed her, for in her darkness, she had found light and the way to illuminate the lives of others.

O Paladine, O Father of Light, a journey has been set before me, a path dark and stony, leading to a place I'd never thought to go. Is this your will?

In her mind, in her heart, she saw the images of her dream. Rain fell, silken, soft, and whispering of hope. Her skin reveled in its touch, so long unfelt. Her lips tasted honey. Out from the rain, from the hissing, sighing rain, a tall figure stepped, hooded, its face hidden. Man or woman? Who could tell? Then the figured cupped its hands, holding them out as if to offer . . . a gift.

Almost, almost she thought she heard a voice. Dark or light, man's or woman's? She did not know. In her heart, where hope never died, she believed she heard the dream being sigh. And then it turned to walk away, as ever, only this time it stopped and looked back over its shoulder.

Crysania gasped and her hands fell from the box.

"Paladine!" she whispered. Her hands flew to the medallion at her breast. It lay heavy and cold. "Paladine," she said, softly pleading.

Then came a sense of him, like an ember in a banked fire. But, ah he was so distant!

She reached for the box and opened the lid. She touched the stone Dalamar could never touch without pain. She smiled to feel the light of great goodness at her heart. Was this her answer, her god speaking to her through this long forgotten artifact? Or was this only hope trying to become an answer in itself?

From the window behind her came the sound of a voice raised in greeting, then sudden alarm. Crysania's heart leapt. The one voice became two, then three, then more. Outside the study, other voices rose, and footfalls, and the slap of leather on marble.

She heard a soft tap at the door, the sound of a step within.

"My lady," Seralas said. "Forgive—

Her hands suddenly shaking, she said, "Who has come, Seralas?"

"Lagan Innis, my lady. He's back from the High Clerist's Tower."

Lagan. "Only he? Where is Nisse?"

Crysania heard the elf swallow once, then again. She heard footfalls on the floor, then breathing as the cleric came closer. "Lady, please come. He's hurt and . . ."

And his news was not good.

Chapter Five

Once more Valin pushed his friend gently back down onto the pallet in the dwarf's small cell. "Be still, will you? Let me see to your wounds."

Brown eyes glinting, his hand a fist not of anger but frustration, Lagan Innis tried to hold still and failed again in the moment they heard Crysania's step at the door. He sat up, shrugged away Valin's hand, and rose to his feet.

"My lady," he said. Valin put a hand on his shoulder and pushed him back to sit on the edge of the cot. "My lady, I'm sorry . . ." Words failed him, and he tried again. "Nisse is—lady, Nisse is dead."

Silence fell like darkness into the room. Then softly Crysania whispered, "Paladine accept her graciously into his heart."

"He will, lady. I know it. He will, for she died well and—in his cause."

"How?" Her face white as marble, her hands folded to conceal their trembling, she said, "Lagan, how did she die?"

The sound of chanting flowed in through the door, through the windows, a deep, soft, fluid song of praise to the god. Lagan swallowed hard. "It never should have happened, lady, and yet it did. It did. She died on the road home."

He stopped to still his shaking voice and Crysania came to sit beside him, her hand lifted tentatively.

"Tell us your tale in one piece, Lagan. But in a moment. May I?" she said, asking the permission she always sought before touching the face of another.

Lagan nodded, and her fingers touched his face gently on the rough bandage wrapping his head, on the blood matting his red beard, the small touches seeming like a blessing, Valin thought, for pain and sorrow seemed erased from Lagan's face. The mage took advantage of his friend's stillness and this time managed to unwind the bloodstained, dirty bandage. A deep cut gaped beneath the cloth, unstitched, unhealing, red with infection around the edges.

"Lady," Valin whispered.

Crysania nodded as though she could see what he did. "Have you been treated, Lagan?"

Lagan nodded. "Sir Thomas had one of his knights get me a poultice and bandages for the cut."

"Sir Thomas?" Crysania sat straighter. "This happened at the tower? Why? How?"

"No, it didn't, lady. It happened elsewhere." He moved to say more but had to stop for some sudden pain.

Valin took his shoulder and firmly pushed him back onto the cot. "Stay," he growled as if to a wandering hound. "I mean it."

Lagan stayed, and Crysania moved closer, lifting her hand as though ready to help with more than poultices and wraps. She drew breath to speak a healing prayer that would close the cut, clean the infection, and take away the dwarf's pain.

She spoke no word before Lagan, greatly daring, took her hand in his. "No, lady. Wait. I—there are things you should know. Let me tell you."

Valin sat straighter, and Crysania dropped her hand to Lagan's. The chanting rose and fell, the plainsong lifted in praise.

"Then tell me, Lagan."

The dwarven cleric nodded, but only to himself, gathering thoughts and, Valin thought, perhaps his nerve.

"Listen," he said, in the way of his kind, a stern word to gather the attention of all. "My lady, when Nisse and I arrived at the tower, we learned that Sir Thomas knew no more than we did of these rumors of war. Ach! Some things we told him even he hadn't heard. When we'd arrived, he was making ready to send out a scouting party, and Nisse and I volunteered to go along rather than wait for them to return with news we could help gather."

He stopped then, looking from Crysania to Valin. What Crysania didn't see, Valin did: Lagan's eyes filling with deep sorrow. And yet what she didn't see, the lady sensed. Wasn't it ever so?

"Lagan," she said, her voice gentle as a balm, "If you can, please tell me what happened."

Lagan snorted, a derisive sound, the scorn meant for himself. "I can tell, lady. That much I can do."

He sat up again, his back to the wall.

"Nisse and I went with the scouting party. We traveled through the Virkhus Hills out onto the plains. All through the pass, we met no travelers coming toward Palanthas. It was—" he shook his head, then winced for the pain that it brought— "it was eerie to see the road so still and empty. Out on the plains, it's even stranger. The heat—the heat has killed everything, lady. Leeched the life out of the ground. Everything is brown and brittle. Nothing is green out there where a sea of green used to be. Not the least bit of lichen clings to the stones, no stream runs, not even a trickle. The corpses of starved animals lay all over, stinking in the sun."

Valin reached for a cup from the bedside table and filled it with wine. He gave it to Lagan but had to help him drink, so badly did his friend's hand shake.

"Can you go on?" Crysania asked, her hand on the dwarf's, offering strength and assurance.

Lagan could. He squared his shoulders and continued while hot breezes came in from the open window carrying the scent of the unrelieved city. And corpses, Valin thought, corpses stinking in the sun. He filled Lagan's cup again and pressed it into his friend's hand. He filled another and offered it to Crysania. She took it, but it sat untasted upon her knee. In the little cell, tension gathered like a storm.

"The plains were like the pass, my lady," Lagan said. "Empty, but worse. Here in the mountains, we are feeling the effects of the heat. But this close to the sea, we still have some small amount of moisture in the air, in the soil. There the land is barren. There is no green. No life."

Valin shuddered. A desert son, he was used to the great golden sweeps of sand that admitted no green. Still, no one who knew how to look closely would say the desert was barren. Life could always be found if one knew how to look. He closed his eyes, trying to imagine the horror of a land meant to be green and abounding with life, now dead.

Lagan took a sip of wine, then another. "We traveled toward the Vingaard River, and there we began to see the first of many travelers. Refugees full of tales of two vast armies heading through the Khalkist Mountains and coming down from the north. Ach! They're bold, those knights! No sooner did we hear this news than we turned north, hoping to collect better information. It wasn't long before we encountered droves of refugees fleeing from Kalaman. They said the city was besieged."

Valin's heart sank, aching. "Kalaman," he whispered. "Lagan, how could that be? Did this army come from the sea?"

"Ah, my friend," Lagan said, "I'm sorry to bring you this news. I know your people make their home in the desert between the sea and Kalaman. I can tell you only this . . . We heard no news of the desert tribes."

And no news, Valin thought, might well be good news in old sayings, but it was worse than bad news to him, leaving him to all the terrors his imagination could provide. How fared his mother and sisters? How fared his brother?

Wind rattled through the trees outside the window. The chanting of clerics had some time before fallen still. Lagan sat in silence, head low.

"My lady," he said, his voice rough and low, "there was a battle on the plains. Our scouting party stumbled upon an enemy army. They chased us. The knights turned to fight and did their best—no one can say they didn't. We stood no chance. Nisse was hit by an arrow. I—lady, I . . ."

His voice trailed away. He looked from Crysania to Valin, then down at the cup of wine in his hands.

"Well, we got away. When we returned to the tower, Sir Thomas had received a courier. North Keep, Valkinord, and Kalaman and all points in between have fallen to this army. It is the army of Lord Ariakan."

Crysania sighed, a small sound like the whisper of a

breeze at the window. The blood drained from her cheek. Her lips trembled. Then, in an instant, those signs of her distress vanished. Quietly she said, "I knew that Ariakan's Dark Knights were growing in strength, but an entire army?"

An army of Dark Knights, sworn to evil, to the worship of the Dark Queen! Valin shuddered.

Lagan, his shoulders slumped, his back pressed to the wall to keep him sitting upright, went on with his tale. He told of Sir Thomas's belief that Ariakan was attacking the east coast with half his army and marching them west through the mountains. His hands shaking, he told how the lord of the Dark Knights besieged the northeast with the other half of his army and would bring those forces south until both halves became one again.

Valin listened, and as he did he tried to imagine a map of the continent, tracing Ariakan's movements in his mind. If this army of Dark Knights had invaded the Khalkists, then Neraka would be virtually deserted. All those creatures of evil who ordinarily populated Neraka would have been brought into Ariakan's army.

He looked at Crysania. Strangely, these dire events were conspiring to lead her into a pact with Dalamar. Feeling cold in the pit of his belly, he realized that his thoughts mirrored hers. He saw it in the sudden light of understanding in her eyes, quickly sprung, as quickly damped.

"On the way, my lady, the armies are gathering strength as they collect allies. His commanders are knights on dragonback, as committed to their cause as the Solamnic Knights are to theirs, and just as honor bound. They lead an army of ogres, draconians, and goblins." His face, till then pale above his dark beard, went gray. "We heard of humans as tall as minotaurs among his ranks, barbarians who will fight to the death and give no quarter. His army is sweeping in a vast arc across the mountains. And they fight side by side with magic-users."

Valin snorted. "You can't be right about that, Lagan. The knights, Dark or Solamnic, have no love for mages."

Her hand on Lagan's, Crysania asked, "Were these Gray-Robed wizards?"

"Yes, lady. How did you know?" Lagan looked from one to the other of them. Quick-eyed, he saw Valin frown and Crysania nod to herself. "The gray-robed wizards—knights, they call themselves—swear their allegiance to the Dark Queen and they go armed, lady. Armed! What wizard on Krynn ever goes armed? Tanis Half-Elven said—"

"Tanis? You have seen Tanis?"

"Yes, lady. When we returned to the High Clerist's Tower, he was there, bringing word to Sir Thomas, an account of the battle at Kalaman. The Conclave of Wizards led the charge against the Gray Knights. The wizards of the three moons were defeated. Justarius was killed."

Valin sighed, suddenly remembering his unkind thought when he'd seen the wizardess Jenna the day before. Dark-eyed and weary she'd seemed, and he had wondered whether she'd passed a long night in her lover's bed or one plotting and scheming to keep their power in balance. She had instead been grieving for Justarius, mourning for the great mage who was her father.

With a weary groan, Lagan Innis sank down in his bed. He'd been long on the road, wounded and unhealed but for chancy poultices and one rough bandage. "Lady, Nisse died of her wounds on the road home."

Valin frowned. That should not have been! Why hadn't Lagan tried to heal her? He glanced at his friend, white and weary. Perhaps he'd not had the strength himself for the work.

Lagan lifted a hand to wipe sweat from his face. His hand shook. "My message to you from Sir Thomas is this. He thinks the two armies will sweep across the mountains and down from the sea and then reunite before turning toward Palanthas."

Crysania sat in silence, her face pale and composed, her hands still, one upon Lagan's arm, the other still holding her untasted cup. Valin waited, not breathing, and then the lady rose.

"Lagan, I'm glad you're home safe. And now you must rest . . . yes!" she said when he drew breath to object, to say he was well, to tell her not to worry. "You must. I will send a cleric to heal your hurts.

"I'm sure I don't need to caution you not to speak of this news you've brought. Panic is the last thing we need now."

She stood, but as she did, Lagan caught her hand, saying, "Lady, please, stay a moment." He glanced at Valin. "Alone, please."

Valin took the cup of wine from his friend's hand. Then he excused himself, leaving Crysania alone with her cleric. He did not go far, though, only to wait in the corridor outside Lagan's cell. Low voices drifted out from under the closed door. Once he heard Lagan's raised up, a dreadful cry of grief and sorrow. In the silence afterward, he heard the sounds of the temple, clerics coming and going, the lilt of laughter in the hall below. And then Crysania's voice, close at the door, as though she stood there with her hand on the latch.

"Sleep now, my friend. You've done well and I am grateful."

Valin stepped farther back into the corridor, not wanting to seem to be eavesdropping. When she came out of Lagan's cell, Crysania's face shone as white as the face of the silver moon itself, drained of all color.

"Lady," he said, going quickly to her side.

She put her hand on his arm. He felt it trembling.

His mouth dried up with fear. "Lady, please tell me what is wrong."

"Everything," she whispered, turning her face to him. "Everything is wrong, Valin. Nisse died because—" She stopped, took a small breath, and continued. "She died because, though he tried with all his strength, Lagan couldn't heal her."

Valin stared, barely understanding.

"He couldn't touch Paladine's strength, he couldn't find it. 'Nowhere to be found,' he said. He said the god is nowhere to be found. And, oh, dear gods, if that is so, I don't know what we will do now."

*   *   *   *   *

In his tower, shrouded in shadow, his eyes glinting, Dalamar the Dark looked into a black bowl filled with water. Upon the surface of that water small figures played, those of Crysania and her desert mage. It had been difficult to keep this little scrying spell together. More energy was needed than usual. It wasn't only Paladine who kept himself at remove from his worshipers. Dalamar's own god, the dark son Nuitari, did not pour out his strength for magic as easily as he had. Still, the energy Dalamar had spent was worth the return. He'd heard Valin and Crysania speaking: *I don't know what we will do now!*

"But I know," he said. "I know what you will do now, Revered Daughter. You will do the only thing you can do, and that is the very thing I wish you to do."

He leaned forward, breathing strongly upon the still black surface of the water. The images broke apart, scattered, and vanished. The Master of the Tower of High

81

Linda P. Baker & Nancy Varian Berberick

Sorcery crossed his chamber, his steps soundless on the thick carpet, his shadow dark and long before him. He poured himself a cup of red wine, then went to his window and looked out, north past the trees of terrible Shoikan Grove, north to where the Temple of Paladine stood.

Smiling, he raised up his cup and he said, "Good journey, my lady." Laughing, he added, "May the gods speed you on your way."

Chapter Six

Crysania sat on her favorite bench in the garden of the temple, the long one of rose-veined gray marble, tucked away on the west side, near the apple grove and the small stand of pear trees. In springtimes past, those trees had frothed with blossoms, the scents so sweet they perfumed the temple for a week and more. Not this year. The flower buds had died of heat on the branch. The trees had leafed, but come autumn, they would not bear fruit. Like the crops in the fields, they would wither and die.

How will we eat come winter? she wondered. Who will provide if crops are dying and the beasts in the forests perish of thirst and hunger?

Paladine's will, said her heart. Trust in the god. He will provide.

She drew a long breath, reaching out with her soul. He

was there, but "there" seemed so very far away when all she could gain was the sense of him, not the touch of him upon her heart. In the deep pocket of her robe, the Dragon Stones lay, one still and silent, the other calling to her.

Lightly she touched it, the warmth of goodness spreading like an ache through her, rising to her heart. She looked for reassurance; she looked for her god. She did not hear his voice, though she felt him each time she touched the stone.

Where are you, O Paladine? My dearest lord, where are you?

No voice came to answer.

Crysania sat still, her hands in her lap, her heart unquiet. It had always been that she could find peace in the temple gardens, surrounded by the soft sounds of breezes through the trees, by gardeners at work with hoe and clippers. She had even learned to distinguish the soft flutter of a butterfly from that of a sparrow, the gentle song of a hummingbird at the roses from the insistent buzz of bees in the lavender. All these things, sound and scent and tender touch, had always worked to calm her soul and soothe her heart when trouble came. And all these things, these soft garden sensations, were denied her now. The hot wind carried barely a whiff of green, and the grass underfoot crackled, brittle and dry.

That crackling now tracked the retreat of a young woman as she departed across the burnt lawn. She had brought a message from Lord Amothus saying that a large shipment of wheat that had been expected had not arrived. It had been grown with great care, using great amounts of scarce water, but it had fallen victim to an ambush on the plains. A shipment by water was similarly late, and there were unconfirmed rumors that a large body of Ariakan's troops had moved out of Kalaman, heading back toward the sea.

"But why?" Crysania had asked. "Why would Ariakan give up the city he'd just conquered?"

The messenger had drawn a long breath and let it go slowly. "Lady, my lord doesn't know."

Crysania twined her fingers together, then untwined them, willing herself to find calm so that she could think. Were Ariakan's ships bound for Palanthas? Would the morning watch soon spot red sails on the horizon?

She had sent word of this latest development to Sir Thomas but did not expect to hear from him yet. And she had sent an urgent message to Dalamar, though she knew she shouldn't expect to hear from him at all. From long experience, Crysania knew the dark elf absorbed all the news he could get but radiated little back.

The sun moved behind the temple, casting cooling shadows. Crysania bent to the basket at her feet, plucking up a strip of clean white cotton. The basket was full of such, and she sat now rolling the strips into tight bundles, rolling bandages for the Solamnic Knights. This task employed everyone in the temple at one time or another during the day, for she had decreed that no hand, not even hers, must remain idle. In every spare moment, bandages must be rolled, for if the Dark Knights did fall upon the city, many of the clerics would go to the tower to help with the wounded there. The least wounded would be bandaged by laymen and healed after those whose lives were more seriously threatened.

Crysania's hands stilled, then busied themselves again. Lagan Innis's cry of grief echoed in her memory: "Lady! I could not heal Nisse! I prayed, I reached out, I sought the god—and he was not there!"

This morning one cleric and then another came to her, whispering of similar failures to touch the god in their prayers. They were ashamed, as though they had committed some sin that caused Paladine to turn his face from them.

"No, my dear one," she had said to each, "never think so. His love is great, and our sins are small. He is with us, he is. Only he is silent now for reasons of his own."

"What reasons?" they'd asked, each in their turn.

She had to admit that she did not know; she had to bid them trust in the god as she did.

A warm breeze rattled the drying leaves in the apple trees. Nearby, the acolyte who served as Crysania's assistant today crouched beside one of the gardeners, the two of them poking in the dry earth, discussing in hushed tones how best to care for the vegetable plots and the herb gardens without wasting water. Their voices sounded faint and far-off.

Crysania put aside a roll of bandages and reached for a new strip when she heard the crunch of footsteps on the gravel path. She raised her face, tilted her head slightly to one side, and then smiled. Sometimes she had to wait for a voice to know who was approaching her. Not in this case. This one's steps, heavy and measured, she knew very well.

"Valin. Come join me here in the shade."

"Lady." He bowed to her. "How do you always know it's me even before I speak?"

She smiled. Her busy fingers came to the end of another roll of cloth and smoothed it down. She pushed the finished bandages into the bottom of the basket and took up another strip.

"Your footsteps aren't like any other's. I always imagine that your feet are not quite happy on our solid ground, that they are wishing for soft sand."

Valin sat beside her on the bench and stretched out his long legs before him. He took the basket from the ground and held it on his knee. "My lady," he said in his rich, deep voice, "I've been called a large oaf with heavy footsteps by many, but never so charmingly."

She laughed aloud, surprised to feel sudden delight, and he found the end of a strip of cloth, tugged it free, and put it in her fingers.

For a long moment he kept silent, still and unmoving. Then he said, "Please tell me, lady, that you're not considering Dalamar's proposition."

Crysania sighed silently. The old question with him, spoken sometimes, haunting always. There were times when she was pleased with the way the mage seemed to almost divine her secret thoughts. This was not one of them. She already knew Valin's opinion of Dalamar, the Dragon Stones, the dark elf's machinations, and Black-Robed Wizards in general. He had made himself clear about all of it since their visit to the tower two days ago.

"I would be foolish not to consider it."

She straightened her shoulders, assumed a calm demeanor that she did not really feel. "Yes," she said, hearing him draw breath to object. "Yes, I know it better than most: Dalamar plays at games within games, and I don't yet understand what he's playing at now. Do I even believe him when he says that the stones, once found, will give me the power to speak to Takhisis? I don't know. I do know this, though. One of the stones he's given me touches my heart like the hand of Paladine himself. How can I doubt the goodness in it? How can I believe that goodness will become so corrupt once the stone is joined to its kin that nothing but evil will prevail?" She put aside her bandages. "Valin, I can never believe that goodness will become corrupted. I am not able to believe so."

Instead of the protest she'd expected, he said simply, "Lady, you are so good. Perhaps you are—"

He stopped so abruptly that she had no doubt what his next words would have been.

"Perhaps," she said lightly, "I am blinded by goodness?"

Uncomfortable silence sat between them until at last he said, "Forgive me."

"No, don't ask for that. There is no need. Must the word go out of the language simply because I live it? Of course not. Valin, I appreciate your concern."

Again his silence, a gap filled by the soft voices of the gardener and the acolyte as they conferred. Then, his voice rough and low, Valin said, "It is not simple concern, my lady. It is—" He closed his fingers over hers, long, supple fingers, rough and warm. "Do you know—you must know how—I feel about you."

"I know that you care," she said, her heart thumping hard in her breast. She knew that, and she suspected more. "And I am grateful for that, and for your loyalty."

In the courtyard between the temple and the garden, a voice lifted in laughter. It was Lagan Innis who had done nothing but mourn these two days past. What had teased the laughter from him? Crysania wondered with one part of her mind, wishing she could go to see. Wishing, oh, wishing she did not sit here with Valin's declaration of love about to spill out and fall upon—upon what? Barren ground? No, not that. Her heart was not barren, never that. Yet she must turn from what he would say. She must.

"Valin," she said as gently as though he'd come to her with some wound in need of healing. "My friend, you must not—"

"Crysania, I love you."

He said it simply. Quietly he laid his heart and his soul in her hands.

And, oh, she wished, selfishly she wished she could take his love and cherish him. She thought of all that she must face, of the threatening war, of the strange silence of gods, of all the loss ahead, and she did not want to lose Valin too. How would it be to love him, the great tall mage from desert lands? How would it be to have him beside her always, in her days, in her nights, the warm, reassurance of his love hers forever?

It would be wonderful. And she would be so very wrong to reach for that.

"Valin," she whispered as she gently withdrew from his touch. Her hands felt cold now, and her heart ached with another loss impending. "Valin, I thank you for the honor you do me, but—"

She could not see him, but she could hear him. His breath hitched as if in pain.

"But you are the Revered Daughter of Paladine, and I am only a desert chieftain's son."

Crysania winced as though from an unkind blow. "I thought you knew me, friend mage. I thought you did. If you knew me, you'd know your birth—no matter if you were the son of the lowest man of your tribe!—would never make you unworthy in my eyes. Your heart is everything, and none is nobler than yours."

Bitterness wrung his voice. "Then what keeps you from me, lady?"

"Don't you know?"

He did. His silence said so.

"There is no place in my life for love such as you offer. Oh, gods, if only there were! But, Valin, you know who I am; you know how much responsibility I bear. The kind," she said hastily, "that I can share with no one. Yes, I am a Revered Daughter of Paladine, as you say, and that title comes at great cost. One of the things I pay in fee is to forgo the life of love even the poorest woman of the city may hope for."

"Your god," he said, still bitter, still hurt. "He comes before all."

"Yes," she said gently. "He does. He must. I have my faith. And my commitment to that faith. I have duties to uphold. I serve the temple and those who worship in it, as well as those who do not.

"Valin, I would not hurt you for all the riches of the world. You are so very dear to me. But I will not give you false hope. I—I'm sorry."

In the courtyard, Lagan Innis called to someone, saying he wondered where his friend, the mage, had gone. The answer came, muffled by distance. It must have sufficed, for Lagan's voice was not heard again. And Valin stood, straight and tall to hide his pain. She knew it. She felt it.

"I beg, lady, that you will forgive me. I was wrong to speak this way to you. I was wrong to burden you with my foolish fancies. Now tell me, please, how I can help you in these hard days to come."

Crysania felt loss sliding over her heart like a cold, deep shadow.

She rose to stand beside him, suddenly deciding. "I need someone to go to Kalaman," she declared. "To assess the situation and report back to me. I ask you to go on my behalf—immediately."

He groaned, a man wounded. "No, please, lady. Don't send me from you. I swear it, I won't speak of my feelings again. There's no need to send me away. I want to be here with you in case there is an attack, or if you decide to go to—"

His voice trailed away. He was loath to speak the name of the evil city in such godly surroundings. She presented her reasoning before he could draw further breath to protest.

"Valin, I must have reliable information. The silence of the gods, Ariakan's gathering armies, the dreadful heat—all these things are connected somehow. I know it. I feel it in my heart. But what my instinct tells me is only warning. I need facts, information. I need to know where my best efforts will be spent. I need you to do this because I trust you. And you know that area much better than any of the clerics here. You're much better equipped to handle yourself if the conditions are as bad as I fear."

What could he say? She had presented her case so well, so strongly, that he could do nothing but agree.

"But I beg you, Crysania, give me your word that you won't leave for Neraka until I return. You will need me even more on that trip than you will on this one."

"I cannot promise that," she said, her voice low and sad.

They stood in silence for a long moment, Crysania thinking that, just as he had said, she did need him. Thinking how selfish that need was. Weighing the selfishness of her need against the needs of the temple and the awkwardness and discomfort of keeping him close by. She almost hesitated. She felt she owed him, at least, some explanation. She breathed deeply, drew upon her self-control, and drew him back down onto the bench.

"Even before Lagan returned with news of Ariakan and his army, I was distressed by these developments and considering you for this mission."

"Distressed? Here is news." He smiled. She heard it in his voice, and the smile was without humor. She heard that, too. "I've never seen anything distress you."

"If I could be what you think I am, my friend, we'd all be better off. But I am who I am, and so I'm often distressed, Valin, and often I go to my prayers."

She paused, touching the medallion at her breast. She began again, and this time as she spoke her voice grew stronger. The words flowed faster. "There are times when Paladine seems to surround me, so close it seems he is part of the room I am in, the air I breathe. Sometimes his presence is less immediate." She gripped the medallion so hard she felt the imprint of the dragon itself on her palm." But now it has been a long time since I felt his presence very strongly. It has been a long time since I felt him as I used to feel him . . . with me."

She paused, swallowing. "This morning as I prayed, it was as if I could barely detect him. No, I can't put it into words. It was as if he were there but not listening."

"Lagan has said the same thing to me."

"He and others are feeling it. It's hard, Valin, to look for the god who for so long sustained me and find only silence."

Valin reached out for her, touched her hand soothingly, offering wordless comfort.

Shuddering slightly, Crysania continued. "Something is wrong. Very wrong. I know it in my heart." She took up the cotton strips again, her fingers moving automatically. "That is why I tell you this. So you will understand how vital it is that I have accurate information from someone I can trust."

"Lady, if you go to Neraka, you must take me with you! Who will protect you?"

Crysania grew solemn. "Anyone who goes with me will protect me, as I will protect him."

"Then you have decided."

She hesitated only a moment. "I believe my course is set no matter how I decide. Events seem bent on guiding me." And she didn't like that, she who was used to guiding her own course.

Agitated, Valin stood. He caught her arm. "Please, lady, walk with me."

Reluctantly she put aside the strip of cloth on which she was working.

The acolyte, seeing Crysania stand, also started to rise, but Valin waved her away. He led Crysania deeper into the garden, away from the temple, away from those who had ventured outside.

"Lady, you know I don't trust Lord Dalamar. He has

his own reasons for what he does. He didn't even tell you about the gray wizards and the conclave! And even if Dalamar persuades you somehow, think of Neraka! You can't be serious about going there." His voice dropped low. "You can't be serious about communicating with Takhisis!"

Dry leaves crunched underfoot as they walked. Crysania reached up a hand and trailed it through the branches of the hedge that lined the path. The few leaves that still clung tentatively to the branches were as lifeless as those that marked their passing. She stopped.

"Valin." She said his name softly, caught his large hand between hers. "It would be best if you go. Now." She looked up to where she knew his eyes to be. "You have lived here with us and borne our scrutiny with charm and grace. And while there are still those who mutter about mages, there are many in the temple who have come to accept you as one of us, without questioning your motives or your beliefs. I cannot but think that they will carry this forward in their dealings with other mages. I have wanted this discourse, this openness between mages and clerics, for many years. You've brought me so much closer to it, and I will always honor you for that. And if you cannot go where I send you now, then I understand. But all the same, then you must go from here."

He sighed once deeply, and she turned to leave him, her step slow and her heart heavy.

His hand fell lightly on her shoulder. She stopped. He turned her around.

She lifted her face, ready to ask a question, and in that moment felt his lips on hers. A gentle kiss, offered in hope of never dying. She gasped a little as her heart roused and warmed to him. He put his hands round her waist.

"No," she whispered, against his kiss. No, she said to

him, and to the sad reality that demanded she not accept what again he offered.

He let her go, took his hand from her, turned his face and let the kiss die.

"I will go on this mission because you ask it," he said huskily, "and I hope you know that you may trust me in all things, no matter what has passed between us here."

No matter, said his unspoken words, what has not passed.

Then he walked away, leaving her alone there on the path, acutely aware of the sound of his footsteps as he walked back up the path.

Her assistant came trotting up as she turned back toward her bench. "Lady, is there anything you need?"

Crysania put her hand to her hair, smoothing it absently, wondering if the flush she felt was visible. "Yes, please. Would you carry my workbasket inside? I think I will retire early."

The young woman bowed and offered to accompany her, but Crysania waved her away. She did not want company now, not even unobtrusive company.

* * * * *

Valin sat a long moment at the small desk, the only other furniture in his chamber beside his bed and nightstand and the small chest he'd brought with him from his home. Ink dried swiftly on the parchment before him, thanks to the heat of the afternoon. The words there were few, a spare message written in haste. A message, perhaps, to draw him into danger. A message, perhaps, to help him learn things he must know. Crysania would never permit this message had she known about it. Valin would take the greatest care to be certain she did not. What he did now was his business. Only his.

To the Lord of the Tower of High Sorcery:

*My lord, I greet you. In days past, you spoke words
of invitation to me, a request that we meet and con-
verse. I will come to you as you request. You may
expect me in the morning.*

He read the spare message again, then penned his
name and rolled the parchment, tied it with a white
ribbon, and marked it with his own seal. He was, after all,
the son of a desert chieftain, one whose sigil, though perhaps not particularly well known in Palanthas, was the
sign of an honorable man and thus proudly made.

That done, he went out into the temple, found Lagan
Innis, and said to his friend, "Please take this to The
Three Moons. And I beg you, my friend, speak to no one
of it."

Lagan frowned, his expression clearly bespeaking a
cleric's reluctance to venture into the mageware shop.

Valin winked. "Never worry. I haven't heard that Mistress Jenna is in the habit of turning dwarves into toads.
But just in case she is, you needn't wait for a reply."

Lagan snorted and snatched the parchment from
Valin's hand. "Good as done."

And Valin knew it was so.

He returned to his room, closed the door behind him,
and murmured a spell. There were no locks on temple
doors, but this spell would guard as well as a lock. Any
who approached with the intent of seeking him would
suddenly remember that they'd seen him elsewhere only
a moment ago and so leave.

The spell set, Valin unrolled a white, closely woven
rug no larger than a cleric's prayer mat. He stretched it
out upon the floor. His hands trembling with pleasure,
with anticipation, he smoothed the rug and took out a

small pouch from the chest at the foot of his bed. His heart sang, his blood tingled. It had been a long time since he'd cast more than a simple spell. Now he would weave one of the most complex.

Stepping carefully, his feet bare and clean, Valin sat in the exact center of the rug. From the pouch came spell components. First he took out four stones—tourmaline, rose marble, granite, and turquoise. These he placed at each corner of the rug, for they were ward stones, bespelled to keep him safe while he worked his magic.

Next he took out two smaller pouches, one of gold velvet, the other of blue silk. Each contained the dried leaves of certain sweet-smelling herbs. He poured the contents of the gold pouch into his hand, from that hand, he let the powdered herb trickle to make a green circle on the white rug. As he did, he whispered words of enchantment, deep words known only to those versed in magecraft. He did the same with the blue pouch of herbs, shaping a circle within the circle, so that he was surrounded and safe.

Drawing a deep breath, Valin summoned his strength and firmed his will. He closed his eyes, feeling magic humming in him, coursing through his blood, skittering along the length of his bones, singing in his heart.

"Wake in me now, silent one. Silent one, awake!"

Deep within himself, he felt a stirring, a rousing. His strength began to wane.

"Rise from me now, silent one. Silent one, arise!"

And the rousing grew stronger, a power gathering. The urge to fall down and sleep lay heavy on him.

"Step forth now, silent one. Silent one, step!"

A breeze sighed at the window; Valin heard it as from a great distance. Upon his skin he felt a touch, as of a familiar hand, but only as a man just falling into sleep feels. By sheer force of will, he opened his eyes and felt the familiar shock of seeing himself standing before him. It was not like looking in a mirror, the act of seeing his fetch. It was more as if he saw himself in a dream, fully dimensional, strong and tall and straight.

"Silent one," he whispered, "you must take my voice and fare forth."

The fetch, a creature born of his own spirit, a being with no will but his, bowed once and made no sound.

Valin drew breath, long and slow, holding on to the waking world with quickly waning strength.

"You must find my brother, wherever he may be, and you must tell him this for me: I need you! Come to Palanthas, to the Temple of Paladine, and seek the Lady Crysania. She will take a long and dangerous journey, and I cannot be with her to ward and guide her. Come and take my place at her side, Brother. On our mother's pure soul, on our father's fiery heart, I swear to the urgency of my need!"

And the fetch, silent, with only those words to speak to only that man, stepped out from the circle, out beyond the ward stones that would keep Valin's body safe while his spirit fared forth.

The white robe sank onto the rug, asleep before he could smell the herbs warding round him. He never felt the fetch leave, nor did he awaken when it returned.

*   *   *   *   *

Crysania crossed through her quiet study to her bedchamber. She opened the windows wide, but the early evening air was hot and still, and the room remained stuffy. Standing before the open windows, she closed her fingers upon the medallion of the golden dragon and took a deep breath. She waited quietly, patiently for Paladine's warmth. But no breath of light and goodness came to fill her soul. She tried to push away the worries and concerns of the day, tried to forget Valin. Lips moving softly in a litany of prayer, she circled the room.

Over and over she murmured, "Lord of all that is light and good, I have choices to make, and they are hard ones. Grant me thy comfort and wisdom."

Dust scraped beneath her sandals. She kicked her sandals off and listened to the sounds of the temple and the approaching night. Bells chimed softly in the garden, voices twined together, murmuring. The silver song of crickets rose from the grass, one calling to another. A gull cried, high above in the hard blue sky, ever hungry, ever hopeful.

A little at a time, her tension eased, like a burden lifting from her shoulders. Ah, she'd been yoked with that burden of worry and fear for so long!

At last she felt better. Yet still she didn't feel Paladine's touch. She put aside her medallion and let her robe fall off her shoulders and pool on the floor. Her linen shift clung to her, damp and uncomfortable. as she washed in lukewarm water. That done, she stepped out of the linen and dressed in a light nightshirt. Only then did she take up the robe, slip her fingers into the pocket, and retrieve the two Dragon Stones. Their magic warmed her hand, radiated up her arm.

The warmth became a tingling, spreading throughout her body.

And suddenly she could feel Paladine as she had not felt him in weeks. So near!

She fell to her knees, her lashes wet with tears.

"Paladine, bless us. Grant me thy comfort and wisdom. Help—"

Like a bright shard of light, so bright it hurt, she felt his presence. But something was wrong. He felt—

Something was terribly wrong!

She knew it, trembling on her knees, that Paladine—her great god, her wide-winged silver dragon—stood in great danger.

The magic prickling began to burn. The burning became painful, like fire on her skin, like flame in her heart. With a cry, Crysania dropped the stones. She released the medallion.

She staggered to her feet, the dust on the floor burning the soles of her feet as though she walked on glowing embers. She gained her bed, sobbing, not knowing whose pain she felt, hers or her god's.

She lay for a long time, shuddering, tears streaking her face, fear wracking her heart. It seemed to her that darkness came with clawed hand, reaching for her, clutching at her. She cried out once. It seemed she'd screamed. But no sound followed, not the questioning voice of an acolyte or cleric. Who could overhear the cries of her heart? Only the god who could not speak to her, who could not seek her.

A long while later sleep overcame her, and yet still she was denied peace. Exhausted, she dreamed of battle light on shining swords, of dark, looping corridors filled with deadly traps. She dreamed of her god, hooded and shrouded and standing alone in a storm.

She dreamed of touching the bright, shining stone given her by Dalamar, the servant of darkness. She dreamed that she felt—for only the briefest moment!—the embrace of her god, the peace of his love and strength.

Then she dreamed no more.

Chapter Seven

With words softly whispered, words to slip from the memory as soon as they were heard, the Lord of the Tower of High Sorcery lighted the candles scattered about his chamber, those on the table, those on his desk, those set upon small stone shelves built into the walls themselves. Light sprang, shadows scurried back, and Valin stood calmly, watching the change.

"Welcome again, sir mage," Dalamar said, smiling a cool, humorless smile. "You grace me with your company."

That much Valin didn't believe. So said his silence, grimly held. He knew his strengths, and he had long ago reckoned his weaknesses, so he had the good sense not to fall into wordplay with one so powerful as Dalamar the Dark.

"Thank you for seeing me, my lord," he murmured and said no more.

Dalamar eyed him, toe to top, a disdainful smile upon his lips. "Well, of course. It is a pleasure." He gestured to the same chairs they'd occupied a few nights earlier. "Please make yourself comfortable."

This time, though, Valin noted, he offered no wine, no banter, no pretense at pleasantry. He kept his place, unwilling to let himself become comfortable here. He must be on his guard always.

"What is this game you're playing with Crysania?" Valin asked bluntly.

Slender shoulders shrugged casually. Dalamar ignored the question.

"I must admit, you are not what I expected." Narrow-eyed, Dalamar scrutinized the human. Again the slender shoulders rose and fell as some opinion was confirmed through observation.

Whatever the opinion, it mattered not at all to Valin.

"I repeat, what are you trying to do to Crysania?"

Dalamar made himself comfortable in a low, deep chair. He gestured again for Valin to do the same. Again Valin refused. The dark elf's eyes flared.

"I said sit."

Valin did, almost before he could think.

"Now," Dalamar said, his voice low and easy, "the matter of the Dragon Stones is between your mistress and me, nothing I choose to discuss with you." Candlelight rose and fell, flickering on the walls and the ceiling. The dark elf sat a long moment in silence, his fingers steepled, his eyes closed. Then, when Valin had thought himself forgotten, Dalamar said, "But I thought perhaps we might be able to help each other in other ways."

Valin sat straight in his chair, unbending in his watchfulness.

"Help each other? How? I was not aware that I needed your help. I certainly never imagined that you would need mine."

"You are mistaken, sir mage, and so you can't see that we want the same thing, you and I. Because we do. We are in a unique position to help each other. And Crysania."

Outside the window, soft moanings sounded, low cries to chill the blood. Here were the sounds of Shoikan Grove at night, the daemons, the ghosts, the terrors that warded the tower at all times. Valin swallowed once, then again, but when he spoke, he made no attempt to hide the suspicion in his voice.

"Assuming that we do want the same thing, my lord, why would you want to help me or Crysania?"

Dalamar nodded, as though at the fair question of an apt student. "Well said. I want to know more about the Dragon Stones. I will admit . . ." He let his voice trail in feigned reluctance to speak further. "Well, I had hoped that I might be able to use them myself. But I could not."

"Because one of the stones is good?" Valin guessed.

Dalamar nodded.

Valin sat forward. "Then how do you imagine Crysania will be able to use the Dragon Stones? According to your legends, one of them is evil. Yes, she is no mage as we are, and so the touch of that stone wouldn't harm her as it would me, but she is still a cleric of Paladine. The touch of that stone would do her no good." He paused, then said, "The goddess you think she will be able to contact once those stones are rejoined is not one who loves her. Nor one she loves."

Dalamar looked at him, an inscrutable expression on his face. "She is sending you away, is she not?"

Valin started at the sudden change in subject. His face flushed in anger and embarrassment. "How do you know that?"

A small stone bowl sat upon the table at Dalamar's side. Water, clear and still, sat within. The dark elf let his fingers trail across the still surface, watching the ripples run out to the sides.

"I know," he said at last, "because I know your lady. I know . . . " He paused, staring at the colorful rug that lay beneath their feet. Yet his mind seemed far away, as if whatever held his attention was far away. When he looked up again, a small light gleamed in his eyes, of laughter perhaps. "So that you will understand, I will tell you a story you might be interested to hear. I first knew Crysania during the War of the Lance."

Valin swallowed, shifting carefully in his chair. He had heard something about this. There were few on Krynn who had not heard it in some form or another, the story of Crysania's adventures during the Blue Lady's War.

His eyes upon the rug again, his thoughts upon some other time, Dalamar spoke. His was a charming voice when he wanted it to be. He wished it so now.

"In those days, your Revered Daughter was new to her faith. But even as young as she was, she was strong and powerful, absolute in her conviction. She was one of the most beautiful women I'd ever seen, and one of the coldest."

Valin opened his mouth to protest what seemed to him a slander. He snapped it shut just as quickly as Dalamar continued.

"Like ice she was. As cold and beautiful as a glacier. As unreachable. Or so she seemed to me. And yet there was fire in the ice. The woman is made of contradictions. She told me once that she had an unusual ambition, a sense of purpose, that burned like a flame in her. Her goal was to bring goodness to the world. She felt that she had been called upon to confront and destroy all evil. So she went into the Abyss."

Valin nodded. This he knew, yet even so, the name of that dark and terrible place still had the power to make him shiver.

Dalamar seemed not to notice. "You have heard of the mage Raistlin Majere?"

"I have," Valin said. "Who has not?"

A look passed over the dark elf's face, one to make Valin think of a man in the grip of old hauntings. "Very few. With Raistlin accompanying her, Crysania passed through the portal. Raistlin went to find the power to rule the world. Crysania went to find the strength to bring the world goodness."

Dalamar looked up, caught Valin's glance, and held it.

"Now, a fine mage such as you are surely knows that the portal has been sealed by my own hand, but at the time, the portal was thought to be impassable. No seal warded it because the ancients, thinking to make impassable what they could not seal, had set a spell upon the gate. To gain entrance required a Wizard of the Black Robe and a cleric of Paladine, working as one. They thought it impossible that one so dark-hearted and one so good would work together, trusting each other implicitly."

Silence settled, long and deep. Not even the moans from without could be heard. Then Dalamar smiled, a cold gesture from a chill heart. In that smile, Valin understood that the dark elf knew a secret none but he and Crysania knew. He knew of a silent, secret kiss, stolen and cherished in the temple gardens.

"You see," Dalamar said, "the ancients had not considered the folly of the human heart."

It was all Valin could do to keep his eyes upon Dalamar's, to keep himself from looking away like a schoolboy caught doing what he should never have done. He managed, but the effort left him sweating and cold.

Dalamar's voice softened, as if he knew Valin's pain. "Thus Crysania went into the Abyss with the man she loved. Raistlin Majere."

"Raistlin!" Valin had heard the stories about the connection between Raistlin and Crysania. Tales of Raistlin were told around campfires and whispered wherever mages gathered. The most often told, the darkest and the most wonderful, was that Raistlin Majere had fought the Dark Queen and prevented her from entering the world, at the sacrifice of his own life.

Dalamar trailed his hand in the water again, making ripples, watching them expand.

"She never told you this, did she?"

Valin admitted it.

"Well, I suppose it's a thing you should know about her. Her faith and strength and Raistlin's power took them through the portal. Her faith and strength protected Raistlin. And when he had no more use of her, he abandoned her to die there."

Valin groaned. He'd heard that, he knew it, but to hear it now, in this place, was to hear it for the first time.

"As you know," Dalamar said, gauging Valin's reaction and smiling over what he reckoned, "the lady was near death when Caramon brought her back through the portal."

"Raistlin's brother," Valin murmured. These names were well known throughout Krynn. Raistlin and Caramon, Tanis Half-Elven, these were among the nine Heroes of the Lance, men and women who had plumbed the depths of their souls and found the courage to battle the Dark Queen and save the world.

"Yes." Dalamar nodded, remembering. "Tanis Half-Elven and I were here, on this side of the portal, when Caramon came back through. It was, in the end, his love that saved his brother. It can be said—it has been said—

that his love saved us all. Some even say Raistlin's love had a part in that salvation, his love for his brother Caramon and for Crysania. Raistlin faced the Dark Queen alone, holding her at bay until Caramon could bring Crysania to safety."

Valin sat still, enchanted by the tale.

"And then Caramon sealed the portal with the Staff of Magius. I was near death when they came out. When it was over, when they were trying to save her and me, Tanis said Crysania wept and told of fires and burning, how her flesh was burnt from her bones, the bones burnt black and splitting in the tremendous heat."

Valin closed his eyes, trying to shut out those words, trying not to imagine the pain his lady had endured. And yet he could not close his heart or the grief that raged there.

"She said this," Dalamar sighed. "But there was not a mark on her. Except for one thing."

Valin opened his eyes. "Except that she went into the portal sighted and came out blind."

"Yes. Her faith and that of her clerics helped her to heal from the experience, but nothing could return the sight the gods themselves had taken. I sealed the portal, and no one has passed through it since."

He rose to his feet, an incongruous smile on face. "Well done of me, don't you think?"

Tears stung Valin's throat. How childish he had been, how innocent, how foolish, to think himself worthy of Crysania! How she must have laughed—but, no, she wouldn't laugh at him. She wouldn't even pity him. She had known the great legends in the flesh. She had compassion enough to save the world. He swallowed, afraid that his voice would not serve him when he spoke.

"What does this have to do with what is happening now?" he managed to ask.

Dalamar crossed the room, took a delicate blue crystal cup from the sideboard, and filled it with wine. He made a show of offering the same to Valin, but Valin shook his head.

"What does this old tale have to do with what is happening now? With wars and Dragon Stones and the strange silence of the gods? Can you not guess, sir mage? Well, I will spare you the effort. You asked how it is I can imagine that Crysania will be able to use the Dragon Stones if the goddess they bring her is Takhisis herself." He lifted his cup as in salute. "I tell you I imagine that anyone who has in her the strength Crysania has can do almost the impossible."

Valin almost believed that himself, and so his next question had not to do with that. His next question was the one Crysania herself had been asking. "Tell me, my lord, what do you think to gain by giving a Revered Daughter of Paladine the chance to speak with the Dark Queen?"

Dalamar shrugged as though the question were of no importance. "Don't worry about that, sir mage. I'll never tell you, and you will never guess. But listen! You know her; you know she will go. She must, for she will not be searching to speak with my queen. She will be searching, always and ever, for a chance to speak with her own god. So let us get down to business, the business for which I called you here."

A chill ran in ripples along Valin's spine. Dalamar's mask of graciousness fell from him, leaving his face white, his eyes like a midnight sky.

"I can make it so that she will never send you away," Dalamar said gravely.

Valin's heart jumped. "But what could you do that would make her love me? And even if you could cast such a spell, I would not want to force her—" He stopped himself, his feelings too raw.

107

Dalamar laughed, a sound from dark caverns. "I did not say I would make her love you, desert mage. Only that I could fix it so she would not send you away. Although it isn't impossible to think that with my help, you might find a way to earn Crysania's love."

It was all he wanted! Everything he dreamed of, the very thing he worked for!

His voice hoarse, his throat dry, Valin said, "What could you do to . . . to give me this chance?"

Dalamar settled comfortably in his chair and set the blue crystal cup on the table beside him. "I told Crysania I would pick the guide for the trip to Neraka. You could be that guide."

Valin's hope sank. "How? She has already said she will not take me."

"I will cast a spell to alter your appearance."

Valin shook his head. On his feet now, he prowled the room, restless suddenly, wishing he hadn't come here and certain he must not make a deal with this mage. Beyond that certainty, however, lay something else—his urgent heart, his love for the Revered Daughter of Paladine. Like the ancients, he had not reckoned on the foolishness of the human heart. Dalamar knew this. Valin understood now how completely his love bound him to this path he now stood ready to take. Still, he objected. He must try to find a hole in Dalamar's plan, all the while hoping there was none.

"Make me look like someone else?" he said. "Crysania won't be taken in by that trick."

The dark elf smiled, almost benignly. "Not make you look like some*one* else, mage. Like some*thing* else. Let Crysania send you away. I will give her a gift for her travels. A tiger. A white tiger of the desert to take your place, to serve as her guardian and companion."

Valin stopped his prowling. Behind him gaped the

window, and beyond lay Shoikan Grove, a place as filled with traps as this tower chamber seemed to be.

"Of course," added Dalamar, "there are drawbacks. You will have only a limited ability to communicate. And—"

Valin held his breath, waiting for him to continue.

"—and the spell will not be reversible. It will have a limited life, however." He stopped, his eyes gleaming. "It will last only until the lady proclaims her love for you."

Valin struggled, like a fly caught in a spider's web, knowing himself doomed, fighting because he had to.

"This is absurd! What would be your reward for such a spell? And why should I agree to such foolishness?"

Dalamar shrugged, then settled back, his long thin fingers again steepled. "You will agree because you love her, and I offer you the only chance of being at her side on this dangerous quest. I offer this chance because, as I told your lady, I wish to know the fate of the Dragon Stones. You will be my eyes and ears, reporting back to me as you travel."

He would never do it. He would never go with her disguised, constrained to tell Dalamar about their every discovery, each hope, each turn in the road. Never!

So he would lose her, she whom he could not bear to lose.

Valin bowed his head. His eyes on the carpet that earlier had so interested Dalamar, he whispered, "I will accept your spell."

And may all the gods help us, for our hearts are good and our hope is strong.

It was an old prayer, one of the first he'd ever learned. Valin repeated it now in his secret heart, but it gave him no comfort.

* * * * *

Lagan Innis looked up from his packing, dark eyes alight with his determination. "Yes, I am going with you. Don't bother arguing."

Valin sighed, making his point for what he hoped was the last time. "Lagan, the lady will need you here. She's asked only me to go out to Kalaman, and I'm not asking you to accompany me."

"No matter," the dwarf said. "I'm going anyway. I've been on those roads, Valin! I know what's going on there, I know you will need a companion. And the lady will agree once I put it to her that way."

He stopped, looking around the small cleric's cell at the spare furnishings, the bed, the nightstand, and the one small wardrobe in the corner. He didn't look like a man who would regret leaving comfortable quarters. Valin knew his friend too well to think that. He looked like a man trying to ask a difficult question.

"What?" Valin asked, gently because he guessed what Lagan would say next.

A gull cried loud in the sky over the gardens, and another answered. Beyond the walls, beyond the temple, the low, constant sound of the city rose and fell as Palanthas woke to another day of rumor and fear and burning heat.

"Valin, you . . ." Lagan stopped. He cleared his throat. "It's not that I failed Nisse, is it? That's not why you don't want to take me along. Is it?"

Valin closed his eyes, ashamed. He'd lied to Crysania this morning when he told her he'd undertake her mission to Kalaman. He had to lie, for it was important to his plan that she believed him gone. He'd stood so close to her, lying, that he couldn't imagine she'd detected his breathing, a little edgy, a little ragged, and not known him for a fraud. Still, she hadn't, and she'd accepted his word and thanked him with all her heart. It had been hard to lie to her, and now it was no easier to lie to Lagan.

"Listen," he said, making the word heavy with importance, as Lagan himself might. "Lagan, I don't think you failed Nisse. I could never think that. I know you did all you could do for her, and I know your prayers are good ones, my friend. If Paladine had been near to hear them, he'd have granted you the strength you needed to heal Nisse's wounds."

"Ach! If this, if that!" Lagan shoved a small pouch into his pack, then took it out again, hefting it in one hand, then the other, as though weighing it. It was a lovely thing of purple velvet, embroidered in silver dwarf runes. In the pouch he kept the few small talismans of his calling, a flake of sliver he swore was a paring from one of the scales of the silver dragon that was one of Paladine's avatars, and a little book of prayers he had himself transcribed from ancient texts.

Valin took Lagan's pack from the bed and sat down. "You can stitch the world with 'ifs,' my mother says, and still what is, remains what is. In this case, Lagan, 'what is' isn't pretty. It is an ugly picture of a war storm brewing and a silence of gods. We must all do what we can, and I don't think anyone will do more than the Revered Daughter of Paladine."

Lagan nodded, still tossing his rune-marked pouch from one hand to the other. "She's going, isn't she? She's going to take that journey to Neraka."

Valin nodded. "And I won't be able to be with her. But I hope — Lagan, I hope you will be. I've asked her only this morning to take you when she goes."

The dwarf asked softly, "Will she?"

All his heart was in his eyes, his sorrow over a death he once would have been able to prevent, his fear that his god—no matter what anyone said to the contrary!—had found him unworthy, that now Crysania must feel the same.

111

Valin forced himself to laugh and, laughing, he cuffed his friend on the shoulder. "Yes! Of course she will. She said she'd intended to anyway."

That was truth, and so much easier to speak than the lies he'd been telling since he returned from the Tower of High Sorcery.

Lagan drew a long breath and let it out slowly. "All right, then. But I wish you weren't going to Kalaman. I wish you were going on Crysania's quest." He kicked the pack on the floor and sent it skittering across the room. "Ach! I wish no one was going anywhere!"

"Well, I suppose we can stitch the world with wishes, too, and not much would change."

For a long moment, silence stood between them, and then Lagan said, "Maybe she'll change her mind about you, desert mage."

The color rose to Valin's cheeks, but he said nothing.

"It's been known to happen," Lagan said, "that a woman reconsiders things when enough time has passed."

Valin snorted. "Does everyone know how I feel about Crysania?"

"Not everyone. Just me, and that's because I know you. Has she given you any hope?"

"None."

Hand to hand, Lagan tossed the pouch, the silver runes twinkling in the early morning sunlight falling through the window. "That doesn't mean you haven't taken any, though, does it?"

Valin got up from the bed and picked up his own pack. Lagan's questions cut too close to a truth he dared not reveal. "I take hope where I can, my friend. You learn to do that early when you live in the desert. I hope there will be water. I hope there will be grass for the horses. I hope the woman I love will love me."

Lagan laughed, a low warm sound, and took Valin's pack from his hands. "I hope she will, too, my friend. But now it's time to get you on your way."

Valin followed Lagan out of the small room into the hallway. The temple was quiet and dark, filled with only the small sounds of clerics waking to their day. He'd not chosen the hour of his leaving. Crysania herself had, deeming it important that his journey remain a secret for as long as possible.

"Lagan," he said when they came to the gates opening out to the city, "there is one thing I need you to do for me."

"Name it."

"I have sent for my brother, and he will arrive here soon. I've asked him to be part of Crysania's quest, to guard her as I would have done. He will come here looking for me, but someone must tell him what has happened to send me away, and someone must present him to the lady. Will you do that?"

Lagan put Valin's pack into his hands. "I'll do it, and don't you worry about it."

"And Crysania . . ."

The dwarf nodded. "I'll look after her, too. Now go— go, and Paladine's blessing be on you, friend mage."

And so he'd done all he could do in the service of doing . . . perhaps what he should not be doing. Valin pushed the doubt aside, bade his friend farewell and good luck, and went out to take the road he had chosen . . . for good or for ill.

Chapter Eight

In the small hours after sunrise, Valin walked the streets of Palanthas, drinking in the sights and sounds of the city. He was to present himself at The Three Moons at the fourth hour of the morning to Mistress Jenna, who would convey him to the tower. Until that time, he must occupy himself and keep out of sight of those who might know him and speak of having seen him when all at the temple believed him well out of Palanthas and on his way to Kalaman. To that end, he broke his fast with bread and cheese purchased from a vendor in the Old City market and took it to a quiet quarter of the city where once fountains had sent plumes of water leaping into the air. Nothing moved in those fountains now; water could not be spared. There he'd sat, on the wide edge of a silent fountain, eating his meal.

A last meal as a human, he thought. Then hastily he amended the thought. A last meal for *now* as a human.

The assertion rang hollow, even as he made it. He had no warranty that Crysania would ever speak to him the words necessary to end Dalamar's spell. He had, in fact, every warranty that she wouldn't.

"Valin," she had said, "I would not hurt you for all the riches of the world. You are so very dear to me. But I will not give you false hope. . . ."

Or any hope at all.

What hope was to be had, he must find for himself. And that's what he would do today. He would submit himself to the magic of Dalamar the Dark and hope that one day Crysania would know him and love him and set him free to walk the world in human shape again. Until then—he tossed the remains of his meal, crust and rind, into the gutter—until then one more tiger would walk abroad on Krynn.

* * * * *

Jenna stood quietly beside the window, her back to the opening, to Shoikan Grove. The pallor Valin had lately seen on her cheeks had vanished. He did not imagine she was done grieving for her father, but she had come to terms with the cold, bitter fact of it. That much Valin could tell by observing her lips firmly pressed together, her eyes dry of tears.

"Sit, mage," she said to Valin as he prowled the room. "Dalamar isn't fond of people roaming, even in so confined a space."

Valin sat, but as quickly rose to his feet again. Where was Dalamar? He'd been waiting in the dark elf's chamber for nearly an hour listening to the water clock, trying not to listen to the moans winding up from Shoikan

Grove. Each moment's passing wore on his nerves, scraping by with leaden feet, and fear sat coiled like a snake in his belly.

Smiling without humor, Jenna said, "He'll be here soon."

Valin shot her a startled glance. "It's as if you read my mind, mistress."

She inclined her head, a small bow. "It's just like that. Now, sit."

He sat, and this time he did not rise until he heard the soft sound of a footfall outside the door and Dalamar came into the room.

The dark elf had nothing to say for a long moment, only stood eyeing Valin, reckoning something about him. The sum of his reckoning he kept to himself.

"You are ready, then," he said finally, his voice silky and the more menacing for its quietness.

Valin swallowed once, refusing to let fear make his hands clench into fists. "This is my only choice, my lord. It is the right choice."

Dalamar shrugged as though it little mattered to him whether Valin thought his choice rightly made or ill conceived. "You understand, I cannot reverse the spell?"

His mouth dry as dust, Valin said, "I understand."

Smiling as though he were certain Valin understood exactly nothing, Dalamar took the desert mage's arm and turned him toward the door. "Come with me, then. We will begin."

Valin looked once over his shoulder to see if Jenna would follow. She would not, for she no longer stood near the window. She stood nowhere in the room, and only a small whiff of dried rose petals and pungent spice remained, hanging on the air like a whisper barely heard.

* * * * *

Dalamar opened a door and showed Valin into a small featureless room, empty as an execution chamber, damp as a room this far down in the tower must be. No wall hanging softened the four stone walls; the floor bore not even the meanest scrap of rug. No light illuminated the place other than that straggling in from the open door until Dalamar spoke a word of magic. In a breath, light sprang up in the far corner, pale and giving off no warmth.

"It should be comfortable for you here." Dalamar eased the door closed but did not latch it. "I will take care of your things."

"I have nothing," Valin said.

He'd left his pack at The Three Moons for Jenna to dispose of, telling her to give his clothing to beggars, thinking it best that someone have the use of clothing he would not need. She had laughed, as at a child, and reminded him that it would do him no good if people from the temple saw a beggar on the street dressed in too-familiar clothing. And so he'd told her to do what she willed with his pack and kept back only the gold bracelet given him by his parents when he passed his mage's test in Wayreth.

That bracelet, glinting in the heatless light, hung on his wrist now. "The only thing I have is this."

Dalamar's smile was much like the one Jenna had given him, and after a moment, Valin realized what the dark elf meant. With a shrug, he stripped off his clothes, folded them neatly, and set his bracelet on top of the pile. The amethyst, set like an eye in the gold, winked at him.

Dalamar touched the bracelet. "I will use this to make you a pendant," he said. "An anchor to connect you to your old life."

Valin barely heard him. The air in the room brushed cold against his skin, raising shiver bumps. He closed his eyes, willing away fear as Dalamar took the pile of his clothes and stepped outside the door to set them on the landing. When the dark elf returned, he shut the door tight.

Mage light glowed in the corner of the room, casting long shadows across the dark elf's face, weaving a mask to hide his every expression. His voice low, he said, "You will be more comfortable if you kneel or sit."

Valin knelt.

"Don't panic if you become disoriented. I will keep watch over you."

Valin drew a long breath into his lungs and let it out slowly. His spine straight, his head high, he steeled himself.

Unimpressed, Dalamar merely smiled. He spoke a word softly, and the mage light dwindled almost to nothing. He withdrew something from the deep pocket of his robe and held it carefully in one hand while he took something else from the other pocket. The scents of bitterroot and ashes, of pearl moss and celodyne, twined in the air as the dark elf brought his palms together, rubbing gently. He dipped into his pockets again, once more bringing his hands together, adding artemisia and wolfsbane to the mixture.

Valin's head began to throb dully. His eyes ached, his stomach turned, as Dalamar held up his cupped hands and blew into them gently.

Like a man who stood too close to a lightning strike, Valin felt the hair on the back of his neck rise up, the skin of his whole body prickle and tingle. Dalamar began to speak.

Wordless words, sounds without shape, weaving together and writhing, these were the words of power, the words of magic, and they resounded in the little room, rolling like thunder down the sky.

Shivering, shuddering, Valin groaned aloud at the first touch of magic. It stripped him of his calm, planted seeds of fear in him that swiftly grew into terror to tear at his heart, his soul. He gasped, rocking back on his heels. He reached deep inside himself, scrabbling around like a man hunting for treasure in a deep well, desperate to find a talisman, a word, a name, an image to hold on to.

Crysania!

Had he shouted her name aloud?

Crysania!

And he saw her eyes before him, soft gray as a dove's wing, sweet and wise and trusting.

"This is right," he managed to say. "Right." He repeated that word over and over again, a mantra to keep him anchored as Dalamar's voice swirled around him, rising and gathering like the wind.

The room spun madly, whirling and raging.

Sparks from the dim light floated down onto him, spreading across his flesh, taking away his voice in the very moment he knew he must scream or die. They wrenched from him his humanity, and he screamed voicelessly to feel it go, leaving behind only the pain of the ripping as all his bones broke apart and reformed. He heard his spine crack, like glass crushed.

He opened his mouth again to scream, but no sound came out.

The room whirled faster and faster. Gray chasing gray chasing gray. Gray haze and red agony. Tendrils of fire spread into his limbs.

Valin tried desperately to breathe. He tried to cry out, and now he had his voice, full and roaring: Crysania!

The room spun faster until finally—an hour, a day, an age later—his screaming became silence.

* * * * *

119

Hunger sat on the white tiger like a storm crow on a corpse, clawing, cawing, raking at his belly and blocking out all sense of anything else. He rumbled deep in his throat, an angry sound, an uneasy sound, a sound of warning.

He pushed up from cool stone, his powerful muscles bunching. Beneath him lay a blanket, rough, wadded. It stank of human scent and elf scent and all the odors of the fibers and dyes that went into the making of it.

He smelled water, and his growl became a questing sound, a low roar. Four walls confined him; a ceiling hung above, a floor lay below.

He lifted his head, breathing in the scents. An elf had been here, a male. The room stank of him. Woman scent hung on the air, human.

He smelled blood!

His belly clenched, his hunger renewed.

The tiger shook his head. His mind wasn't working right. His thoughts came disjointed, one pushing out the other, rushing at him with each new stimulus.

Marble smell . . . harmless.

Elf smell . . . dangerous.

Carefully he prowled the room, head low, ears cocked. He found the water. It lay nearby in a bowl of painted clay. Red clay, fire, onion skin dye. His own scent clung to the bowl and swift came the image of him drinking from it.

The tiger staggered. Vertigo rocked him, wrenching an enraged howl as images collided. A tall, brown-maned human stood upon two legs, the clay bowl in his hand. A white, gray-striped tiger stood upon four, lapping at the water where the bowl sat upon the floor. Each, man and beast, occupied the same place in space and time.

The tiger reached for his senses, those powers which, for man or beast, are anchors to time and place.

Blood smell. His stomach settled, the vertigo eased. Blood. Somewhere was fresh kill! He was hungry.

He swung his head, and his shoulders moved smoothly, powerfully. The blood smell came closer, carried on the scrape of footsteps and the creak of the door opening. The scents of elf and human, one male, the other female, roiled on the air. Light poured in from the open door.

The tiger growled, feeling a threat, scenting danger.

Blood smell, meat smell!

Again he growled in anger and warning, for these two were dangerous, these two were enemies. And yet they were not. Confused, the tiger tried to sort among his senses and reactions, tried to think.

Enemies, yet not enemies. Bargains struck, deals made. For Crysania, for himself.

He heard a step upon the floor, and the woman came into the room holding a bowl. She avoided the tiger's eyes, as any sensible person would, for only those with a death wish gazed into the eye of the tiger. With great care and exaggerated motion, she tilted the bowl toward him so he could see its contents.

Sense-reft human! Did she think he couldn't smell the meat there?

The tiger took a pace forward, then halted. He growled again and shifted. The muscles in his legs bunched again, coiling to spring as the elf came into the room and put himself between the woman and the tiger. He said something, the elf, and the tiger knew he chided the woman for having come in first.

The smell of raw meat hung in the air, distracting, tantalizing. The white tiger coiled to spring. Food! He vaulted forward. The elf stood his ground, no fear stink on him as he stepped to one side.

"Valin!" the dark one said sharply. "Valin!"

121

He dropped to one knee, bringing his face close to the tiger's. His breath smelled of dead things, of salt and food ruined by fire. Greatly daring, the elf put his hand on the tiger's head, smoothing his fur. The tiger smelled soft flesh—succulent flesh—and soap and fibers dyed the color of night.

"Do you know where you are, Valin?"

Valin.

Images collided again, man and beast each existing in the exact moment, the exact place. The tiger, the man— their images shimmered in the beast's mind, merging. Meaning tumbled through Valin's brain, attaching itself to the sounds the elf made. Like the bright shards of color and light in a child's kaleidoscope, images formed around the sounds, making patterns, making language. The tiger recognized the sounds coming from the elf as words. One was his own name.

"Yes," the elf said, satisfaction, even triumph in his voice. "Now you know what's happening, don't you? Valin—you are Valin."

It was so, the tiger knew. Valin knew, and he remembered every moment of his transformation, each scream of pain, each cry that became his lady's name: Crysania!

"Do you know where you are, Valin? It's been three days. Do you remember the spell?"

Valin shook himself. He looked around the room at the bare gray walls.

Dalamar, he soundlessly said.

The elf didn't move, didn't seem to know his own name. No, that couldn't be right.

More strongly, and yet still silently, the tiger said, *Dalamar!*

"Yes!" The elf nodded, scratching the tiger's ear.

Valin pulled back from that intimacy, growling. Dalamar didn't try it again.

The elf only laughed and turned to the woman still standing behind him. "He knows his name, and he knows mine. He thought them both, and I heard them in my mind."

Dalamar slid closer. "Valin, do you know where you are?"

Valin shook himself again, impulses conflicting in him. He could answer, or he could eat. His silent voice a dangerous growl, he said, *Hungry.*

Dalamar laughed softly. "I suppose you are." He reached back and took the bowl from the woman.

Jenna!

"Yes," the dark elf said. "Jenna is here."

The tower.

"That's right." Dalamar set the bowl on the floor. The smell of rich, red meat filled Valin's nostrils, setting his mouth to watering. He fell upon the meat, devouring it swiftly, all the while looking round himself to see that no other predator dared to come near.

None did. Dalamar and Jenna kept their places, watching in silence.

The food consumed, the tiger's appetite sated, Dalamar reached into a pocket of his dark robe and what he brought out, he held up for Valin to see: a leather collar, marked in runes. Dangling from it was a pendant made from the remnants of his former life, a small dragoncast in gold, its eyes the amethyst cut in two. Not until the tiger had scented it and tasted it with his tongue did he permit the collar to be fastened round his neck.

Annoying thing. It rubs my fur.

"You'll get used to it," Dalamar said. "Easy as wearing clothing. Now, are you ready to be reunited with your lady?"

Valin answered him in his mind with an obscenity, and the dark elf threw back his head and laughed. He clipped a short leather leash to the collar and murmured soft words of magic.

Wind whirled, the world spun in light and color, fragmenting, then reuniting as Dalamar's transport spell set them down in the city a short distance from the temple.

An overwhelming riot of scent screamed in Valin's brain—dwarf and human, elf and gully dwarf. Rats and—minotaur! Garbage rotting in the sun, food in the market stalls, cattle, the sea. Fish!

"Easy," Dalamar said, his voice low, his touch calming. "It will never do to run rampant in the city, friend mage."

Valin held on to his self-control and bade his senses be still. To his surprise and great relief, that wasn't hard to do, and soon he was able to walk calmly among people, who, stinking of fear, stopped to stare at them, a tiger padding alongside a black-robed mage.

Dalamar laughed and leaned down to whisper, "By tonight, there will be no one left in the city who has not heard of you. Now come down this road and around this corner. It's only a little way."

You need not waste time on directions, Valin said coldly. *I know where I am.*

In moments the wall that surrounded the temple grounds came within sight. The wide gate swung open to admit them, and the great columns of the temple loomed overhead. As they mounted the steps, Dalamar released the snap on the leash and pocketed the length of leather.

Valin paused just inside the wide doors, as he had in the past, to wait for his eyes to adjust to the gloom. But he didn't have to wait. Surprised, he looked around. He could see well into the depths of the hall. The change in his vision was as powerful as that in his sense of smell. Delight and fear both raced through him.

What man could know or even guess how it felt to

move with muscles that worked with power and grace? None! Who but he knew how the world truly smelled, what the world looked like through a tiger's eyes? None!

And who, he thought slyly, casting his thought into wordless emotion, who could know what it was like to make the Master of the Tower of High Sorcery step back a respectful pace when he lifted his head to growl?

A cleric approached them, surprised to see Dalamar the Dark in the temple. "Lord Dalamar! How may I assist you?"

He spoke to the dark elf, but his eyes were fixed warily on the tiger.

"I've come to see the Revered Daughter."

"She's with her advisors, lord." The young man hesitated, giving ground before the mage's long strides. Clearly the Revered Daughter was not to be disturbed. Just as clearly, a tiger was not a normal visitor. Nor was Dalamar.

Dalamar paused before the high, wide oaken doors of the great hall. "I have brought a gift for her. Please tell her I'm here."

The cleric obeyed reluctantly and returned not with Crysania, but with Lagan Innis. The dwarf stood on the threshold, eyeing the tiger, eyeing the dark elf. Valin grinned, a wide, terrifying pulling back of lips from fangs. Lagan stepped quickly back.

"My lord," he said, his darting glance going quickly from the mage to the beast. "The Revered Daughter asked me to conduct you and your, uh, gift to her study. She will join you there shortly."

Dalamar gestured acknowledgment, but Valin stepped forward before the mage could move. He brushed up against his friend, nearly knocking him off his feet. Laughing, not caring if Dalamar heard that, he put his head squarely under the dwarf's hand.

Lagan, too proud and stubborn to show fear, held his ground, looking desperately up at Dalamar for direction.

The dark elf made a sound of exasperation and jerked his head at the tiger. "I believe he wants you to pet him. But take care," he warned abruptly. "He doesn't like it when you scratch his ears."

Lagan, in the act of doing that very thing, froze. Valin, still chuckling mentally, tried something new with a voice that till now had only growled and roared. Pleased, he discovered that he could indeed purr.

"This way, my lord," Lagan said, scratching the tiger's soft round ears gently as he conducted the mage and his strange gift through the marble halls.

Valin noted that his friend was very careful not to smile when the dark elf could see him.

Chapter Nine

Paper rustled, whispering. Hot wind stirred at the window, rousing the odors of oak bookshelves and rows upon rows of texts, old parchment, and new ink.

What gift, Crysania wondered, has Dalamar brought here? Were the Dragon Stones not enough?

Out of some far distant tale from childhood came a muttered warning: *Beware the gifts of mages, for nothing is offered unless something is taken.*

She put her hand to her pocket, touching the Dragon Stones she was never without. Her fingers touched gingerly, the very skin and bone of her remembering how those stones had burned and stung the last time she laid her hand on them. They sat calmer now, warmer, more peaceful.

Paladine . . .

The god said nothing.

The hot breath of summer touched Crysania's neck, making her hair tickle at her cheek. She raised a hand to brush back the hair, then settled against deep cushions in the window embrasure. One cleric and another murmured, discussing plans for the running of the temple in Crysania's absence. Their papers and maps covered the large round table near the window, artifacts of their work as they planned what they would do if the army of Ariakan turned toward Palanthas. They discussed where the clerics would be most needed, how many to keep in the city, how many to send out onto the plains, how many to Sir Thomas at the High Clerist's Tower. It might be that the God of Goodness and Light kept silent before the prayers of his faithful, unable to lend his strength to their healing efforts, but each cleric of the temple had good, strong knowledge of the healing craft involving herbs and potions.

The voices of the clerics rose and fell, washing over Crysania like the sound of a distant sea.

And I am almost gone from here, she thought. They talk and they plan and they will do fine, but my mind is already on the road.

Away first to the High Clerist's Tower to speak with Sir Thomas, to let him know she was leaving the temple and Palanthas itself, though perhaps not why. How could she tell him that she would go out from the Temple of Paladine in hope of finding her god, in fear of finding the Dark Queen herself?

I am going on quest, my lord, to see what I can see.

Crysania smiled, privately and without humor. She might just as well say that as anything. No matter what she said, Sir Thomas of Thalgaard, that good and loyal knight, deserved to know that the Revered Daughter of Paladine was leaving her temple. For a while.

Clerics murmured, the wind sighed, and papers whispered from one hand to another. Someone said to her neighbor, "I wonder where Valin is now. I wonder what news he'll bring from Kalaman."

I wonder, Crysania thought, how he fares.

Unbidden, memory of the mage, of his declaration of love, tugged at her heart. For her, he would do anything. She knew it. He would go to Kalaman in search of news, he would spy upon dragonarmies if need be. He would race the war storm and come back to Palanthas with news so badly needed. And she would be gone when he came back, away upon her journey.

What was that, sadness whispering in her heart?

Not at all, she told herself, unless it was sadness for all the world poised on the precipice of war.

The heavy wooden door of the hall creaked on its brass hinges. Into the quiet came firm footfalls, those of Lagan Innis. The dwarf stood a moment at Crysania's elbow, waiting for her attention. She turned from her thoughts, lifting a finger to her lips.

Softly, trying not to disturb the discussion around him, Lagan said, "Lady, Lord Dalamar and his . . . gift are in your study."

"Thank you, Lagan. I will come."

She rose, and the dwarf fell into step beside her, ready to assist should she need him, silent as night should she want to walk only with her thoughts.

* * * * *

Upon the threshold of her study, Crysania stopped to gain a sense of those who waited within. She placed Dalamar at once by the darkly mysterious scent of the spell components that clung ever around him, by the brush of his robes on the marble floor. Mingled with his scent was

129

another, stranger one, the musk of animal, the heaviness of warmth and sun.

Something moved, something not as tall as she and yet much larger.

"Good day, Lord Dalamar. And good day to whoever is with you."

Dalamar came to her, his companion keeping pace beside him with heavy footsteps. "My lady, I have come to you with a gift."

"A gift, not a guest? Well, your gifts abound. You are too good to me, my lord."

Robes whispered, and the scent of the air changed as the dark elf came closer. "Not at all, lady. I have promised you a guide to go with you on your journey, and I have come to keep that promise."

Footfalls padded behind the mage, came beside him. And with them, a new, powerful, bestial scent.

At Crysania's side, Lagan kept still, but she felt his wariness. For the gift or the giver?

"Lagan," she said, and the dwarf put his hand on her arm, gently guiding her forward until she stood before Dalamar and his gift . . . her guide.

"It is a tiger, lady," Lagan said, taking her hand and, with her assenting nod, placing it upon a broad head.

Soft fur, warm fur, animal musk, breath as hot as the wind outside in the streets. The tiger stood beneath her hand. She heard his tail swishing in the air, back and forth, a slow swinging motion. Crysania's other hand came up, reaching for the animal, finding its soft round ears.

"He won't harm you," Lagan said. "Be easy. He's a handsome beast, white—a desert tiger—and he has the faintest gray stripes in the same pattern as his golden jungle kin. His eyes are like emeralds." Dropping his voice low, he said, "He likes to have his ears scratched."

Crysania smiled and stroked the tiger's ears with the

gentle, rhythmic touch that delighted cats of all kinds.
The tiger could not help but acquiesce, Dalamar saw. Her
goodwill established and accepted, Crysania moved her
hand to the tiger's broad head, his shoulders, and his
back. He smelled clean and wholesome, as all beasts do
who are not sick or injured.

"Dalamar, this is a handsome beast. I can feel his
strength and health. But I don't know why you would
bring such a creature to me."

Robes rustling, the mage came closer. In his voice, she
heard a sardonic smile as he said, "But you do know, my
lady. I promised you a guide for your journey. This animal
is it. He will take you where you need to go."

The tiger rumbled suddenly, moving restlessly.
Sudden, instinctive fear clutched at Crysania's belly. By
force of will, she kept still. She put her hand on the tiger's
head, stroking. It quieted instantly. Beneath her hand lay
a broad, soft leather collar, and Lagan came closer to turn
the collar beneath her fingers so that she felt a pendant.

"It's the image of a tiger," Lagan said, "cast in gold,
with two chips of amethysts for eyes. Not dwarf craft," he
said, and she could imagine his eyes narrowing critically.
"But good enough."

Crysania turned the pendant in her fingers, feeling the
smooth metal, the cool stone, the delicate carving of a
miniature tiger. She smiled, genuinely amused.

"Dalamar, what am I to do with such a creature?" She
had a sudden image of the huge tiger among her clerics,
scattering them like so many fluttering birds. "It's a fierce
gift for one such as me."

The tiger leaned into her, bumping against her legs so
that she had to take a step back to hold her balance. Even
after she had steadied herself, it brushed up against her.
She could feel its heartbeat, its slightest movement, its
power and majesty.

"Do with it as you will, lady," Dalamar said coolly. "But remember why I bring it to you. This tiger can lead you to Neraka and the Dragon Stones. Without him, you will not find what you seek. This I know, though I can say no more. Of course, if you have already made the choice not to go . . ."

Crysania ruffled the tiger's ears. "My lord, you must not think I have chosen not to go simply because I haven't yet found the time to advise you of my decision."

She could feel him smiling. She had not seen his face in many years, but the image of it had never faded from her mind. And so she knew that Dalamar's smile was accompanied by an arched brow, a small sign of surprise at the peppered reply from one whose words were ever soft and sweet.

"Of course you will do as you wish, lady. And I will leave you to become acquainted with your guide."

He turned to go. She fell into step with him. The tiger padded close beside her.

"I should thank you for the gift, my lord. Tell me, what is the tiger's name?"

Dalamar took her hand to guide her toward the wide, sweeping staircase leading down to the first level of the temple.

"I haven't named him," he said, "That's up to you." He put her hand upon the smooth polished banister. "Perhaps you could call him . . . Valin."

Valin. The name fell like a sudden stone into a still pool of water.

"Where is that foolish white robe anyway?" Dalamar continued hurriedly, a small note of satisfaction in his voice for the quiver of emotion he sensed. "He's usually lurking nearby."

"Valin is attending to his duties this morning," Crysania said. "And I can't imagine why you think I would name the tiger after someone in my temple."

Dalamar chuckled, but Lagan said quickly, "It's not a bad idea, lady. You don't have to name him Valin, but perhaps you can call him Tandar. Lord Dalamar did say the tiger's from the desert. And that's Valin's family name. He told me once that the word means 'desert king.' I think the naming would amuse Valin. And I'm sure he would be honored."

So it might, Crysania thought. She imagined his voice filling with laughter when he learned the news. And then she remembered she would not be the one to tell him that she'd named a tiger after him. Nor would Lagan. They would be far away by the time Valin came back from his mission.

"Tandar," Dalamar said smoothly, as though he'd not noticed the lady's silence. " Not quite 'desert king,' master dwarf. A closer translation would be 'master of the sand.' "

The tiger rumbled in his throat, as if he recognized his new name.

"Tandar it is," said Crysania as she descended the last step. "Will you stay to take some refreshment with me, my lord?"

"Thank you," he said curtly, almost rudely. "I must go."

She yet had a hand on his arm, and so she could feel how he stood like a man tensing against pain. She knew how uncomfortable it was for him to be on temple grounds. She could easily imagine how much the dark mage must loathe coming into contact with the light. So had she felt each time she visited him in the Tower of High Sorcery.

"Then I won't detain you." She gestured to Lagan, a silent request that he leave her alone with the dark elf. When the dwarf stood at some remove, she said, "Dalamar, you haven't mentioned the conclave's battle with the Gray Wizards."

133

He permitted just the tiniest twitch of his muscles. She wouldn't have sensed it, and only felt it because she still touched his arm.

"There is little to say about that, lady. We gambled. We lost. We must regroup and try again."

"And you lost many who were loyal to you."

He snorted, a soft sound of bitter regret. "Don't try to heal my hurts, lady. Even you couldn't do that. What is done is done."

"And cannot be undone. I know it. But surely there is more to tell. What do you know of these wizards, these Gray Knights?"

He stopped just inside the great front doors. Crysania and the tiger waited.

Dalamar no longer paid any attention to the animal. It was as though the beast, now Crysania's, no longer existed for him.

"They are powerful sorcerers, lady, who obey no laws of magic save their own. A rogue order, and named rightly. They have somehow earned the favor of the Dark Queen. And we must find a way to stop them."

"We," she said, investing the word with no emotion, not even shaping it as a question.

"Very well. *I* must find a way. That is why I am helping you make the trip to Neraka for the rest of the Dragon Stones. I confess, when I first found the two, I thought to use them in the battle." He made a soft sound, the kind that accompanies an impatient wave of the hand. "I cannot use them as they are. Perhaps once they are rejoined, one of us can."

Yes, Crysania thought, but will you use them or will I, master mage?

"Of course," he said, as though guessing her thought, "It all depends upon which god answers your call, doesn't it? The Dark Queen, who seems to be so active in the world these days, or yours, who is so . . . silent."

The tiger, almost forgotten by her side, pushed against Crysania insistently, growling.

Dalamar bowed. "Now I must go, lady. I don't imagine you will send me word of your departure, but I do wish you a safe journey."

"I'll see you out, my lord," Lagan said, suddenly at Crysania's side. "I'll return in a moment, lady."

With quick footsteps, they were gone, leaving Crysania where she stood. She heard slowing footsteps about her in the hallway. Her clerics, as they went about their business, must certainly be startled to see this great white tiger pacing at her side. None approached her; all buzzed softly, whispering their wonder.

Crysania put her hand on the tiger, on Tandar. She felt his large head moving from side to side as he breathed in what must surely be strange scents. It struck her then that he found his way in the world much the same way as she, by scent and by hearing.

"Well, then," she said to the beast. "We are certainly a couple of well-matched companions, aren't we?"

Tandar rumbled, a powerful, strangely comforting presence. How quickly she'd become comfortable with him! She might do well to wonder whether she could trust this beast, this guide of Dalamar's choosing, but she did not. Against all wisdom, instinctively, she did trust the tiger.

Tandar's head came up. His tail twitched in warning.

Softly came the step of Telassa, an elven cleric, then her voice, steeled to courage as the tiger rumbled deep in its throat. Crysania touched the tiger, gently imposing a silence the beast instantly accepted.

"What is it, Telassa?"

"I've come to ask if you will return to the library or whether we should continue our work tomorrow."

Crysania said she would, indeed, return to her work, and quietly, she made a request.

"The tiger's name is Tandar. Please take him to the stables and ask Divad to find him a comfortable place— away from the horses!—with plenty of food and water."

Telassa swallowed audibly. To her credit, she overcame her fear and walked to the lady's side. She accepted charge of the tiger and went out with him, her step calm, her will steeled to show no fear.

* * * * *

Crysania dreamed.

Rain fell from the sky. Droplets formed into tears tasting not of salt but of honey. She turned her face up to the sky and sighed to feel the cool, wet rain soak her skin, plaster her robe to her body. The honeyed rain and enchanted tears mixed with salt tears, her own tears on her face.

"Paladine!"

With all her heart, from every corner of her soul, she cried out to her god, her face and her hands upturned to the sky.

No answer came, not a voice to shape words of comfort, not the embracing warmth of Paladine's love.

Out of the rain came terrible, unyielding heat. The drops of rain sizzled through the sky, hissed when they touched her body, evaporated as they hit the ground. The scent of rose petals filled her nostrils. The air, rippling and shimmering, gathered into a tall, hooded shape.

Paladine!

The dream wight came toward her, walking in darkness, in heat, in rain. It lifted its hands, cupped in offering.

"Paladine!"

It was he! She knew it. She felt it in bone and sinew, in

heart and soul. Paladine stood before her, but he was not as she remembered him. His eyes shone darkly, as holes in the fabric of the world, empty, aching, silent cries.

Horrified, she lifted her face, her hands, as though she would offer to the God of Goodness and Light the healing blessing she offered to anyone in pain.

Dark, almost empty, Paladine looked down upon her, then he turned his head away.

Walking, the god seemed to take the sky with him, the rain and the clouds, the very firmament. All the world stretched, featureless, around her, and then—with wrenching suddenness!—the black sky grew stars. Not a great field of them sweeping over the face of the world, only a few to form one constellation.

The five-headed dragon of Takhisis spread out across the sky, each head with a burning eye, each eye the color of the fabled Dragon Stones.

Crysania screamed, falling as if from a great height.

She woke before she hit the ground.

* * * * *

The air in Crysania's chamber clung, stifling. Her hand lay on soft fur. Half afraid of what she would find, she moved her fingers slightly and touched what felt like the cold, damp nose of an animal.

"Tandar," she sighed.

The tiger moved his head against her hand, blowing his hot breath across her body. His breath smelled of raw meat.

Crysania drew a ragged breath, hard to do with tears choking her.

Paladine! What had happened to him? Why had he stared so balefully at her? What pain was he in, what desperate trouble, that he'd come so darkly into her dreams?

She reached out to her bedside table and grasped her medallion, then turned her head on the pillow and closed her eyes.

"O Lord of Light and Grace," she whispered, "I have heard you calling me in my dreams. I will find you. I will never abandon you, as you have never abandoned me!"

And she would have prayed for him, for the strength he must so need, but how does one pray for a god?

Tandar stirred, pushing his nose against Crysania's arm to offer comfort in the way of dumb animals. She touched him, stroking his soft, rounded ears.

"I believe you know what I'm thinking, don't you?" she asked him softly. And it seemed she could hear the tiger's answer, like a whisper in her mind. Wordless comfort. After a moment, the tiger backed away. Tandar lay down on the floor, so near to her that she had only to drop her hand off the bed and her fingers would brush his broad back. She could feel the tiger's heartbeat drumming against his ribs.

He must have escaped Divad and come in through the open window.

The tiger breathed softly, snuffling against the floor. The sound was the last thing she heard as she fell asleep.

Chapter Ten

In Palanthas these days, the people never slept . . . or so said the people of Palanthas.

The heat of the night was the same as the heat of the day, thick and heavy and unending. Few could bear to stay indoors, and so the city streets were always full. Vendors hawked their wares at night. Merchants kept their shop doors open, receiving more customers in the hours of darkness than in hours filled with blazing sun. Carters with torch boys in front and back went down to the bay to unload whatever goods the ships brought and went right back up the hill to set up their booths.

In the high streets where the wealthy lived, grand homes perched on the hill, once set there for the view, now the envy of their less fortunate neighbors for the occasional breeze that came off the bay. Men and women and children revived the old custom of promenading, strolling up and down the streets. Only now they didn't stroll in hope of being admired by their fellows; they hoped for a breath of air, even the illusion that the city was cooler out-of-doors at night.

In the low streets, things were much worse. Fetid air hung over all. Footpads and thieves went about their business, preying on those who roamed the lanes and byways looking for someplace cooler than their stuffy little houses. Heat-weary citizens filled the parks, their tempers frayed, their hearts nearly drained of hope. Babies wailed and children snarled, and mothers and fathers spoke in low whispers of their burgeoning fears. All those fears were actually one: How will we survive? How will we feed our children if there is no harvest? What will happen to us, fed or starving, if the stories of dragonarmies preparing to descend upon the city are true?

All these things the Lord of Palanthas saw, all he heard. A prudent man, he doubled the watch and tripled the patrols. For all that, he fretted each day that the grumbling rising up from all quarters was the harbinger of riot, a fear-fueled rampage that would tear the city stone from stone. When he didn't worry about riot, he worried about fire, for the buildings of the city were not all of grand marble and glorious stone. Most were constructed of wood, and many were very old and dry. And there was the matter of impending war. Each day Lord Amothus conferred with Lady Crysania, the two of them sharing their news, the rumors that had come to them that day, their fears.

And each night, before he went to his bed, Lord Amothus stood upon his balcony and looked out upon his city, listening and hoping. Last, before his night was done, he turned to that quarter of the city where the

Temple of Paladine rose high above the ground. He offered up prayers to the god, the same words every night, words made heavier by the repetition, invested with his fear.

"Lord of Light, God of Goodness, I pray you look upon your city and the people who love you. I pray you grant them rain, I beg you grant them comfort. O Paladine! I beg that you stretch out your hand and keep the dragons of war from us!"

To that old prayer, he added another, one he trembled to make and yet must offer.

"Look kindly upon your Revered Daughter, my god, for she will soon set out upon a journey none of us would wish for her."

As his words fell into the darkness, he knew he didn't pray alone. In her temple garden, the Revered Daughter echoed, if not his words, his need.

Please the gods, all our prayers winding together will be sufficient to hold back the dark tide swelling.

* * * * *

"I am haunted tonight," said the Revered Daughter of Paladine as she walked in her midnight garden. "Tandar, I feel like every prayer ever lifted in this city is a ghost. I hear them crying, flying, seeking the god."

The white tiger kept step with Crysania, walking always on her left, always close enough to brush her robes and let her know he was there. Crysania smiled. In only a few days, Tandar, warm and strong and dependably ever present, had become so comfortably a part of her life that any who saw them must surely think she'd raised him from a cub. She, who used to enjoy her untouched moments, now enjoyed the solid, comfortable weight of the omnipresent tiger pressing gently against her.

141

In the hot, close hour of midnight, Tandar paced solidly beside her, his broad head swinging from side to side, attending each sound and scent of the garden. In these hot nights, the people liked to come here from the city in search of quiet and a place to escape the constant anxiety of their fellows. Some, it was true, sought only a shady place to sleep, but these, too, were welcome.

Tandar heard them all, the strollers talking quietly, the lone walkers, the sleepers. And he heard the slither of the snake at the edge of a nearly dry pool, the chirp of a cricket, a nightingale's liquid song dropping down from a branch. All these the tiger heard and judged.

"You are the best of companions, my friend." Crysania touched his shoulder, her hand resting on the soft white fur. "Perhaps the more so for your silence. We will journey well together."

To Neraka, she thought, unwilling to name the unholy city aloud in this garden of peace and solace. In the morning, she would travel to the High Clerist's Tower to speak with Sir Thomas. Darkly came images from her nightmare.

Paladine standing helpless in the driving rain. The god's face hidden and hooded. The sense of danger and pain she'd felt so strongly

Paladine!

She put her hand into the pocket of her robe and touched the Dragon Stones. Their warmth flooded through her, offering assurance and strength.

After she returned from the High Clerist's Tower, she would start out upon her journey. Lagan Innis would accompany her, and she would choose two other clerics from the temple. Her heart warmed to think of Lagan's acceptance of this quest. She'd told him little but that they must leave the temple and that her journey would be perilous.

"I'll tell you more when the time comes closer to leaving. And you should know before you accept this journey, my friend, that I don't know what end I will find. All I have is hope."

He'd remained very quiet. She knew he was considering all she said and wondering about all she did not say. At last he came and sat beside her. Greatly daring, he covered the Revered Daughter's hand with his own.

"Not all, lady," he'd said with typical dwarven simplicity. "You'll have me."

And by this he meant he would follow her to the end of the world itself if that's what Crysania required of him. She did not wonder that Lagan and Valin had become such good friends. They were much alike, the mage and the dwarf, each the possessor of a strong and loyal heart, the kind upon which gods could depend. If so gods, why not she? With this good company, she would set about the task of finding the remaining Dragon Stones and fitting all five together.

What god would she speak with—Paladine or Takhisis? Crysania could not know. She did know, though, in the very depths of her heart, that she must risk the one for the chance of finding the other.

The tiger twitched an ear, ready to go on, but Crysania halted. They had come to the quietest corner of the gardens. It was the darkest, most shaded place. She felt for the bench she knew would be there, old marble, once snowy white, now—so they said—bearing the inevitable marks of age, the stain of lichens, a chip at the edge, a blunting of the frieze carved on the back. Crysania sat, and her fingers found the frieze, a crude carving of the burial of a Solamnic Knight.

The knight himself lay stretched upon his bier. Beside the bier, twelve knights stood, their weapons raised in salute, an honor guard to mark the passing of a comrade fallen bravely in battle. Crysania had had the bench brought to the garden many years ago, in the days of the building. She'd heard one story and another about the depiction. The one she liked best said that this frieze was made to honor each Solamnic who died honorably in battle, and every one who would do so, down all the ages of time.

"All the ages of time, Tandar." She smoothed the skirts of her robe, felt a roughness in the embroidery at the pocket, and told herself she must remember to have it mended. "How many ages do you think there will be?"

The tiger settled at her feet, silent.

"No matter," she said, answering her own question. "However many there will be, they must surely have men as brave and honorable as these."

She settled in silence, her hand reaching automatically for the dragon medallion at her breast. She always reached tentatively now, wondering if the god would be there. Her fingers closed round the cool metal, and every tension eased from her, washing away like dust in rain.

Paladine!

He said nothing, but he was near, and that must be enough for now.

Crickets scraped in the grass. The nightingale flew up in a small whir of wings and alighted upon a low wall, singing again. Heat pressed all around, like Crysania's anxious thoughts.

This morning's conversation with the Lord of Palanthas had revealed more rumors and few truths. "And if rumors were fishes," he'd said, "we'd all eat well."

"Fishes, my lord?" She'd been prepared to smile at that jest. What he said next would not let her.

The head of the fishers' guild had been to see him, warning that catches, always generous, were becoming smaller. The water was too warm, killing the tiny sea creatures the fish thrived on. And so the fish fled the bay and went in great schools out to sea in search of food and more comfortable breeding grounds. The nets of the fishers came up not even half filled.

Amothus was as frustrated by this as by the dearth of news coming into Palanthas. The lack of people coming in from the heat of the plains, travelers to the city, packmen with their mules laden with wares, their heads full of news, was inexplicable. What did it mean? That the buildup of Ariakan's army was not so bad as they'd been led to believe, or that everyone had been killed?

Fear touched her, a cold finger on the back of the neck. She had sent Nisse to her death. Now she had sent Valin out there into the plains. How did he fare? Was he well?

"I had hoped," she said to Tandar, "that I would hear word from him by now."

The tiger snorted, shaking his head, then suddenly tensed.

Footsteps approached, the sound of two strollers going quietly. Tandar growled low in his throat and rose smoothly to his feet. Crysania touched him to silence.

"Peace," she whispered, sitting still herself. She saw no reason these midnight strollers shouldn't have the privacy they seemed to want.

The tiger fell quiet, but he did not stand at peace.

The two walkers spoke in low tones, their voices those of young men. They argued, the matter obviously of great concern to each. They separated. One went back the way they had come. The other hesitated. The steps of the latter changed, from boots against sandy cobblestones to the whisper of leather on grass as he advanced across the temple lawn.

Tandar rose and put himself between Crysania and the young man.

She felt the young man's eyes on her. She turned her face to where she thought he stood. On silent, padding

145

feet came the return of her melancholy feeling that she walked among ghosts this night.

The young man stopped. Footsteps sounded again as his companion came back to join him. The first moved again. A sword rattled. The sound was the first she'd heard of weaponry, and so Crysania knew he'd taken care to muffle the voice of his sword.

Her heart rose. Perhaps he was a knight with news of the battles on the plains. Or perhaps he came here to ask Paladine's blessing on this achingly long battle eve. If that were the case, she must not hide in shadows.

Crysania stood and turned toward the men. Tandar growled roughly, unhappy that she went so boldly to approach these strangers. All sounds of footsteps halted. One young man muttered a warning. Both froze.

Crysania stopped, too. That voice—she knew it, despite having never before heard it. She'd heard the voice of his father, though, and that of his uncle. Caramon Majere was the father. The uncle . . . ghosts, Crysania thought. The uncle was Raistlin Majere, dead in the Abyss.

It had been a long time since Crysania had spoken to those men, but their voices were not soon forgotten.

Tandar growled, and one young man said to the other, "It's a tiger. About ten paces behind you."

Crysania stepped forward, Tandar at her side. "Don't be alarmed, gentlemen. This is Tandar my guide. He won't hurt you."

One, smelling of roses and spices, was surely a mage. Palin, she thought, Caramon's son. With the voice and the scent, he could be no other person.

"A mage," she said, "and a knight. I presume you are not lost wanderers, then, but on some sort of mission. Have you come seeking Paladine's blessing?"

"L-Lady," said the mage, a charming stammer to mark his surprise as she stepped out into the moonlight. "My

Lady Crysania, how—how did you know us for a mage and a knight?"

"I see what I can, young mage, and the eyes aren't the only way to do that. I know you are a mage because I can smell your spell components. I guess your name, because to hear you speak is to hear the voices of your father and your uncle. That your companion is a knight became clear once I heard his sword rattle. And because I know your two brothers are knights." She turned toward that silent young man. "Are you Sturm, sir knight, or are you Tanin?"

Silence stretched long between the three. Tandar shifted beside her, nervous, tense, his powerful muscles flexing. The unnamed knight sighed, as one does who makes a difficult decision. He stepped forward, and Crysania had the sudden impression that two others were with him, though she heard no sound of footfalls on the path. Haunted!

The feeling passed as, in a rush of words, he said bluntly, "I am neither, Revered Daughter. I am Steel Brightblade, Knight of the Lily. I serve Her Dark Majesty."

Palin whispered something, a swift wordless sound of dismay. Tandar echoed the sound with a growl, voicing his displeasure. Crysania, caught between surprise and sudden apprehension, said, "A courageous act indeed, Steel Brightblade, for a Dark Knight to brave these temple grounds. Your Queen is no friend to my god." Then she added, "How have you come here, Palin Majere, in company with a Dark Knight?"

The young mage kept his silence for a long moment, then softly, he said, "Lady, my brothers are dead. There has been fierce fighting," His voice broke. "And they acquitted themselves well."

Involuntarily she whispered, "Paladine be with them!"

147

"I am Steel Brightblade's prisoner, taken in the battle near Kalaman and honorably bound to accompany him here to seek ransom."

"Not here in Palanthas, you aren't." A chill touched her, prickling on her arms. "You're going to the tower."

Tandar shifted under her hand, head up.

"You think me credulous, young man. Your captor will get no ransom from Lord Dalamar. You would do better to go to Wayreth."

"I am where I must be, lady," Palin said, gently but firmly. "It is a matter of honor, and I have sworn to say no more than that."

Nor would he be budged from that stance, this son of Caramon Majere. Crysania let the matter go.

"If your honor binds you, then I must not interfere. But know this, You will be walking the Shoikan Grove."

She shuddered, remembering her own long-ago journey through that horrible place. Her first thought was that he would never survive, but when she chased that fear away and stood calmer, more quiet in her heart, she felt the inner goodness of the young white robe, the light of Paladine's blessing shining on him.

She felt more ghosts, and a sense that Palin walked some path whose end no one might guess. It was nonetheless a destined path. Tandar moved restlessly against her. She stilled him with a touch, then reached up to close her hand round the medallion of Paladine. For too many weeks it had been so strangely quiet, the energy of this talisman, but only moments ago she had held it and felt the warmth and comfort of the god, far distant as he was.

Shine now for this mage, she prayed. Guide him, O Paladine, as you have guided me, for I feel that though the start of his journey is dark, it may yet end in light.

Her fingers agile and light, Crysania unfastened the clasp of the chain. She held out the necklace that had not been out of her possession for more than thirty years.

"Palin, take this, for you will need it if you go to brave the undead guardians of Shoikan Grove." For a fleeting moment, she wondered if she should simply send them to Jenna's shop, but thought better of it. Jenna was undoubtably tiring of the traffic through her store.

"Oh, lady," Palin said, his voice low and thick with emotion. "I cannot take such a gift from you. This journey I make—lady, you don't know—"

"I know this: There is no evil in you, Palin Majere. You are making this journey because you must." She pressed the medallion into his hand and closed his fingers over it.

The resistance went out of him. "Thank you."

She heard the rattle of the chain as he slipped the silver dragon over his neck.

Steel took advantage of their silence to step forward, urging Palin on.

Crysania had almost forgotten the other one until he spoke, until she felt his strange presence once again. He bowed to her, offered to see her safely back into the temple.

"You are kind, sir, but as you see, I have my guide beside me. But tell me, how will you enter the Shoikan Grove? Your queen does not rule there. Her son, Nuitari, does. "

"I have my sword, lady."

Such sweet, simple courage! She recalled what Tanis Half-Elven had told her of the Dark Knights years ago, that they were as brave and honorable as their Solamnic counterparts, but dedicated to evil.

Paladine help us if we must face an army of such men!

Crysania stepped forward and touched him graciously. The breastplate of his armor was hot from his body. Swirls and curves of engraving met her fingers. Swirls of fog pushed at her mind. He started, but did not move away. He was a big man, as tall as Valin. Again she felt that this one was attended by others besides Palin Majere. As Palin walked in the light of Paladine's blessing, this man walked under the conflicted guidance of two masters, one dark, one light. Darkness of heart, lightness of soul. She did not understand how he bore the strain.

"Two want to guide you, sir knight. One dark and one light. Which will you choose?"

He groaned a soft sound of torment not meant to be heard.

"My blessing goes with you both," she said.

They bowed to her, the mage and the knight, and each spoke in courtesy, wishing her godspeed along her own path as she had wished for them.

Almost she smiled, thinking that her path and theirs could be no more different. Theirs led to the Tower of High Sorcery.

Tomorrow she would take the first steps of her journey away from it.

"May all our steps travel so," she murmured to Tandar, faithful at her side. "May all our steps travel toward the light!"

Chapter Eleven

Crysania stood upon the second story balcony of the temple with the medallion of Paladine in her hands. She'd wakened to find it in her bedchamber this morning, the metal cool to her touch and, paradoxically, imparting the warmth of the god's presence. The warmth was not as strong as she was used to feeling, but still it was there, assuring her that Paladine yet walked in the world, yet watched over his children. She'd sat a long time with the medallion in her hands, praying. And when she'd done praying, still she wondered how it had come here, into her very bedchamber. Certainly the young mage hadn't returned it. No case could be made for that. And so it must be that the god himself had seen his talisman home to her once Palin had no more need of it.

"But how did he fare?" she whispered now to the

white tiger close at her side. "Is my medallion returned because Palin made his way safely through the grove?" She shuddered, turning sightless eyes toward the tower and the grove. "Or is it returned because he did not? " She sighed, "Paladine, be with him, wherever he fares."

Hot wind blew, carrying grit and dust and a faint scent of the sea. Oh, when would the weather break? In the city, they were talking about heat madness, about a citizenry whose nerves were frayed raw by heat and the dread of war. Amothus worried about riot, and he wondered whether the citizens would be able to resist the dragonarmy or simply fall before it. And Crysania prayed, day and night, for the strength Palanthas would need in the face of war.

Tandar put his head under her hand, a reminder of companionship, then returned to his watch. His large head moved from side to side as he observed the people in the courtyard below. Anyone seeing him, she thought, would be forgiven for thinking he knew what was happening, that he'd understood all she'd said to her clerics earlier, her explanation of the coming battle and the High Clerist's Tower need for help. From time to time, though, he left her side, pacing. He stopped—she heard it—at the south end of the balcony, looking away across the city to the plains beyond.

"What is it?" she had said to him the first time he'd done that.

He'd only switched his tail, slowly back and forth, the mark of a tiger's unease.

Now he turned his head. He didn't growl. His stance relaxed as the footfalls of Lagan Innis sounded heavily on the tiled floor. For all the years he'd been at the temple, Lagan still walked like a hill dwarf, planting his feet upon mosaic-tiled floors as though he yet roamed the rocky hills of his homeland. He stopped to scratch Tandar's ears, then growled, "Go on, you," when the beast leaned so hard against him that it nearly knocked him from his feet. It was a game with them, and already it seemed to Crysania that of all her clerics, Tandar liked Lagan best.

"My lady," Lagan said, his hand still on the tiger. "They're bringing the wagons around now. Telassa made sure most of the supplies were brought out and ready to load."

Crysania nodded. She heard the movement, the heavy thump of supplies being thrown into the wagon beds, the soft nicker of the horses, the rattle of wheels. Over all, she heard the excitement of her people, and she knew she had made the right decision to send clerics and supplies to Lord Amothus and more on to High Clerist's Tower. The waiting had grated on everyone's nerves. These tasks, though somber ones, released energy too long spent in anxiety.

"Lagan, is there any sign of Firegold yet?"

"None, lady, but the dragon will come." He said that easily, for her sake, but Crysania knew he'd be just as happy to be inside when Firegold arrived. Lagan might get on well with tigers, but he was known for being less than fond of dragons.

"And you should know," he said, hurrying past the talk of dragons, "that two people have come to see you. They seem to be from the desert lands. They say their errand is urgent."

"Please show them to me, Lagan."

She heard him go, then heard others come through the study and stop by the open door. Crysania turned her back to the garden, motioning her visitors forward. Tandar slipped out from under her hand, returning to his watch over the courtyard, showing tigerish disdain for the arrival of visitors whose comings and goings would be of no consequence to him.

Steps sounded as someone came forward. The weight of those steps told her this was a man—human, perhaps, for elves were usually lighter of foot. The second visitor kept still. Light breathing, a uniquely female scent—it was a woman keeping back in the shadows. The man knelt before her, and when she extended her hand, he took it gently in his and kissed it.

"Lady," he said, his voice low and carrying the faint tinge of hoarseness one sometimes hears in desert folk who spend much time shouting against winds as wild as any found on the sea. "Lady, I am Jeril ar Tandar."

The tiger rumbled deep in his chest.

"Valin's brother," Crysania said. "Your voice has the sound of his. Be welcome here in the Temple of Paladine."

He rose and thanked her, and when he stood silent, she lifted her hand to where she imagined his face might be. "May I?"

He lowered his face to accept her touch.

Her fingers told her he was much like Valin in appearance, with high cheekbones and eyes nearly as large as an elf's. His mouth was one stern line, and his hair hung in a long braid over his shoulder in a warrior's braid.

"My lady," he said when she had finished her inspection, "I have come at my brother's request." A steel blade sang out from a scabbard. "My sword is named Desert Light, and I lay it now at your feet. I am yours, Revered Daughter. I will serve as you choose."

Take me with you on your journey, would be more to the point, Crysania thought as she accepted his sword in her cause. Her next thought was to wonder when Valin had found time to summon his brother before leaving for Kalaman.

She neither accepted nor rejected Jeril's offer. She still had a question that needed answering. She looked toward the doorway where the silent visitor stood.

"Who is the lady with you?"

Jeril spoke a word in a language Crysania didn't know. Light footsteps touched the stone floor as his silent companion came forward.

"I am Kela, lady. I am a mage like Valin, and I have come with my husband from the desert to serve you."

"Your husband?" Crysania managed to keep surprise from her voice. Valin liked to talk about his family. He missed them in this foreign city. The Revered Daughter knew a good deal about his father, about his sisters and his brother, about his mother. She hadn't heard that Jeril was married.

"We are newly wed, Revered Daughter. How could I let my husband leave me so soon after the wedding feast?"

She said it with a smile in her voice, as one woman to another, and Crysania politely returned her smile. But Tandar rumbled again, and this time the tiger didn't sound pleased. Was he voicing his opinions of her guests, or was she only imagining his displeasure?

"We're readying for battle," Crysania told them. "As you can see. Some of the clerics are preparing to move to the High Clerist's Tower. I'm sure Valin has told you about . . . recent developments."

From the sound of his voice, Jeril might well have been smiling. "He told me, lady."

"Then you've seen him? Is he well?"

"I have seen him, but not lately."

"I don't understand."

Hot wind blew across the balcony. Out over the sea, a hungry gull cried. "My brother is a mage, lady. He sent word by a fetch that you would soon set out upon a journey."

A fetch! Crysania shivered to think Valin had sent his own ghost out to find his brother with this message.

"Lady, he told me you would send him upon a mission that would keep him from here for some time. He begged me to come to take his place in your company. He swore to his need on our mother's soul, on our father's heart. That is a strong oath, lady, the strongest we desert folk know. And so I have come, and I will follow you on your quest. I will protect you with my life."

All this he said as though he were a subaltern speaking to his commander. This tall warrior might look like Valin, but he hardly sounded like him. Had Valin inherited all the good cheer in the family?

Jeril crossed the balcony and stood looking down. "We have heard of the army massing on the plains. I assume this fact and Valin's journey are connected. Down there, in the courtyard—is this the expedition we will join?"

The tiger rumbled, pacing once more along the balcony.

"No," Crysania said, making her decision to accept this dour desert warrior and his wife. "We will form our own party. There will be but five of us." She dropped her voice low. "You will soon know where we are bound, but not until the time to leave is upon us. At that time you may decide whether you will go with me or stay here."

Jeril snorted. "I've sworn an oath to protect you on your journey, lady. It matters little to me where you go."

Crysania waited, and into the silence, Kela said, "I feel as my husband does."

"Do you know why I take this journey?"

Kela kept quiet, letting Jeril answer.

"Valin said nothing about that. It doesn't matter. My sword is yours, Revered Daughter. Whatever cause you take up, it can only be for good. I have said it,I will serve as you bid me."

"You are kind," she said, "and you are generous. I accept you, Jeril, and you, Kela. The first thing you must do is find food and drink, for surely you are hungry and tired from your journey. After you have rested, please find the cleric Seralas and tell her all you might have learned, rumor or truth, on your way from the desert. Anything will help, for we have no overabundance of information here."

Jeril started to say something, but he cut himself off in midword with a gasp of surprise.

"What is it?"

"Lady, a gold dragon comes!"

"Ah. That must be Firegold."

The dusty scent of leathery dragon skin filled the air, and the dragon's voice spoke quietly in her mind.

I am here.

In the courtyard, horses snorted and stamped. Voices raised up in greeting and awed delight as Firegold spiraled down from the hot blue sky to the temple grounds.

"Lagan," Crysania called, "are you there?"

"Always," he said, coming out from the study to ask for her orders.

"Continue loading the wagons. I want them on the road so that they can make it to the tower before nightfall."

"And you, lady?"

"I'll be back soon."

Firegold extended a broad, long wing out to the balcony. Crysania reached back and was surprised to find Jeril's strong arm ready to brace her as she sat on the railing as swung her legs over it. She clambered easily, if not gracefully, up the dragon's wing. Firegold wore a saddle wide enough for her to rest her feet upon the bottom.

Once she was comfortably settled, the dragon said, "Lady, you have a tiger nearby."

"I do," she said, "and I ask your indulgence to let him ride along. He is my guide."

Firegold considered the matter for a long moment, then agreed.

Tandar climbed out on the dragon's wing, careful not to dig in his claws as he stepped upon the dragon's great shoulder to take his place behind Crysania on the broad saddle. He leaned hard into her to keep his balance as Firegold pushed with her mighty wings and powerful legs and vaulted into the air.

Air, hot and dry, buffeted them until they were aloft, and the dragon curved toward the mountains. Now the wind streamed across Crysania's face, making her eyes form tears and her hair whip about her shoulders. The tiger leaned more tightly into her, and she reached out to reassure the beast, looping her arm about his powerful shoulders.

She held the tiger so until at last they slowed, descending to the Tower of the High Clerist, and the beast could set paws to ground again.

* * * * *

The Revered Daughter of Paladine, her white tiger at her side, followed the young knight through the winding corridors of the tower. Here the air was blessedly cool, for the walls were of thick stone. Not even the heat of this terrible summer could penetrate them. It was a balm, the coolness, like a tender hand upon a feverish forehead.

The knight led her past a ward room, past barracks from which flowed the sounds and smells of men preparing for battle. Whetstones sang on the edges of blades, and the scent of leather polish hung in the air. And there were many voices. Men young and old, warriors all, spoke of their readiness for battle, some of them with certainty that victory would be theirs.

"Well, it *must* be so," said a very young, very assured voice.

Oh, Crysania thought, had that boy's voice only lately broken? Had he only lately kissed his sweetheart farewell and gone laughing to his barracks to prepare for battle?

"Victory must be ours, you see, because we are Solamnics. Our god is Paladine, and he is all that is good and right. How can you lose when you are on the side of good and right?"

If anyone answered the boy, Crysania didn't hear it. Her knight led her past those rooms and into other corridors. Up the stairs they went, winding and high, and at last the knight halted. Sounds of dispute rang out from a corridor to their left. Among the angry voices, Crysania recognized one as that of Tanis Half-Elven. She recognized the snap of anger in his tone, and that didn't surprise her. Her old friend had no trouble expressing his feelings. What surprised her was to hear that anger rise in defense of the Lord of the Tower of High Sorcery.

"Lord Dalamar comes in good faith," Tanis was saying. "I swear it. I will answer for him with my life if need be."

Crysania put her hand on Tandar's shoulder, urging him forward, obliging the knight to follow.

"My lords," she said, "I will swear as my friend Tanis swears."

In the corridor, the knights dropped to their knees, swords rattling, armor clanking. A great welling of affection rose in her for these proud men who humbled themselves before Paladine's cleric. The words of the young knight so assured of victory returned to her, and she wondered how men such as these could be defeated.

"Please," she said, "gentlemen, rise." Crysania smiled and turned in the direction from which she'd heard Tanis's voice.

She turned her head slightly, picking out Dalamar by his scent and the shimmer of magic. With a touch, she asked Tandar to guide her to the dark mage. She heard the knights mutter in surprise to see the Revered Daughter guided by this great white tiger. Their muttering changed to silence as, his voice only slightly edged with sarcasm, Dalamar took her hand and bowed over it, saying, "I thank you for your affirmation, Revered Daughter." His lips brushed her hand lightly.

Crysania inclined her head in acknowledgment, then turned to the knights and asked that they escort her and her friends to Sir Thomas.

As Knights of Solamnia, the men served Paladine, and so they were obliged to obey her wishes, but she had never felt such a show of reluctance. Clearly they didn't want Dalamar anywhere near their beloved commander.

"Gentlemen," she said, giving the word the weight of command.

"My lady," the commander snapped, as he would to a superior's order.

He ordered his men into formation, then led the way for Tanis, Dalamar, and Crysania. Tandar angled to keep himself between her and Dalamar.

"How did you know I would be here, Revered Daughter?" Dalamar asked. "Are my movements being monitored by the temple?"

"Paladine watches over all of his children," she said, "as a shepherd watches over all his sheep. That includes black sheep."

She heard his swift intake of breath. She felt his annoyance, like the tingle of lightning on the skin. Smiling, she said, "No, sir wizard, I did not know you were here. It is only coincidence that sets our paths crossing today."

She felt his suspicion increase. She knew he wondered why she was here and not on her way to Neraka. Well, she thought, let him wonder. He has been trying to direct my path for too long now. He will know I am gone when I have left.

Yet even as she thought this, she felt a twinge of regret. Had none of them learned anything after all the years of war and strife? Tanis and his wife, Laurana, had been trying for years to unite all the races and end the suspicion between White- and Red- and Black-Robed mages, between mages and clerics and knights. Dreamers, they were called, and simple-hearted, and things much worse than that. Crysania sighed. It seemed the only time people could agree on an alliance was when they were forced into it by having to choose between joining together or dying separately.

Dalamar moved closer. "I take it, then, Revered Daughter, that your god still has nothing to say to you about what is transpiring in the world?"

She stopped. Tanis slowed his steps, listening. She knew that by the sound of his breathing. At her side, Tandar made a low rumbling sound in his throat, not quite a growl but certainly a warning.

Dalamar spoke more gently. "I do not ask out of some vindictive sense of triumph, Revered Daughter. My own god, Nuitari, has been strangely silent of late, as have all the gods of magic."

"What about . . ." She hesitated over the name, then chose the honorific instead. "What about your Dark Queen?"

He took a long moment before replying. Concocting a half-truth, she wondered, or wrestling with the need to admit what he doesn't like to admit? In the end, he said, "I don't know. All I know is that Nuitari's power wanes, and as a consequence, my own power has been affected. The same is true of Lunitari and Solinari. All mages report this phenomenon. It's almost as if the gods are preoccupied."

Crysania took a deep breath. "You are right, my lord.

When I heard these rumors, I took them to my god in prayer. He made himself . . . distant." She paused. "You see this talisman I wear around my neck?" She touched the dragon reverently, reaching for its warmth, barely finding it. "Whenever I prayed to Paladine in the past, I felt his love surround me. This medallion would begin to glow with a soft light. My soul would be quieted, my troubles and fears eased."

She stroked the medallion with one hand, feeling the comforting shoulder of the tiger with her other hand. She sensed Dalamar and Tanis waiting for her next words as they walked slowly along the hallway.

"Of late, the medallion has remained quiet. I know Paladine hears my prayers; I feel that he wants to comfort me. But I fear that he has no comfort to offer."

"Perhaps," Dalamar said, "we may find an answer to our questions soon." He hesitated, then continued, his voice so low that only she and Tanis could hear. "Palin Majere has entered the portal."

Tanis drew a sharp breath.

At her side, the tiger growled softly.

Crysania's heart sank as she remembered her midnight encounter in the temple gardens. "Is this true?" she whispered. "Or are you at gamesmanship again, my lord?"

Dalamar made a small sound of regret. "No games this time, my lady. What I say is so."

Such finality when she'd hoped for a riddle in reply!

"How did he get in, Dalamar? You sealed the laboratory. You posted guards."

"He was invited, my lady. I think you can guess by whom."

Tanis took her arm, not to guide but to assure her of his presence. "You let Palin go inside? You should have stopped him."

Dalamar's laughter rang sharply in the corridors. Ahead, the knights did not react though Crysania could not doubt they felt the chill of it, one and all.

"I did not have much choice in the matter, Half-Elven. All of us know firsthand of Raistlin's power. You better than some, eh?"

Tanis bristled, the dark elf chuckled, and Crysania said into the silence, "Raistlin Majere is dead."

She gently withdrew her arm from Tanis's hand. At her side, Tandar leaned against her legs. "You know it as well as I do, Dalamar. He was granted peace for his sacrifice in the Abyss. If Palin Majere has been lured into the Abyss, then it must be by some other force."

"You seem so certain, lady."

"I am," she said. "You forget, my lord—I was there."

He didn't accept that. She knew it, but he said no more. They went on in silence, the corridor ringing with the footsteps of their escort, until they came at last to Sir Thomas's chamber.

The commander threw open the doors to the chamber in which the Knights Council had been convened. Three knights from each of the orders, Rose, Sword, and Crown, sat at a table opposite the doors. Each rose to greet her and accept her blessing, and when Sir Thomas expressed his surprise at seeing her, she told him she'd come to learn what she might, and to let him know that he would soon be receiving a contingent of clerics from the temple, each skilled in the healing craft.

"They will come fully supplied, Sir Thomas, and I pray they will return home having had little to do."

It was a courtesy, a hope, a gentle gesture. It was accepted as such by all but Dalamar, who laughed softly.

"My lords," said the dark elf, his voice low and dangerous. "The Revered Daughter is good to hope, but you would be wise to hear what I have come to say. The

Knights of Takhisis will attack this fortification at dawn tomorrow morning."

Voices rose to challenge this bold assertion, the angry, stern voices of men who'd been seeking news about the enemy and had found little until one they considered a foeman walked into their keep and delivered it with a smile. At her side Tandar moved restlessly, his tail switching.

Her voice calm, her hands still upon the table, Crysania said, "Tomorrow, my lord? How can this be?"

"What is," he said coolly, "simply is, my lady. That's how it can be. There is more: Dark clerics entered the haunted ruins and summoned the shades of the dead to join the fight. They stopped in Dargaard Keep, and I have no doubt that you will find Lord Soth and his warriors among the attacking forces." There were a few snorts and chuckles of disbelief, and Dalamar continued. "Lord Ariakan is their leader. You trained him yourselves. You know his worth better than I do."

They knew, each one of them, and so they knew the forces allied against them were the most formidable any of them had ever faced. And yet . . . and yet theirs were the boldest hearts, the strongest, the most daring. They were Knights of Solamnia, terrible in battle and glorious in victory.

Sir Thomas leaned forward and said, "Your news is grim, my lord. The storm of war is upon us, and it may be that none have seen a darker time than will soon be here. Yet I say this to you: The Tower of the High Clerist has never fallen while men of faith defended it."

His fellow knights murmured agreement, heartening each other, but an aching chill sat upon Crysania's heart, like creeping ice. All the pieces of the picture fell suddenly into place. The rumors that once haunted her now became truths. With a flash of understanding, she knew what was about to happen.

"My lords," she said, wishing she could offer hope instead of what she must, "perhaps that is because men of faith have never attacked the tower."

Dalamar was quick to understand. "The Knights of Takhisis have been raised together since boyhood," he said. "They are unswervingly loyal to their queen, to their commanders, to each other. They will sacrifice anything, including their lives, to advance their cause. They live by a code of honor as strict and pure as yours, Sir Thomas. Indeed, Lord Ariakan patterned it after your own. "And so you see, my lords, that you have never been in greater danger."

Crysania lapsed back into silence as the discussion heated up over the strength of the advancing army. The knights were caught off guard. No reinforcements were expected; messengers had been sent to the eastern lands and returned with the hard news that the eastern lands were already under siege. The size and speed of Ariakan's army was cause for genuine alarm.

Sir Thomas remained undaunted by the discussion. He straightened. "We are prepared, my lords, my lady. The fewer the numbers, the greater the glory. Paladine and Kiri-Jolith are with us."

"Their blessings on you," Crysania answered, and the words she had spoken so often seemed freshly minted now, filled with all her good will and hope.

Yet that hope seemed forlorn. Sir Thomas and his gallant knights could not know what she and Dalamar knew. Not even Tanis seemed to understand.

Perhaps the gods upon whom they all depended had no aid to offer.

Chapter Twelve

Crysania knew something was wrong the moment she opened the door to her study. Something didn't feel right. The word "invader" leapt to her mind, raising the hair on the back of her arms.

Behind her, Lagan Innis uttered the kind of sound he'd likely not made in years, a low, angry growl. He took her arm and held her back.

"Lagan, what's wrong?"

"Wait, lady!" The dwarf got in front of her, keeping her from the room. "Someone has been in here. The chairs are all overturned, the pillows scattered."

She would risk tripping and falling if she ventured into that chamber, whose rigid order, now disturbed, was meant to allow her to walk easily and safely.

"Someone's gone through your desk, lady." He made

a sound of disgust. "The door to your bedchamber is open. Come away. Whoever did this might still be here."

Crysania shook her head. "I don't think so, Lagan. The room feels—how shall I describe it?—it feels wrong, but it also feels empty. Guide me, please. I want to go in."

Another unclerical sound escaped from Lagan, but the dwarf obeyed his lady. He guided her round the mess of pillows and toppled furniture to her desk. All the drawers were open; the few things she kept in them were spread out on the desktop.

"What are these?" she asked, touching sheet after sheet of paper.

"Maps—the ones you keep in the right-hand drawer at the top."

Thanking him, she neatly stacked the maps that her advisors sometimes used in meetings, then put them back into the drawer. The quick movements disguised the shaking of her hands.

"What else is here?" She ran her hands over the desktop again.

"Nothing more." Lagan came close. "What would anyone have been looking for in here? Who would do such a thing? The Revered Daughter's own study—her very bedchamber!"

If greater scandal were known, it seemed Lagan couldn't imagine it.

"What were they looking for, lady?"

She almost said she didn't know. She passed her fingers across the Dragon Stones in her pocket. But who knew about them? Dalamar, of course, and perhaps Jenna. Valin did, but he was days gone and far away with an enemy army between him and Palanthas. Tandar knew, but he . . . She would have thought, but he is a tiger. She amended that, realizing that he was sent to her by Dalamar.

Impossible! Even though he was Dalamar's gift to her, she could certainly trust her own instinct about the beast, the instinct that told her he was trustworthy. Or was that hope, not instinct?

Crysania purposefully discarded that thought. She must not mistrust her own instinct. Yet the fact remained that someone had wanted something from her chambers badly enough to defile the temple for it. The idea sickened her.

"Lagan, will you do me a kindness? Please find Jeril and Kela and bring them here to join me."

"And leave you alone, lady? No, I—"

Softly, behind him, came the loud breathing of a tiger. Tandar stood in the room, growling.

"I won't be alone," Crysania said, smiling. "Please, will you do as I ask?"

Of course he would, and he did so in good time. Crysania had no sooner found the chair to her desk than she heard voices and footsteps coming down the hall to her study.

"It's time now," she said to Tandar, speaking as though the beast could understand her. The last cold tendril of her doubt left her as the tiger came to her. He stood close as the others entered the room, his head under her hand as they ranged themselves before the doorway, one to either side.

"My friends," she said, "it's time to talk about our journey."

She slipped the Dragon Stones from her pocket and lay them upon the naked desktop.

"Lagan, come take up these stones."

He came close and held out his hand, his breath catching in his throat as the Dragon Stones nestled into his palm.

"Ah, lady," Lagan sighed. "What wonders are these?

Is the god himself in them? I haven't felt such peace in a long while. Not since before . . ."

He stopped, but Crysania knew what he meant. Not since before he tried to heal Nisse and failed.

Lagan held the stones a long moment before reluctantly passing them to Jeril. The desert warrior held them, rolling them together so that they clicked against each other in the silence.

"They are stones, lady. What of them?"

"You don't feel them, Jeril?"

He passed the stones to Kela with a word, then said, "No, lady. What should I feel?"

At once, a wave of loss, of regret—a sudden flash of anger!—washed over Crysania. She wanted to snatch the Dragon Stones back, to thrust them deep into her pocket, to send these people from her chamber. Shaking, dismayed, she clenched her hands into fists, which remained hidden beneath her desk. She had not expected to feel such possessiveness!

"Power," Kela breathed, answering Jeril's question. Her words came breathless with awe. "Power such as we seldom feel in this life."

Jeril laughed, the first such sound Crysania had heard from him. "Oh, well, if that's it. Valin always says I'm a lump when it comes to magic. I've never felt any of it."

Tandar pushed up against his lady, breathing heavily, unhappily. Crysania forced herself to wait a decent moment before extending her hand to Kela, silently asking for the stones back. Once they sat in her hand again, all tension drained from her.

Hush, she told herself, it is the day that makes me feel like this, the rifling of my chamber, the growling of war at the gates of the city.

Crysania motioned for the others to sit. "My friends, we must start our journey. You have all agreed to come with me, and none of you has asked where or why. The time has come for you to know, and I tell you now, whoever wants to decline this journey may do so with all my goodwill."

Silence filled the room. Outside, the city's heartbeat sounded—the rise and fall of countless voices, the rumble of wagon traffic, the clatter of a horse beyond the temple walls.

"I have learned that Ariakan's troops will attack the High Clerist's Tower at dawn. His forces are strong, and though ours are good and brave . . ." She stopped, unwilling to condemn Thomas's knights with her doubts. "I must go and find the mates to these stones, that we may hope to use their power for the coming battles."

The tiger rumbled unhappily. No one else made a sound.

"Seralas will be in charge of the temple while I am gone. She will follow the plans we have worked on these past weeks and give the tower as much aid as we can. We five will be gone from here tonight."

"Gone where, my lady?" Lagan asked.

"To Neraka," Crysania said, the name falling like a dark stone into their expectant silence.

Neraka! The city of the Dark Queen, the fortress of her baleful champions, the place where her dark temple sat, twisted and ugly as some abomination, ill-born and evil.

"Any of you who want to stay here, please speak now."

Someone sighed. Crysania thought it was Kela by the sound. No one else made even the slightest sound.

"Jeril," Crysania said, her heart swelling with love for these friends and their quiet courage, "can you lead us east out of the city without taking us near the Westgate Pass?"

There was a rustle of leather and a rattle of steel as the man stepped forward. "Yes, lady. We'll have to go through the desert. There's a way. It's not well known, but the tribes have been using it for decades. Along the shore, through a pass, then skirt the mountains through the desert."

"Is there no shorter way?" Lagan asked.

Jeril snorted. "Plenty of them. It makes better sense to take this longer way, though. I'm sure your lady would prefer adding a couple of days travel to her journey to being captured by the Dark Knights before she's even out of sight of the High Clerist's Tower."

No one disagreed with that, and no one had more to say.

"Take what you need for the journey," Crysania said, her voice gentle. "But remember that we are traveling light. I want to make up those extra days in speed. We will leave after the sun sets."

In her hand, the Dragon Stones warmed. It was as though they'd heard and understood.

* * * * *

Hooves clattered on cobbles, the sound echoing eerily from building to building as the five seekers set out from the Temple of Paladine. They went in simple garb, lightly cloaked and hooded against the sun, looking like nothing so much as a group of travelers bound home from the city. Gone were the white robes of the clerics, replaced by the rough clothing of wayfarers. Only Kela retained her normal attire, with robes doubtless as white as Valin's own. Gone too was Firegold, on a reconnoitering mission for the Solamnic knights. The memory of her brushed Crysania's mind like a caress of his wing.

And how are you, Valin? Crysania wondered. I would like to have seen you one more time, my friend. . . .

The thought surprised her. She put it quickly aside.

Jeril rode in the lead, Kela in the rear. Crysania and

Lagan shared a mount, a fine strong gelding the dwarf had chosen himself from the stables. With Lagan up front and Crysania behind, they managed well enough, for Lagan had insisted on leaving off the saddle. "We'll do better that way," he'd said, "neither of us bumping the horn or the back."

Tandar, unswerving, loped alongside the gray, keeping close to his lady.

Crysania marked their progress from the temple grounds, through narrow back streets noisome with unhealthy odors of rotting food, waste, and worse. She knew by the cleaner scent when they passed by the gardens of the Old City and those of New City. The rank smell of rotting fish and brackish water told her they passed along the docks to the bay.

"Ach!" Lagan said, his voice muffled against his sleeve as he pressed his arm to his face in hope of hiding from the scent. "The breeze off the water is like a furnace wind. I hate this Anvil Summer!"

Crysania smiled grimly, agreeing silently as they veered away from the bay and the stink of rotting fish, and up into the foothills to the west.

The air cooled from the burning of sun on sand and water to the shade of small trees as they climbed along a narrow hunting path. The cooler scent of the forest pervaded now, the light fragrance of oak and maple and elm twined with the tang of evergreens and the poignant aroma of moisture lifted up from earth long covered in leaves.

Sometimes Crysania managed to let her mind range freely, seeing in memory sights she'd not experienced in more than thirty years. Light and shadow and trees, all called up by their scents. Other times her mind returned to the one question that had haunted her since she first accepted the Dragon Stones from Dalamar: When she found the rest of the stones and connected all five, which god would answer her call?

She remembered the warmth of Paladine's voice as she had known it for so long, the deep, rich tones as he spoke to her of love and compassion. And she did not forget the sound of the Dark Queen's voice, the harsh crowing laughter, the raking shrieks of rage, the full-throated roar of power. She'd heard that voice thirty years ago. She had never forgotten it.

"There are ferns in the shadows, and that must mean water somewhere," Lagan said. "The squirrels have made nests high up, and they are new. They must be finding nuts from last year's hoard. I wonder how they will fare next year?

"We are on hunting trails, lady. We are on narrow paths, with stones jutting out from the sides. Jeril is scowling so deep you'd think he was born with the mask of a daemon glued on his face. Your Tandar never leaves our side. . . .

"Lady," Lagan said when the gelding halted. "Jeril has found us a campsite."

He slid from the horse's back and reached up to help her down. The muscles in her back and legs had long ago started aching. It seemed everyone must hear them screaming by now. Water gurgled nearby and she said, "Lagan, will you guide me?"

He did, the tiger close beside them. She knelt, reaching for water, and had to reach farther than she'd imagined. The stream was but a narrow ribbon.

"It's happening everywhere," Lagan said. "The streams are getting smaller."

"I was hoping we'd be farther along before we stopped," she said. She dipped her fingers into the lukewarm water and washed her face and hands. Beside her, Tandar lapped noisily.

"We're within an hour of the pass," he answered. "Jeril says it's too dangerous to try to navigate it at night. We'll go through early tomorrow morning, and then we'll be in the desert. The timing is good."

She nodded and made her way back to the campsite. Already the party was settling into a pattern that she thought would hold in the days to come.

Jeril carefully cleared a large circle on the forest floor, leaving nothing but dirt in its center. Kela started a small fire in it, using softly spoken words of magic. The essence of it passed over Crysania's skin, awakening a tingle from the stones. Lagan pulled out their supplies, and Crysania made them tea to go with their bread and cheese, while Jeril unpacked their bedrolls.

Despite the tension urging her to move on, Crysania was tired, and she thought she'd have little trouble falling asleep soon after she'd eaten. She curled up on her bedroll, shifted several times until she'd gotten all the sticks from beneath it, yet still she lay awake.

"There are stars, lady," whispered a voice from out of the night . . . Lagan's. "I see the constellations, and they are like diamonds sewn into a swath of blackest velvet." His voice fell still. Crysania heard him breathing. So quiet was he that she believed he'd fallen asleep. Then, satisfaction couching his words, he said, "I see him, lady. Paladine's dragon shining."

"He looks down upon us," she whispered. "He sees us."

"Yes, he does."

Jeril made some slight sound in his sleep. The fire hissed, and a log fell to ashes as Kela poked the flames awake. The only one missing from their group was Tandar, gone hunting for his supper.

"Good night, my friend," Crysania said to Lagan.

Lagan's soft snoring was his only answer, and she barely heard that before falling asleep herself.

* * * * *

The tiger roamed the night by the light of two moons, the red just rising, a crescent of the silver already shining in the sky above him. The taste of hare, three fat bucks lingered in his mouth. His belly had stopped rumbling after the second kill, the yearning for blood-rich meat subsided soon after. He'd have been happy to have more, but no more hares, or game of any sort, were to be found. His tigerish scent hung in the air like a threat.

Fed, he wandered the night, keeping close to the place where Crysania and her companions passed the night. He heard their voices low against the silence, and when those voices fell still, yet he heard their breathing.

From a distance of twenty paces, he paced the campsite round, a silent warden at the perimeter, keeping back all creatures of the night who might prey upon his sleeping friends. He paced, and knew his pacing to be a delay. There was a thing needed doing tonight, a thing he'd agreed to. He must reach out with his mind and speak with the Master of the Tower of High Sorcery.

Did he doubt he could do that? No, he didn't. The ability lay within him, unused since the dark elf had changed him from man to beast. He felt it like a throbbing somewhere deep in his mind, like a light pulsing. He'd need only reach for that light, that pulse, and he would be able to speak to Dalamar in his tower.

He hesitated, pacing round and round the clearing, caught between his obligations. He'd made a promise to the black robe, one that must be kept. And it was a promise he hated, for it seemed to him that to report to Dalamar about this journey was no less than spying upon his lady.

In the clearing, Jeril and Kela traded places, the woman going to her bedroll while her husband stood watch.

Her husband! Tandar shook his head, growling low in his throat. He could not doubt his brother's word that the woman was his wife. But who was she really? He didn't recognize her as a woman of his tribe. Perhaps she came from one of the neighboring tribes, or from a band wandering through. The wind blew from the west, warm and carrying the scents of all those in the clearing. Tandar lifted his head, breathing deeply.

Why hadn't Jeril told his brother in far-off Palanthas of the impending wedding? Why hadn't his parents let him know so he could come and stand by Jeril's side at the ritual, as was right and proper?

The tiger shook his head again, growling once more. It might be that the answer lay in what he well knew—that Jeril was impulsive, quick to friendship, quick to anger, quick to love.

I will trust you, Brother, the tiger thought.

It was more a wish than a promise, though.

Moonlight spilled down upon the beast. Solinari would soon set. Lunitari would hang on into the morning sky. Time passed; the stars in their constellations turned, wheeling toward night's end.

I will do what I must, Tandar told himself.

He paced once more round the clearing, listening to the night, to the birds deep in the forest, to the breeze rattling through the dry grass. Jeril sat straight and tall, Desert Light unsheathed and set across his knees. All would be well with him watching.

In silence, the forest barely aware of his passage, Tandar left his watch and found a small glade. There grass still grew green, fed by an unseen underground stream. He lay down in the middle of the glade, in the cool grass. Moonlight poured down on him; the shadows of trees fell over him. He was, he knew, nearly invisible in that light, his white pelt but a splash of Solinari's light, the gray bars but shadows of branches.

He settled. He closed his eyes. He slowed his breathing.

He reached deep within to the light and the pulsing, and when he touched it, he felt himself drawn out from his body, out from the world itself.

He stood upon a twilight plain, a place with no shadows, no sun, no moons, no stars. He felt no breeze; he sensed no other living creature. In his belly, fear clenched, and at the same time a kind of exhilaration welled in him.

He called, *Dalamar!*

And a dark figure came walking in the eternal twilight.

Dalamar!

I hear you, said the figure.

Tandar squinted into the chancy light, never seeing more than the outline of the dark elf. He smelled nothing on this strange plane, tasted nothing on the air, felt no breeze on him, heard no sound that was not Dalamar's voice. This was a plane between the waking world and the sleeping world, a magical place.

He did, however, have another sense, a sixth sense that seemed native to this magical plane, and that told him the mage was weary. Weary in body, weary in spirit. He felt like a man who'd been too long observing some terrible thing.

Blood. Screams. Terror.

Tandar growled uneasily, then fell still.

I am here, the tiger said, remembering he was a mage, remembering he'd once had the power to create a spell like this one. His tension eased.

As am I, Dalamar said, no hint in his voice of what Tandar had sensed. *Speak.*

Tandar told of the journey from the moment they'd set out from the temple. He said nothing of what had happened before, choosing to take his orders literally and seeing no need to tell the dark elf of the rifling of Crysania's quarters. He half believed Dalamar had something to do with that, or at least knew about it.

It is all very ordinary so far, my lord.

The figure in the twilight stood still, hands folded deep within the sleeves of his robe, head low, a man thinking. When he lifted his head, his eyes shone bright and startling.

Something puzzles you, sir tiger, he said, his voice in Tandar's mind as softly dangerous as ever it had been in waking life. *You are wealthier by one sister-in-law and you don't understand why.*

Tandar admitted it was so.

Well, the mage said, *perhaps it is the usual reason. They love. Or,* he chuckled, *they loved too soon and now must mend the matter with a wedding.*

It might be. No doubt my brother has his reasons.

Unruffled, Dalamar agreed.

With no other word, the dark elf turned and walked away across the empty plain. He did not vanish; rather, he dwindled, growing thinner, losing dimension, finally shrinking to a tiny point of what could only be described as dark light.

The kind, Tandar thought, that glows in the heart of a black crystal.

The tiger found himself suddenly alone, lying in a glade from which all moonlight had vanished. Only the stars hung in the sky now, and by their light and the scents on the hot night air, the beast made his way back to the camp.

He went round the campsite, passing near each of his companions. As he passed Kela, asleep on her blanket, he sniffed the air, breathing deeply. Then he snorted. Dalamar was right—the woman was with child. Only lately so, he knew by the scent of her. Perhaps she was not even a month along. He looked once at Jeril, still sitting his watch, in his mind laughing to imagine what conversations must have raged in his father's tent when Jeril told their parents the reason for his sudden wedding.

The big warrior glanced his way, nodded respectful greeting, and tossed another log onto the failing fire. Yawning mightily, as only such beasts as he can do, Tandar padded to Crysania's bedroll. She lay asleep on her side, the curve of her hip gently rising, the whiteness of her neck gleaming. Her dark hair clung in wisps to her damp cheek.

I am near you, lady, the tiger thought as he lay down beside her.

He pressed his back into the curve of her own. It felt like stolen intimacy, and yet he didn't change position. He fell asleep listening to her heart beat.

Crysania, he said to her, in the silent voice of the heart. One day you will say that you love me, my lady, and then no intimacy will be stolen.

Crysania!

Chapter Thirteen

Crysania woke with her heart racing, her pulse pounding. Sweat rolled down her cheeks, tickling along her ribs. These things she felt only barely, for in her memory, in her mind, rang the echo of her own name cried aloud.

Crysania!

Again that voice in her mind. Without thinking, she reached for the Dragon Stones and found them safe in her pocket. She let their warmth wash through her. The sense of well-being and security she felt reassured her.

And yet there was that voice. Remembered or dreamed? Blessedly, her sleep had been free of dreams, or if it had not, those dreams had been the stuff of normal sleep, wisps of images floating, nothing bearing the weight of import or nightmare.

She frowned, sitting up. Tandar lay alongside her

bedroll, head up, tail switching. She touched his shoulder tentatively.

Crysania, said the voice in her mind gently.

"Tandar?" she whispered.

He snorted, a sound like a harrumph of affirmation. At the same time, a feeling of reassurance formed in her mind, not in words but as abstract emotion. Was she dreaming? A moment ago she'd had the definite feeling that he'd been speaking her name when she woke.

Crickets chirped in the forest. From the direction of the little stream floated the sound of a frog croaking. Nearer, Lagan snored gently. Kela sighed in sleep, while Jeril hummed softly, some desert song to remind him of home as he tended the fire.

After a moment, feeling as foolish as a lonely old woman speaking to one of her dozens of cats, she whispered in her mind, *Tandar, can you hear my thoughts?*

He answered with words this time, ragged and straining, but real understandable words. *Yes. When they're very loud.*

She stroked the smooth fur on his shoulder, feeling somehow better connected to his answer when her fingers were touching him. She smiled in delight at the concept of loud thoughts.

And you can talk to me?

It seems I am learning to.

But why now? Why not before?

The tiger lay a long time silent. Then he answered, *Perhaps Dalamar has done this. I—I kept my word to him, lady. I've spoken with him tonight.*

Crysania put her hand on his head, absently scratching behind his ears. He stretched his neck in pleasure.

And does your vow to him demand that you keep from me what was said between you?

A tumbling delight ran through her mind—the tiger's laughter. *Why, no, lady, my vow doesn't make any such*

181

demand. He had little to say, and I not much more. I told him of our journey, but not of what happened at the temple, the attempt at theft. I told him who are our companions, and he asked no more.

Crysania patted the tiger gently. *Good night, my friend.*

He sighed, a deep groaning satisfaction.

She lay back down and shifted until she was as comfortable as she was going to get lying on a blanket on the ground. She fell asleep to the sounds of Jeril tending the fire.

*   *   *   *   *

Too soon for her aching muscles, Crysania heard Jeril walking about the camp, stopping near each sleeper to wake him. Lagan came awake with a startled gasp, Kela with a sigh. At Crysania's side, Tandar sat, her guardian at watch.

"Early up, my lady," Jeril said, stepping wide around the tiger. "The sun's not yet risen, but the sky is past gray, and light is soon coming."

Her hand on Tandar's shoulder, Crysania rose. "How can I help with breakfast, Jeril?"

He made a soft sound. She imagined he was smiling. "By packing up all the food we have left over from last night. We're eating on the road, lady." He paused, and Crysania heard a soft whisking sound, as though someone were sweeping the ground. "That's Kela, wiping away our tracks with a branch. The fire is out, the campsite cleared, and soon there will be no sign that we've been here."

They had little time for waking, less for getting ready to ride again. Crysania, once the one to whom all would have looked for orders, heard the others going to Jeril for instructions. She set herself to work as willingly as Lagan saddling the horses and Kela breaking camp.

The heat rose, sweat breaking out upon the back of her neck, trickling. By these signs Crysania knew the sun had come up over the horizon. Lagan brought the horses, rested from the night and dancing with impatience to be on the way. Once the dwarf had mounted, Jeril lifted Crysania easily to sit behind him.

On the morning air, the ringing neighs of the horses sounded loud, like trumpets. The joyous song lifted Crysania's heart. The feel of her mount's muscles, power-ful beneath her, gave her the feeling that the horse could run forever. Lagan didn't let that happen, though. He let the gelding stretch its legs, then kept it firmly in hand, conserving the beast's strength. They settled into a com-fortable pace, the kind that lets a horse cover distance without tiring, and soon Crysania understood why Jeril hadn't wanted to attempt the pass through the mountains at night. A pass, they called it, but it seemed to her more like a very long, very narrow hallway than a canyon.

"Narrow as a widow's bed," Lagan said. "Who's to wonder why it's so little used!"

Behind them Tandar loped, and a wave of amusement washed over Crysania as the tiger heard that comment.

But listen, lady. He's right. I've never seen so narrow a space and still heard it called a canyon.

Crysania did listen, hearing the sound of their passage echo from stony walls stretching up hundreds of feet. Once she slipped an arm from round Lagan's waist and reached as far as she could. She touched a wall. She changed hands and touched the other, feeling stone and soft lichens, a plant growing right out of a crevice. She lifted her hand and smelled a light, musky fragrance. She'd touched the spent leaves of a columbine.

They went single file and Crysania knew they rode in a shallow riverbed. Sometimes she heard the sucking sound of hooves in mud; other times she smelled water, clean and fresh. All the while the sounds got closer and closer as the canyon walls narrowed in.

"Watch your knees," Lagan said.

Stone snagged her skirts, scraped through to her flesh. Soon the riverbed grew so narrow that the water reached almost three hands up her horse's legs. Ahead, Tandar stopped and shook himself, no doubt deeper into the water than the horses.

"It's not safe to travel this route in wet weather," Jeril said, his voice echoing back to her. "A heavy rain will send a rush of water along the canyon. That's why the walls are so jagged, from being washed out."

High up, a raven called. Another answered. Crysania shivered and imagined a wall of water rushing down that narrow passage and no way to get out of its path.

"I hope it doesn't rain," she said to Lagan.

The dwarf laughed grimly, saying he hadn't heard anyone voice that wish in a while.

Up ahead, Tandar snorted, shaking himself vigorously. They came, at last, out of the water and turned sharply right, onto a dry, stony path.

"We're within sight of the mountains," Jeril said, his horse beside Crysania's. "But we can make better time if we ride in the sand. It won't be comfortable, but—"

"No matter," she said, steeling herself. "We will follow, Jeril. Lead."

The heat, as they came out of the stony canyon, hit like a wall. It poured down from above, then radiated off the sand so that it seemed to be coming at her from all directions. Wind moaned, then shrilled, then dropped low again, like the sound of ghosts. Crysania shivered, an unwonted thought striking her. That wind sounded like the voices of Shoikan Grove, the moaning, the sobbing, the shrieking of tormented souls forever trapped.

The sand whipped at her face, crept into the folds of

her gown, beneath the fabric, scratching. It clawed at her eyes, coating her lashes until she had to ride with her eyes closed.

"Lagan, are you all right?" she asked. "Can you see?"

"Barely, lady. I'm following Tandar, and glad enough he's white-pelted or I'd never be able to see him."

Jeril still rode ahead. She assumed Kela was yet at the rear. The sounds of them riding were all muffled by the sand, torn away by a rising wind.

She coughed and spat sand from her mouth. Clinging one-armed to Lagan, she wiped her face, and the moment she breathed, her mouth and nose filled with grit again.

"Lady. Here." Kela came alongside, murmured a word to Lagan, and the gray gelding halted. "Turn your head toward me."

Ahead, Tandar stopped. She sensed curiosity and caution from him. The feelings came faintly, though, as if he tried to keep his thoughts to himself.

The mage's strong fingers touched her face, her chin, brushing the coating of sand away. Then she slipped Crysania's hood down and rearranged her scarf, wrapping it around her head so it sat securely. The hem draped down over her eyes, brushing her lashes. The bottom wrapped across her mouth and nose, but comfortably. Then Kela pulled the hood back up over all of it.

"There. That should feel better."

Crysania moved her head experimentally. It did feel better. "Thank you," she said, expecting the folds of cloth to slip from her face. They stayed securely in place.

"You look like a desert woman now, lady," Kela said approvingly.

"I suppose I do. If only I could manage the affection for heat and sand you desert folk seem to have."

Only cool silence answered, and the woman dropped back to take her place at the rear of the party.

185

"Where's Tandar?" Crysania asked.

"Just ahead of us, lady," Jeril answered. By the sound of his voice, he wasn't far ahead. "That's a strange pet you have."

She laughed. "Pet? No, he isn't that. Tandar belongs to himself. He is more of a friend."

"And a good thing for us all that he is." Jeril's horse fell in beside hers. Lagan whispered encouragement as the gray gelding sidled away. "I can't imagine you'll come to any harm with that great beast near. How did you come by him, lady?"

"He was a . . . gift."

The gift stopped still where he was. Horses snorted, picking up some scent that startled, then frightened them.

Lagan cursed a very unclerical curse, managing to rein in their mount, but barely.

Crysania sniffed at the air, but all she smelled was sand and sun and her own sweat.

A moment later Lagan cried, "Jeril! What's that?"

His voice was tight, and Crysania had her arms around him so she could feel him tensing. Fear, unspoken, ran through him and into her.

Like thunder across the sky, Jeril's voice tore into the silence.

"Ride!" he yelled. "Ride for the hills!"

Crysania had time to cry out, "What is it?" before Lagan whipped the gray with the reins, drumming the beast's ribs with his heels.

Ahead, Tandar roared, the sound of rage.

"Lagan! What is it?" She clung to him, off guard, off-balance, and afraid every moment of falling to her death beneath the horse's hooves. "What's happening?"

Lagan whipped the horse again, urging all speed.

"Barbarians, lady. The blue-skinned barbarians of Ariakan's army!"

Chapter Fourteen

Crysania wrapped her arms tightly around Lagan's chest and only loosened her grip when she heard his hoarse, choked breathing. Sand flew up into her face. The gelding surged forward, then turned abruptly. She slipped, falling sideways, then righted herself just in time to keep from spilling herself and Lagan onto the sand.

High and terrible, a shrieking war cry rent the darkness. Her blood ran icy in her veins. Her heart thundered.

"Hang on, lady!" Lagan shouted. Then, to the horse, "Go! Go, you! Go!"

She slipped again, head reeling as she fell sideways. She cried out. Just as she reached the point at which her falling weight would have been too great for her to regain her seat, a strong hand, Kela's or Jeril's, caught her shoulder and shoved her back.

"Are you there?" Lagan shouted over his shoulder.

"Just barely," she said, her voice a desperate croak. She grabbed him again, terrified, helpless, and out of control.

She heard shouts, booming hooves. Running feet coming closer!

The terrain under the gelding's hoofs changed, and the sand that Jeril's horse was plowing into the air dissipated. The scent of green fell suddenly all around her. Trees loomed, and stone clattered under galloping hooves.

"Hang on!" Lagan shouted as the gelding surged up.

She did hang on, though she had no idea how her trembling arms managed the strength. Lagan sawed to a sudden stop. Strong arms reached up and caught her round the waist, dragging her to the ground.

Tandar was almost beneath her, tangling with Jeril's legs.

"Get out of my way!" he snarled at the tiger. "Let me get her up there."

Lagan dropped heavily from the gray's back and slapped the horse on the rump, sending it away. Between them, Jeril and the dwarf got Crysania up a steep slope, guiding her as best they could past bushes and trees. Branches slapped her face, scratched and clawed at her clothing. Her skirt ripped; her hem snagged. Roots seemed to reach right up from the ground to trip her.

Behind her, Crysania heard Tandar's harsh breathing as they gained level ground.

"Here!" Jeril shouted back down the hill. "Kela! Come to high ground!"

Crysania moved. Jeril wheeled her around and slammed her back against something hard and jagged with sharp edges.

Tandar growled.

"Where are we?" she demanded, choking on dust, gasping for breath. "How many are they?"

Jeril rumbled a curse. "Twenty or so. All mounted. All with swords. Didn't see any crossbows."

He turned away from her. He snapped instructions, and she could follow to some degree what was happening around her. He placed the two others, Kela on her right, Lagan on her left, then Jeril took up a position between them, on the point of the rise.

"Don't let them draw you away. Don't let them get between us." Then, in sudden surprise: "What the hell is that?"

Lagan's laughter rang out, incongruous and thoroughly heartening. "Battlefield leavings, I think you'd call it."

Jeril snorted. "Are clerics allowed—?"

Voices, rough and coarse, shouted from below. Heavy bodies smashed past the small trees.

Tandar leaned closer, his body taut, his breath coming in slow, menacing drags. Crysania put her palm on his great head. The passion simmering in him communicated itself to her, making her shake as the adrenaline in her own body responded to his urgency. She wrapped her fingers around her medallion.

Only the lightest touch of calmness embraced her. Fear clutched at her with cold, bony hands. He was far away, her god, distant again.

"But you will hear me," she said, so quietly that only the tiger heard. "Near or far, I know you will. O Paladine, protect us."

The others ranged out in a loose circle about her. In a voice loud enough so that they could all hear, as crystal clear and cool as a mountain stream, she warned, "Tandar will protect me. Don't concern yourselves with me."

Jeril said nothing. Lagan muttered something in the

language of hill dwarves. She didn't know that tongue well, but she imagined it translated to something like, "No chance of that, miss."

Hoarse voices shouted words in an uncouth language.

Under all, Crysania heard Kela murmuring to herself, her voice low as she sought the spells she had committed to memory.

The barbarians were close now, their breathing harsh on the air, the smell of their painted bodies rank and acrid. A chill swept over her. This was an alien smell, not at all like the scents of humans or dwarves or elves.

On the air, Crysania felt the vibration of their cries as they ran up the slope.

"Stand your ground," Jeril ordered. "Don't let them separate us."

The first attacker met Jeril, shrieking with battle lust. Sword rang against sword in terrible battle song. Kela quietly spoke the words of a spell. Heat, smelling of sulfur and the metallic singe of the air after a storm, rushed past Crysania.

"Paladine help us all," she whispered as screams of pain and rage rang through the roar of the fireball.

Lagan met the battle cries with one of his own, a deep-throated bellow so fierce Crysania hardly believed it came from her quiet, scholarly cleric. All sounds became one, the hideous howl of war. Steel belled on steel; blades sang their blood song. Lagan raged, battle fury and triumph, and that voice was as alien to Crysania as the barbarians'. Kela's voice joined Lagan's, louder now, full-throated, confident as she began another casting.

Jeril laughed, a sound to freeze the heart. "Come on! Try it again if you must!"

A second wave of barbarians reached them.

Jeril shouted, "Lagan, hang in!" Then he was gone from Crysania's side. In another instant, so was Lagan, borne away by a tide of enemies. No one stood by her now but Tandar, snarling at all comers.

Crysania heard the crunch of bone, a shrill, high scream of agony from not an arm's length away.

She fell back against the cliff wall, its sharp edges cutting into her shoulders. Tandar pressed against her, his body between hers and the fighting. She closed her fingers around her medallion and tried to concentrate. But the sounds of dying and killing came at her faster and faster. Bodies crashed against bodies, against ground.

Kela's voice grew louder and more desperate. The electric sizzle of sparking swords hung on the air, mixing with the odor of spellcasting, the heavy stench of blood. Screams and battle cries, alien voices, familiar voices, all mixed.

Crysania grasped the medallion in trembling hands, clutching at the words of prayer as though she clutched a lifeline.

A deep masculine scream pierced the air. The smell of blood washed over her. Jeril? It couldn't have been Jeril. It wasn't his voice. She surged forward and Tandar pushed her back.

A body crashed in close, stumbling. A sword's blade clanged on stone near her shoulder.

Tandar roared, a huge, terrible sound, like an earthquake, an explosion in her mind, firing her nerves. The tiger leapt, great claws curled, teeth bared, a red haze of wrath clouding his mind, clouding her own. The need to protect Crysania was uppermost in his mind, and she felt it. His body soared on muscles strong and graceful and invincible.

The huge human before Crysania screamed as the tiger hit him. He fell back under the weight, rolled as fangs snapped at his neck and claws raked open his belly.

Crysania flung herself back. Her head thumped off the

191

rock wall, and her mind found the words. "Paladine, protect us!"

She clenched one fist around her medallion and grabbed at the stones deep in her pockets with the other. A warm light, pale compared to what it should have been, filled her soul. It insulated her mind from terror.

And it gave her sight.

No, I must be mad. I must be hurt and wit-wandering!

And yet she saw. It was a strange kind of sight, hazy, wavering, as if she peered through water. She knew at once this was not her sight returned to her. She saw through someone else's eyes, and through those eyes the world had no colors, no sharp edges.

Tandar!

He did not reply, but the vista changed, as though the eyes, the head, of whoever granted this sight turned, surveying the land. And so Crysania saw that she stood on a rise, against a rocky outcropping. Beyond was desert and plains and sky, all gray and tan. And close, too close, raged the battle.

Jeril, tall and strong, wielded his sword with the power of two men. Kela, small as a girl and delicate, stood with her hands lifted to the sky, chanting spell words and magic. Lagan Innis fought at Jeril's back, with a torch in one hand and a war axe in the other.

No, she realized. Not a torch . . . a clerical spell of light.

Paladine! For that much strength we thank you! For more, we beg you!

Dry in the mouth, Crysania closed her eyes, and the images stayed with her. Odd, off-kilter images.

"Please," she breathed. "Paladine, protect us."

In her mind, Tandar roared, wordless fiery rage.

Her eyes snapped open as Jeril shouted a warning.

Two huge blue-skinned men bore down on Lagan, ignoring his god-granted light, covering their eyes and charging him. Lagan's light fell. He grasped the helve of his found war axe, his stance wide, his face as white as snow above his dark beard.

"Tandar! Help him!" Crysania dug her fingers into the tiger's shoulder and pushed him away.

Tandar bounded toward Lagan, his massive body beautiful, gray stripes shifting with the play of muscles beneath his white pelt. He leapt at the last moment, paws hitting one of the attackers in the chest. He landed, solid and balanced, on the ground. Thundering, he turned to meet the other attacker, but Lagan was already there, wielding the war axe. He called upon the god for light again, and light sprang to his hand. He flung the flaming ball at the barbarian, and when the barbarian threw up his arm to ward his eyes, Lagan hacked at him with the axe. Blood spurted from the wound between the man's ribs.

Crysania closed her eyes, sickened by the blood and the fury, and the sight of Lagan's face, wild with battle rage as he turned to face the next attacker. The hands of the dwarf who had lovingly translated ancient prayers now were awash in blood. And yet, eyes wide or shut, still she saw, for they were not her eyes looking.

Tandar! Is it you?

He did not reply, and all she felt flowing down the mind connection between them was rage and a passion for blood.

Crysania's lips moved in silent prayer, not for herself but for her friends. She clung to the medallion as she heard Lagan dispatch another attacker, accompanied by a high-pitched, rending scream of agony.

"Paladine, protect them," she gasped. "Bless them. Bless them all."

She was who she was, and so she prayed not only for her people, fighting with such ferocity, but also for the

193

attackers, those who were dying around her with such terrible screams of fury and hatred.

Out from the fire storm, Jeril's voice rang: "No, Lagan! Don't kill him. We need information."

It was as though that bellowed order was also the order to stop. Quiet seemed to descend around Crysania, settling upon the hill like deafness. As suddenly as it had begun, the battle was over.

* * * * *

Crysania heard weeping and realized the sobbing came from her. She wept for the battle just fought, for the battles and the death that must even now be howling around the High Clerist's Tower.

Palanthas! Were they fighting there?

And all this fighting, this raging, was it but the echo of another, greater battle in the realm of gods?

"Lady?"

Lagan's voice came from above her, calling her back from her sorrow. He breathed heavily, stinking of blood and sweat. Kela was nearby on the ground, her teeth chattering, shivering with exhaustion. Jeril came up the hill, growling in a voice every bit as deep as Tandar's as he wrestled with the barbarian he'd kept Lagan from dispatching.

Only Tandar made no sound. He lay beside her, against her, reeking of blood.

Softly Lagan said, "Lady? Are you hurt?"

Slowly Crysania released her grip on the medallion. She let her prayers fall away. Slowly she stood, wiping away her tears.

"I'm all right," she lied. Who could be all right after such a battle, after all that killing? She took a deep breath, cleansing her body of fear and tension. "I'm fine. Is everyone else . . . ?"

"Yes. We're here." Lagan took her hand, and there was blood on his fingers. His hand shook. "But I—I have a small cut."

Crysania freed her hand and touched him gently, finding the wound. A cut, yes, but it was no small one. It ran the width of the dwarf's strong arm, pulsing blood. Praying, pleading, Crysania closed her hand over the wound, calling upon the healing strength that Paladine used so often to allow her.

Would he hear now? Distant and distracted, would Paladine hear her prayer and grant her strength?

Holding her breath, Crysania waited. Waiting, she was rewarded. The warmth of the healing, the joy of it, washed through her. A strength that was of her and from without her passed through her veins and nerves and into Lagan Innis. The wound closed, disappearing as though it had never been.

Lagan sighed, unabashed tears rolling down his cheeks. Not for his pain or his healing, Crysania realized. He wept for the friend he'd been unable to save with this very prayer.

"Why is it like this, lady?" he said, his voice low and rough. "Why does the god ignore us and then hear us?"

Crysania shook her head. "I don't know, Lagan." She put her hand into her pocket, touching the Dragon Stones, thinking that perhaps she could ask him directly soon.

In her mind, Tandar growled as he came to lie down beside her.

Shivering, she remembered the feel of his bloodlust. The cool tigerish joy of his leap into the air, of knowing that he was stronger than his enemy. She heard, as if in memory, the euphoric singing in his pulse as the smell of his enemy's blood filled his nostrils.

Crysania . . .

He sighed her name like a prayer, and she saw herself

in his mind, precious and to be protected, even at the cost of his own life. Moved, her heart filling, she lay her hand on his head, soothing him with wordless emanations of peace and calmness.

"Lady. " Jeril crouched beside her. "We should go."

She straightened.

"The barbarian Lagan captured . . ."

The hesitation in his voice as he said the last word almost made her smile. She remembered his shout to her cleric. Captured? Spared was more like it.

"He says this group was in the rear of the army, and they were separated. Looting, I think," he said with disgust. "They were trying to catch up with the main body of the army, which they thought was several hours ahead. We should go now, while the plains are quiet."

Crysania nodded, pulling herself up with the arm that was looped around Tandar's neck, although she knew that Jeril probably had a hand extended. They started down the slope, and Lagan fell in beside her. She almost didn't ask, because she wasn't sure she wanted to know, but she had to. "You didn't kill him, did you, Lagan? The barbarian?"

"No, lady," the dwarf said grimly. "But he'll have such a headache when he wakes that he'll be wishing I had."

Lagan helped her to sit on a log. He wiped the blood from her fingers with dry leaves, then went to help Jeril round up the horses. Tandar wandered away, too, panting, in search of water. Kela came and sat beside her, silent and weary.

"Are you all right?" Crysania asked the young mage.

"Yes." Kela's delicate voice was hoarse and ragged. She cleared her throat and tried again. "Yes. It's just extremely tiring, casting spells like that. I need to rest."

"I will ask Jeril to delay." Crysania reached over and lay a hand on the woman's arm. The muscles under her fingers were trembling, the bones under the muscle as delicate as a bird's.

"No." Kela drew a long, shaking breath. "We should go on while we can. I'll manage."

Crysania nodded in wordless approval of the woman's determination. "Perhaps I can heal your tiredness," she suggested. The arm beneath her fingers shivered.

"No, lady. You must conserve your strength, too." The mage pulled away gently and went to help the others find the horses.

* * * * *

The sun beat down with relentless, pounding heat. Crysania pulled her hood up to shield herself from it, but after a while the air was so hot against her mouth and nose, she pushed it away again. They traveled in silence, each alone with his or her own thoughts. After a time, missing Lagan's description of the land around them but loath to disturb him, she reached out for Tandar with her mind.

It was your sight I had, there at the battle, wasn't it?

It was. I know you didn't like to see what I showed but, Lady, you needed to see it. For your own safety, you had to know.

I thank you for your care if not for the sight.

A ripple of wry laughter shivered in her mind.

Can you show me the plains?

She felt him bend his mind to the task, concentrating as he scanned the vista before them. The hazy landscape she saw in her mind was not what she'd have seen if she'd been sighted. The vantage was low to the ground, the range farther and wider than she remembered being able to see. Everything was bright but colorless, sparkling with blinding white highlights overlaid on a landscape of dull, lifeless brown.

That's how a tiger sees, lady.

The land was dying. The magnificent plains, once lush with grass, alive with flowers and streams, rife with birds and deer and hares, were now dead and dull and brown. The brightness, tingeing to an unnatural red in the north, was the sun pounding down, burning the land almost as she watched.

The tiger glanced around once again, giving her a hazy, rolling view of the land and her party. Kela was behind them, pale and blonde, slumped and exhausted, but alert, watching the land and the riders in front of her at the same time. Jeril was in front of them, riding high in his stirrups, alert to the movement of every blade of grass. And Lagan Innis, covered in the blood of his enemies, rode up before her, tense and wary, eyes darting left and right. He still carried his found weapon, the war axe, across the horse's withers.

Tandar, weary and distracted, couldn't hold the vision long. The last thing Crysania saw was Jeril. Her heart contracted, with fear, with some regret she yet had no name for. How very like his brother Jeril was! Brown-haired and dark-skinned and broad of shoulder, they weren't alike enough to be twins, but no one who saw them could doubt their kinship.

As if he felt her thoughts, Jeril slowed and allowed his horse to drift back.

For a moment, his big body shaded Crysania's, and she sighed with momentary relief. The sun was no longer directly overhead, but still its heat was relentless. The folds of her robe, moving with the slow gait of the horse, were hot against her skin. Even the strands of her hair were hot beneath her fingers as she smoothed them back from her forehead. Her skin felt dry and tight. Her lips were cracked and bleeding.

Lagan laughed aloud, recalling Crysania from her

thoughts of the heat. Jeril leaned close and said something to the dwarf, evoking his laughter again.

"Might be," Lagan said in response to the comment Crysania hadn't heard. "Might be you don't know all there is to know about clerics."

Jeril grunted. "I know they don't come battle-ready, Lagan Innis."

"No," Lagan said, "we don't. But I wasn't always a cleric. My father taught me my skills, just as he did my brothers. I can build a high forge fire. I probably even remember how to do a bit of forge work. The axe . . . well, the war axe and I were old friends once a long time ago."

Tandar snorted, blowing dust and air and dead grass against her horse's legs. The animal shied away from the tiger.

Crysania let her attention drift from this conversation between new friends. She thought of the battle they'd just won, of the battles to come that they might not win.

They rode in companionable silence for a while, and after a time she could not measure, Jeril said, "Lady, the day's growing old. Let's stop here for the night. We're all tired, and it must be another hour or two to the river."

It didn't seem that late to Crysania. She tilted her face up, and she could tell the sun hadn't set. The heat on her head had dissipated slightly, but it was still discernible.

"We could go on for a while yet," she protested. But the others were already dismounting.

Kela, especially, was quick to climb down.

"We're all tired, lady. The animals are tired." Jeril came to Crysania and offered her a hand to climb down.

"No fire," he told Kela. "We can't chance it. It's too dry out here. And it would be visible for miles."

As she walked away from her horse, Crysania's knees threatened to fold. She settled to the ground beside Kela, her muscles throbbing with weariness. She smelled water and leather as Kela pressed a waterskin into her hands. Warm and flat, the water tasted sweet as spring wine on her lips.

Jeril brought her pack and dropped it at her feet. She rummaged through it for the food she had so carefully packed. She took a share of the dried meat and hard bread, then passed it on to Kela. The others gathered nearby, grass crunching underfoot as they spread out their bedrolls. She unrolled her own blanket and lay down to rest.

Tandar, who had been circling the camp, sniffing audibly of the air from all directions, came and lay beside her as he had the night before. Near the edge of her blanket, Lagan and Jeril discussed the round of watch, agreeing that Lagan would take the first turn, then wake Kela for the second. After her watch, Jeril would stand guard.

"Agreed, then," Lagan said. "Go on off to sleep now, you two. You've earned it."

Jeril yawned, as though the mere suggestion of sleep had pulled it out of him. "Wake us when—"

He said no more, the thought left unfinished as the sky erupted with wind. A choking storm of dust and dead grass whirled up into the air. From several yards out onto the plain, Kela cried out.

Before Crysania could move, Tandar crouched beside her, leaning at an awkward angle to shield her body with his own. Her arm came up to protect her face as the storm of particles blown by the wind hit her, biting into her skin.

Kela shouted again. Crysania rolled onto her hands and knees, bumping into the tiger, pushing him from his protective crouch over her.

Tandar, what's happening?

Firegold!

In the same moment, Jeril cried, "Dragons!"

The tiger stepped back. A hiss of steel against leather,

and Jeril sheathed his sword. He helped Crysania to her feet.

"There are dragons, lady! The sky is filled with them!"

She saw them, not with her eyes but in her imagination, stroking wings and sinuous necks and sparkling scales. Silver dragons swirled above them, weaving and diving.

"How many are there?" Lagan cried.

"Ten!" Kela shouted. "No! Twenty!"

Jeril answered her breathlessly. "More. All silver." Then he corrected himself. "No, there are two gold ones in the pack."

His voice tight, Lagan, the scholar, said, "Wing. A group of dragons is called a wing."

Jeril laughed. "Whatever. They are magnificent! And one is coming down. A gold, lady."

And Crysania heard the voice of an old friend: "Yes! Lady, I am here!"

Crysania steadied herself with a hand on Tandar's shoulder. With the other hand, she brushed at her robe, at her hair. The wind of broad long wings sent the dark strands flying again.

"Revered Daughter." The dragon's great voice vibrated through her very bones, made her stomach quiver. The great golden dragon dipped her head in a bow. "You are not safe here. The last of Ariakan's army is coming down the river."

"We encountered a band of barbarians yesterday," Crysania said. "One of them said they were in the rear and had become separated from the main group."

Firegold rumbled, a sound of disgust and disdain. "No. He spoke only of his group. Or he lied. This force is not large, but they started to move before dawn. They will sweep across the plains like brush fire. We come from Dragon Mountain. These silver dragons were guarding the tomb of Huma and were ordered to the High Clerist's Tower. We journey with them. The knights have need of us soon. But we will carry you to safety first."

"Ordered? Who dared order away this honor guard from Huma's tomb?"

"Huma himself did, lady."

Silence fell upon the group, as though a ghost came walking.

"Firegold," Crysania said, her voice taut. "Can you tell me what is happening?"

"Ariakan has taken the tower," the dragon said. "But he will not keep it for long. He will face a foe far stronger and more evil than any he might fathom."

Crysania grasped her medallion. "I don't understand. What is happening? What foe?"

Lagan moved to her side. "The tower has fallen? Palanthas will be next. The temple."

The dragon spoke quietly, simply, answering Crysania. "The Irda have broken the Greygem. Within it was imprisoned Chaos, who some say is the father of all the gods. He is now loosed upon the world."

Chaos! Crysania's heart quaked. Chaos, the Father of All and of Nothing. If that were so, the fight these dragons faced would make those of the past seem like skirmishes.

"Paladine?" Crysania murmured, as if she were afraid to hear the answer.

"Our father fights his own battle," Firegold said. "As do all the gods, against Chaos."

"I don't understand," Jeril said. He had the sound of a man looking from one person to the other, seeking an answer. "What is Chaos?"

"Not just what, young one," the dragon said. "Who and what and when. Chaos is the father of the gods, who forged the pillars of good, evil, and neutrality upon which our universe is set. The gods emerged from Chaos, and if he has his way, they will return to it."

Crysania stood still and silent, her fear so strong she could say nothing. The heat of the day before was nothing compared to the air she tried to pull into her lungs now. She fumbled at her medallion, hidden in the folds of her robe. It steadied her, and she was able to draw breath again.

The news was beyond anything she'd expected to hear, despite the foreboding of her last contact with Paladine. It was also, paradoxically, a relief. At least she knew now what she hadn't known all these weeks. She knew why Paladine had been so distant, why she had felt him to be in grave danger. For a moment, knowing alleviated the pain, the uncertainty of the past weeks. Then fear rose up in its place, hot and strong and sour.

The gods truly did battle each other. What would become of the world?

Tandar leaned against her, offering his support. She clenched her hands into defiant fists, determination filling in to brace against the fear. She straightened her spine, loosed her grip on the medallion. Somewhere Paladine fought for his life, for the life of the world. An image from her old nightmare came sharply to memory—the hooded figure standing in the rain, hands outstretched to offer her a gift.

The Dragon Stones were the gift, she was certain. Were they a gift of power, or one to lead her to understanding? Whichever the truth, Crysania believed it in her heart that the two Dragon Stones she'd received from Dalamar were a gift from Paladine. And so, then, was this quest to find the other three. Did he summon her? Had he sent her these two stones so that she would find the rest and come to him?

Crysania didn't know, but she would go and find the answer.

"Firegold, the news you bring indicates that I am a part of this battle of gods."

"As you say, lady. How may I serve you?"

" In Paladine's own name, I ask, Will you take me and my companions to the mountains?"

Long and loud, a bugling carol, Firegold trumpeted to her watch.

Around her, the air filled with the thunder of wings as the second gold and one silver dragon came spiraling down from the sky.

Chapter Fifteen

Oh, lady, I'm an earthbound beast! Oh, lady!

Firegold dipped and climbed with the air currents, wings wide, then tucked, then soaring wide again. Behind Crysania, pressing hard for balance, quivering, Tandar closed his eyes, and so darkened the sight he again lent to Crysania.

Can you open your eyes?

He did, and again Crysania saw the Plains of Solamnia rushing by beneath them. The scene was colorless, as before, but even so it took her breath away. So long! It had been so long since she had been able to know with certainty what lay around her without having to touch, to taste, to listen, to smell.

Oh, gods! What a gift!

And the gift was gone, vanished as Tandar closed his eyes tight once more and moaned.

The great dragon swiveled its head back to glance at her. "Lady, I assure you I will not let you or your friend fall," she rumbled. "Tell the tiger he need not grip so tightly."

She brushed her hair back as it whipped across her face. "I think he's doing his best not to hurt you."

Firegold snorted, as if to say it didn't feel as if he was doing his best, but she let the matter drop.

Tandar, show me our friends. Can you?

The tiger groaned, then sighed to find the matter easier than he'd imagined. Through Tandar's eyes, Crysania saw her companions. Lagan rode a swift silver dragon, a young female named Chase. He clung to her, wide-eyed, seeming as desperate to be down from the dizzying height as was Tandar.

"Well done, Lagan!" she cried, calling him to give him courage.

He might have heard her, but if he did, he dared not turn his head to acknowledge her words. His face was marble white, rigid and unmoving. She thought she saw his lips moving in constant prayer.

Kela, who had been delighted by the idea of going aloft, rode with Jeril on a golden male named Goldstrike who easily kept pace with Firegold. They were beautiful together, those two natives of the desert, hair wild and flying, faces flushed with delight. Once Crysania saw the mage fling back her head, laughing. What wonderful stories they would have to tell their children!

In her mind, Tandar rumbled, a grim, wordless sound of unhappiness. He did not like the mage, that much was clear.

Why, Tandar? She fought well and hard for us. She's been a good friend.

A companion, he amended. *Look, lady, is that the river below?*

It was. It showed as a brown stripe on the land, no wider than her finger. Far away, the mountains scored a dark blue streak between the tan of earth and the blue of sky. To the north, a hazy smudge of gray caught Tandar's eye, thus hers. A thumb shaped smear reached into the sky.

"What's that?" She pointed, then realized that Firegold couldn't see her arm. "To the north. The gray streak."

The gold dragon turned that way. "Fire."

"We must go and see," Crysania said. "There is a village at the bend in the river. If they are in danger, we must warn them. Or help."

"As you wish, Revered Daughter."

The great leathery wings beat an extra turn, and Firegold rushed forward, leaving Crysania's stomach lurching. Tandar made a piteous sound, then settled to groaning. Firegold bugled one long cry to the others, then separated from the wing. She banked gracefully, turning toward the smoke on the horizon. Swiftly the others followed.

Wind screamed past them, tearing at their hair, their clothing. It was deliciously cool so high up.

Not so below, though.

In the village below, one of the huts was on fire, its thatched roof flaring, flinging sparks into the air. A bare circle of ground formed a common area, where villagers and blue-skinned barbarians fought. Even so high up, Crysania heard the terrible song of steel on steel, the screams of the dying, the groans of the wounded, for she heard all that in her heart.

Tandar roared, the sound fierce and warlike. Firegold answered, trumpeting.

Crysania leaned over the dragon's neck. *Tandar! What do you see?*

Linda P. Baker & Nancy Varian Berberick

He showed her, and her stomach turned. Mixed among the blue-skinned attackers were creatures from nightmare, terrible things that were part human, part dragon.

Firegold cried, disgusted. "Draconians!"

The Dark Queen's creatures! Twisted beings created from evil magic and born of the stolen eggs of dragons. They were the terror unleashed during the War of the Lance. Thirty years later, they were not the force they once were, but even a band of them could savage an unsuspecting village or town.

They've come out from Neraka, lady. As we've guessed.

On their left, Goldstrike banked hard, coming in low over the fighting. Villagers and attackers alike fled as the huge dragon dropped down from the sky. Tandar roared again. Jeril's battle cry tore the air. Chase, with Lagan hanging on tight, followed, the rest of the watch spreading out around them. Only Firegold held back.

"Take me down!" Crysania cried. "Take me down, Firegold!"

The gold obeyed, but in her own time, circling the village once and again as the attackers scattered. They were a good-sized unit, but the way they broke up, running for the plains, leaving some of their kind to fight alone, made Crysania think they had no leader.

Firegold took the second turn, then landed in the center of the village beside Goldstrike. Goldstrike stayed only long enough for Kela to get to ground, then leapt to the sky again, joining the others. Crysania looked up through Tandar's eyes and found Chase, with Lagan still firmly in his seat. Sunlight glinted off the edge of his war axe. Whatever fear he'd felt being on dragonback burned away in the fires of anger as he looked below and saw the devastation.

Together Chase and Goldstrike raced to join the other dragons in pursuit of the enemy across the plains.

Upon the ground, tears sprang to Crysania's eyes. All around her rose the groans of the wounded, the sobs of the terrified. The silence of the dead. Tandar pressed close, warm and heavy against her legs, putting his head under her hand. She hardly felt him.

She prayed, the words coming all in an instant, and even as she did, she wondered whether the god would hear this time, or whether he was too far away, too tangled in his own battles.

* * * * *

A woman lay dead upon the ground near a burned hut, in her arms a wailing infant. A nearly grown boy, covered in blood, staggered among the ruins of his home, trembling, eyes wide, seeing horrors. From behind the well on the common, a howling cry lifted, then fell suddenly silent as a painted barbarian died of his wounds.

Tandar left his lady's side, prowling a tight circle around her, tail switching, ears back, growling. The screaming and the stink of blood and smoke ran like knives along his nerves, pulling him one way and another.

Go and fight! Stay and protect!

Villagers tried desperately to pull down the burning huts before they could set fire to others, to the plains and all the tinder-dry grass waving in the hot winds. An old man lay dead in the dirt, his blood soaking into the thirsty ground. A woman fought a scaled, fanged draconian, meeting the creature's sword with a pitchfork. She fell under a barbarian's axe, killed from behind.

Tandar roared, but he kept his place.

Crysania put her hand on his shoulder. The connection between them, that deep bond of the mind, flickered and vanished. Too much else roiled his senses now.

"It's all right," she said, stroking his head. "Take me to the wounded."

Her voice and the cool determination of her thoughts steadied him. He hesitated. They were nearly all wounded. The man lying only a few feet away was probably already gone. Another man sprawled just on the other side of him. Beyond lay a woman, a sword cut in the belly pulsing thick, red blood.

Tandar, take me to help them.

Her thought touched him like peace, with sweet understanding. He jerked into motion and led her across the road to the bleeding woman. The man beside her moved with enough life left in him to moan. The woman lay too still. Whispering prayers, her voice thin and trembling, Crysania knelt beside her. She put out her hands, feeling blindly across the still body until she found the deep wound, the wellspring of blood. She lay one hand on the wound and gripped her medallion with the other.

The purest light surrounded her, the light of hope, prayer light.

"Paladine, grant this woman your healing strength—"

A roar of anger drowned her prayer. A draconian came at her in a rush of cursing. Winged, it leaped and glided on the smoky air. Laughing, shouting obscenities, the creature swooped low, bellowing, "This one is mine!"

Tandar tensed to attack, but Firegold beat him to it. One blow of a powerful wing, and the dragon swiped the draconian from the air. It flew backward, hit the ground with a crunch, and did not move. Tandar growled. A villager came out from behind a hut, running for the body.

With the same wing she'd used to strike the creature from the sky, Firegold held the human back. None too gently, his voice tinged with disgust, the dragon said, "Don't go near it. The bodies are treacherous, even in death."

Tandar snarled, watching the body melt and smoke, oozing noxious liquid to burn the grass with a hiss and acrid stench.

Crysania coughed, her throat burning. The prayer light surrounding her dimmed, but she kept her thoughts focused, touching the place where a sword had pierced the woman's side. The woman sighed and stirred. The flow of her blood slowed, then stopped.

Crysania touched the woman's forehead briefly, then was up, reaching for Tandar to guide her to the next person.

Kela is near.

She stopped, then turned to the sound of the mage's footsteps. "Kela, find the worst of the wounded. Have them brought to me if they can be moved, or mark them if they cannot."

Unhesitating, Kela ran to obey.

Fire crackled, then roared. Smoke belched up into the sky as some nearby village men dragged a hut's burning thatch to the bare ground. The walls fell inward, collapsing to the ground, sending up sparks to fly, hungry, to the next thatched roof. Wind off the plains fanned the fire. Flames leapt up from the thatch.

Choking on smoke, Crysania bent to lay her hands on another man. He moaned as she prayed, reaching up to grasp her hand, trying to touch the soft light surrounded her, the gentle prayer light. He tried to add his racked and torn voice to hers in a plea to the god for his life.

Tandar wheeled, trying to keep Crysania in his sight and to make sure no enemy approached. The scent of fire clawed along his nerves. Sparks, like tiny, glinting daemons, leapt from the burning hut, riding the wind outward.

Lady! More wounded come!

He tried to lend her sight. He hadn't the strength.

"I hear," she said aloud.

They came staggering, some clinging to Kela's hands, the rest leaning on each other, on sticks, on hoes and tools. Mothers carried their babes. The sobbing rose like a haunting. They came to the light. They came to the Revered Daughter as though called.

How not? That prayer light surrounded her, a beacon of purity and hope in this terrible place of grief. They came to her, starving for her aid, for the strength they must feel pouring out from her with the light.

One side of the burning hut collapsed outward. The villagers ran to it, stamping the licking flames and beating the burning grass.

Tandar! Where are Jeril and Lagan? Do you see them?

He looked upward, unable to share his sight. He could not see very far into the sky. *They will be well, lady. The dragons won't let them come to harm.*

Crysania added the names of her friends to the litany of her prayers. Across the way, the roof of another hut collapsed. The man inside it disappeared, screaming. Dust and sparks shot skyward.

Kela, a sobbing child in one hand, a wailing infant in her arm, stared, helpless, horrified. Tandar wheeled frantically, looking for help, someone to go to the man's aid. In his mind, Crysania said, *Go! No one will harm me while Firegold stands guard!*

The tiger ran. The smoke was worse near the hut. It filled his lungs, thick and gray, and coated his eyes. He leapt through a hole in the flaming wall. Smoke blinded him; fire singed his skin. He roared in rage, in fear. Outside, someone sobbed, a child cried out, "Da! Save our Da!"

Tandar found the man crumpled near a burning wall. He grabbed a mouthful of tunic and backed away, dragging him. His muscles bunched, knotted. He pulled until he came up against something hard and unyielding. The wall. In the smoke, he'd lost his sense of direction. Pain ran searing along his leg up to his hip.

Fire!

He roared in agony. He grabbed the man once more, backed away again, toward where the smoke was light gray instead of dark. Hoping he'd found the break in the wall, he pulled, he dragged, growling around the mouthful of tunic. The muscles in his shoulders and legs screamed for oxygen and got none. Then bright light stung his eyes. Suddenly air swirled into his lungs, and he fell to his knees, wracked with coughing.

Someone took the burden from beneath his chin. Someone else nudged him farther back, away from the hut. In the clearer air, he smelled his own burnt flesh, the stench of burnt fur.

Then he smelled Crysania, dusty and covered in sweat, in the blood of others, yet inexplicably still retaining the faint scent of the temple. Incense, flowers, herbs, the cool, crisp scent of linen.

Tandar shook off the hands that were trying to help him. Snarling in pain, he dragged himself to his lady. His own breath wheezed in and out. Crysania touched him. He groaned.

Something seeped into him, into his heart, his bones, into his very soul. Tiger soul, man soul. It wasn't really warmth. It was tingling, a coolness, a healing, an energy flowing inward, flowering into health.

The pain clawing at his lungs eased. His eyes cleared.

The man he'd dragged from the flames lay still beside him. Tandar backed way from Crysania's hand.

Go to him. She hesitated. Again he roared into her mind, *I pulled him out of fire! Heal him!*

Crysania tightened her grip on the tiger, held him for a moment with her head against his shoulder. She felt his

213

exhaustion, his sorrow. He felt her tears on him, wet and warm.

"I couldn't." she said softly. "I'm sorry. He's dead."

Tandar groaned.

She turned, reaching for the next wounded person. Tandar moved slowly to her side. He couldn't hear her thoughts anymore. He was too tired for that. All around them the village continued to burn.

In the sky, the full watch of dragons circled overhead, one gold and a phalanx of silvers. Firegold trumpeted; the watch bugled back.

Victory!

And a child died, choking, while his mother wailed out her grief.

Chapter Sixteen

The villagers, in thanks, gave them food and water. They gave them a place to sleep in whatever huts remained whole. In a small hut near the center of the village, beside the stone well where water bubbled up from far below, Crysania slept. Lagan did without, his back propped up against the hut, watching. Kela and Jeril had a hut to themselves. Crysania had insisted, saying that they might well want the comforts of husband and wife this night. No one imagined they would do more than lie exhausted in each other's arms.

Tandar prowled the edges of the village, listening to the night, the ravens on the plain, the wind racing. He looked often to the sky, to where the watch of dragons had disappeared into the distance. Not even Firegold remained. Something had called them, the great gold had said that much, promising to return. Now, in the west, the sky hung dark and sullen. The stars seemed dulled, though no bank of clouds ran before the hot wind. In the north, as though the sun were rising where no dawn should be, the horizon gleamed. Not rosy, but orange.

Tandar growled. Something burned, something big, something wide. Everyone had seen it.

Beneath his feet, the ground seemed to rumble. Not as with an earthquake, not as with a storm. It rumbled, he imagined, to the sound of a thousand war machines on the roads, with horses, with the hordes of the Dark Queen marching to war.

The red moon rose. The silver was but a narrow paring in the sky. In Tandar's mind, a call sounded, soft, dangerous, insistent. It was the call of magic, the voice of the spell laid upon him so many long days ago. He made one more pass around the village. Lagan Innis sat awake outside Crysania's hut, his war axe across his knee. He scraped rhythmically with a whetstone borrowed from Jeril.

The tiger padded softly away, out into the high grass beyond the village. Groaning with weariness, he lay down, concealed. Water trickled somewhere not far off. A thin stream, by the sound of it. He closed his eyes and sank deep into his mind, letting the trance overtake him. When all the sounds of the night were gone from his notice, when even the rustle of grass against his own pelt went unfelt, he found himself once again upon the twilight plain of magic.

Dalamar!

Silence answered. The sky shimmered purple. Here stars seemed brighter, sharper. Nothing moved on the gray flat plain, not even light from the sky.

Dalamar!

Small, thin, a shape grew up from the ground, grew out from the sky itself.

I am here.

He was hooded, dark, his face barely seen, his eyes only small glints. He seemed to have less substance than the last time Tandar had called to him.

My lord, I have come as you require.

You stink of blood. You're liking this new shape of yours, aren't you? The power, the speed, the hunter-lust.

It was so, and Tandar didn't deny it. Sometimes he forgot to think of himself as Valin, and once, dreaming, he had seen himself not as a man but as this white tiger. He raised his head, sniffing along this strange plane as he would in the waking world.

Smoke. Terror. Fire. Blood. Sweat.

My lord, he said, his voice twisting wryly. *You, too, stink of war. How are you liking that?*

The image of the dark elf shivered. It might have been with laughter. *Never mind me. Tell me what has happened to make you reek like this.*

Tandar did. In spare images, he sent the mage mental pictures of what had taken place, the battle, the dying, the fires all around. *And there is something else . . . something in the sky. The horizon looks strange, there in the north.*

The dark elf came closer, walking along the twilight plain. His form grew more substantial, deeper somehow, stronger. Then it flickered, like a candle in the wind, bending a little this way and that.

Dalamar!

I am here. Can you feel it, sir mage? Can you feel . . .

His voice faded, the shape of him shrank as though— unthinkable!—as though Dalamar the Dark, the Master of the Tower of High Sorcery, could not hold the simple spell of mind-reach.

And then he was gone, the twilight plain empty.

Dalamar!

Nothing answered but the wind on the plains, the

rustle of grass, a raven laughing high up and far away.

Tandar woke, shuddered. He rose, shaking himself, and looked to the north. It seemed the sky was on fire out there, far away. Cold fear washed over him. What could it mean? What lay out there, so vast and wide, that the burning of it would light up the sky?

* * * * *

Crysania woke at the first gray light, feeling as though she had not slept at all. She groped around for Tandar, but she didn't find him. She tried to remember whether she'd felt him near in the night, the heaviness of his body near hers, the sound of his animal breathing. She had not.

Tandar?

Near, Lady.

Have you spoken again with Dalamar?

I have, but not for long this time. His magic is working no better than anyone else's.

She nodded, a weary gesture. *I take no comfort in that.*

Take comfort in me, Lady. He moved closer, coming out of the shadows at the back of the hut. He lay down beside her, the length of him heavy against her body, his heart beating strongly against her. It was comfort, and she took it.

The wind shifted, bringing the sudden scent of roasting meat. Her stomach convulsed, growing with hunger. She rose to her feet, feeling her way with her hand on the wall. Her skin was sticky with sweat and grime; her clothing reeked of blood and smoke. She sighed, longing for the cool feel of linen sliding along her skin, the first splash of water from her washbasin.

Tandar, are the dragons back?

No, lady. We watch for them.

And the sky?

It burns.

Outside, she heard Lagan and Jeril speaking, their voices low and quiet. The song of the whetstone had long since ceased, yet it seemed to Crysania that she heard it still, scraping in her mind. She reached for her pack and felt through it for her comb. She untangled her long hair as best she could, with fingers and the teeth of the polished wooden comb. That done, she caught her hair back in a wooden clasp and brushed at her robe. Who would know her, what citizen of Palanthas used to seeing the Revered Daughter in her impeccably brushed robes, with her hair arranged perfectly, her hands still and white and calm?.

She ran her thumb along the broken nails of her left hand. No doubt, she thought, I stand in real need of a washing behind my ears, too.

Soft came a footstep at the door. The scent of a mage drifted into her hut, rose petals and spices and secret oils.

"Good morning, Kela."

"Lady, I've come to see if you need anything."

Crysania managed a grim laugh. "I need *everything*, but I will do with what I have. Is there water?"

Kela took the lady's hand and put it in the crook of her arm. "There is water, and the villagers have found some food out on the plain. They're roasting a springbuck. Come eat."

With Kela guiding, she went out the door. Lagan stood near, and he greeted her quietly.

"Did you sleep well, lady?"

Wind sighed in the grass, moaned down the sky. Somewhere nearby a child sobbed, a mother murmured soothing words that did not soothe.

Into Crysania's silence, the dwarf said, "Neither did I."

Kela stepped aside, leaving the two clerics in private.

After a moment, Lagan said, "It's not like I've ever imagined, lady, this business of war. You know . . ." He

219

stopped, then forced himself on. "I have done a fair amount of translating in my day. Prayers, and before that, before the temple, some of the finest battle poetry a man can find. The songs of the Solamnics, the hymns to glory, their heart-wrenching hero songs. I've translated the chronicles of the minotaurs, even a fragment of one of the ancient texts of Istar that tell of their wars and their triumphs. . . ."

"And none of it looks like this, does it, Lagan?"

"No," he said, a man just discovering the difference between reality and the dreams of heroes. "No, none of it looks like this. Ah, Lady, but I am with you every step of this journey. You know that."

"I do," she said gently. "And you are thinking no one wants to get home from this quest more than you do."

He made a small sound of agreement.

She sighed. "Lagan, my friend, I think you're wrong about that. Someone else wants to get home at least as much as you do."

The good rich smell of roasting meat drifted between them. Fat sizzled, hissing into a fire. People spoke, voices low and weary.

"Who wants that more than I?" Lagan said.

"I do, my friend. Now"—she put her hand on his shoulder, asking him to guide— "let's go eat. Perhaps we'll feel better if our bellies are full."

The food was warm and good, the water cool from the deep well. They found shade beneath thatched roofs, and no better meal had they taken since leaving Palanthas. Tandar came to sit near them, his breath smelling of the blood of his own meal. And, gods be thanked, it wasn't until the end of their breakfast that the dragons returned.

"Come, lady," Jeril said, "Firegold awaits you on the plain."

Crysania accepted his arm and let him take her to the dragon, Tandar padding behind, Lagan, not so eager, following.

"Lady," Firegold said, her voice like thunder. "I have come to tell you that we dragons must be gone from here now, and in haste."

Crysania's heart sank. "But I thought you'd come to take us to the mountains."

"We cannot, Revered Daughter."

Silence fell all around her. She barely heard the breathing of her people and the hissing of the wind.

"Forgive me, lady. There is no longer time. We must go to the aid of the knights at the tower. The forces of Chaos will attack there soon. And—some of your people will have seen it—the Turbidus Ocean is on fire."

Crysania jerked her head up, looking north with her sightless eyes.

Firegold lifted her wings, gently stretching. Dust whirled up from the ground. "We have just learned. Fire springs from a vast rip in the ocean, out of which pour horrific creatures, born of Chaos. Fire dragons and shadow creatures, all of them created of fire and magic. Wights and daemon warriors." The dragon shook her head, the sound like thunder. "As I speak, Chaos's forces ride to assault the Tower of the High Clerist. Already they battle the dwarves in Thorbardin. Dalamar and other members of the conclave go to determine whether there is any way to fight these magical creatures."

"And you," she said, "you must go to fight these same creatures at the High Clerist's Tower."

"Yes, lady. We must."

And, she thought, if we hadn't stopped here, we would be well on our way, riding in the mountains. . . .

She closed her fingers round the medallion of Paladine, the silver-wrought dragon. This will have to be the only dragon we have, she thought, but it will be enough.

Even as she thought this, a tremor of doubt rippled through her. She had not dreamed of the god in several nights, and now this news of Chaos. All the more reason, she told herself, all the more reason to go on. And quickly.

"A dangerous journey, Firegold. I pray Paladine's blessings go with you."

She felt the air stir as the dragon bowed. "Thank you, my lady. On the way back, we saw your horses. They aren't far. Send your people to find them and you can travel as you were."

Beside her, Jeril muttered something to Lagan, who made a sound of assent. "We'll go, lady," the warrior said, "and we'll have them back in good time."

"Paladine be with you, Revered Daughter," the dragon said.

"As he will be with you, Firegold."

The dragon backed away before leaping skyward. Dust and grass blew about their faces as the other dragons followed her.

Crysania stood a long time silent, the wind blowing around her. Tandar stood nearby, and Kela, but it seemed to the Revered Daughter that she had never been so alone.

* * * * *

The plain smelled of dusk, of day's end and twilight coming, when Lagan and Jeril came back with the horses. The morning would see the return of their journey, their trek to the mountains and the stronghold of the Dark Queen. The companions went silently to their beds, no one wanting to think about what lay ahead. Tomorrow would be time enough for that.

Tandar patrolled the edge of the village, sniffing at the night air. Their silent watch, their faithful ward.

Crysania lay between waking and sleeping, listening to the tiger walking, thinking of all that had happened. To the east and west and south, the sky was dark. But to the north, it bled. Tandar had shown it to her reluctantly, a glow that seemed to be burning on the mountaintops. She tried to imagine the sea burning. Water boiling and hissing away to steam. She tried to imagine dragons of fire and could not.

In the darkness, half in dream, Crysania felt something move. Something touched her, sliding against the edge of her robe on the bedroll. The touch burned like fire, like one of the creatures Firegold had said was spilling from a wound in the earth. It was touching along her legs, feeling for something. Its fingers crawled on her skin, burning her through her robe.

She cried out, "No! Get away!" and her cry made no sound. She thrashed, trying to get away from the thing that reached with fiery fingers. The movement woke her, and at last a frightened cry erupted from her throat.

Questions filled the darkness outside the hut, Kela's voice, Lagan's, Jeril's.

Kela spoke a word of magic, and Crysania felt heat flare up in the small hut.

"What is it?" Jeril demanded. "Lady! Are you all right?"

Crysania sat up slowly, her fingers twisted in her bedding.

"Lady? What's wrong?" Lagan asked. He dropped to his knee beside her. She smelled the tang of his war axe.

Crysania reached out, found Tandar beside him. Her voice rough and ragged with fear, she said, "Someone was here. Something was—I thought someone was touching me while I slept."

Tandar growled, but Kela said gently, "No, lady. I stood watch outside your door. No one came in. No one

223

was here." She touched Crysania's shoulder. "I don't know why we're all not having nightmares these days."

Crysania nodded slowly, but she shivered as her skin remembered something moving inside the folds of her robe, searching for the pocket in which she kept the Dragon Stones. She sniffed the air, trying to tell whether someone had come into the hut. Had she imagined it?

"Lady?" Lagan said, uneasy.

"I'm all right. Kela is right. I was dreaming."

But she hadn't been. She knew that though there was no way to explain it to the others. There was no scent of a stranger in her hut.

Her skin crawled, her heart ached.

The person who had been touching her was in the hut this moment, and that person was one of her own people.

Chapter Seventeen

Crysania rode in silence behind Lagan, listless and with barely enough strength to cling to him. From time to time, he turned to remind her. "Hold on, lady. Don't fall asleep. Hold on."

She tried, with the sun beating down on her, the gritty wind clawing at her face and eyes. She tried to hold on, to keep her grip so Lagan didn't have to fret about her. And then her arms would weaken, her hands come unclasped. Nodding, her head would fall forward, a moment of blessed sleep before Lagan turned to whisper, "Hold on, lady. Don't fall asleep."

"It's hard," she confessed, forcing herself awake. "The sun . . ."

Always the sun, burning down, beating upon them. Like a hammer beating iron stock, so the saying had gone in Palanthas. She had thought the land dead before, when Tandar had been able to afford her glimpses of the world around him. Then they'd been near the mountains, near the brown, muddy river. This greater devastation she sensed without his help. The air smelled dry. Nothing more. It carried in it no hint of life, no scent of green. Beneath the horse's hooves, sometimes not even dead grass crunched. Sometimes there was only earth, cracked and hard.

They seldom found water anymore. When Tandar scented a stream, they headed for it. When the horses did, they trusted the beasts. Never was there enough to fill all their water bottles and still accommodate Tandar and the horses. After the horses had drunk, after Tandar had lapped, often what remained was enough for one water-skin only. This they shared, passing the skin around so that each might take a scant mouthful. For food, they had what Tandar hunted, small rodents, once a large fowl of some kind. On this they lived, but not well.

The sun, the wind, the heat—they were a relentless enemy from which no escape could be possible. Not even at night did they find relief. Despite her coverings, Crysania's skin was burnt to blisters, stinging at the mere touch of her gown, at the slightest breath of air. She knew the others were in as much pain as she. Who could sleep when the smallest motion burned, when all the body ached for the touch of cool water? Not she. She lay quietly on her blanket, still and staring blindly up, trying to imagine stars, sometimes thinking that the hiss of night wind in the grass was the first sigh of rain come at last to heal them.

When the rain didn't come, when no blessing swept down out of the blackness, Crysania's throat would clench tight with pain and the longing to weep. However, she had no tears. The sun had burned them all away.

One night, aching with that unshed burden, she'd felt Tandar move close to her, pressing against her back.

Tandar, who are you?

She felt his amusement, a glitter of laughter across her mind. *Don't you mean, 'What are you,' lady? I am a tiger. I am your tiger.*

But she told him, no, she didn't mean "what are you." *I mean what I ask. Who are you?*

The glitter faded. The tiger lay still, his heart beating. *I cannot say, lady.*

She smiled, softly, without rancor. *You choose your words carefully, Tandar*

As should we all.

Across the fire, burning each night for cheer, for light against the darkness, for the sake of the sighted, Lagan snored gently. Jeril and Kela, asleep on their shared blanket, breathed in unconscious rhythm.

They are so lucky, Crysania thought, the feeling surprising her.

Soft, testing, Tandar's voice in her mind: *Because they have each other?*

She lay still, feeling the beat of his heart, the rise and fall of his breathing. She would ignore that question. It was intrusive. Almost she thought it was impertinent. It didn't deserve an answer.

Yes, because they have each other.

And you, lady. Have you no one, waiting in Palanthas for you to return?

All of Palanthas, it might be said, awaits the return of the Revered Daughter.

He was a long moment silent, his thoughts only smoky feelings of longing, the kind she'd never felt from him till now. Who was he?

I have a friend, she said to him in thought. *A man of the desert. A mage. He is gone, though, and I don't know how he fares. This war . . .* She stopped and chose honesty. *I sent him away.*

Because he displeased you.

No. Because . . . because . . . She sighed wearily. *I don't even remember why anymore.*

But she did remember. Of course she did. She wouldn't have said so that day in the temple garden, but she knew now: She'd sent Valin away because he'd come too close. And maybe she'd sent him to his death, her devoted friend who would go anywhere, even to his death, if she required it.

Ah, gods! If she could ask for one boon this night and receive it, it would be the ability to weep.

The tiger sighed deeply, and soon Crysania felt him sleeping. She was left alone in the night and the eternal dark, wondering how Valin fared, wondering whether he still thought of her, or whether he had seen the impossibility of what he wanted from her. Wind hissed in the grass, not sounding like rain now, but sounding like fire.

"Valin," she whispered, her throat closing up again with tears she could not shed. "I hope you are well, friend mage. I miss you."

The tiger moved a little away, and soon after Crysania did sleep and, sleeping, she dreamed of Valin. She heard his voice; the scent of him filled the dream. She felt his hands as though she were holding them, and they felt the same as on the day he'd offered her his love, warm and trusting.

"Is it true?" he said in the dream, who'd never spoke those words in the waking world. "Is it true that you, lady, whose love for all those who need you is boundless, have not enough for one more?"

In the dream, blessedly, she was able to weep. In the dream, she did. But when she woke in the morning, her cheeks were dry, her tears unshed. Beside her, the tiger slept, his heart keeping beat with her own. She slipped her hand into her pocket, closed her fingers round the Dragon Stones.

For these I am here, she told herself, for the power they will give, for the chance to speak once again with Paladine. And it *will* be he with whom I speak.

She said so to herself, in perfect faith, she who had given up much for that faith. What else to do but trust her god?

After they broke their fast on tough, dry rodent, they resumed their journey northeast toward the city of the Dark Queen. It was then Crysania began to gather her strength, her courage, for the thing she must do before entering Neraka.

* * * * *

Jeril dropped back to ride beside Lagan and Crysania, letting Tandar range ahead, letting Kela guard from the rear. Crysania, head nodding in the noon heat, let the sound of quiet conversation wash over her, Jeril's voice low and gruff, Lagan's weary. She had come to love those voices, to know them as though they were the voice of her own heart.

"You make a fine fighter," Jeril said.

Lagan snorted. "For a cleric. For a poet."

"Well, yes, for a cleric. Among my people, though, the poet who can't use his sword as well as his pen isn't accorded much respect." He chuckled. "You, my friend, would not go unrespected in my father's tents. My brother," he said, "has chosen his friends well."

"Paladine be with him," Lagan said, the words heartfelt.

It seemed to Crysania that words such as those had come too easily to their lips in the past, easy blessings, convenient prayers, spoken almost without thought. Who among them now didn't feel the words of each prayer offered? Who among them, out in this burning land, didn't crave the god's blessing, for himself, for his kin and friends?

She reached for her medallion. It sat cold in her hands.

"So, cleric-warrior," Jeril said, laughing. "What will we do with you after all this journeying is done?"

"No one need worry about that." Crysania, her arms around him, felt Lagan's quiet laughter. "Comes the end of this journey, comes the end of my fighting days. I want nothing more than to return to the Temple of Paladine and bury my nose in old books and parchments again."

"And make your translations of antique prayers and even older hero stories?"

Crysania heard Lagan's sigh. "Yes," he said, "that's just what I want to do. And I want the easy rounds of ritual and prayer, the sound of the chants rising up all around me, the smell of the incense—"

Suddenly startled, the horse snorted, shying from Jeril's mount. Lagan got the gray in hand and turned, saying, "It's Tandar, Lady. Come running back."

There was a flurry of hooves, and Kela's mount surged past. The mage flung a word to the others and urged her horse to speed.

"She's gone to follow Tandar," Lagan said. "He's found something."

The mage's voice came back to them, sudden and clear and joyous. "Mountains! We've come to the mountains, lady! And water! There is water!"

"All the gods be praised," Lagan sighed. "Come, hang on tight, lady."

* * * * *

At last she could breathe! Crysania pulled in lungfuls of air that had no gritty dust mixed with them. Hot it was, but clean and almost smelling of the trees that grew here. Perhaps those trees did not thrive, but they did survive. The trickling sound of running water brought an ache of joy to her heart. The horses gulped, Tandar lapped, and the waterskins made the most wonderful sound, gurgling as they filled. The water tasted like stone, like earth, sweet and clean. Crysania drank until Jeril had to warn her to stop.

"There is plenty, lady, but you'll make yourself sick if you don't drink slowly, and not so much."

Crysania forced herself to do as Jeril warned. She drank, listening to the world around her. She heard a bird call, another answer. They might have been wrens, for their songs were a lovely liquid complexity of notes seldom heard from other birds. She heard rustling in the brush, and that certainly was supper.

"The sky," she asked Jeril. "Does it still burn?"

It did, far away to the north where the sea itself burned.

"We must go on," she said. She reached into her pocket and cradled the Dragon Stones in her palm. She expected to feel the power of them weakened, as so much of magic had become. They felt as strong in her hand as on the first day Dalamar had presented them to her.

For that, she thought, the gods be thanked. From these stones, she would find the strength to do what soon she must do, the needful thing before entering Neraka. She listened to her friends, their beloved voices, as they spoke one to another.

I will have the strength, she told herself, to do it. They will understand. . . .

They went on, the land climbing, the air cooling slightly. Tandar hunted and brought them hares and once a grouse. It was not the season for nuts, but to their meal of meat and water, they added dandelion greens and

231

nettle leaves, found growing bravely in the cooler air of the mountains. Better fed, their spirits lifted, and it seemed that all would be well.

At noon of the third morning since gaining the foothills of the mountains, Crysania felt the presence of Neraka. Nor was she the only one to sense it. Lagan, uneasy before her, said he felt as though everything were dark and bruised.

"The air, the ground, the sky itself. It all feels like pain."

It did, for now they approached the precincts of the Dark Queen, of Takhisis herself. The wind sounded like her voice, rasping, grasping, filled with evil. Crysania shuddered. None here but she had ever heard that voice. Thirty years before, it had raked her, shrieked at her, laughed at her, mocking her every hope, torturing her every prayer.

Did she ride to hear that voice again? Would Takhisis greet her once the Dragon Stones were reunited?

Paladine! She reached for her medallion. It sat still in her hands, as though it were nothing more than a beautifully wrought decoration.

She rode with one arm around Lagan, one free so she might hold the medallion, feel something of its warmth and strength should . . . should its power ever return. In that way, they came to Neraka, riding out of the hills to the edge of a deep, shadowed valley where the city of the Dark Queen lay before them.

Unlike Palanthas, or even rough Sanction to the south, Neraka was not an old city. In truth, it could be only rightly called a sprawling village, a collection of tents and rude huts and crooked buildings around a gaping wound that had been—that still was, despite its ruin—the Temple of the Dark Queen. All around that temple rose the Khalkist Mountains.

A whisper insinuating itself into her thoughts, the memory of Dalamar's words: "It is told that almost one thousand years later, the dwarves found the magical Dragon Stones the elves had cast deep within the mountains, and shunning magic as they do, gave the stones to a red dragon, who in turn ordered that the stones be hurled into the caldron of Darklady. Darklady then erupted, forming the Lords of Doom, the ring of volcanoes that surround Neraka. It is said the explosion of color from the stones became the eyes of Takhisis's constellation."

So, Crysania thought, weary and sweating, staring blindly down at Neraka, we have come almost to the end of our journey.

Lagan shifted and turned, speaking to Crysania. "It's not so old, the city, is it?"

"Not so old as some might think."

Its origins lay in the time of the Cataclysm, when the gods destroyed the Kingpriest who would have raised himself up in their image. After the Cataclysm, when the gods took all the true priests away, faith had left the land for a time. It had taken the Dark Queen to set about the turn of events that brought the return of faith in the gods. Takhisis had taken up the foundation stone of the Kingpriest's temple from Istar, the city of the Kingpriest, and set it down on the plateau that spread out before them. Her temple had grown out of it . . . and her evil.

"Full of evil, though," the dwarf said, shuddering. "I feel it like a shadow on me, lady."

Beside them, Jeril's horse shuffled. Behind, Kela's mount snorted and danced. Even the beasts felt the dark touch.

Crysania pressed her hand to her medallion but felt no warmth or comfort. Still, she prayed. What else to do? Paladine would hear, she trusted he would. He had never turned from her, not in the waking world.

Around her, her friends kept quiet, some praying their own silent prayers, others simply lost in their own thoughts. Only Tandar moved, pacing.

Crysania said softly, "Dear ones, from here I go on alone."

Her words trailed silence in their wake, deep and stunned. Then Jeril cried, "No!" and Lagan said, "Lady, you can't mean it."

She meant it, however, though it took all her might to hold on to her resolve. These friends had come so far with her, lending her strength and courage, their faith like a balm. Now she must leave them.

"From here on," Crysania repeated, her voice quiet, "Tandar and I go on alone."

"Lady . . ." Lagan stopped, still too surprised to find words.

Crysania laid her fingers on Tandar's head, seeking reassurance, seeking support. She found it in the soft vibration of his breath.

"This is my quest, Lagan. You've risked too much already. All of you." She shuddered, feeling the darkness of Neraka like a maw opening before her. "I won't—I can't ask you to go into that place."

"Your quest?" The dwarf had found words now, and they came fast and strong. "You talk as if we didn't all undertake this journey. As if we haven't all risked ourselves already."

Crysania's heart ached under the burden of that truth. She who had no tears on the burning Plains of Solamnia had them now. They pricked at her eyes.

"I know you have, Lagan, and I thank you for it. But I must go on alone."

"No," Kela said, speaking for the first time. "Whether or not you like it, we stay with you."

Silence fell, the surprise of those who would never

234

have spoken thus to the Revered Daughter of Paladine.

Kela went on, undismayed. "We've come this far together. It's the only way to continue. Jeril," she said. "Jeril, tell her."

Jeril moved his horse to Crysania's side. "Lady, know this: We are not going back without you. And if you don't let us ride beside you, we will follow." With a sweet simplicity to remind her of his brother, he said, "We are sworn, lady. Should we now forswear ourselves and break our vows to Paladine?"

Tandar's thought touched hers, wordless urging she could not fail to understand.

Ah, but how could she take them with her? How dared she take them, these brave souls, these courageous hearts, into the city of the Dark Queen?

How did you dare take them this far?

How indeed?

"Very well," she said, helpless before them, undone by their love. "We go on together."

On down the steep hillside, the horses slipping on the scarp, on tumbling stones. On and down into the shadowy vale, leaving the light behind them. They rode until they came to a crossway. There Tandar moved close to Crysania.

Four roads, winding and uncertain, as though painted with a trembling hand, led into the village, joined at the center by the black Temple of the Dark Queen. It seemed to Crysania that the air trembled around that place, wavering between the twisted spires, the warped walls. So heavy, the burden of that evil!

Nothing moved on the road. Not a cart, not a rider, nor anyone on foot. Not even a raven sailed the sky.

"Ariakan's army came through here," Jeril said. "He would have recruited from the inhabitants. Maybe the city is unoccupied."

"No," Crysania murmured softly. "It is not empty. I feel it. There are people there, souls there. Each," she whispered, shivering, "each in evil's grasp, in torment."

Night came as they spoke, creeping down the hills, merging with the shadows until all lay dark and still. Blackness lay all about them, except for the angry red glow from the north, just visible over the mountaintops. The sea still burned.

They made an unlighted camp and ate what little they had from the morning meal. Though Tandar offered to hunt, no one was interested in eating the game he'd find in this evil place. In the darkness, Crysania listened to Lagan and Jeril and Kela discuss whether they should approach Neraka by day or by night. Either way, they were exposed, vulnerable, for a grassy plain surrounded the city. They would find no concealment. She let them talk, thinking it through, but when they seemed no closer to a choice, she made one for them.

"Night," she said, "is the best choice. Even in this foul place, it will offer us cover, however scant, as we ride. We will go now."

With no fire to put out, the small meal eaten, they mounted again in solemn silence and set out, downward into the Dark Queen's city.

* * * * *

All the while they rode out onto the Plains of Neraka, slowly making their way toward the city, they saw no movement. No light shone. No shadow glided across the darkness. The temple loomed above the walls of the city, darker than the starless sky. Crysania shivered, chilled to her bones by a coldness that seemed to be moving around them, coming closer. Her uneasiness communicated to the gray gelding, who danced sideways, ignoring Lagan's attempts to quiet and steady him.

"What is that cold, lady?" the dwarf asked. He shivered as she did.

"I—I don't know. It's—"

Evil, Tandar said, his voice low and dark in her mind.

It was evil, and it moved like a miasma on the wind. Even as Crysania realized that, the coldness surged toward her.

She cried out and let go her grip on Lagan just as the first touch of ice brushed up against her skin. Her heart came up in her throat as hands like bones and ice grasped her, lifting her into the air. It seemed as if ice was boring into her bones.

Jeril called her name. "Lady! Crysania!"

Tandar roared.

And Crysania fell, down and down.

Breath blasted from her lungs as she hit the ground.

Lagan shouted to her, to the panicked horse. Jeril cried, "Kela!" and the white tiger snarled his battle cry as Crysania gasped for breath, trying suck in air and finding nothing. Tandar hit her once, butting her in the back with his head. He hit her again, and air came back into her lungs.

Steel hissed against leather as Desert Light came out from its sheath. Crysania pushed herself up, shouldering past Tandar. She ignored the groan of her spine, the sharp pain in her left shoulder where she'd struck a rock.

"Something is here," she gasped. She felt it, cold creeping malice. "Something evil . . ."

Kela's shrill scream tore the air.

The others wheeled, surrounding Crysania, weapons outward. The icy nothingness came closer, again reaching for Crysania. The circle around her tightened, horses snorting and dancing, weapons still gleaming. Lagan cursed as one suddenly stung. He held his place, horse in grip, war axe firmly in hand. With Tandar's eyes, Crysania saw a white patch growing across the dwarf's neck, like the dead skin of frostbite spreading. Then her sight faded suddenly.

Crysania's heart thundered in her breast. What fell thing had touched him? Her breath came ragged and raw.

Horses danced all around her as riders struggled to make them hold their places despite the terror they felt.

Tandar! Let me see! Tandar!

Light burst upon her, the bright, colorless sight of the tiger.

"There!" Kela cried. She pointed into the darkness, barely managing to keep her seat as her horse danced and twisted. The beast was as frightened as she by the thing that stood in the darkness, that was part of the darkness.

Jeril whirled to where she was pointing. "I can't see anything!"

"There! Eyes. Red eyes!"

Through a forest of legs, Crysania saw two lights in the night. They were not red, as Jeril had said, but dead white and glaring, for she saw through Tandar's eyes, she saw what the tiger saw. Then the lights vanished, and she saw only darkness and the city beyond, barely visible in the dim glow from the north.

"There!" This time Lagan saw it.

Crysania's blood ran cold to see the terrible, glaring white eyes that hovered above the ground. If they were a man's eyes, the thing would have been taller than Jeril. The others wheeled to see, but it was gone again, shifting, floating, flitting about them.

"What is it?" Jeril demanded. "Damn it! The thing's circling us! Kela—there!"

And then Tandar left her in darkness, roaring as he bolted from the circle. The eyes vanished.

"It's a daemon warrior," Crysania said, huddled and shivering. "Firegold spoke of them. She said they were cast up from the darkness of Chaos."

The creature came nearer, the cold of it flowing.

"Begone!" Kela cried. Gasping, she called out words of magic. A flare of light erupted from her fingertips. Crysania felt the heat of her spell, smelled the tang, like lightning's scent. The cold darkness danced backward from the flames, almost mockingly.

Jeril swore, rubbing at his eyes, blinded for a moment by the brightness. "Damn, woman, warn me when you're going to start throwing fire!"

Kela laughed, a high, nervous sound. "If I warn you, I warn the enemy. Keep yourself ready and you'll be all right."

Now the thing suddenly appeared in the space between Jeril and Lagan, rushing forward. Crysania felt the coldness, the blackness as deep as the Dark Queen's evil.

Sight vanished again, leaving Crysania disoriented and dizzy. Tandar roared.

The daemon rushed forward, a river of cold pouring in Lagan's direction. Crysania heard the dwarf shouting battle cries and prayers all at once. The axe's blade whistled through the air. Lagan cried in pain. Crysania heard the terrible sound of steel shattering. Tandar flung himself down upon her, pounding the breath from her lungs again, leaving her gasping as the shards of Lagan's blade whirled through the night, a hundred tiny blades.

Kela flung out another casting. The icy flow surged back. Crysania struggled to her feet, staggering blindly among the legs of terrified horses. Tandar wheeled, circling. Suddenly Crysania could see through the tiger's eyes once more. What little Crysania saw, she saw in a mad whirl of light and dark all tangled up, as though by the light of a guttering torch being whirled around someone's head. Her stomach churned. Dizzy, she groped for the white tiger and held on to him hard.

"It's trying to reach Crysania," Lagan roared. "Protect her!"

Crysania tried frantically to see the dark, cold thing, the glaring eyes, the blackness. The daemon surged toward Kela. Jeril and Lagan closed in to block its movement.

Kela cast a spell again, hurling balls of bright fire the size of a man's head, driving it back, but her horse had taken all it could bear. It bucked, reared, then bolted, with the mage clinging to its back. Darkness swallowed them both. Crysania heard a high-pitched cry, then only the sound of the horse as it galloped away.

"Kela!" Jeril cried after her, even as he shifted in place, trying to fill the gap. The daemon warrior came toward him, moving more deliberately this time. They were one less, and now they had no magic to defend them.

Jeril met the creature, war cries raging from him as wild laughter. Desert Light whirling above his head, he charged. His horse kicked and bucked; he struggled to maintain control and failed. The beast bolted before he got both feet from the stirrups, dragging the warrior behind it.

Tandar twisted and turned, keeping his body against Crysania's legs, trying to see from where the next rush would come.

She saw, in that wild, flickering way, Lagan on his feet, braced and defiant, nothing but the haft of his war axe in hand as the swirling darkness reached him. He screamed as the daemon touched him, howling as though he were on fire. Head back, he screamed, and—horrible!—the darkness reached out snaking tendrils, swirling into him, stabbing into his eyes and mouth.

Lagan staggered. The oaken haft of his war axe fell from his grip. Eyes wide in wordless agony, he clutched at his throat and fell to his knees. White as marble, white as snow, all the color leeched from his cheeks, from his hands, from all his flesh. Lagan Innis was dead before he hit the ground.

Crysania cried out in grief, in rage of a kind she'd never felt before. And inside her, in her mind, in her very heart, she heard grief's echo as Tandar roared. *No! Gods, no! Lagan!*

The wildly whirling sight was ripped away from her, leaving her in darkness, shuddering and weeping, unable to move. The pool of icy nothingness flowed all around her, reaching, seeking, touching.

The stones! Lady! The Dragon Stones!

Tandar's cry roared in her head. Crysania, on hands and knees, tried desperately to snatch the Dragon Stones from her pocket. Each time she moved, she fell, disoriented, sightless, and feeling the cold of the daemon warrior seeking her. Tandar was all over her, whipping around her body, trying to cover her from all sides.

The Dragon Stones!

Did he warn that the daemon was coming for the Dragon Stones? Did he cry out to protect this treasure they'd risked so much for?

Gasping, panting in the night that was at once burning hot and riddled by icy cold, Crysania commanded stillness from herself, ordered herself to breathe, to move with purpose and to trust Tandar to keep her safe. With one trembling hand, she took the two stones from her pocket. The one sat still, humming to itself, unaligned. The other greeted her as if she were an old and good friend, with warmth and love.

She lifted her fist, the stones in her grasp. All the warmth she'd ever felt in Paladine's goodness, all the comfort, all the strength—dear gods, all the courage!—poured into her and flowed out from her again, a power directed, wielded as a weapon.

No one knew what the Dragon Stones were meant to

do, and anyone who said he did was only guessing.

Crysania lifted her hand, and she lifted her heart, her will, her faith.

"Begone!" she cried. "Evil cannot touch me, for I have Paladine as my shield!"

A scream tore the night, an inhuman sound like glass exploding. Like fury and blood and razor-sharp wire scraping over her skin. Tandar roared in triumph, and the night changed. The inhuman coldness of the daemon warrior fell away, vanished on the air, as though it had never been.

Shaking, sobbing, Crysania fell to her knees, the stones still clutched in her fist.

Chapter Eighteen

Tandar moaned, a low, piteous sound.

He's hurt! Crysania thought. Dear gods, he's been hurt!

Softly the tiger's voice came into her mind. *Hurt to death, lady, and dying of grief.*

At the tiger's feet lay a small dark shape, like a bunch of rags piled up. Crysania's heart cringed at that pitiful shape.

Lagan.

She listened keenly and heard no snuffing nearby, no stamping. She no longer smelled the stable scent. The horses were gone, running free.

"Where are Jeril and Kela? Tandar, do you know?"

Tandar looked around in the night, showing her that neither the warrior nor the mage were there, not injured, not killed.

*Kela's horse ran off at the start of the fighting. Jeril . . . I
don't know where he is. I saw his horse bolt, too, and he tried to
jump free.* Tandar shuddered. *I don't know what happened to
him either.*

"Go and look," she said.

No. I won't leave you.

Crysania put her hand into her pocket, touching the
stones. "I think I'll be all right here, Tandar. I have the stones,
and they've served me once to drive off the darkness."

He protested, but in the end, he did as she commanded. In the doing, he took his sight from her, leaving
her once more in blindness.

Groping, Crysania reached out and touched the body
of the loyal, brave dwarf. "Oh, Lagan," she whispered,
her voice caught in wrenching sobs. "How far from home
we have come."

She put her hands on the haft of the shattered war axe,
the smooth, strong oak. She touched the dwarf's robe,
travel-stained, bloodstained. Under her hands, she felt
the small pack he'd carried, which held the few things
he'd brought from the temple, the most precious to him
the purple velvet pouch embroidered in silver dwarf
runes, marks that said, *Where light is, dark may not enter in.*
There was in that pouch, he had said, a paring from one
of the scales of the dragon that was Paladine's avatar.
There was in there, tucked away carefully, wrapped up in
cloth, a small book of prayers that he had translated from
ancient, crumbling texts.

*To the God of Light and Goodness, I commit my work, my
life, my self. . . .*

So said the first page of that little book.

A dry rustle of wings whispered near her. A click of
claws upon stone rattled. Crysania's heart jumped, then
settled uneasily. She recognized the stink of a carrion bird,
the growling caw of a raven.

"Go away," she sighed, heart-weary. "The daemon warrior has taken everything."

In a whir of wings, the raven left her, its cry like curses on the night. The hot wind blowing across the Plains of Neraka brought the distant sound of horses neighing.

Crysania swallowed hard against her sobbing. Her tears rained down. She reached and took Lagan's pack. With great care and trembling fingers, she undid the clasp and withdrew the velvet pouch. Did it indeed hold a relic of Paladine? She sighed, a shuddering sigh that wracked her whole body.

No, that was no holy dragon scale, or surely the daemon warrior would never have been able to come near enough to Lagan to kill him.

But there were, in that pouch, relics of Lagan, talismans to remind her of her good and faithful friend. Crysania took the Dragon Stones out from her pocket. She pressed one to her lips, and then the other, finding comfort in spite of sorrow.

Where light is, dark may not enter in.

"Lagan, my friend, come the rest of the way with us, in your spirit if not in your body."

She slipped the Dragon Stones into the pouch and cinched it shut. Then she tucked it into her pocket, the small weight comfortable against her hip. For a long time she knelt there, her heart spilling over with wordless prayers as the night deepened around her. She heard the wind among the trees, the ravens in the sky. She heard, once, Tandar's wild roar, and then she heard him coming back to her.

He had found nothing to tell him what had happened to their friends. No sign of Kela, none of Jeril.

"No track?" she asked.

None. No scent, no sign at all. It is as though they have vanished.

245

But they hadn't, of course. They couldn't have, unless by magical means. From that thought, Crysania took hope, imagining that Jeril and his wife had found each other after the fighting, that Kela had erased their tracks and all sign of them with a spell.

"And if that is so, Tandar, they will find us if they are able to, for they know where we are going."

Tandar growled low in his throat, and Crysania felt it at once that he was uneasy in that hope.

"You don't trust the mage, do you?"

He rumbled again, tail switching dangerously, but he gave her no words to confirm or deny her statement. Still, the feeling remained, as it had always been—unease, mistrust. And fear. Of these feelings, Crysania shared not even the smallest part.

We haven't much of the night left, lady. We should go on now if we are going.

Crysania put her hand on his shoulder. In trust, she went where he guided, down the hill into a dark and evil place.

* * * * *

Water sat in the dark bowl, roiling with the one image it had held since first the Turbidus Sea erupted in flames. Fire, raging, roaring, reaching high into the sky with such fury that its glow could be seen from out the window of the Tower of High Sorcery itself.

All around the room candles flickered and died. On the wall, the torch Dalamar had just lighted—with flint and steel, by all the gods of night!—was the only light to trust. No enspelled candle held its light in this night of flickering magic. By that light, smoky and flaring, he looked into the scrying bowl and saw the image of awakening Chaos.

He had hoped for more, for a glimpse of the white tiger and the Revered Daughter of Paladine. He had hoped, and his hopes had been disappointed. Only fire showed upon the scrying waters, and sometimes things of darkness that looked like daemons dancing.

His mind-reach spell connecting him to the white tiger had also failed. Only an hour before, he'd felt the beast nudging in his mind, insistent. Each time he tried to reach the mage, to walk onto the lightless plain where the two could meet and talk, he had been held back, shunted aside. Kept out. Dalamar ground his teeth. Like the enspelled candles, this bit of his magic was failing now.

And all around him, the world tore itself apart in fighting.

He heard a soft sigh behind him. Jenna put her hand on his shoulder. "Love," she said, "come to bed."

Outside the Tower of High Sorcery, Palanthas the Beautiful had fallen to the Dark Knights. Beyond the mountains, the Tower of the High Clerist was falling, breaking under the relentless attack of Chaos. And out upon the sea, a rift gaped wide, vomiting fire and creatures that seemed to be born of rage. What terrible game of the gods was afoot?

"Come," Jenna said, her voice gently insistent.

Dalamar laughed, a cold sound, never taking his eyes from the fire on the water. "With all the world falling down around your head, dear Jenna, can you think of nothing better to do?"

Her fingers caressed, light and warm along the nape of his neck.

"I do what I can do, Dalamar. What I can do now is lie in my bed. Alone, or with you."

He rose and turned his back on the bowl, where only fire showed. Let her do what she would, and he would do what he must.

When he told her of his plan, she didn't weep. She knew him, and so she believed in him. And Jenna wasn't one to weep easily, no matter that he said he had decided to go out onto the sea, out to the fire, and then to enter the rift from which the creatures of Chaos spilled.

Because he must know, he said. He must know what was the nature of these terrible creature of Chaos flung out into the world. Nothing seemed more important to him now, and certainly not the doom of the white-robed mage he'd changed into a tiger, nor the fate of the Revered Daughter of Paladine.

Not even the mystery of the Dragon Stones seemed worthy of his concern when all the world seemed set to tear itself apart under his feet and all magic leaked out from the gaps.

* * * * *

The night hung dark, with no moon to show Tandar the way into Neraka. Red Lunitari had yet to rise. Solinari was shining, but as the slenderest crescent, with no light to spare. Regardless, Tandar led his lady with confidence, surefooted on rough ground. His were a cat's eyes, made for moon-reft nights. And should his keen sight fail, he could still explore Neraka by the feel of the place.

Are you well, lady?

She said she was, but he didn't believe that and he told her so.

"You seem to know so much about me, Tandar."

It's my task to know you, lady. And my pleasure.

Oh, his pleasure, yes. He sometimes thought that if she never spoke the words to release him from Dalamar's spell, if she never said, "Valin, I love you," still he would be happy to keep near her, to ward her, to share her thoughts.

To lie beside her, a beast, not a man; her pet, not her

lover. Yes. Valin would do that, if he must, all the days of his life.

Yet, he dared hope, it might be that she would speak those words of release. He could not forget the sigh in her voice, the note of longing when, a few nights before, she'd spoken of him, of Valin, whom she'd sent from her.

Into his silence and thinking, Crysania now spoke, softly saying, "Tandar, was there no sign of Jeril out on the plain, no scent or track? What could have happened to him and Kela?"

My brother, the tiger thought.

Kela.

He shook himself, aware of how he distanced himself from her, even with words. She was his brother's wife. In law, she was due all the respect he'd accord his own sisters. That status demanded more of him than he had given her, an acceptance he was unable to offer. He didn't trust her. She felt wrong. She smelled wrong, like someone hiding secrets.

Let us pray they are safe.

He padded through the shadows, guiding Crysania, thinking his dark thoughts on the way to Neraka, until at last black, twisted walls rose up before them. They clawed at the sky, like fingers reaching to rend and tear. These were the walls of the Temple of Takhisis. Clustered around those temple walls lay rickety buildings and tents and stalls.

A scrabbling came out of the darkness, a wild laughter twisting up to the starless sky.

Crysania gasped. Tandar growled, putting himself in front of her. Something, someone, went scurrying, weeping and laughing all at once.

An ogre, lady.

Her heart thundered. She took a breath to steady herself, then let it go in a sigh, sorrow for the poor thing, that member of a race once the most beautiful of all those upon Krynn, now fallen and broken. Such were the servants of the Dark Queen.

We must go with care now, Crysania. You must keep as quiet as you can.

She pressed his shoulder, assenting.

Tandar went on, Crysania at his side. They took a broadly circular route around the broken buildings, keeping to the deep shadows, until he found a gate that appeared unguarded. Like a madman's maze, the city had many gates, all writhing and weaving. How was he to know which gate to take, which to trust? He laughed, deeply, in his mind. No gate here could be trusted, so it mattered not at all which one he chose. He took the first one he came to, hoping. That led to a second, and then to a wall. They must go right or left.

The air of Neraka hung like poison around them, groping fog fingers leaving foulness in their wake, a stench of sewage, sickness, and blood, of rotting food, decomposing corpses. The stink of madness and despair.

"Do you know where we are?" Crysania whispered, her voice muffled behind the arm she held over her nose and mouth.

No. We can go one way or the other. There is a building in the center, dark and large. It looks almost as if it's reaching for us. In places, it is rubble, as if the walls have fallen. In places, the walls appear straight, but from the way we have been walking, they cannot be.

Crysania said softly, "Tanis Half-Elven told me that the temple exploded, after he and the others escaped during the War of the Lance, but he said it didn't fall."

Which meant that the shadowy shape looming over them was new. Something regrown, perhaps, as the original temple had grown from the foundation stone, as a twisted caricature of itself.

"Tanis said there was something about the corridors inside the temple. A spell made them seem straight. We're not inside the temple?"

No. We're still outside, between buildings. But it seems twisted. Do you have as to where the rest of the Dragon Stones are?

Silence greeted the question, deep and frightened. The hair rose up on his nape.

Her voice, small as mice, she said, "Dalamar said—he said *you* would know where the stones are."

In the alley behind them, dark laughter sounded. A woman's voice rose up, then suddenly fell still. Tandar turned, growling. Ahead, the laugher rose up again, wild and terrible. Behind, sobbing pulsed in the night, like blood pouring out from a wound.

Heart racing, rage building, Tandar growled, *Lady, Dalamar told me nothing about the stones. He told me to guide you here. He charged me with that and your safety.*

Her breath shuddered, shivering on her lips, the sound of hope fading.

Beyond the crooked walls, moans rose and fell. A scream pierced the night, falling away into babbling, then sobbing, then stillness. What hope could live in such a place as Neraka? None, none at all! And who could not forgive hope's death, even the hope of one such as the Revered Daughter of Paladine?

Tandar growled. *Lady, lady, don't despair. Let me think, let me . . .*

Her hand rustled in her pocket as she reached for the Dragon Stones, now settled in Lagan Innis's purple velvet pouch among the pages of his prayers. *Where there is light,* said the runes on the pouch, *no dark may enter in.*

Soft came a thought to the tiger, a hope. Tandar had tried no magical spells since becoming a tiger, none since he'd stopped thinking of himself as Valin. He'd reveled in

251

the glory of his animal being, the strength the power, and magic had not seemed like a thing a tiger could work. But he didn't know that, not certainly. Yet what would be revealed should he try magic?

Lady, wait. Give me a moment. I think—I think I can find the way.

"How?"

He laughed, a warm sound in her mind. *You asked me what I am, lady, not so long ago. I will tell you one of the things I am. I am one acquainted with the ways of magic.*

He felt her surprise as she reached out a hand to touch him. Still, she trusted him, and when he pushed her, gently with the pressure of his shoulder, toward the deepest shadows against the near wall, she let him guide her. She didn't complain when her back touched something cold and slimy. She didn't wince when rough stone scratched at her skin. She simply stood, still and quiet, where he bade her stand. So well did she trust him.

Water gurgled, slow and turgid, somewhere nearby. Wind moaned, winding through the mazes, carrying scents metallic and rotting. A rat scurried, squealing. Upon the twisted wall overhead, a murder of crows ranged, laughing down at them, lost travelers in a damned city.

In his secret heart, where his thoughts were heard by no one, Tandar called up the words of a seeing spell. Quivering, he waited. Breathless, he hoped. Had he forgotten the words, the cadence? Had he—

Magic flowed through him, as warm and sweet as it had ever been! It sang in his blood, bright and glittering, and before his eyes, the walkway's curving turn lay revealed. He stretched, with magic-touched senses, and he felt the tug of something he couldn't name. A tingle not unlike that which he'd felt when he held Crysania's stone, only this was different, strong and dark.

He looked around him, wanting to growl, forcing himself to keep quiet. In the shadows, Crysania waited, the brightest thing in all this darkness, sure in her faith, trusting. It might be anything, that tug, and very probably the springing of some wizard's trap. He shuddered. What if it was the Dark Lady herself?

Trust!

Lady, a large building lies ahead. It's sturdier than the others nearby, and a squat tower sits upon it. I think—I think this is where we must go.

After a moment, she nodded, pressing on his shoulder.

Along dark corridors they went, past even darker doorways and rooms where the voices of the Dark Queen's servants slithered out beneath the doors. He took her out into the night again, through what might once have been a market, now fallen to broken, sharp-edge wood and rubble. They went around heaps of garbage where things scuttled on clawed feet. All the while he was guided by the pull of something he could not identify and yet must trust.

Crysania stayed with him, unquestioning, pulling the hood of her robe up and tucking the folds across her mouth and nose.

Into his mind her voice came, sweet as a breeze across sandy dunes. *Where are we?*

Close.

A chill rose up now. From the stones of the stairs, it seeped out from walls, weeping moisture, growing stronger the farther down they went. The cold wrapped ghostly streamers around their legs, as though trying to prevent them from moving on. Crysania's breathing came raggedly, echoing harshly off the narrowing walls as they came to another corridor, this one curving wide and lighted by a sputtering torch at each end.

Light, he said, and he showed it to her in her mind.

Not good, she said.

He agreed, for light meant someone was near to attend the torch.

The monotonous drip of water came from somewhere ahead, and voices, deep and guttural.

Go on! she said when he hesitated.

He did, all his instinct afire in his blood, urging him to turn back. Beside him, Crysania went quietly, gracefully, the only sound of her passing the brush of her robes on the filthy stone floor and the uneven whisper of her breath. Cold rose around them like waters in a drowning sea. The unflagging tug of whatever called to him—a dark thing, an evil thing—grew stronger.

Tandar went faster now. Crysania had to work to keep up until at last he halted. He gave her sight for the briefest of moments. An archway rose to frame an alcove. Guarding the arch was a heavily carved wooden door.

Crysania reached out, touching the crudely carved oak, the rough stone of the arch. Her fingers found an iron latch. She eased it up, breath held as the door swung open. The room beyond was of medium size, dimly lighted by two smoky torches and a handful of candles scattered about on the floor.

The room reminds me of Dalamar's study, lady. It's filled with bottles and boxes, open spellbooks and jars of spices. I think it's a mage's room.

Why not? Where else would one hide the Dragon Stones but in a mage's room?

Tandar herded Crysania into the room quickly, pushing the door shut with his body. She stopped, her hand on his shoulder, the other slipping into her pocket.

Is it here? Do you still feel it?

Yes! Like the stones you have, only different. I don't see it, but I feel it. It's here somewhere.

He scoured the room, starting from where he was and

circling it. The magic of evil clawed at his skin, moaning in his mind, words too terrible to remember. Though he went in tiger shape, he was still a White Robe, and the stench of dark magic was like sickness in him. He prowled the room, senses extended, as Crysania felt her way across the room, hands held before her. She found a low worktable scattered with books and jars. She touched one thing and then another, working purposefully from one end of the table to the other. All the while she wore the expression of one who searches a sewer.

Tandar circled.

They could search for hours and not find three little stones! Panic crept into him, icy and laughing, a jeering dark voice to tell him there were too many places to look. Boxes and drawers. An entire evil city of nooks and crannies.

And then, in a voice darker than that of panic, deeper, stronger, the stone cried out, a wordless roar.

Lady! I feel it! Among those books! Behind you—a shelf!

Crysania turned, stumbled against a stool, then righted herself, her hands on the bookshelf. She felt along the edges, running trembling fingers carefully across the things she found there. Statues, crystals, but still no stones.

Her fingers touched a small square box. She gasped and pulled back. Then, smiling grimly in the guttering light, she plucked the box from the shelf.

This is it, he heard in his mind, her voice shaking.

She held out the box so he could see it, small and square, with rounded edges and no design or pattern worked on the top or sides. It had two small rounded balls on the front of it, one above the other, and a line of wood separating them. Pulls for two tiny drawers.

Be careful, Crysania!

Breath held, she opened the first drawer. Two stones lay there, clacking against each other as she tipped the

255

box for Tandar to see. She reached in to touch them and drew back her fingers with a sudden cry.

It burns!

The dark one—don't touch it again! They're just like the two you have, except for the color. One is dull and rough and gray. One is smooth and shiny and black.

I only sense two. Is there a third?

No, just the two stones. Maybe in the other drawer?

Her fingers trembled as she opened the second drawer on the little box. It was stuck. She pulled with gentle force. The drawer slid open, jerking. It was as empty as a broken hope.

Can you feel anything else?

No. This is what I feel. But the red one must be here. Check where the box was again.

She felt all along the shelf as Tandar stalked the length of the shelves and around the room. His hackles rose with sudden dread. It had been too easy, finding the stones. Much too easy.

He felt her sudden surprise rippling in his mind. She pulled a second box from the shelf, one identical to the first.

Wait! Here . . .

Behind Tandar, the door creaked and started to swing open. In the instant of hearing, he leapt back, found Crysania and knocked her sideways, down onto the floor and out of sight as the dry, leather stink of a draconian flowed into the room.

The draconian was one of the ones without wings. It stood more upright than most of its fellows, and its face was almost, horribly, human, with dark skin like that of the plains peoples, high cheekbones, and startling blue eyes. More human than the woman behind him, whose grayish skin and deep-set eyes were ogreish in appearance. Their faces were turned toward each other as they entered, the draconian speaking over his shoulder.

As Tandar growled a warning, they turned toward him with almost comical surprise. The tiger met them with a snarl. He leapt before either had time to recover from shock. His front paws hit the draconian in the chest. It was like hitting granite. The creature, overbalanced by the blow, rocked back on its large tail and remained upright. Tandar's claws reached for a hold on the metallic armor.

The draconian roared and swiped at him with a massive, taloned hand.

Tandar fell sideways, dull pain thudding through his head. He twisted in midair, regaining his balance, and landed, ready to spring again. This time, he aimed for the woman, whose lips moved in spellcasting. He caught her, as he had the lizard man, midtorso. This body gave easily, falling backward, with him atop it. The draconian swiped at him again as he fell past. The clawed blow sent the two of them, tiger and woman, tumbling into the hall. The woman hit the ground hard, taking the brunt of the draconian's blow and Tandar's weight.

Bone snapped, and she screamed in pain.

Tandar swiped at her throat. She twisted, desperate fear in her eyes. His claws raked her shoulder, tearing robe and flesh.

He wheeled, hearing the draconian at his back, clumsy and stumbling as it tried to turn in the doorway to avoid stepping on the woman's legs. It lunged, and as he whipped around, the draconian did too, its tail whistling through the air. The scaled, fleshy appendage, thick as a tree trunk, smacked Tandar on the side of his head. Blood roared in his ears. Pain like lightning rushed along the pathways of his nerves. He echoed the woman, screaming his pain.

In his mind, he cried, *Crysania! Stay down!*

If she answered, he didn't hear her voice during the long tumble into darkness.

Chapter Nineteen

Crysania staggered, then went gasping to her knees in the moment Tandar fell. The two boxes tumbled from her hands as pain washed over her, channeled by her connection to his thoughts. She doubled over, confused and frightened.

Tandar!

A groaning slid along her nerves, then sighed away. Nothing came to her now from Tandar's mind but a low, soft moaning, barely heard and wholly unaware of itself.

The tiger was unconscious.

Groping, she found the two boxes. Hands shaking, steeling herself against the crawling sense of evil emanating from the dark stone, she plucked it and the non-aligned stone from their drawer. From the second box, she took the fifth stone, certain of it by the emanation of cool

and neutral magic. She dumped all the stones unceremo-
niously into Lagan's rune-marked pouch. The pouch she
buried in the depths of her pocket. She shoved the two
small boxes away, under what seemed like the lowest
shelf of a bookcase.

Reaching carefully, she discovered the wide desk and
pulled herself along its side, slipping underneath. She
crouched there, not knowing whether she huddled in
plain sight.

Heart thundering so loud she thought it must be
heard in all of Neraka, Crysania knew she was trapped.

She tried to make sense of the thunderous racket she
heard, angry voices and running feet. Hoarse voices
shouted questions, swords rattled, and the sounds all clustered at the doorway. A hundred prayers on her lips, she
drew back as far as she could into the corner under the
desk, crouching to make herself as small as possible. Footsteps came into the room, the sounds of them making it
impossible to count how many persons were there. Armor
clanked and rattled as people ranged themselves around
the room, some at the door, others right near the desk.
Breath held, Crysania heard at least three different voices,
one hobgoblin, one guttural and feral. A draconian?

"How did it get in?" the hobgoblin asked. The stench
of him filled the mage's chamber. Crysania pressed her
hand to her nose and mouth. "What was it doing in
here?"

A human spat, then growled, "Check the stairwell—
and don't forget to check the hallway! Make sure it was
alone!"

Feet scuffled on cold stone, kicked aside furniture, the
sounds spreading throughout the chamber. Feet in leather
boots passed right by her, then paused at the corner of the
desk. A foul odor, of unwashed body and crusted filth,
assailed her nostrils. It was no thorough search, however,

only a fumbling around the room. Soon the sound of foot-steps moved away. The room cleared as everyone moved back into the hallway. Someone kicked the door shut, but still she heard their voices beyond.

"Well, it seems to be alone. What do we do with it?"

"Lock it in the dungeon until Lije comes back."

Another voice, weak and whiny, protested. "Are you going to carry it down the stairs? It's huge."

Raucous laughter faded as their voices became a low, wordless rumble. Once Crysania heard the voice of the injured woman moaning in pain.

She imagined them staring down at the tiger's body. What was she going to do? What if they decided to kill Tandar where he lay?

She gathered her skirts, moving back to the edge of the opening. She crept out from under the desk and stood slowly, carefully. Her knees ached, they were cramped and sore from staying hunched over for so long. She wanted to go to the door, to press her ear against it to see what was happening, but she dared not take the chance.

She must go a step at a time, make careful progress. She took one step, reached to be sure of the second. She took a third step, and in the moment her foot touched the floor, Tandar woke.

His consciousness slammed into her with battering force. She reeled back against a table. She pressed her hands to her head as she felt the sharp pain in his left ear. The coppery scent of blood filled up her senses as it flowed into his. Whose? The woman's? His own?

It was his own, trickling down beneath his ear, tickling his fur. Confusion. Where was he? Anger. Pain. Sharp toe of boot prodding his ribs. Rough voices coming at him from the ceiling. He got up, dizzy but alert.

Tandar! I'm here! Be still . . . hush, be still. I'm still in the mage's chamber.

Stay there. Stay quiet.

She clutched the table, willing herself not to think of being lost in this place without Tandar to guide her. But if he could escape—*Get away if you can!*

Laughter snarled through her mind. *I'm going with them.*

She heard his growl through the heavy door as he taunted them, trying to draw them away from the door.

No, Tandar. Don't. They'll hurt you.

Again that snarling laughter, that sense of him despising his opponents. *Don't worry. They think they're herding me.*

Then, in an instant, she saw it all through his eyes, the dance, the game. One of the humans came too close. She almost laughed to see the man skitter backward as Tandar lunged. They herded him, so they thought, the captors moving with swords and daggers drawn, a winged draconian with strange pale eyes, a hobgoblin and three humans. They were all dressed in varying degrees of ragged, dirty black.

They followed him away from the door, crowing their delight with the ease of their task as they herded him away from her and down the long dark corridor. At the end of the corridor, two of the humans took the lead while the others crowded close, poking at the tiger with daggers. Crysania closed her eyes, but it didn't help the sensation that those sharp silver points were coming at her. One of them pricked him, the blade skidding across his ribs.

Tandar roared, pain erupting like fire in him, in her. Gasping, Crysania felt the powerful play of his muscles as he took a swipe with a big paw.

The man yelped. The dagger flew end over end through the air and fell, bouncing off a wall and clanking down steps. Yelling, prodding with sword point and dagger, they closed in on him, forcing him into a dark, low-ceilinged stairwell.

She ran to the door, tripping over something small—a chair, a stool—and tore at the latch. One of her nails turned back on itself painfully.

Tandar! If they take you into the dungeons, I'll never find you!

I'll be alone, alone. And I have been so long alone . . .

Then she was through the door, a frenzied blur of White Robes and flashing silver medallion.

Tandar! Run now!

She wheeled back the way they had come, then ran in darkness. Surprised shouts followed her, curses and cries and the thunder of running feet.

Tandar snarled. Someone screamed in pain.

Crysania, stop!

It was a command, plain and simple. A sound to be obeyed, and she obeyed it, her body reacting without conscious thought. With unquestioning trust. She stumbled to a halt.

Turn left now. Up.

He skidded into her, past her, smacking into something. She put out her hand. Less than an arm's length away was the wall.

Go up!

He was beside her now, guiding her.

She climbed as fast as she could, with him struggling along beside her. The running footsteps sounded close now, echoes bounding off the walls and tangling with harsh gasps for breath.

Keep going—straight up!

Tandar swung away from her, turning back to meet their attackers.

Crysania grasped the wall and kept climbing, stumbling on slick steps, staggering to her feet again, lifting up one foot after another.

Cries of pain and surprise and anger echoed behind her. Swords whistled through the air, some ringing against stone, missing their target. The stink of sweat and dirt and terror hung on the dank air. Rage, wordless, incoherent rage raced like wildfire through her mind.

The tiger roared, and someone screamed. Furious joy surged into Crysania's mind even as she reached for another step and found—nothing. The shock of having her foot come down so hard shook her to the teeth. She flailed out wildly, finding only air. Gasping, murmuring prayers beneath her breath, she scooted along the top step until at last she found the cold, weeping stone of the opposite wall. It continued on to a landing.

Where did the stairs lead? She could not recall, and so she started back to the other side. In the instant she reached the wall, Tandar leapt to her side, thrusting his head under her hand. Blood, hot and sticky, matted his fur.

This way.

He led her to the left, out into open air. Now they ran on level floor, Tandar listing to one side, stumbling and off-balance. Footsteps thundered behind them. One of the men made the landing, huffing and trying to gather his breath.

Tandar wheeled again, leaving her to stagger to a stop and grope for a wall. A shout rose up, angry and frightened. A sword's steel blade hit something solid and hard, ringing against wall or floor. Another cry, warbled upward, then the crunch of flesh and bone.

Then . . . silence.

Tandar bumped against her, barely waiting for her to shift her hand to his shoulder before he was loping again, bumping against her clumsily, but still leading her.

You're hurt.

He didn't answer, only leaned against her to turn her around a corner as the halls behind them filled up with more shouting, more footsteps.

Faster, Crysania!

Her lungs burned, demanding oxygen. Her heart pounded, crying for more blood. Her legs wanted nothing but to stop. Crysania reached down into herself and drew on strength she didn't know she had to keep pace with the tiger. The pursuit came nearer, curses following them like arrows as they burst through a doorway and out into the hot air of Neraka's midnight.

This way!

Tandar turned under her hand. He lead her across a yard. Dried grass crunched under her feet. They turned, then turned again. He slowed, then stopped.

Under here!

He slipped from under her hand, crouching, and she dropped down and followed on hands and knees. Gasping, she felt for him, encountering sticky wet fur, his head slick with blood.

She put her arms around him, leaned her head into his shoulder. His warm blood touched her forehead. *You saved my life. Thank you.*

He shuddered, bearing her weight for a moment before he pulled away.

I haven't done that yet, lady. We're still not safe.

She listened a moment, as he did. No alarm rang through the courtyard. She heard no sound of footfalls behind them, no cries off to the sides, not even a whisper to warn of secret men surrounding them. Wind, the hot night wind, sent leaves and trash skittering across the ground. No other sound did she hear, not a rat scrambling, not a carrion bird scratching the night with its cry.

But they were not alone.

Crysania shuddered. Tandar growled.

Something was near, a presence colder than death.

We're near the temple, Tandar said, *almost past it.*

Crysania shuddered. *Something in there—someone—*

knows I'm here. She sidled sideways on hands and knees, out into the open. *We have to go.*

Not yet. Not yet. Not until we're sure it's safe.

We have to go now!

He climbed to his feet unsteadily, following the insistent tug of her hands. *There's a gate ahead, about a hundred yards away.* As he took a step forward, he stumbled and went to his knees. He stood quickly, still shaky, and tried to move forward.

Tandar!

She dropped to her knees beside him.

The draconian in the hallway hit my ear. I can't hear on that side, and it's affecting my balance.

She touched one side of his face, his soft rounded ear, and found blood there, too. She could feel a swelling there, above his jaw, a lump that filled her palm.

You can't risk a healing prayer, Crysania.

She knew it. There was no time. And outside this terrible place, outside the world itself, the gods battled among themselves. What attention dared Paladine spare from his own desperate need to listen to the prayer of one lonely woman for the healing of a tiger?

Lead, Tandar.

He did, and she followed him as he eased toward the gate. She felt him sigh with relief when they were through and the cold, knowing regard of the temple receded slightly. Her own pent-up breath slipped free in the hot night air.

Before she had the pleasure of even one quiet, clear breath, the alarm they'd dreaded went up behind them. Shouts filled the night, and again, the thunder of booted feet.

Run!

As she followed him, he turned and she slipped. He slipped also. They both skidded several feet before regaining their balance. They turned again and again in the writhing maze of Neraka's walls and gates, losing their footing several times.

She felt grass beneath her boots, then something like cobblestones. Grass whispered again, then vanished to become bare dirt. Tandar turned, shoving her until she felt stone against her back. She understood at once, shrinking as far back as she could, veiled in shadow and night.

The running feet went past, breath huffing, curses growling on the night air.

A moment later Tandar lurched away from her and back out onto the path. He led her at a fast walk, the two of them stumbling on the bare dirt. He slowed, edging forward a step at a time.

Crysania, we're going through another gate. It's the north gate out of the city.

Out into open grassland where they would be visible to their pursuers, two small, stumbling figures fleeing the Dark Queen's wretched city.

High and shrill, a woman's voice cried, "There they are! At the gate!"

They burst past a wall. Crysania grazed it with her arm, the rough surface catching her sleeve. Neraka was pulling her back!

"No!" she cried, her voice bursting from her. With a wrench, she pulled free, tearing her sleeve, leaving fabric and blood behind.

Run as hard as you can, Crysania! Straight ahead!

Then he slid away from under her hands.

Trying to stop, to reach for him, she fell hard to her knees. Groping, she turned and crawled back to him, guided by panting and groaning. Led by the smell of his blood, she found him. He lay on his side, ribs heaving with the effort to breathe.

"Get up!" she shouted at him. "Get up. They're coming!"

Go on, he moaned.

Crysania shook him, as much in desperation as anger and fear. "Get up! I won't go on without you! They'll get me, too, if you don't get up!"

His exhaustion, his pain, these things were as her own, mingling in her mind with terror as he struggled to his feet. She felt him reach down deep into himself, seeking strength.

"If you make it to the forest," she promised, gathering up her robes, "we'll be able to rest. I can heal you."

You can try, he said wryly.

"I *will* heal you," said the Revered Daughter of Paladine through clenched teeth. "Now get up!"

How far across the plain? How far until they were among the trees? The clash of swords, the tangle of cursing voices and crashing footfalls boiled up behind her as guards poured through the city gate. Tandar's balance was even worse than before, but he ran along beside her, keeping pace.

An arrow whizzed past her. Crysania heard it like a wasp, and she heard the thud as it drove into the ground. She hooked her fingers in Tandar's collar, steadying him, pulling him along almost with the strength of her will alone. The attackers' footsteps jarred the ground beneath her feet. Before her was another sound, another . . .

A horse! Tandar cried.

She veered to the right, away from the sound that was thundering down on them. Tandar slammed to a stop. Crying out, she slid on the grass, struggling for balance in the utter darkness and finding it by the grace of good luck.

Whatever was coming at them skidded to a stop just inches from her. The smell of horse washed over her. Small feet hit the ground, and a familiar voice, cried, "Lady! Get up behind me! Here's my hand!"

Kela! And Jeril? Crysania's heart soared, listening for the sound of another voice, another horse. She heard neither.

Kela grabbed her hand, pulling, but Crysania backed away.

"Tandar's hurt. I have to try to heal—"

"The tiger? Leave him." Kela pulled again at her wrist.

Crysania snatched her hand free, reaching for Tandar, for her medallion.

Kela wheeled away, remounting. Behind them, Neraka roared with the fury of pursuit, and Crysania thought for a moment that the mage meant to leave them. But she only urged her horse forward, putting herself between them and the city and its charging guard.

Tandar groaned, *Leave me!*

"Be still!" Crysania hissed.

She shut herself away from his thoughts, raised up a barrier of prayer so that all the sounds around her were naught but the murmuring of a distant sea.

"Paladine, heal this . . ." She hesitated. She'd almost said "man." "Paladine, hear my prayers. Grant your healing power to this noble being who has so well served your servant this night."

Kela's voice rose up in a chant. The scent of rose petals, of spices, of other unrecognizable spell components hung on the hot night air. Shouts of anger and pain came distantly to Crysania's awareness. Her medallion glowed against her hand, but faintly. The warmth she had known all her life sputtered like a failing candle. She had no hand free to seek the white stone in Lagan's rune-marked pouch, nor would she have dared risk touching the dark stone.

"Paladine, hear me!"

Tandar groaned under her hands, moving as though he was stretching, arching. The soothing power of the

God of Goodness and Light swept over her, a grace that eased the pain in her muscles, the doubt and fear in her soul, surging into the bruised and bloodied flesh under her hands.

Tandar rumbled, a vibration of new energy and life. He moved again under her hands, this time to climb to his feet.

It's enough. I can go on.

She ran her fingers over him. Checking the wounded ear, the cuts on his face and side. The swelling was almost gone, the two wounds closed.

Kela was several paces away. Crysania could hear the snap of her reins and the dancing, pawing footsteps of her horse. This time she gladly accepted the hand Kela offered and climbed up behind her.

"Head low, lady," Kela shouted.

Crysania burrowed her head into the mage's back just as Kela called one last spell.

Something whooshed through the air, smelling of lightning and fire. As Kela's horse leapt forward into a gallop, Crysania closed her mind to the piteous screams behind her.

Fire enveloped the guard of Neraka.

* * * * *

As she felt the first brush of branches overhead, Crysania realized that she and Tandar would have never made it this far alone.

"Kela," she said, "I thank the gods you found us."

The mage said nothing, guiding her horse carefully over the rising ground. Tandar loped alongside, ducking back now and then, then racing ahead, but always coming back to run beside her. They went on in this way until the horse, labored from the run, began to lose its footing and falter.

"We need water," Crysania said. "Kela, find a place to stop and rest."

Silent, the mage did so, stopping at last in a small clearing where, by the sound of it, a trickle of fresh water ran. Kela helped her down, then dismounted herself. She led Crysania to the water, and the two women drank gratefully from a small pool, then made room for Tandar and the horse.

"Is it night still?" Crysania asked, settling her back against rough stone. She wrapped her arms around her drawn-up knees, hunching over a little, shaking.

"It is," Kela said. "And the fire in the sky grows brighter every moment, lady."

Tandar came near, settling beside Crysania with a deep groan.

Silence stretched out around them. Even the night creatures were still. At last Crysania said, "Kela, where is Jeril? Did you find each other after the daemon warrior attacked?"

Tandar lifted his head, his tail switching a little.

A moment passed, and then another. Then, her voice wooden, Kela said, "Jeril is dead. A daemon warrior—" She stopped, her voice breaking, choking with tears. "He died well."

And under Crysania's hand, Tandar went suddenly still, as rigid as stone. His thoughts, always near, receded, as though fleeing from her. Then, with terrible suddenness, she felt him again. She felt a roaring, terrible grief, sorrow raw as wounds.

Jeril! My brother! Jeril!

Brother?

Crysania gasped, then made herself still. Kela said something, speaking the tale of her husband's death, giving it in short, spare words. Crysania tried to listen, replying occasionally with words of comfort. All the while one word ran round and round in her mind: *Brother.*

Oh, dear gods. Oh, dear gods . . .

Kela, unaware, rose to her feet, her movements quick, sounding like a woman wanting to walk away from pain. "You will excuse me, lady. I must tend the horse."

"Yes," Crysania murmured, hardly hearing her own voice for the grief surging through her mind. Tandar's grief. Oh, Valin's grief!

Beneath her hand, the tiger lay, unmoving, awash with sorrow so deep she thought he would drown in it.

Valin . . .

In her mind, he roared, a beast's rage. *I am not Valin! I am Tandar! Voiceless Tandar, who can't recall the last word he spoke to his brother in life!*

He *was* Valin, the man become the beast, the white-robed mage become the white tiger, Dalamar's gift to her. How had it happened? By what evil had Dalamar wreaked this change upon the desert mage? Her mind roiled with questions, none of which she dared ask now.

Gently, careful of his sorrow, Crysania said, *I will name you as you wish, my friend.*

He spoke no word in her mind, made no move under her hand. He simply lay where he was, groaning as he had not groaned when swords cut him and knives bit him. In this way, he had mourned the death of his friend, the loss of Lagan Innis. In this way he mourned now the death of his brother.

Crysania leaned down, asking no question, guessing much. Softly she whispered. "Valin. Valin, I'm here." He could grieve, the tiger, but he could not weep, and so she wept for him, lending him her tears as he had lent her his sight.

So they stayed a long time, twined in grief, until at last Kela stood before them, her horse stamping and shuffling at the lead.

"Lady, the night wears on. We have to go someplace, for we cannot stay here. The guards of the city will find our trail before long. Where shall we go?"

Crysania wiped her face on the hem of her dusty gown. Her hand on the tiger's head, she tried to think.

When she began the journey—more than a month ago—she thought little beyond finding the Dragon Stones. On their run through the city, across the plain, she'd thought little beyond escaping with their lives. And now . . .

The tiger stirred beneath her hand. He climbed to his feet and shook himself.

Now we must do what we came here to do, Crysania. Good men have died in this cause, losing their lives to give you the chance to call upon a god. That we must do.

They must. She must bring all of the stones together and take the risk Lagan and Jeril died to allow her. She would call upon a god . . . but which god would answer?

Takhisis, or Paladine?

No matter. This was the risk she must take, the chance her friends had died to allow her. She must find a safe place to engage the magic of the Dragon Stones, a sacred place. Into her heart came the memory of an old story, a tale of grief made sacred by the tender touch of Paladine's gracious hand. Tanis Half-Elven had told that tale to her a long time ago when they passed a quiet hour in the stillness of an autumn evening. A tale in the days soon after the War of the Lance.

"Godshome," Crysania said quietly. "We're going to Godshome."

Chapter Twenty

Crysania rode behind Kela, clinging to the mage with both arms. No outcry from Nerakan pursuit sounded. No rumble of a mounted troop shook the earth. Crows did not cry in the sky, the wind had no will to move, no voice to use. It seemed, each time she listened, that all the world had lost the ability to make even the smallest sound.

And then she would hear the softest rustle on the still air, the smallest clatter, as of pebbles rolling. Each time, she whispered in her mind, *Do you hear it, Tandar?*

He smelled nothing, for no breeze carried a scent forward to him. He saw nothing, though a time or two he went aside from the narrow path, dropping back to see what might be found.

We are being followed, he said the second time he returned. *But I don't know by whom. Or by what. We must go*

*with care, lady, and you and I should keep our suspicions to
ourselves for now.*

But what about Kela?

He growled, not aloud, but deeply into her mind. *If she
hears what we do, she's saying nothing, and I would find that
strange, wouldn't you? If she doesn't hear, we'll tell her when
she needs to know. Or events will.*

His heart had not softened toward his brother's
widow, though Crysania had thought that, if nothing
more, shared sorrow would assist that change. If anything, it seemed his mistrust of the woman had grown.

I trust no one but you, lady. It seems the safest route.

Reluctantly Crysania agreed to say nothing to Kela.

The Plains of Neraka had fallen well behind them
before the sun got halfway to noon. The path rose ahead,
and Tandar led the way with certainty.

Valin saw the way, he'd said as though speaking of
someone other than himself. *On a map in the Temple of Paladine. We won't be going the way your friend Tanis went all
those years ago. We'll be taking the back door, coming in from
the opposite direction. Trust me, I'll get you there.*

So he did. By the time the sun began its journey down
the sky, he led the two women right to the pass that
opened into the Misted Vales. Beyond there, according to
all maps, lay Godshome.

"Perhaps these Misted Vales were well named at one
time," Kela said as she let her weary mount stop to crop
the small tufts of tough grass growing between the close-
sitting boulders crouching at the head of the trail down
into the valley. "But it's been a while since any fog or mist
hung here."

All the year long, without doubt. Crysania smelled
only the dust of the day, the dryness of parched grass, and
the ache of trees gone barren in this terrible year. The
horse stumbled, weary of its double burden. Crysania

lifted her head, breathing the hot air.

"Is there water, Kela?"

"Up ahead. A little stream and an even smaller pool." She moved, as one trying to look back over her shoulder, then made a small sound of impatience. "Where's that tiger of yours got to now, lady?"

Crysania reached out with her mind. *Tandar?*

Here, behind you.

What do you hear?

Nothing. But we're still being followed. I feel it.

That was good enough for her. To Kela, she said, "He's dropped back. Look again. He's right behind us."

So he was, padding along behind the horse as though he'd been there all along.

The horse swayed and Crysania clutched the mage to keep her balance. "We should stop here for the night, Kela."

The mage stiffened. "But there are hours left of daylight, lady. We should push on."

If you do, Tandar said, *you'll be going afoot.*

Firmly Crysania said, "We'll stop beside the water, Kela. I'm going to need rest before I attempt . . ."

She let the thought trail away. She didn't want to talk to Kela about the Dragon Stones and her hopes for the magic she would find. Tandar's suspicions are infecting me, she thought, and I have no reason to believe there is cause to mistrust this woman. She rode with us almost all the way to Neraka and would have gone the distance if events had not prevented her. She fought well to defend us before that, never leaving us in battle. And yet . . .

And yet if she had no reason to mistrust Kela, she had every reason to trust Tandar—Valin!—so she said no more, only pleaded exhaustion and decreed the day done.

Behind them, she heard Tandar snarl. She felt the rush of his pounce. A small squeal of pain rent the air, then vanished in death. The tiger came near, and Crysania heard Kela's humorless laugh.

"He's good for hunting, lady," she said. "When all's done, you should keep him around. He'll make a fine amusement in Palanthas, don't you think?"

Tandar growled around a mouthful of prey, then padded on ahead.

* * * * *

Fire crackled, and the scent of roasting meat and pinewood perfumed the air. Tandar had brought down three hares, two for the spit and one for himself. Crysania and Kela had each eaten one, the two women shredding meat from the bones of their meal as contentedly as though neither had heard of the invention of fork and knife. As they licked rich juices and fat from their fingers, Tandar lay near the little pool, cleaning the blood of raw meat from his broad paws.

Delicious! he said, purring in Crysania's mind.

Raw? Delicious? She shuddered.

He laughed, but the sound fell bitterly. *I am a beast, lady. A tiger. Of course the blood of the kill is delicious to me.*

You are a man, she said gently. *Valin, won't you tell me what's happened to you? Did Dalamar . . . ?*

He yawned noisily. He got up and stretched. Then he walked away, tail switching, silent. For a brief moment, he gave her sight, showing her the vale and the rising trail they would follow in the morning. When he took the sight away, she heard him prowling the perimeter of their camp as had become his habit, a silent sentinel.

What do you hear?

Nothing behind.

Perhaps it's gone, whatever was following.

The tiger let scornful silence answer that hope, and he

prowled, softly padding, giving special attention to the trail leading back the way they'd come.

"Lady," Kela said, her voice quiet as she put another dry branch on the fire, "will you show me the stones the dwarf Lagan and my—my husband died for?"

A pang wrenched Crysania's heart, so painfully did the words "my husband" seem to fall from Kela's lips. So newly married! So newly made a widow.

"Of course," she said. She reached into her pocket and took out Lagan's velvet pouch. She traced the runes, in her heart repeating the words they shaped: *Where light is, dark may not enter in.*

May it be so, she prayed as she opened the pouch.

She tumbled the five stones out onto the blanket. The dark one still tingled and burned her fingers, but not so strongly as it had in Neraka.

"You found them all," Kela said, a little catch of excitement in her voice.

"Yes, the three aligned stones are all here now, and the two nonaligned ones."

"And you found a pouch for them, I see. It's a pretty little thing."

"It is—was—Lagan's. I thought that since he started out with us, something of his should continue on with us."

"How poetic," Kela said, her voice chill. "I suppose the dwarf would have appreciated that. I found nothing of Jeril's, not even his sword. The daemon warrior got it all."

Kela reached, perhaps for the pouch, perhaps for the stones themselves. Startled, quickly ashamed, Crysania felt the motion, and she felt within her the same resentment, the same jealousy that had surprised her in her study at the temple the day she'd passed the Dragon Stones from one to another of her friends. With what she hoped was a casual gesture, she picked up the Dragon Stones.

Tandar's voice rumbled in her mind. *Put them away!*

Again Kela put out her hand.

Crysania, put the Dragon Stones away!

And Kela said, "What will you do with the Dragon Stones at Godshome, lady?"

Crysania spoke with more hope than she'd felt in days. "I will pray, and my god will hear me."

Fire crackled as the last bit of fat fell from a spitted hare, sizzling in the flames. Kela said nothing for a long while. Then she said softly, "Such faith, lady! I am envious."

Perhaps she was envious of Crysania's faith. Perhaps she was envious of something else. And perhaps, Crysania thought, I am letting myself become as suspicious as Tandar, with as little reason to be.

Nevertheless, Crysania sent the stones sliding into Lagan's pouch once again. She tucked the pouch deep into her pocket, then she rose and bade Kela good night. She was a long time at falling asleep, though. She listened to the fire dying, to the thin trickle of water creeping into the small pool, to the horse snuffling and stamping. She heard Tandar out in the night, but she was not comforted.

* * * * *

They found the last path out of the Misted Vales, the rising road to Godshome, well after noon on the next day.

No one needed to tell Crysania of the nearness of the place. She felt it because the Dragon Stones let her know. As ever, they rolled and clacked together in Lagan's velvet pouch, the sound of them speaking with the same rhythm as the movement of the horse, but now she felt them through the velvet, through the fabric of her robe.

She felt them as though they lay against her naked skin, glowing, humming, tingling with power. No longer could she distinguish one stone from the other, black from white from red, aligned from nonaligned. The sensation of their power, their voices, merged to sing one song. It seemed to her that this song had but one word, for all its varied rhythms.

Godshome!

We are still followed, Tandar warned as they stood at the head of the path.

You're certain.

I am.

We will go forward, she said.

We will.

Up they went, up through the mountains, out of the dense shade of the foothills and into the sparse growth of high altitude. The air was thinner, the underbrush thicker. Crysania had hoped they would find relief from the unending heat in the higher ground. Her hope failed early. Without shade, it seemed the pitiless sun had grown stronger, even larger. The higher they climbed, the harder Crysania found it to breathe. Her temples throbbed for most of the afternoon, but as they drew nearer to Godshome, the stones sang brightly, rejoicing, and so she forgot her pain. She took the rune-marked pouch out from her pocket and rode with one arm wrapped round Kela's waist. In her other hand, she held Lagan's pouch close against her breast.

"We'll be there soon, lady," Kela said, her voice sparkling with excitement.

Soon, Tandar said in her mind, his voice a dour counterpoint. Then he swung away, padding back down the path the way they'd come.

Anything?

No sign, but we are followed.

Crysania held the velvet pouch closer, praying.

When they found the high canyon walls, her hope surged.

They are gray, Tandar assured her, *as Tanis Half-Elven told you.*

It must be the mountain peaks surrounding Godshome. Crysania breathed deeply. The place smelled clean and wholesome and hopeful, of pine sap and fresh air and sunshine that did not burn.

It all seems like one seamless wall to me, Lady. Stay a moment and let me venture on to find a way through.

He found it in good time, loping back to her only moments after leaving. *The way through is narrow, lady. Only a little wider than your shoulders. You won't be able to ride. Tell the mage to help you down from the horse.*

With Kela's willing help, Crysania put foot to ground. Kela dropped down behind her, leading the horse and guiding her up the stony path to Tandar.

"We'll have to go single file," she said. "You go ahead. The horse and I will follow."

Crysania hesitated, reaching back, expecting to feel Tandar's head beneath her hand. She felt only air, empty and hot.

"Tandar, where—"

Like lightning falling, something hit her, hard, in the center of her back. The blow slammed her forward. Breath blasted out of her lungs as she fell under the weight of the blow. Gasping, she found no air.

Tandar!

She lay stunned, without breath, a weight pressing on her back, trying to collapse her lungs. She opened her mouth, gasping like a drowning woman as Tandar roared behind her. He was right! They'd been followed from Neraka.

She felt the heat of his breath on her neck. It reeked of blood and his wild fare.

The weight lifted from her back. Air slammed back into her lungs, filled them with the metallic smell of her own blood, and of magic.

Knees dug into her back, crushed one of her hands into the gravel. A hand—Kela's!—grabbed her arm and tried to drag her to her knees. Crysania staggered, then fell again. Wildly she cried, "Tandar!" even as she felt shame for having doubted the mage. How could she have? Here was Kela, as swift to her defense as Tandar ever was.

A dagger hissed free of its sheath with a satin hiss.

"Get away," Kela shouted.

Crysania pulled away, thinking to give the mage room to fight.

Kela held tighter. "Keep still," she hissed. "Or I'll kill you right here."

Ice ran in Crysania's veins, the ice of terror. She clutched Lagan's pouch, the Dragon Stones, protecting it as the mage pulled her. Her chin dug into the ground. Rocks and dirt scraped the palms of her hands and her knees. The top of her head hit something hard.

In her mind, she screamed, *Tandar!*

Kela got an arm around her throat and used the grip to pull her to her feet and turned her around. Snarling threats and curses, she steadied Crysania against her body.

Somewhere, out in the dark that was her world, Crysania heard the tiger's hot breath, his growling and snarls. She arched, gasping for breath, and the arm across her throat tightened. The sharp point of a dagger dug into the tender flesh below her ear.

"Get away," Kela shouted, "or she dies!"

Tandar took a step toward the two women, snarling. Kela stepped back and aside, dragging Crysania with her, using the Revered Daughter's body as a shield against the tiger.

"Kela," she gasped. "What are you doing? Have you lost your mind?"

"Shut up!" the mage hissed in her ear. "Tell that tiger of yours that if he comes any closer, I'll water this dry ground with your blood." She pressed the dagger closer for emphasis.

"He won't come closer," Crysania assured her, arching her neck, thrusting her jaw up in an attempt to relieve the pressure. "Why are you doing this?"

Kela laughed, the sound like a raven cursing. "For the Dragon Stones, you idiot."

Crysania groaned as Kela snatched the bag from her hands. It was as though she'd stolen something more than velvet and stone. It was as though she'd reached into Crysania and snatched out her heart.

"Please," Crysania cried. "Don't! You don't know what you're doing."

"Oh, yes, I do," Kela said, sounding much calmer now that she had the pouch in her hand. "I know better even than you. I knew when Dalamar was so interested in them that they must be important."

"How did you know about Dalamar? None of my companions knew of his interest."

The tiger snarled again, his tail whipping the air.

Kela laughed harshly. "You are wrong, lady." She spat. "My husband knew. His brother told him everything in that sweet little message he sent along with his fetch. And naturally he told his new wife everything. The trusting fool. When he no longer served my need, I got rid of him."

In her mind, Tandar's voice raged.

Crysania's heart sank. There had been trusting fools in this tale, she thought bitterly, but poor Jeril was the least of them.

"You there in Palanthas aren't the only ones who've noticed what's going on in the world, nor the only ones to put together the pieces of the puzzle. The growing army. The gods at war. Dalamar's interest in the stones. You can't hear your god. Dalamar can't hear his. I can't hear mine."

Crysania's heart thundered against her ribs.

In her mind, Tandar whispered, *I will kill her, Lady. I will rend her flesh from her bones!*

"My magic's been affected," Kela said, caressing Crysania's throat with the dagger's keen blade. "Did you think I am so poor a mage that all I could do was throw fireballs and lightning? I have always been able to do much more than that. But something is wrong. Something is draining my power."

The dagger's edge pressed tighter. A small drop of warm blood slid down the length of Crysania's neck.

"Don't you feel it? They're leaving us!" Kela hissed. "Just like the Cataclysm. Our gods are leaving us."

She dug into the pouch of stones and pulled them all free. Clutching them in one hand, she shook them against Crysania's face. "The gods are too busy with their own battles. And they're losing. That won't matter to me, though. With these, I'll be powerful. The gods can all go back to Chaos, and I'll still have magic."

Lady!

One word he cried, and in it, Crysania heard all this thought. As clearly as though she were again sighted, she saw in her mind a picture of his sudden, desperate intent.

Tandar leapt, roaring like thunder breaking open the sky.

Crysania reared back, bringing her elbow down and her head up. The elbow caught Kela in the thigh. The back of her head slammed into Kela's chin. The mage gurgled, head snapping back, arm snapping back. The sharp, cold edge of the dagger slid across Crysania's throat. Her skin split.

A single thin line of blood oozed from the cut and trailed down her throat.

Crysania dropped, sliding out of the other woman's grasp and rolling to the ground. Just as Crysania rolled free, Tandar struck Kela in the chest with all his weight. The dagger flew from her hand, the blade ringing on stone where it fell.

The mage screamed, the scream cut short as her head hit the stony ground. In the silence, the Dragon Stones tumbled from her hand and rolled across the ground.

Tandar! Don't! Don't do it!

He hung there in the moment, poised between dealing death or dealing mercy.

"Tandar," she said aloud so that her words hung weighty on the air. "Tandar, don't kill her. Come help me."

He didn't move.

"Valin," she said gently, "please come help me."

Silent, he came to her, stiff-legged, quivering in his rage. Silent, he stood near, braced to let her pull herself up by her grip on his shoulder. Once on her feet, she went to Kela, feeling to see if the mage were dead or living. The pulse beat weakly in her, but steadily.

"We will leave her," she said, picking up the dagger and slipping it into her belt. "By the time she regains consciousness . . . " She stopped, excitement and fear twining around her heart. "By that time, what we go to do will be done. Now, help me find the Dragon Stones."

He led her to the stones. She knelt slowly. Her body ached with scrapes and cuts and bruises, but by the time she'd gathered all five of the stones into her hand, she barely felt the pain.

"We have to hurry now," she said. She wasn't sure from where the sudden, aching urgency came. Still, it was there, real in the tightness in her shoulders, the jittering along her spine that must be obeyed.

In silence, the white tiger led her along the rising path. He guided her carefully, so that she walked as easily as though she trod the smooth marble floors of the Temple of Paladine. Wordless, he took her to the crevice he'd found in the high gray wall. She reached out with her hands and found that he hadn't exaggerated when he said the opening was just barely wide enough for her shoulders.

It was too narrow for her to walk with Tandar beside her, and for a moment, he hesitated.

"There is no danger ahead," she said calmly. "But there are two dangers behind."

He lifted his head under her hand, a silent question.

"Kela," she said, "and whomever—whatever—has been following us these two days past."

He couldn't argue, so he dropped back to let her pass.

Crysania put out her hands, one to each side, feeling her way along the narrow passage like a rock climber blindly descending. Rough stone, layered and sharp-edged, passed beneath her hands, scraping her skin. One step at a time, she went slowly through the crevice, feeling the weight of the stone around her. She smelled lichens and felt them beneath her hand, brittle sketches on the stone. She smelled the rock, and in places the dry, dusty scent smelled sharper, deeper, stone remembering rain.

By the time she emerged into open air, her right hand was scraped raw and the heel of her left hand was bleeding. Tandar came through behind her and stopped. She put a hand on him and felt him quivering. His thoughts were like a sigh of wonder.

"Show me," she whispered. "Will you show me?"

He moved out into the wider space, and she went with him. He gave her sight slowly, and when at last she saw what he did, she took her hand from him. In her pocket, the Dragon Stones hummed and sang their word-less songs of power. Songs of joy, songs of enchantment, songs to fill up the heart and illuminate the soul. She took out the pouch and held it close to her heart.

"Oh," she whispered softly, as though she were at prayer. "Oh, Valin . . ."

Godshome stretched out before them. Sentinel stones ranged round a crater, a bowl. A sacred chalice! Twenty-one stones stood there, thick and close together, each to represent one of the gods. She smiled, remembering the first time she had heard Tanis tell the tale of Godshome. Hearing it, she had determined that she would place twenty-one columns in the great hall of the Temple of Paladine. And he had said to her that the bowl that lay beyond the stones seemed made of night, of a sacred emptiness that existed only to be filled.

"But it isn't an emptiness," she said to Tandar. "Tanis told me. He said the bowl is black and hard as obsidian. It's a kind of mirror, he said, but what's reflected there is no simple image. What you see there . . ."

The Dragon Stones sang, the energy of their power a physical vibration she felt right through the velvet pouch.

What do you see there?

"You see gods," she whispered. "You see them in the stars. And you know, if ever you doubted, that all the stories played out in the constellations are not stories at all. They are truths, and you feel them in your heart and in your soul." She sighed, remembering Tanis's story. "You feel them in your very bones. Tanis said 'All things are holy in this place, even sorrow.' "

And he felt sorrow in this place?

"Yes, he did, for his dearest friend died here, in the arms of Paladine."

Tandar sighed. Soft along the channels of his thought she heard him whisper, *Jeril* . . .

An ache of foreboding touched her.

The sky spread out, black as moonless midnight. And naked of stars.

Tandar growled, his tail switching. *Where are the stars?*

"It's all right," she said, her hand shaking so she had to clutch the Dragon Stones more tightly. "Tanis said the sky looked different from here. He said that when he came here it was raining, out there beyond the sentinel stones, but it was not raining in here."

Yet as she spoke, she found no comfort in those memories, for Kela's words, spat in rage, overwhelmed the sweet solace of the old tale.

They're leaving. Just like at the Cataclysm. Our gods are leaving us.

"Take me to the stones. We must get past them and into the bowl."

I don't know how we can get past them. They're all pressed up against each other. Like a wall.

"We can go through. Tanis told me the way is clear once you see it."

Doubting, uneasy, the white tiger guided her, leading her carefully across the stony ground to the great tall wall of stone. Sighing, grateful, she found just what Tanis had said she'd find. The sentinel stones only looked as if they were locked together. She squeezed through the space between two of them easily. Tandar came through behind her.

Her hand on the tiger, Crysania moved forward, walking confidently toward the black, shining bowl. In her hand, the Dragon Stones sang, the velvet of Lagan's pouch growing warm and tingling from the energy of their power as they drew close to the edge of the dark chalice.

"We'll see the stars once we're there," she assured Tandar.

Tanis had told her. Even in the bright blue daylight, he saw the stars reflected in the shining black pool. And he had seen the three moons of magic, even the black one that was visible only to powerful Black-Robed mages. He'd told her how Paladine's constellation had appeared as the wizard Fizban bore the body of the dwarf Flint heavenward, and how the constellation had disappeared again when the avatar of the god returned. "I knew him then," Tanis had said. "I knew I'd been in the company of a god." Crysania shivered now to recall how Tanis's voice had softened with wonder, with awe, as he told her that tale.

"Tandar," she said. Her hand rested softly on his shoulder. "Valin . . . show me the stars. Take me to the moons." Once again she saw through the eyes of the tiger.

He moved forward in awe. He took her to the lip of the bowl and looked down.

No . . . he groaned.

"Oh, dear gods. No," she sighed, her breath trembling on her lips.

No moon shone in reflection on the black surface of the bowl. No star glimmered, not in its proper constellation, not alone.

The gods are gone! Kela had said it. Dalamar had feared it.

Crysania dropped to her knees at the edge of the black bowl. She held the stones clasped against her breast, against the medallion that she had worn for more than thirty years. Dalamar's warning came back to her, his laughing admission that the mage who had enchanted these stones was one of his dark order.

And what, he had asked, if it is Takhisis you call up?

Then I will stand in her presence, Crysania thought now.

But she didn't believe she would. She recalled in her

mind the image of the figure in the rain, the hands reaching to offer her an unseen gift.

"This is your gift, Paladine," she whispered to the god some said was not there. "These stones, born of that dream I once thought a nightmare. This is your gift, and I am here to use it."

Clutching the Dragon Stones in both hands, feeling their power, their sacred strength singing in her heart, in her bones, she leaned forward. She felt over the edge of the bowl, the stone, rough at the lip, becoming smooth as glass beyond. Her heart full of prayer, she tumbled the stones out of the velvet pouch and into her cupped hand. One by one, she lay them carefully on the lustrous surface of the bowl.

The black stone stung, like a scorpion's bite. She placed that one first, whispering Lagan Innis's hopeful rune prayer.

" 'Where light is, dark may not enter in.' "

Next to the black, she placed one of the nonaligned stones.

The red stone felt to her like the cool regard of one who observes and records, distant and powerful. She set it so that the nonaligned stone stood between it and the black.

" 'Where light is, dark may not enter in.' "

Beside the red, she place another nonaligned stone.

Last, Crysania took the white stone. It filled her up with hope, and when she placed it in the configuration, she lifted her face, her sightless eyes to the sky, and cried, " 'Where light is, dark may not enter in!' "

Power ran round her, skittering on her skin, finding an echo in her heart.

"Paladine, " she said, her voice ringing like bells against the sentinel stones. "Father of all that is good and light, hear your daughter!"

Beside her, Tandar stood still. She didn't hear him breathe.

Somewhere beyond the tall stones, the wind picked up and ran singing along the tops of the sentinels as though through the boughs of trees.

In the black bowl of Godshome, the chalice of the gods, no star shone, not one of the three moons glimmered. No light flickered in the unfulfilled emptiness.

Chapter Twenty-One

Crysania's hair blew around her cheeks. Her hands where they lay clasped on her knee shone white as marble. Fear rose up in her, a dark dread like none she had ever felt outside of nightmare. It came from within, from her own heart. The velvet pouch fell from her hands. Crying out, Crysania fell forward onto her face. Wind snatched up Lagan's rune-writ pouch, stealing it away. The silver embroidery glittered wildly in sudden strange light.

Heatless light, it offered no warmth, no cheer. Glaring and swelling up from the ground, down from the sky, it fell cold upon her, with a touch like death.

Someone wailed, the cry a terrible shriek, empty of all but blackest despair.

Dear gods, dear gods . . . the wailing was hers!

Tandar growled. The sounds of his fear vanished in the rising wind. The wind howled, it laughed, shrieking in abandon. Crysania lifted her head and saw Tandar crouching—cowering!—beside her. She pulled herself to her knees by sheer strength of will, by inches moving until she knelt again at the lip of the dark bowl.

The wild wind whirled around her, tearing at her robes, her hair, stinging her cheeks raw.

"Paladine!" she cried, the sound of the god's name falling dead upon the ground.

Dark, mocking laughter roared out from the wind. "Not he, Crysania! Not he!"

Crysania flung herself back from the bowl, from the wind. She stumbled against Tandar, and he cowered no more. He pressed against her, his heart galloping. The tiger was the only warm thing remaining in the world.

She knew that voice! The blood in her veins turned to ice. She knew that laughter. It had been the anthem of her torment so many years ago, the voice of the Abyss.

Takhisis!

The wild wind took shape; the madly whirling darkness became a terrible beauty. A woman's form rose up from it, barely visible against the black, empty sky. She wore stars in her long black hair as though they were diamonds. All the world stood reflected in her black eyes, a world of hate and harm, of pain and fighting and dying. In this world, evil ruled.

Crysania pressed her hands to her eyes, begged Tandar to take his sight away. She felt it leave, yet still she saw. Blind she was, but all folk, blind or sighted, must see a god when a god stands before them.

Tandar reeked of fear, a thick musky odor. Even so, he put himself between the Dark Queen and Crysania. The gesture amused the Dark Lady, but it affected her not at all. Takhisis stood where she willed, and she willed to be where the Revered Daughter of Paladine could see her in all her dark glory. She laughed, not the hideous, shrieking laughter Crysania had once heard. This laughter was throaty, quiet and intimate.

Do not be afraid, daughter.

The words whispered in Crysania's mind, like the footsteps of death stealing near. The counterfeit gentleness stung, like bile rising in her throat.

"I have answered your call," the Dark Queen said. "What is it you wish of me?"

Beware the gifts of mages!

The old warning rang thinly in Crysania's memory. Even now, huddled on her knees before the Dark Queen herself, Crysania still wanted to believe—she *must* believe!—that the gift of the Dragon Stones, no matter how strange, no matter how terrible, came to her from Paladine himself.

She had seen him, in her dreams she had seen him, his hands cupped as though holding something, reaching out to her, as though offering something.

Crysania's heart thundered in her ears, a terrible sound, like something about to burst. She got to her knees, staggering, and then she made herself stand straight and proud. She was the Revered Daughter of Paladine, even if that counted for nothing before this dark goddess.

Beside her, Tandar kept as still as the surrounding stones. She felt his terror, the fear running like fire in him. She put her hand on him, and he became still.

"Dark Lady," she said, her voice catching in her throat. "I have come with a question."

"Only that?" Her eyes flared, dark fire. "Not with gifts?" She looked down, her eyes on the tiger. "Not with some small sacrifice of blood and death to amuse me?"

Crysania's hand shook. Her voice became dry in her throat. She swallowed, willing herself to speak.

"No, lady. Not with any kind of sacrifice. I have come with the Dragon Stones to call upon a god so I may ask a question. The stones you see before you. Will you hear my question?"

Darkness gathered round Takhisis. It was as though she pulled all the lightless sky down to be her gown. "Speak."

"The gods—we have heard—we have heard that what wars are fought here in the world are also being fought among the gods. Some have said that the gods will soon go away. Lady, is it so?"

The Dark Queen smiled, a bright feral baring of her teeth. "Don't be afraid, my child. And you are my child, though perhaps you don't like to think so. Still, it is true. All of creation belongs to the gods. Know this: The gods have gone nowhere, for the gods are immovable. It is your heart that has changed."

Crysania drew a breath and boldly said, "Then if the gods have gone nowhere, let me see Paladine." Her heart warmed only to hear his name. "Let me speak with him."

Cold as winter midnight came the laughter of the Dark Queen. Crysania's heart quaked as Takhisis rose up before her, as immense as the sky, seeming to fill up all the world around with her terrible glory.

"Who are you," Takhisis cried, "to question the ways of the gods? You stand at the bottom of the well of your ignorance staring at the patch of sky above and think to question me?"

"I am—" Crysania shuddered from the cold, as though the hand of death lay upon her "—I am the Revered Daughter of Paladine, and you are the Mother of Lies. I reject you! I reject your evil! I know the truth, and it is this: Where light is, dark may not enter in! In the name of that truth, I say, let me see Paladine."

All the world became still. In Godshome, no one breathed, no one dared move. Even the Dragon Stones fell still, their gleaming power song unraveled into silence.

The darkness changed. It was as though the edges of Takhisis's midnight gown were folding in upon themselves. Beyond those edges, light grew. It seemed, in the first moments, to be a silver satin border on the darkness, gleaming as satin does. Then the edge became brighter, as light encroached upon dark. Like inevitable dawn, that light progressed, with slow, stately certainty that nothing could stand before it.

Tandar's breath came rough and swift. Crysania felt the fear lift from her heart, as foul fogs lift when the sun comes to warm the earth. She wept, her tears pouring down, for hope returning.

Tandar groaned, a deep animal sound, and the sound of it fell away gently as a voice came out of the light.

"Do not weep, daughter."

Crysania turned her face up to the sky, tears streaming even as she lifted her heart in laughter, absurd, delightful, incongruous laughter that rang around the stony enclosure like peals of joy.

"Father, you have come! Oh, I have been so afraid!"

"For yourself?"

She admitted it. How could she not? He who saw into her very heart must know the truth of her fears.

"And," he said, very gently. "You have been afraid for me." He held out a hand to her, light shining all around.

Beware the gifts of mages! She smiled, and in that moment, as though her joy had given him shape, the god Paladine stood before her, turning her smile to sudden laughter.

For here was no shining dragon. No eternal warrior stood before her, girded in armor and wielding divine weapons.

Here, eyes slightly puzzled, hands fumbling in the pockets of his robes, stood an old avatar indeed.

"Fizban," she breathed, her heart light as a child's.

The old one looked up, as though suddenly startled. Fizban, indeed, absentminded, good-hearted, and slightly testy. So had Tanis Half-Elven seen the god, in this very place, more than thirty years before.

"The very same," he said, frowning at her as at an impertinent child. "And why not? I have been here before. Like this. I think. Girl," he said, suddenly startled, "there's a tiger behind you!"

She laughed again. "Yes. He's my friend."

The old wizard cocked his head, squinting as he fumbled in his pockets again. "You're certain? I can change him into a mouse . . . or something."

"I'm certain! Yes, I'm sure. He's a friend."

He grunted, as old men do, and then he fell silent. Above, the clouds flowed wildly, and it seemed that they ran into each other from all the quarters of the sky.

"Father," Crysania said, "I have come here with a question."

He grunted again, but now it seemed that something had changed. He yet stood before her as Fizban, his absurd pointed hat falling over his eyes, his hands quivering like an old man's. His eyes, though, gleamed brightly.

"Ask."

Tandar pressed against her, warm and assuring.

"Father, I have heard from dragons that you have fought a battle with Chaos. I see you here now—Father, are you well? Did you win?"

He looked at her long, then turned his face to the tumbling sky, the clouds all running madly above them.

"Yes, daughter, we've won. Chaos is defeated. He has fled this world."

The words were the right ones, the ones she wanted to hear, yet they seemed to sigh under a weary burden of sadness.

Her breath caught in her throat. She reached for Tandar and found him, as ever, beside her. She felt his ribs rising and falling with each breath.

"My child," said the old wizard, "the Father of All and of Nothing was defeated, but the price he demands for leaving this world in peace is a high one. His children must go with him."

Crysania's breath left her in a sudden sob. "No!"

In the sky, the clouds boiled, roiling and tumbling madly. On the ground, no shadows mirrored their wild dance.

"That is why I have come to you," Fizban said. "To say good-bye. I must leave this world."

All the hope draining out of her heart, Crysania cried, "No! Oh, Father, no!"

He looked up at the sky, frowning as an old, be-fuddled man. He lifted his hand as though to cast a still-ing spell, then let it fall again.

"Child, I must do what I have agreed to do. We do not find it easy, we gods, to leave this world and the children we have created. We have fought for you and over you. Above all else, we have loved you. But we will not hand you over to the wrath of Chaos, and so we must leave the world. It is the sacrifice we make to save you."

Crysania felt a touch upon her cheek, tender and sad. "The others have already gone, and I must follow."

"What will we do? How will we survive?" Crysania cringed, thinking of the long days without Paladine's loving presence. She could not comprehend the rest of her life stretching out before her in silence and darkness. Without Paladine's bright and loving warmth.

"You will survive, my daughter. You must survive.

The world will have need of your compassion and wisdom." He looked at the white tiger beside her, and it seemed to her that the smile lighting his eyes was one of sudden, amused satisfaction. "You will find new ways, new magic. My blessing goes with you always."

She felt him start to go. It was not like anything she'd ever experienced. This going was the sun dwindling, withdrawing. This was true darkness, a cruel blindness without even the distant flickering gold of his presence.

"No!" she moaned. She could not bear it. She could not. This could not be. It was a dream. A nightmare. She would awaken and go to her window and kneel down in the warmth of the morning sun and pray, and he would touch her with warmth.

But he never would. He'd said it. He would never come here again. He must leave the world.

She fell to her knees, grieving. Clinging to Tandar, she sobbed, her heart wrenching in her breast as all the light of her world receded. She knelt that way for what seemed like an age before she heard Tandar's voice in her mind, low and warning.

Crysania!

The gods were gone, Takhisis and Paladine, and so she expected to look up into blindness again. It was not so. The sky had settled. No clouds raced there now in mad, windless dances. Instead, she saw lights shimmering. She blinked, trying to look away. She could not. The lights hovered above the dark glassy bowl, taking on all the colors of the world, the sky's blue, the forest's green, the gold of desert sands, all those and more, mixing and mingling into a rainbow that cast no reflection in the mirror surface.

"Valin," she breathed.

He pressed close to her, his heart beating hard.

The lights coalesced into one bright ball of flame, then

parted, flowing out to become three distinct rivers of color: white, red, black. The rivers ran, and they took shape against the sky, two male figures and one female, each dressed in one of the robes of the Orders of Magic. They were human in appearance, tall and strong. She knew, though, with certainty, that if she were an elf, she would have seen them as elves. Were she a dwarf, those gods would have shown themselves to her in dwarven shape. They wore shapes for the comfort of those to whom they appeared.

Red Lunitari stepped forward from among her kin. "We have come for the Dragon Stars, Lady Crysania. We thank you and your companion for gathering them for us."

"Dragon Stars?"

Nuitari laughed, a dark sound, like storms.

"Dragon Stars," Lunitari said again. "For they are soon to be more than stones, child."

Solinari stepped forward now, and the three divine children made the barest motion with their hands, a gesture in perfect concert. The line of five stones began to rise, turning and dancing in the air.

"They are not of this world," Lunitari said. Her voice was like blood singing in the veins, like silk sliding on soft skin.

The stones began to circle, rising higher, until they hung above Crysania's head. She stepped back. Tandar moved with her, his eyes on the stones. The stones formed a perfect circle in the air, no beginning, no ending, whirling faster and faster until she couldn't distinguish one from the other, their colors blending as the lights of the gods had blended, into one golden disk.

"Valin," she breathed.

My dearest lady, he said, deep in her mind. The words danced in her heart as the lights of magic and gods had danced before her eyes.

Streaming yellow light flowed out from the golden disk, streams of power feathering out from it.

In her mind, Tandar cried out, stricken in pain. *They are going! The gods are going from the world! Magic! It is going—*

A scream rent the god-wrought silence.

Crysania jerked and turned. Tandar wheeled, growling.

Just then the mage Kela slipped between the warding sentinel stones, running toward them.

Tandar leapt sideways, putting his body between the mage and Crysania, bracing for the attack. Kela didn't even glance at him. Wailing her woe, she ran wildly past him, her fists opening, reaching desperately for the golden disk, the gods, and the magic.

And behind her—oh, all you merciful gods!—behind her ran another, a big man who followed with staggering steps.

"Jeril!"

Crysania cried his name, but Jeril never stopped. She saw him with a vision that dimmed as the three gods of magic receded from Godshome. He ran limping, stumbling from old wounds and one new one, a sword slash across the ribs. From that wound, his life poured, scarlet blood soaking the stony ground. He knew what Kela was about to do. Crysania saw the bitter, terrible knowledge in his eyes.

Crysania understood in the same heart-wrenching instant.

"Valin," she cried.

Her sight failing, dimming, she saw the tiger leap for Kela, and she saw the mage dart swiftly around him, laughing and weeping all at the same time.

Jeril screamed, "Stop! Kela! Stop!"

Tandar turned, blocking the staggering man, holding him back. Bleeding, Jeril had no more strength, none to resist. He fell to his knees, bent low, his hands pressing against the sword cut as though he could hold back the flood of his life's blood.

Kela leapt as her feet touched the edge of the glassy surface, arms outstretched, grabbing at the flowing yellow disk. She screamed as she touched it, agony and ecstasy wedded into one terrible sound as power erupted out around her. The golden light streaming out from the magical disk split apart into separate colors. Red and green and white and blue and black. The streamers of color snarled, coiled high into the sky, became flame, became scaled leather.

A voice, deep and sensuous and horrible, whispered, "Yes. Come to me."

Tandar roared.

Crysania screamed in fear.

The lovely mage was swallowed up in a burst of power as the five colors of Takhisis coalesced.

Wind whipped Crysania's robes around her legs, roaring in her ears. She closed her eyes, and when she allowed herself to look again, the disk was so far up in the sky it seemed like nothing so much as a pale yellow moon set amidst the stars.

Stars!

She gasped, reaching out as though she could touch them. These were new stars, not like the old. The gods were gone. Magic was gone. The world lay all around her, empty of their presence, and as she realized that, darkness closed in around her, the old curse, the old gift, blindness returned in the absence of gods.

Someone moaned, a sobbing of pain. Jeril.

Crysania groped in the darkness, reaching for Tandar, for Valin. He put himself under her hand, allowed her to use him as she climbed to her feet.

"Take me to him," she said. "Take me to your brother."

Even as she said it, her heart faltered. What would she

do when she got there? She would kneel beside him, she would offer him comfort. She had no more, for all the healing magic had left the world with the gods.

She stumbled along beside the tiger, weak and weary. She reached out and touched blood, hot and running.

"Jeril," she whispered.

"Lady," he groaned.

"We thought you were dead."

He made a sound like coughing, and only when he spoke did she realize it was a bitter kind of laughter. "We? You and your faithful tiger?"

She found his cheek, and in blindness she touched it, rough and dirty and bearded. "Yes, me and my faithful tiger."

Shuddering, he drew a shallow breath. "Lady—lady, she is dead, isn't she?"

Tandar lay down close beside him, as he used to lie beside her. Jeril's shivering eased as the great beast's body warmth enveloped him.

"Yes, Kela is dead."

He swallowed, and she heard the clicking sound in his throat like a death knell. "Then so is our child."

"Oh," Crysania moaned. "Oh, no. Not that . . ."

Jeril moved, twisting under her hand, twisting away in pain. "I . . . loved her. I loved her . . . and I didn't know what dark passion drove her . . . until . . . too late."

She had tried to kill him, Jeril said, one night after the attack of the daemon warrior. She had told him of her need for the Dragon Stones, of her fears, of her plans. His brave heart would have nothing of those dark plans, and so she'd tried to kill him, and almost she had succeeded. But her stroke had been clumsy and fast, her dagger unsure in the dark. He had lived, he had managed to escape, and he had followed her, his wife of only weeks. The mother of his child.

"To save her, lady. To save our baby."

And so it had been Jeril following behind in the Misted Vales, a lover questing to rescue his beloved from herself. Crysania touched him gently, only for comfort. She had no healing to give.

"She would not be saved," he sighed. He shuddered, then moaned as the tiger pressed closer still, a gentle weight against him.

Brother! Tandar cried, but only Crysania could hear. *Brother!*

"Oh, Paladine," Crysania whispered. "Oh, Father, you left us too soon!"

And now this good man would die.

She rocked back on her heels, turning her face up to a sky in which new stars sparkled. She was glad she couldn't see them.

Something touched her face, something cold and wet. As she reached up to wipe it away, another drop splashed across her cheek, breaking into tinier drops and bouncing up into her lashes. And then another. She held up her hands as more drops fell.

"Is it—is it rain, lady?" Jeril sighed.

She cupped her hands, as the image of a god had done in her dream. She let the cup fill, then she said, "Yes," offering the gift of sweet, clean water to the dying man. "It is rain, my friend. Drink, with my blessing."

Perhaps he heard her, but she didn't think so. Soft into her blindness, into the familiar darkness, came a tiger's mourning groan.

* * * * *

They could not bury Jeril, neither could they make a decent cairn. Tigers cannot lift stone nor dig in the earth. A blind woman cannot. And so they left him in

Godshome. They found his sword outside the ring of stones, washed clean of his blood by the sweetly falling rain. They brought it back to him, and they placed it upon his breast, his hands clasped round the grip. Desert Light would keep him company in this place where no gods would come again.

"It is a fitting place for him," Crysania said.

The tiger said nothing.

"Come," she said, her hand on him, stroking his soft fur. "Take me out of here, Valin."

He did, in silence, his grief heavy. He led her between the sentinel stones and back down the trail to Misted Vales. There they found shelter from the rain in a small cave, and there they lay down together to sleep.

They dreamed the same dreams, the tiger and the woman, their hopes and memories all woven together. They dreamed of rain, they dreamed of gods. They dreamed of clouds that ran at each other from all the quarters of the sky. She dreamed of sight. He dreamed of blindness. And sometimes they dreamed of the dead, of Jeril and Lagan Innis and Kela the mage, who could not be rescued.

In this way they passed the night, Crysania asleep on the stony floor of the cave, the tiger stretched out beside her, a warm, familiar weight. And when they woke, each had the same image in mind, that of a befuddled old wizard staring at them, shaking his head, wondering what in the world was going on around him now.

"He looked at you so strangely," Crysania said, her cheek on the tiger's broad head. "Do you remember? As though he knew something about you. Something amusing."

I don't know what he might have known about me to amuse him. My life has been less than that, lady.

"Perhaps," she said, whispering, "he smiled at something that has not happened yet."

Outside, it still rained, pouring down as though all the dry and terrible summer must be amended. Crysania shivered, for this morning sat much cooler on the world than mornings had for a long time. She wished for a fire, and she curled up closer to the tiger.

I wish for one, too, he said.

"Well, our luck is bad, then. I can make no fire, and neither can you. We must sit here and wait for the rain to stop and keep ourselves warm as best we can."

He said nothing and she knew that he shuttered his thoughts from her. In silence, she lay down beside him again, and after some time had passed, she said, "Will you tell me, Valin, what happened to change you into a tiger?"

He growled a little, she felt the sound like a vibration against her.

I made a bargain, lady. With Dalamar the Dark.

"Tell me. I want to know."

He told her, with images bright and sharp, all she wanted to know. He told her of his journey to the Tower of High Sorcery. He told her what Dalamar had offered—a way to accompany Crysania on her journey to Neraka— a chance to win her love.

A way, dearest lady, to be with you always. To guard you, to run beside you, to hear your voice. He sighed, a deep animal sound. *A way to lie beside you at night . . .*

Rain fell, hissing and sighing, smelling like life and hope and all good things.

Crysania sat up and touched his head, stroked his cheek. She thought her heart would break, so deeply, so terribly did it ache. This much he'd wanted, and she had refused him. This he had asked for, one day in the garden of the Temple of Paladine, and she had turned him away, saying, "No, you can't have that." Into Dalamar's hands she had sent him, because he wanted what she would not give.

"Valin," she said, her voice breaking around her sorrow. "Is there a way you can become free again?"

The sound he made fell like a weight into her darkness. *There is a way, lady. There is always a way.*

She reached to touch him, then withdrew her hand.

"What way?"

He stirred, sitting up. He allowed no hope to color his thoughts.

"What way?" she asked again. "Tell me."

Words must be spoken, certain simple words, and I will be Valin again.

"Words! Spoken by whom? By Dalamar?"

The sound of his breathing changed, grew quicker, then, as he mastered himself, slow again. *Not by Dalamar. By you.*

"What words? Tell me!"

I cannot. If you speak them, I am free. If you never do, I remain as you see me.

"Do you know the words?"

Yes, he said. *I do, but the geas of the spell forbids me from telling you what they are.*

Tears spilled, rolling freely down her cheeks. Words and words and words—the world was filled with them! Which words, in which language, in what combination, would free Valin from his mage-built prison? Her breath caught in sobs; she moaned in pain, in sorrow, in guilty grief.

The task was impossible. It could never be accomplished.

She put her arms around his neck, her cheek upon his head. There she wept, bestormed by grief, while outside rain fell gently, patiently, nourishing the parched earth as her own tears nourished her waking heart.

"I'm sorry," she said against his cheek. "I'm so sorry, Valin. I will search for the words, I will hunt the world over. I swear it. Perhaps Dalamar didn't survive the wars. Perhaps his tower is fallen to the ground. No matter! If it is fallen, I will find the spellbook he used to make this terrible magic. I will search the rubble. I will take the ruin stone from stone and find what we—"

She sat up, wiping her face with the dirty hem of her robe. Was it laughter she felt, Valin's laughter glittering in her mind?

"What? Why do you laugh?"

Crysania, why would you do that? Tear a ruin stone from stone?

She shivered, chilled by the dampness of the morning, by her sorrow. "I will do it, dear Valin, because you have done so much for me. You have guarded and defended me. You have risked your life for me and for our friends. You have lent me sight. You have—" She stopped to catch her breath, to catch her courage. "I will do it because I love you."

He sighed under her hands, his whole body rising with it, falling with it. In the air, a tingling came, a vibration running along her nerves.

"Valin—"

He drew in a tight breath and held it.

Under her hands, his body moved. No—shifted. Broke. The shape of him was changing, and the sensation of tingling became burning, deeper.

He cried out in pain—a tiger's voice, a man's—and it was her name he cried as the changing came upon him, her name as his bones reshaped and realigned and all his senses dimmed, settling back into the range of humans.

Crysania!

The name rang in her ears, bounding off the little cave's walls in echo. And it roared in her mind, booming, then softening, too, into echo. And then he was gone from her mind, the connection between them fallen to empty silence. She was alone.

307

"Valin," she sighed.

He whispered, "Here, lady," and his was the deep familiar voice of the desert mage. He came closer. She heard his bare feet on the dirt floor. She heard him shivering, and she thought, Oh! The poor man's naked! She snatched up her sleeping blanket and handed it to him, tempted by the slide of the fabric on his skin as he wrapped himself in it.

"You're not alone, Crysania," he said, sitting beside her. Warmth from his body enveloped her arm and shoulder. She smelled the blanket and the familiar scent of his hair. "We're far from home, the two of us, and maybe it is that we don't even have Palanthas to return to, but I love you, Crysania, and as long as I live, you will never be alone."

Rain fell harder outside. A chill, damp wind swept through the cave's entrance. Crysania shivered, and Valin put his arm around her, never hesitating. She moved closer so she could put her head on his shoulder. Only once did he kiss her, a soft touch upon the lips. But this kiss lingered, for she did not pull away as once she had. And so they sat, he listening to the rain and she to the beat of his heart. At some point, she looked up and realized she'd been sitting thus comfortably for a long time, as though they had long been lovers, his arms used to filling up with her, her heart well versed in the rhythms of his.

"What will we find out there, Valin? Who has survived the wars? Who has fallen?"

He held her closer, his hands stroking her arms in slow, gentle rhythm. "I don't know, Crysania. I don't know what the world has become. I only know this: We will go out and we will go down to Palanthas, you and I, and maybe we'll find the world a wild and changed place, god-reft, magic-reft. But however it is, we will face it together."

She touched his face, traced the shape of it, and kissed him tenderly. With him she had gone into battle, she had braved the daemons of Chaos. With Valin beside her, she had stood before the Dark Queen herself and come back alive. How, then, should she be daunted by the wars and strivings of mortals as long as he was near?

She said, "I'm cold, Valin. Will you share your blanket?"

He smiled. She felt it against her mouth as he kissed her, his lips curving against hers. "I know another way to get warm," he said.

She touched him, running her hands along his arms until she caught his big hands in hers. He shivered, not from cold.

"Show me," she said, as the rain poured down and the wind prowled lonely outside the little cave.

Gently he took her into his arms.

THE DRAGONS OF A NEW AGE TRILOGY
by Jean Rabe

Volume One:
The Dawning of a New
Age
$5.99; $6.99 CAN
8376
0-7869-0616-2

Volume Two:
The Day of the Tempest
$5.99; $6.99 CAN
8381
0-7869-0668-5

Volume Three:
The Eve of the Maelstrom
$5.99; $6.99 CAN
8385
0-7869-0749-5

Krynn struggles to survive under the bleak curse of Chaos, father of the gods. Magic has vanished. Dragonlords rule and slaughter. A harsh apocalyptic world requires new strategies and new heroes, among them Palin Majere, the son of Caramon. This series opens an exciting page into the future.

RELICS AND OMENS:
TALES OF THE FIFTH AGE®

Edited by Margaret Weis and Tracy Hickman

The first Fifth Age anthology features new short stories exploring the post-*Dragons of Summer Flame* world of banished gods and lost magic. *Relics and Omens* showcases TSR's best-known and beloved authors: Douglas Niles, Jeff Grubb, Roger Moore, Nancy Berberick, Paul Thompson, Nick O'Donohoe, and more. The anthology includes the first Fifth Age adventure of Caramon Majere, one of the last surviving original companions, written by Margaret Weis and Don Perrin.

$5.99; $6.99 CAN,
8386
0-7869-1169-7

The World Needs Heroes!

You've read the adventures of Ansalon's greatest heroes—
now it's time to join them!

Unlock the secrets to the Saga's greatest mysteries with
the DRAGONLANCE®: FIFTH AGE® dramatic adventure game,
a storytelling game that emphasizes creativity, epic
drama, and heroism. It's easy to learn and fun to play,
whether you want to roleplay characters from your
favorite DRAGONLANCE stories or spin new tales all your
own. Best of all, the DRAGONLANCE: FIFTH AGE boxed set
and supplements offer a treasure trove of engaging source
material not found in any novel!

Knights, freedom fighters, mages, and mystics—the heroes
you play rise above the ranks of common folk to discover
the wonders of magic and defend Ansalon from the
dragons that threaten it. Come, hero! Make your mark on
this Age of Mortals, and be remembered forever in legend.

Find the DRAGONLANCE: FIFTH AGE game and supplements
at your local book, game, or hobby store. To locate the
store nearest you, call Customer Service at (800) 324-6496.
See our website at **www.tsr.com** for more information.

DRAGONLANCE® 1999 CALENDAR
MAY 1998

Twelve of the year's best DRAGONLANCE fantasy art covers. Artists include Larry Elmore, Todd Lockwood, Jeff Easley, Keith Parkinson, and more! This calendar will contain major Krynn holidays and birthdays of popular characters, sure to be a favorite with DRAGONLANCE fans.

$12.99; $16.99 CAN
8899
ISBN: 0-7869-1193-X

THE ART OF THE DRAGONLANCE SAGA
SEPTEMBER 1998

The ultimate coffee table art book that set the bar for all others is reissued due to popular demand. The visual creation of the DRAGONLANCE world is depicted through artists sketches. Also included is commentary on the processes behind creating the many characters, dragons and artifacts of the DRAGONLANCE novels and game products. This book is being reprinted with a new foreword by Margaret Weis and Tracy Hickman.

$19.99; $25.99 CAN
8447
ISBN: 0-7869-1181-6

THE SOULFORGE
MARGARET WEIS

The long-awaited prequel to the bestselling Chronicles Trilogy by the author who brought Raistlin to life!

Raistlin Majere is six years old when he is introduced to the archmage who enrolls him in a school for the study of magic. There the gifted and talented but tormented boy comes to see magic as his salvation. Mages in the magical Tower of High Sorcery watch him in secret, for they see shadows darkening over Raistlin even as the same shadows lengthen over all Ansalon.

Finally, Raistlin draws near his goal of becoming a wizard. But first he must take the Test in the Tower of High Sorcery—or die trying.

THE CHRONICLES TRILOGY
MARGARET WEIS AND TRACY HICKMAN

Fifteen years after publication and with more than three million copies in print, the story of the worldwide bestselling trilogy is as compelling as ever.

Dragons have returned to Krynn with a vengeance. An unlikely band of heroes embarks on a perilous quest for the legendary DRAGONLANCE!

THE LEGENDS TRILOGY
MARGARET WEIS AND
TRACY HICKMAN

In the sequel to the ground-breaking Chronicles trilogy, the powerful archmage Raistlin follows the path of dark magic and even darker ambition as he travels back through time to the days before the Cataclysm. Joining him, willingly and unwillingly, are Crysania, a beautiful cleric of good, Caramon, Raistlin's brother, and the irrepressible kender Tasslehoff.

Volume One: *Time of the Twins*
$6.99 US; $8.99 CAN
8307
ISBN: 0-88038-265-1

Volume Two: *War of the Twins*
$6.99 US; $8.99 CAN
8308
ISBN: 0-88038-266-X

Volume Three: *Test of the Twins*
$6.99 US; $8.99 CAN
8309
ISBN: 0-88038-267-8